GOING DARK

GOING DARK

A LIBERTY UNIT NOVEL

GEORGE K. MEHOK

atmosphere press

Visit George Mehok online at georgemehok.com

George Mehok is the founder of ApertureXI Technologies, LLC, a leading technology consulting company specializing in intelligent robotic automation. For more information, visit aperturexi.com.

Edited by Dawn Isus

Map artwork by Rhys Davies

Cover design by Matthew Fielder

Copyright © 2024 George K. Mehok. All Rights Reserved

Going Dark is a trademark of ApertureXI Technologies, LLC

No part of this book may be reproduced, distributed, or transmitted in any form or by any means, including photocopying, recording, or other electronic or mechanical methods, without the prior written permission of the publisher, except in the case of brief quotations embodied in critical reviews and certain other noncommercial uses permitted by copyright law. This is a work of fiction inspired by real places, persons, and events. While these elements may intentionally resemble reality, they are fictionalized and not intended to represent actual occurrences or individuals.

Atmospherepress.com

This book is inspired by the historical events and the remarkable individuals who have shaped our world with their fortitude, compassion, and determination.

To my late father, George K. Mehok, who passed away during the revision phase of this novel. His love for family and country was evident in his honorable service in the United States Air Force during the Korean War. His dedication and bravery were recognized with the Korean Service Medal, United Nations Service Medal, and National Defense Medal. His passion for learning and reading inspired my writing and this work.

Thank you, Dad, for always being there for me.

Jouett's Journey
1781 Map of the Colonies
0 10 20 30 40 50
miles
NEW YORK
West Point
New York
Hanover
NEW JERSEY
Trenton
PENNSYLVANIA
Valley Forge
Philadelphia
Havre de Grace
Baltimore
MARYLAND
DELAWARE
Delaware Bay
Mount Vernon
VIRGINIA
Fredericksburg
Chesapeake Bay
Atlantic Ocean
Charlottesville
Cuckoo Tavern, Louisa County
Monticello
Williamsburg
Richmond
York Town

PROLOGUE

> "Once vigorous measures appear to be the only means left of bringing the Americans to a due submission to the mother country, the colonies will submit." — King George III, 1781

JUNE 4, 1781 – SIXTH YEAR OF THE AMERICAN REVOLUTION
LOUISA COUNTY, VIRGINIA COLONY

A pine branch reached out, raking Jack's face, its needles stabbing his neck like a swarm of angry yellow jackets. With instincts honed by a lifetime in the saddle, he ducked low, clutching his horse's slick, heaving neck. Another branch whisked overhead, failing in its attempt to decapitate him.

Captain John "Jack" Jouett spurred Celer onward, pushing his prized colt to the limits of his endurance, thundering through the dense Virginia forest. He approached the end of the grueling forty-mile ride from Cuckoo Tavern, tracing a southwest path along the North Anna River toward Charlottesville. Bypassing the main road, he chose the less traveled, overgrown trails. For falling into British hands meant either the noose or—perhaps worse—confinement aboard the *Whitby*, the hellish British prison ship anchored in Norfolk.

Catching his breath, Jack inhaled the pungent scent of pine resin mingled with the damp, earthy soil. He wiped the remnants of the night's rain from his face. The deep cuts left by the unforgiving branches burned, and he noticed the dark blood on his riding glove reflecting in the full moon's bright silver glow.

He knew the unmarked westward trails that snaked deep into the Blue Ridge better than anyone, apart from his father,

PROLOGUE

who had taught him the trails, hunting and trapping throughout the bountiful Virginia backcountry. Together, they bartered pelts, fowl, and venison with the wealthy Richmond merchants. Those peaceful days, however, were now just a distant memory, shattered by the British, who had captured his father.

Suddenly, the canopy of trees cleared, unveiling an endless blanket of stars stretching across Virginia's night sky. In stride, Celer shifted his weight to his hind legs and, with a powerful leap, hurdled over the fallen pine log that lay hidden in the moonlit shadows. Jack clenched his teeth and rose from the saddle, bracing to absorb the landing. However, his gloved hand slipped from the pommel, sending him tumbling from the saddle.

His knees struck the rocky riverbed with the force of a hammer on an anvil. He slammed the water with an open hand to expel the pain and quickly reached to his side, checking that his prized hunting knife was secured to his hip. Forged by his closest friend, Ben, the knife's tempered blade served Jack well on the battlefield and promised to prove its worth in times to come.

Jack glanced over his shoulder, his eyes piercing the darkness of the backroad for any sign of Tarleton and his notorious Green Dragoons. The memories of the Battle of Charlestown and Tarleton's ruthless slaying of prisoners remained vivid. His heart raced, knowing too well that they could be closing in at any moment. He was determined to warn the governor of the Virginia Commonwealth of the imminent threat marching toward his Monticello estate. Jefferson's capture could turn the tide of the war, compelling the Continental Congress to seek peace, an outcome Jack could not and would never accept.

Drenched, Jack tasted the gritty mixture of blood, sweat, and river water that dripped down his face. He pushed back his long, wet hair and put on his dripping fur-felt hat, ready to continue his urgent mission.

Several yards downstream, Celer stood gulping water, his reddish-brown coat shimmering in the moonlight. Jack took swift, long strides through the fast-moving, knee-deep water, grabbed the pommel, and threw himself back into the saddle. With a firm kick, Celer obediently responded with the prowess of a champion racer, bolting up the steep, muddy bank, hooves digging deep into the soft, slick clay, searching for firm ground.

As they reentered the dense forest, the canopy shrouded the narrow trail in shadows, prompting Celer to slow his pace. Through the twilight, Jack spotted silhouettes of distant riders approaching. He rubbed his eyes and attempted to shake the overwhelming fatigue from his mind. His hand instinctively rested on the knife's handle.

Celer stopped abruptly with his ears probing forward and his body tense.

Ahead, approaching shadowed silhouettes punctuated with tall hats signified the dreaded British grenadiers, the enemy's elite soldiers. Jack's back stiffened, and his hand clenched the knife's handle. Quietly, he guided Celer into the concealing darkness of the tree line.

The soldiers drew closer, oblivious to Jack's presence.

Jack couldn't believe his eyes. Was exhaustion playing tricks on his mind, or had the forest conjured remnants of spirits lost, wandering, searching for something or someone? He had heard of the folk stories told by the native elders—souls of the dead warriors forever trapped in the mortal world, roaming for eternity.

The horsemen were hovering inches off the ground.

How could that be? Spirits? A dream?

He watched motionless as the ghostly riders passed, and his wonderment was suddenly replaced with profound grief. Among them, he recognized one of the men—wrists shackled, gaunt shoulders rounded, and head hanging down, bobbing in rhythm with the horse's slow trot.

Flanking the solemn prisoner were apparitions of British soldiers, sitting tall and rigid in their blood-red uniforms, leading Jack's father toward the sea.

SACRIFICE

> *"The American people are the ones who pay the taxes which fund the planes that bomb us, the tanks that strike and destroy our homes, the armies which occupy our lands, and the fleets which ensure the blockades. Whoever has stolen our wealth, then we have the right to destroy their economy."* — Osama Bin Laden

28 NOVEMBER, 0415 HRS
LAKE GENEVA TOWNSHIP, ILLINOIS

Hassan stared at the spiderweb of cracks on the oil-stained garage floor. The slow, rhythmic moan of the air raid siren grew louder. A siren only he could hear.

He grappled with his harsh reality: he was compelled to make the ultimate sacrifice. As images of his mother surface in his memory, he fought against letting his mind wander down the path of no return. He had made a solemn promise to look after her youngest son, to protect him just as she had protected Hassan until her last dying breath.

The mournful cry of the sirens caused Hassan's muscles to tense.

Soldiers must obey. Hassan had sworn that oath to Khalid—the mission's outcome hinged on unconditional obedience.

Khalid's orders were clear and would be carried out.

Yet how could he break a sacred promise he'd made to the woman who'd been through so much to protect him?

He reached behind his head and rubbed the scar that ran along the base of his skull, down his neck, and across his right shoulder. The stretched and mangled skin served as a vivid reminder of his childhood on the outskirts of Damascus. The scar tissue was as smooth as polished glass, the nerves deadened from the trauma of the flames. He ran his fingers across the skin again and again. The sirens slowly dissipated with each pass, quieting to a low hum.

He lowered his arm to his side and clenched his fist. The sirens went silent, replaced by an inconsequential high-pitched buzzing of the overhead fluorescent light.

He carefully placed the heavy-gauge duffel bags into the rear of the late-model Nissan Pathfinder, leaving barely enough space for the remaining bags Yousef was packing inside the house. Based on Hassan's calculations, achieving the desired blast velocity, radius, and pattern required every ounce of the explosive material the two men had prepared.

He stepped back to appreciate his work. The garage light reflected in the Pathfinder's blacked-out windows, and the thick, oily smell of the diesel fuel radiated from the rear of the vehicle.

"Where are you? Bring the bags, now!" Hassan wanted to show his younger brother the patience he'd earned, but the mission's precise timetable could not afford to delay.

"Coming, brother," Yousef said, stumbling out of the kitchen into the garage, struggling to squeeze the two oversized duffel bags through the door.

Hassan's men had surveilled the mission's staging site for weeks near the isolated and sparsely populated Wisconsin-Illinois border. Its proximity provided convenient access to metro Chicago and the necessary supplies.

"They're heavy. Why did you have to pack the bags so heavy, brother?" Yousef said, setting the bags down gently. He bent over, hands on his knees, breathing hard.

Six months ago, following the owner's sudden death, Hassan had paid cash for this 1950 one-story ranch-style house at a foreclosure auction. The house sat a modest distance off the frozen dirt road, partially shielded by decaying century-old oaks and a patchy row of unkept evergreen brush. Dark green moss streaked the weathered gray roof, and the gutters overflowed with seasons of congealed dead leaves. Beige bedsheets covered the large front windows, while cardboard over the garage door windows discouraged curious neighbors' prying eyes.

"No more questions. Please do as you're told." Hassan patted his younger brother on the back. "You are a brave soldier. Redemption for our people will be realized soon. However, we must complete the task at hand."

Yousef smiled, a glint of joy shining in his eyes as he turned and walked back into the house, ready to carry out his orders. At nearly twenty-five years of age, he was still more boy than soldier.

Hassan lifted the forty-kilo duffel bags, one in each hand, his biceps, triceps, and pectoral muscles flexing. His renewed focus muted the pain caused by the damaged tendons in his left shoulder—a remnant from the battlefield. He stacked the bags into the rear of the SUV, creating a third layer that pressed against the vehicle's interior roof.

Grabbing several heavy-duty plastic bags off the floor—filled with nails, screws, and ball bearings—Hassan wedged them between the duffels. He'd incorporated the metal projectiles into the design, primarily for psychological impact. The main blast element—three twenty-gallon marine blue plastic containers filled with diesel fuel thickened with phosphate gel—was behind the front seats.

He'd studied the work of the most prolific bombmakers, including his mentor, Omar Al-Faruq, the late commander of the al-Qaeda Southeast Asia sector. However, Hassan recognized that Al-Faruq was an exception and that most so-called bombmakers were crude amateurs. They foolishly relied on martyrs for placement and detonation, which increased the probability of failure due to the weakness of the human mind.

Proud of the first-of-its-kind remote RF cloaking detonator, Hassan greatly improved Al-Faruq's original ignition design, randomizing the device's detonation mechanism's frequency modulation and effectively rendering it undetectable by scanners or the latest network monitoring devices recently installed by the American's inept Department of Homeland Security.

He couldn't have been more pleased with his ordinance design, emphasizing blast power over incendiary combustion. Blast power was required to breach the reinforced concrete; however, equally important, the device's design would achieve the maximum casualty rate due to its unique composition. The devastating explosive force would create extreme overpressure, instantly destroying human tissue and organs within the planned one-kilometer blast radius.

Preparations were progressing on schedule, precisely according to Commander Khalid's orders.

Hassan turned his head and winced at the strong scent of petrol fumes, reminding him of his homeland's oil fields and refineries. He inhaled deeply through his nose. Tiny flashes of light danced in front of his eyes. He took another deep breath. His lungs burned, and his eyes teared up.

He heard liquid splashing and a plastic container hitting the ground. The pattern repeated. Yousef poured the remaining diesel fuel onto the kitchen's linoleum floor and into the carpeted living room. Hassan's orders were explicit: soak the floors and pour what remained down the wooden basement stairs. The impending burn would eviscerate any evidence of the men's existence.

Hassan glanced at his phone. His mental timer warned him that the time to depart was near. He had one final technical task to complete before the SUV was ready. He paused and glanced back at the door leading into the kitchen toward Yousef.

Dread crept back into his mind, and he felt a hollow nausea. He shook his head. Was it the petrol fumes or weakness?

He reached back and rubbed his scarred neck, refocusing

his mind on his mission.

A soldier must obey.

Hassan opened the passenger door and connected his laptop to the black box. His fingers went to work, entering the final configuration necessary to arm the device.

On the command line, Hassan entered:

Config/settings/armsetup decrement_end=09:11:00

He stopped and looked at the black box Yousef had labored over for days and nights, customizing an ESP32-S microprocessor. A wave of pride washed over him, remembering Yousef pounding the table, frustrated, testing the data transfer to ensure the detonation device's cloaking algorithm rendered the American's listening devices powerless. Yousef had done well.

Six multi-colored wires stretched into the back seat from Yousef's black box, terminating into the ignition devices between the duffel bags and fuel containers.

The moment of redemption approached. Hassan had labored for years in anticipation of this day, following Khalid's orders with meticulous precision. The timer would initiate the arming command at precisely 0911 hours.

Hassan's mission began five years ago when he crossed the border at the Honduran cartel-controlled El Paso trail entry. He traveled in the Mexican cartel's caravan with mothers, their children, and others from around the world north through Texas and Arkansas. Hassan's Central America ISIS handler had bought the cartel's cooperation with crypto furnished by ISIS's Caracas South American command center.

It wasn't difficult to blend in. Hassan had spent two years studying computer engineering at Cal-Poly on a counterfeit student visa. There, he transitioned into the hedonistic American way of living and viewing the world. However, blending in was more difficult for Yousef. He hadn't been hardened or fought in the war back home.

Six months ago, Yousef was smuggled into the States in an Egyptian cargo container following his training mission in France, after which he joined Hassan's unit in Detroit. However, Yousef was only too eager to demonstrate to his older brother that he was worthy. The combination of inexperience and eagerness was dangerous in their line of work.

Hassan closed the trunk, the weight of the mission settling on his shoulders, and pulled his black hoodie over his head, concealing his features in the shadows. With practiced ease, he drew the Glock 22 Gen 5 from its shoulder holster, a motion honed through countless repetitions. The classic design and lethal potency of the G22 in .40 S&W caliber made it his preferred sidearm over the standard German-made SIG 227 favored by his former comrades. The Glock's high-capacity magazine and marksman barrel rifling combined power and accuracy, giving him a distinct advantage. Tapping the concealed Ruger in his pelvic holster, Hassan ensured his backup was within easy reach. The compact but powerful SR45 served as his faithful companion in the most unpredictable situations.

His left bicep tensed, released and tensed again. The rush of blood coursed through the large arteries running the length of his arm.

The moment had arrived.

He glanced down at his grip on the Glock. The veins in his forearm had swelled, appearing ready to burst. He felt a powerful sensation akin to the superheroes he often admired in American movies, like those from *The Avengers*. He imagined himself as Thanos—invincible, unstoppable, on a mission to conquer and avenge the death of his home planet.

Hassan glanced in the SUV's mirror, the hoodie shading his eyes, and slowly whispered his favorite Thanos line. "Dread it. Run from it. Destiny still arrives. Or should I say, I have."

He walked into the house. With each step forward, the

petrol fumes became more pungent.

Perfection.

Bent over at the top of the basement stairs, Yousef emptied the remaining diesel fuel down the steps, turned, and smiled with remnants of innocence and prideful exuberance.

Hassan gathered his thoughts, his courage.

Invincible. You must follow orders. It is your destiny.

Hassan raised his Glock. His brother's smile vanished, replaced with terror, an expression that forced Hassan to pause. Yousef's eyes shifted from the barrel of the gun back to Hassan. Hassan hesitated, momentarily captivated by the brilliance of Yousef's sky-blue eyes.

"I am sorry, my brother," Hassan said.

"Why?" Yousef said, his voice projecting a strange mixture of fear and deep sadness.

Hassan flexed his trigger finger with trepidation ever so slightly, and the gun expelled the forty-caliber hollow point with the greatest force. As if in slow motion, he watched the projectile penetrate Yousef's forehead above the bridge of his nose and explode out the back of his skull. His head lurched back. His lifeless body followed, crashing down the basement steps and collapsing over itself until it landed on the petrol-soaked dirt floor.

Hassan stared at the crumpled body, blood pooling around his younger brother's expressionless and mutilated face. He squeezed the handle of his weapon with all his strength. His arm quivered like a suspension bridge steel cable vibrating under constant pressure, straining to hold the weight of the steel and concrete high above a raging river below.

BUSINESS TRIP

19 FEBRUARY, 0430 HRS — THREE MONTHS LATER
SHAKER HEIGHTS, OHIO

The dark web's incessant chatter had quieted to a low murmur. That's what kept Paul up all night. He'd recognized the ominous pattern during his two tours in Afghanistan—radio silence was always a prelude to an attack.

Paul turned over for what felt like the hundredth time, again careful not to disturb Sara. He cherished her, utterly captivated by the striking contrast of her long brunette hair against the white pillowcase—its deep chestnut hue radiating warmth in the early morning darkness.

The familiar predawn street noise calmed his nerves. The *beep, beep, beep* of the garbage truck reversing and the crashing of bottles and cans had become part of the city's regular rhythm, as normal as a rooster crow in anticipation of the morning.

The garbage truck rumbled as it lifted the dumpster in the neighboring restaurant's parking lot. Paul felt most comfortable in the chaos—stillness and silence set his nerves on edge, especially that morning. He so desperately wanted to—no, needed to spend these last few precious moments in bed with his wife. The thought of leaving her, with the looming threat of another attack, was almost unbearable.

The calling cards were obvious. Paul's research yielded multiple hits, but nothing concrete regarding the method, actors, or probable targets. He tried to push the problem out of his mind, wanting to forget it all, cancel his trip to Boston, and spend the day with Sara. But that was impossible now.

For weeks and countless expended man-hours, he and his

team had analyzed the network traffic logs and raw 5G base station records. He ran countless queries correlated against the NSA's deep web known-actor profiles. He searched for evidence, patterns, and anomalies that would tie the RF frequencies used by the trigger man or the malware that exploited the surveillance system to known hacker groups: criminals and nation-states. But he still had nothing concrete. And the higher-ups in the FBI, NSA, and ATF wanted results. Heads had already rolled, and more were on the block.

Paul checked the time. He had a plane to catch. The rideshare driver would be arriving soon. He rolled over and rubbed his week-old beard, wondering if he had time to shave. Sara loved it when he grew it out. She'd rub his cheek and then the back of his neck. But that was a long time ago.

More wine and beer bottles crashed as the garbage truck unloaded the dumpster. The silver-white of the streetlights snuck through the narrow opening in the heavy cotton drapery—the drapery Sara had chosen to match the ivory comforter.

They'd spent years rehabbing and decorating that old house. She loved the historic home's woodwork, and he was glad she'd insisted on maintaining its original character. She also loved the Heights—the architecture reminded her of old Europe and the trips abroad they took together during their college years. The home reflected the classic tradesmen—woodworkers and stonemasons from Germany and Italy who'd learned their craft from generations before them.

Paul closed his eyes, remembering the simpler times. Those days at MIT, they'd run the trails that lined the Charles, past the dozen rowing clubs, and through the heart of Cambridge. She'd been a track athlete and later developed a passion for triathlons. The person who pushed Paul to places he didn't think he could reach. They'd talk about their ambitions and dreams on those crisp autumn morning runs. She would say to him when they were in a good place, "*Dreams are forever but are equally fleeting.*"

After grad school, Paul planned to stay in Boston because that's where the action was—the East Coast's technology capital. Boston, a city that forged entrepreneurs and where he'd established a network of computer geek friends who would take over the world, creating software more advanced than anything anyone had ever seen.

But that was a long time ago, before 9/11—the day that changed his life's path, ended the lives of thousands and shattered countless more.

He tried to lay still, but his mind wouldn't let him.

Why didn't his software spot the warning signs? How did it miss the leading indicators?

"How?" Paul said, realizing he'd spoken out loud. "I don't want to leave," he whispered to Sara, not wanting to wake her. "But I'm missing something. Something big. It's right in front of me. I have to go to the lab. Maybe Dr. Clark can shed light on the data I'm seeing—or, I should say, 'not' seeing."

He closed his eyes, wrestling with the thought of leaving her. She had been his rock, the one who understood the emotional wounds inflicted by his father's passing and his time on the ground in Iraq and Afghanistan.

Paul pushed back the blanket and sat on the edge of the bed, thinking about the recent attacks as the memories of 9/11 resurfaced with renewed intensity. He reached for his phone on the nightstand, accidentally knocking over the empty bottle of Maker's Mark. His hand darted out, catching it just before it hit the floor. As he stared at the thick, hardened red wax on the bottle's neck, he hoped the whiskey would help him cope. But it didn't.

He couldn't stay—they'd strike again soon, but when and where? Hundreds had been killed, and they wouldn't stop now that they had proven they could inflict immense damage. Affiliation was of little consequence—Al-Qaeda, ISIS, IRGC, or the Taliban, their hatred for the West transcended human decency.

Now, their tactics had escalated to an even more dangerous level by entering Paul's digital world. He had hard evidence that the enemy had graduated to using sophisticated cyberattacks to preempt and augment their traditional terror tactics. And he thought his software—the most sophisticated machine learning cyber-tech in the world—could identify them before they attacked.

The Thanksgiving Day massacre had thrown the country into chaos, massively disrupting air transportation and crippling an already weakened economy. The FBI and local authorities worked nonstop to locate the perpetrators, but they hadn't made meaningful arrests despite hundreds of leads.

Paul had to get to the MIT lab. He'd hit a wall, and Dr. Clark could help make the breakthrough he desperately needed.

"I'll be back in a couple of days." His thoughts drifted to his daughter, Emma. She was another reason he wanted to go. He had to make sure she was safe. Yet, he wondered—would she even speak with him again?

Paul stood, momentarily forgetting about his ankle. The sharp twinge of pain broke his train of thought. The damn thing had never healed properly—a constant reminder of his late father and the so-called camping trips. His father always said those trips would toughen Paul up, just as his grandfather had done for his father. He looked down at his ankle, flexing it from side to side, lost in thoughts of his father—a solitary man who never spoke of the battles fought in the jungles of Vietnam as part of the 506th Infantry Regiment, 101st Airborne Division.

But his father had died a long time ago.

Paul put pressure on the ankle and gingerly walked to the window. The cold air penetrated the decades-old glass. Outside, a light dusting of snow fell as the garbage truck pulled away, revealing a white cargo van parked across from the house. The orange glow of a cigarette shined through the darkened driver's side window. There were no visible markings on the van.

Was he being paranoid? He had been trained to spot anomalies. To see what others couldn't. It's what kept him alive. And right now, his gut told him that the van was out of place.

His phone vibrated, signaling it was time to go. Paul hesitated before turning to say goodbye to Sara. However, like every morning, he hoped to wake up from this nightmare. He closed his eyes briefly before taking one final look at Sara.

The bed was empty, the sheets on her side neatly tucked—just as it had been since the day she died.

REBEL HUNTING

JUNE 4, 1781 – DAY FOURTEEN OF THE BRITISH SOUTHERN CAMPAIGN
BELVOIR ESTATE – ALBEMARLE COUNTY, VIRGINIA COLONY

Lieutenant Colonel Banastre Tarleton surveyed the troops with his Light Dragoon saber held firmly, sitting tall atop his battle-proven stallion. The magnificent steed boasted a finely sculpted muscular frame, its crow-black coat shimmering under the midday sunlight.

The severed head of a rebel tumbled across the ground, forcibly parted from the lifeless body by the swing of his cavalryman's saber. Tarleton's slow clap demonstrated a rare sign of approval.

Two of his infantrymen engaged in target practice, unleashing the thunderous blasts of their Brown Bess muskets upon the unsuspecting dairy cows. Each precisely aimed headshot felled the beasts in quick succession. The Welch Fusilier soldiers—adorned in the traditional red uniforms with burnished buttons and black leather hats—stood poised, their bayoneted weapons at the ready. With each blast, a resounding cheer erupted from their ranks.

Tarleton wiped the beads of sweat from his forehead, unfastened the top buttons of his white ruffle shirt, and removed his velvet Green Dragoon riding jacket, securing it to his saddlebag. A searing pain radiated from his wounded hand, a constant reminder of the past. He gingerly opened his blade hand, the healing process far from complete. It had been six weeks since the bloody clash with General Greene's Continentals at Guilford Courthouse, where a musket ball had struck his knuckles, leading to the amputation of the fore and middle fingers.

In the spring of 1777, a few days shy of his twenty-fourth birthday, Tarleton arrived in America as a low-ranking cornet. The commission had been secured for eight hundred pounds, a sum he had borrowed from his mother. Though it marked the lowest commissioned rank, it presented the young man, thirsty for adventure, with an opportunity to join the esteemed 1st King's Dragoon Guards—the most distinguished regiment in the British Army. He ascended the ranks from the moment he stepped foot on the New Jersey shore. He fearlessly led his men into battle with unwavering courage, earning his unit the notorious nickname "Tarleton's Raiders."

Tarleton issued commands to the assembled force with a stern voice, buoyed by an inexhaustible supply of battle-forged confidence. Seventy infantrymen from the 23rd Regiment, accompanied by two hundred loyalists from the 17th Light Dragoons, stood ready to heed orders.

"Men, please demonstrate how we deal with traitors. Then we shall go hunting." He surveyed the field, anxious to resume the hunt for his notorious quarry and traitor to the Crown.

Two days ago, a skirmish with General Lafayette's rear guard yielded the capture of a Continental Express rider, including a letter from Lafayette to Jefferson, which indicated a planned meeting in Charlottesville. Lieutenant-General Cornwallis, Commander of the Southern forces, ordered Tarleton and his Dragoons to capture the unsuspecting governor, Thomas Paine, Daniel Boone, and other Virginia assembly members, a task Tarleton most eagerly accepted.

Tarleton ordered two infantrymen to bind another captured rebel and a young Dragoon corporal to perform a "ruby necklace." At the expense of his victims, he applied this deadly training technique to test his young cavalry recruits' emotional toughness and equestrian skills. Did they have the mental fortitude to kill a man and the strength and agility to cut, with a single blow, through the stout bone of the neck? If the rider misjudged the timing or angle, the saber would strike the victim in the face or the ribs, at times lodging in the body and ripping the blade from the rider's hand. Disgraced, the rider would be ordered to make a second and sometimes a third pass before the victim was cleanly decapitated.

"Bring the traitor to me," Tarleton ordered, pointing his blade at the whimpering rebel.

Tarleton demanded respect as he uttered the orders; respect earned not due to rank but rather from his daring battlefield exploits, having killed dozens of American turncoats with his blade and musket.

"Secure him to the post." The force of his voice sent an ominous tone reverberating throughout the ranks. "Corporal, why do you linger? Take your position and prepare your mount. Now, Corporal, or you will join the rebels in hell!" The scar that ran down Tarleton's square jaw from his ear to the corner of his mouth stretched with every word.

"And, Corporal, if the cut is not neat, consider yourself bound for prison ship duty." The floating prisons anchored off the Carolina coast were the most dreaded assignment in the British army.

"Yes...sir, Colonel. I am ready," the corporal said, his voice quivering. The slender young loyalist struggled to maintain his balance in the saddle as he reached for his sword.

Tarleton met the soon-to-be victim with a stare and a wickedly charming grin. "Traitor, prepare to meet your death!" He hoisted his sword to signal to prepare to charge.

Suddenly, the loud creaking of a wooden barn door swinging open commanded Tarleton's attention. He pulled firmly on the reins, and his stallion wheeled left, allowing his master to witness the sudden commotion. Two rebels raced from the barn into the cow pasture, desperate to escape into the woods.

Tarleton's second-in-command, Captain Champaigne, lodged his boot heels into his gray and white gelding, spurring the magnificent beast to rear up and bolt into action. Champaigne pulled his long-curved saber, holding it high overhead, the polished blade glistening in the morning sun. His horse closed ranks on the desperate escapees, and with a single blow, the saber met its mark, splitting the skull and sending the lifeless body crashing to the ground.

"Bravo!" Tarleton clapped, concealing the pain radiating from his wounded hand.

The second rebel scoundrel frantically ran toward the forest's tree line, yet his deer leather farming pants and heavy boots rendered the attempted escape futile. Sensing his fate, the doomed coward threw himself to the ground, burying his face into the thick grass.

Captain Champaigne pulled hard on the reins, commanding his horse to come to a halt, and, without hesitation, thrust his sword into the rebel's back.

"Stake the rebels' heads on the fence posts. Defying the Crown will never be tolerated," Tarleton commanded.

With a pleased grin, he promptly ordered his men to burn the barn, food stores, and the farmhouse.

The fire raged, sending thick black smoke billowing into the sky. Tarleton wheeled his horse around, signaling his light infantry officers to assemble the men and resume a quick march pace to Charlottesville and the ultimate prize— Virginia's rebel leader, Thomas Jefferson.

BOMB FACTORY

28 NOVEMBER, 0545 HRS — THREE MONTHS AGO
LAKE GENEVA TOWNSHIP, ILLINOIS

Hassan looked down at Yousef's lifeless body, lying below on the petrol-soaked basement floor. Hassan's invincible confidence had evaporated, and the strength that had filled his body moments before disappeared. Like a snake constricting its prey, solemn regret tightened its grip on his soul.

He hurled a chair in a rage, its impact shattering against the kitchen wall. He must not succumb to this momentary lapse of weakness. Success would demand the ultimate sacrifice and an unwavering focus on the mission objective.

He picked up the pack of Camels and the cheap plastic lighter, taking a moment to appreciate the drawing of the small camel, pyramids, and palm trees on the pack. He closed his eyes and held a cigarette up to his nose, rolling it between his fingers and taking in the sweet, earthy scent that reminded him of where it had begun. The smokehouse, located in the historic sector of Damascus, was where Hassan and his friends would sit for hours, smoke narghiles, and listen to the elders debate the legitimacy of the civil war, philosophy, and religion. The smokehouse was where Khalid Ahmed Ghlam, the local war hero, had brought Hassan into the flock.

A sophisticated operator, the regional ISIS commander had perfected what few possessed. His charisma captivated the young men of the smokehouse with his triumphant tales of battle, women, and weapons, skillfully recruiting them with the promise of riches and national glory. Like a concert pianist, Khalid would open with a deep philosophical discussion focused on politics and religion, delving deeply into the injustice and inequities of Western imperialism. He amplified the arch of his persuasive oratory, artfully describing the enemy drone strikes and marauding soldiers pillaging the defenseless villages and closing with a climactic flurry of inspiring visions of a homeland returned to the spiritual and prosperous times of their ancestors.

Hassan paused, his thumb ready to strike the lighter's flame. He studied the worn, petrol-soaked linoleum floor as invisible clouds of potent vapor filled the room.

He relished the thrill of the game. Death was to be embraced, not feared.

Hassan struck the lighter wheel. The flame flickered translucent blue, a reminder of the North Arabian desert sky, before it slowly grew taller, quivered, and darkened into an ocean blue. He closed his eyes and inhaled deeply. The toxic petrol fumes burned his throat and lungs as he waited for the room to ignite into a glorious fireball. It did not.

Again, he had cheated death.

Hassan lit a cigarette and took a long drag, savoring the rich, earthy taste. He drew the smoke in deeply, allowing the nicotine to course through his body, relaxing his mind. He took one last drag and turned toward the garage, casually flicking his cigarette back onto the kitchen's petrol-soaked floor. The rasping crackle of linoleum marked the onset of the violent fire, one that would consume the house—and Yousef's lifeless body.

Hassan pushed open the garage door, and a rush of bitter wind swept in brittle, dead leaves and swirling snow. The icy gusts stung his face as he walked to the driver's side of the SUV. He sat calmly as thick black smoke streamed out the cracks at the top and bottom of the closed door that connected the garage to the kitchen.

As he pulled out of the garage and down the long drive, the heavy vehicle's tires crushed the frozen snow and ice mash, breaking the dark morning's silence. He realized he should get as far away as quickly as possible but couldn't resist the temptation to watch the fruits of his labor.

First, the old bedsheets covering the windows burned like parchment paper, fast and hot, beaming light into the surrounding midnight-black forest. Smoke began to billow from the garage and from under the roof soffits. He closed his eyes, relishing the moment, imagining the brilliant blue liquid flames cascading down the basement stairs and torching the bags of ammonium nitrate fertilizer, stacks of newspapers, and cardboard boxes—a raging river of fire washing over Yousef's lifeless body.

Time was up. In moments, the intense heat would cause the fertilizer to expel massive amounts of nitrogen, oxygen, and water vapor, fueling the inferno.

On the road, Hassan stopped, rolled down the window, and watched the fiery magic unfold.

A bright yellow firestorm burst from the windows as if he had willed it. The heated air blew into his face as the house exploded, hurling burning debris, smoke, and ash into the night sky.

◆ ◆ ◆

Hassan drove out of the neighborhood with his headlights off, watching the brilliant fire illuminate the rearview mirror. He picked up his phone and launched the secure Telegram messaging app:

ENTER PASSCODE:

Hassan quickly typed his fifteen-digit code, which rotated daily.

ACCESS GRANTED

Hassan typed.

To 191_hev:
The rooster crows at dawn
From 191_hev:
The sheep will be brought in at nightfall

Khalid confirmed the secondary passphrase. The connection was now secure and safe for open dialogue.

From 191_hev:
Proceed to 1-bridge view

Hassan closed the app and tossed his phone onto the passenger seat.

He'd been given explicit instructions in the officer's protocol training: all communications would utilize the authorized encrypted messaging app, and voice calls were expressly forbidden. It was well-known that the Americans monitored all voice and standard text messaging traffic.

Hassan turned the corner onto the main road, his eyes drawn to a flurry of bright flashing blue, white, and red lights fast approaching. The high-pitched sirens of emergency vehicles intensified as they neared. Gripping the steering wheel tighter, he braced himself, acutely aware of the thousand pounds of explosive materials lying dormant in the back. His orders were clear: detonate immediately if stopped by authorities. Yet, as the emergency vehicles sped past and their sirens quickly faded into the night, they paid no attention to Hassan's unassuming SUV.

Hassan glanced down at the black microcomputer on the passenger seat beside his Glock. In green lettering, the display read ARMED—SYSTEM ACTIVE.

The designated refueling stop was ninety-five miles north of Chicago in Bridgeview, the location of the Midwest command center.

He had made more than a dozen trips to Bridgeview, each time visiting a different operator to avoid the FBI's surveillance pattern matching. One month, it would be an auto body shop, another a restaurant. However, his instructions never included a mosque or house of worship. Those sites were under satellite surveillance. The NSA's advanced imaging system identified each vehicle visiting a known mosque.

Hassan learned in his Russian-led training that NSA tracking software would create a unique digital signature for each moving vehicle flagged within the thousand-meter geo-fence of surveilled locations.

All places of worship had been preprogrammed into the software, meaning a vehicle would receive a unique digital signature if it entered the geo-fence. From that point forward, if there were the need to identify that vehicle's current location, the NSA's thirty-two low-orbiting tracking satellites would scan for a vehicle with the corresponding digital signature. The software would then correlate the digital signature with license plate numbers gathered from toll road cameras and other cameras linked to the NSA's covert surveillance imaging network.

The in-country protocol defined strict guidelines to mask credit card purchasing patterns; therefore, operatives were prohibited from using unauthorized grocery, bank, clothing, or other retail locations. Surveillance cameras in those locations presented a threat of discovery by Homeland Security and the FBI. Their artificial intelligence-based photo recognition technology analyzed retail store and banking surveillance camera footage to identify targets.

Hassan scanned the road, his mind replaying his brother's body rolling down the basement steps. He remembered how he and Yousef had played football in the street with the other neighborhood boys. So long ago—another lifetime.

Soon, very soon, they will pay.

"Focus. For those who sacrificed for our homeland," he

said, watching the broken yellow translucent lines flash by one after another. He slammed his hand on the dashboard, speaking softly, with purpose, as if his brother was present. "Yousef, I hope you understand. It is better this way. The fruits of your labor are ready for harvest."

However, regret began to consume his thoughts. Hassan had no choice but to obey Khalid. But Yousef had been his only brother.

Focus. I must remain focused.

I am ready.

Hassan's knowledge of the plan ended at this point. He wasn't aware of the final destination. Khalid, the ISIS North America Station Commander, had given him explicit instructions to destroy the bomb factory, eliminate any accomplices, proceed to Bridgewater, and await orders.

His phone vibrated. Hassan's heart pumped.

ENTER PASSCODE:

With his right hand on the wheel, Hassan slowly typed his fifteen-digit code with the thumb of his left hand.

ACCESS GRANTED
432_gew:
On your way from the city. Bring home milk

Hassan replied with the username **291_blk:**

Be home soon

He mentally decrypted the cipher—Downtown Chicago Marriott on Rush Street.

Finally aware of his mission target, he reached into the glove compartment for his gold-rimmed mirrored aviator sunglasses, put them on, and stared intently at the wet road ahead. He pulled his hoodie over his head, the top edge touching the bridge of the sunglasses.

He glanced at himself in the rearview mirror, and a renewed sense of power overcame him, causing his muscles to tense with anticipation. The images of his late brother were gone. Focused on his mission objective, Hassan drove the loaded SUV southbound on I-94 toward downtown Chicago.

◆ ◆ ◆

Snow fell lightly on the windshield, reminding Hassan how much he hated the cold. The Americans were like those bastard Russians—arrogant, living in their frigid cities, thumbing their noses at the rest of the world. They believed their nuclear weapons rendered them invincible, but their hubris had closed their eyes to the truth. America was built on a lie, professing freedom—but true freedom, Hassan knew, lay in the purity of one's beliefs. Americans were prisoners of greed and the desire to inflict their so-called "democracy" on others. They invaded in the name of democracy; however, it was a mockery.

He remembered Khalid's inspirational words:

"We shall not allow the Americans to take our homeland and our way of life. We will strike, and they will fear us. Their tanks, drones, bombs, and soldiers are no match for our will."

Hassan again looked at himself in the rearview mirror and saw a warrior.

His phone vibrated.

ENTER PASSCODE:

This communication was not part of the operational plan. Hassan reluctantly entered the passcode.

ACCESS GRANTED

The passphrases and authentication were completed.

347_uef:
exchange the shirt and buy the jeans

Hassan recognized the cipher to be a new target.

291_blk:
yes, dear.

Hassan swiped away the app and tossed the phone on the passenger seat.

A change to the operational target? Was the original compromised? Or was this part of Khalid's plan to transmit multiple targets to keep the Americans guessing?

Soldiers do not question orders.

Yes, it was part of Khalid's plan. Hassan rubbed his beard.

He is a genius.

And a brilliant target it is. They will fear us.

Hassan approached the I-90 West exit ramp and glanced at the triggering device.

Thirty minutes until the final activating sequence.

A THEORY

19 FEBRUARY, 0555 HRS
CLEVELAND HOPKINS INTERNATIONAL AIRPORT

The rideshare driver pulled up to the TSA's newly constructed guard station, its powerful overhead spotlights reflecting off the freshly paved, frozen piano-black asphalt. Paul welcomed the rush of fresh air as the rideshare driver lowered the window to hand his ID to the guard.

"You're authorized for drop-off only. Make it quick. In and out. Got it?" he said.

Paul recognized the guard's handgun holstered on his belt outside a thick down jacket—an SIG Sauer M17, the Air Force and Army's primary service pistol and SIG's variant of the P320.

The second guard approached the rear of the vehicle, clutching an M4 Carbine firmly in a two-handed grip. These guards were part of a newly formed branch of the TSA, a militarized unit tasked with protecting the expanded perimeters of transportation facilities. In response to the November attacks, the President used his executive powers to close the airports until the FAA and TSA completed facility security enhancements and military-grade perimeter defense measures.

Paul glanced at his watch, a Panerai combat-ready diver with a matte black ceramic bezel. It had been a gift from his mentor, Colonel Wilson—a going-away gift for the first of two life-altering tours in the Middle East. Paul ran his thumb across the watch's sapphire crystal. It brought back memories of the American lives lost in Kuwait, Afghanistan, and Iraq. Lives were sacrificed to prevent future terrorist attacks on U.S. soil. As a young Air Force comms specialist, he'd traveled to and from remote airbases, through hostile territory, under the constant threat of IEDs, Taliban snipers, and ambush attacks. He'd witnessed too many men and women—friends—die or be sent home with horrific injuries.

The 9/11 attacks had been the beginning of it all for Paul. It had been over two decades since the last major attack. But this time, the enemy was more advanced, capable of using technology that had been out of their reach—until now.

The falling snow turned bright red in the stoplight's illumination. Paul thought about the countless times he'd waited at that intersection, the entrance to the International Airport. Traveling the world had been part of his job, but this time was different. The Thanksgiving Day attack had changed everything.

Why didn't I see it coming?

His cyber software monitors, including the remote agents installed in the airport's wireless network equipment, failed to pick up the enemy's advanced chatter—or had they, and he'd missed the warning signs? Unlikely. Was there a vulnerability at the egress or a weakness in the system they exploited that masked their communications?

Or had it been in plain sight all along? Sure, he'd been distracted. The loss of Sara threw him into a tailspin. She was his anchor, holding him firmly to the ground when he drifted. He'd been drifting ever since her death.

Paul needed to enlist Dr. Clark and Emma to help him get to the bottom of it. Knowing Emma, she'd tear into the machine learning algorithms and analyze each log file created over the past six months. Dr. Clark would know how to find patterns in the communication trace files to determine how the enemy encrypted the messaging.

Paul had designed the NSA's cyber matching algorithm to monitor all global communication from any comm source link. "Taps" made it possible, facilitated by telecommunications and social media providers, dating back to the 9/11-inspired

Patriot Act and enhanced by the back doors mandated by the Social Media Privacy Act. The "comm taps" routed message headers to his cyber-monitoring software infrastructure for each inbound and outbound IP communication. His software used massive parallel processing engines to decrypt the messages and applied advanced pattern-matching techniques, continuously building a pattern recognition library comparing the deciphered messages to the ever-evolving recognition "Main Library."

If the Main Library found a match, the system tagged it for high-priority review; the sender's message was flagged, and the Central Command Ops center personnel were alerted to initiate a Level 2 threat review. Hundreds of NSA analysts pored over threat messages, routing their highly classified findings to designated action teams for immediate prioritization.

There was no way the terrorists could hack it, but in Paul's profession, anything was possible.

Since his software's implementation three years ago, the latest cyber threat detection software, combined with the Main Library database, had become the foundation of the NSA's security apparatus. If exploited, the enemy's communications would be rendered invisible. However, it was disturbing that the enemy could use his software to turn the tables and breach the Defense Department's top-secret communications, including all communications flowing in and out of the U.S. National Intelligence network.

An external exploit by a foreign actor, such as the Chinese Cyber Command or the Iranian Red Guard, would explain how the Thanksgiving Day attacks went undetected. But that was unlikely.

Implemented by a joint U.S.-Israeli Cyberpark / USCYBERCOM team, dedicated "taps" monitored the CRI Triad network comms. While it was feasible, Paul had ruled out the CRI as the primary actor behind the recent attack. The more probable scenario was that someone had provided a foreign actor access to the NSA's Main Library and the central processor unit.

That scenario had been factored into the early designs. Audit controls were implemented to prevent such a breach; however, government personnel with top-secret clearance had recently carried out multiple espionage events. These events were perpetrated using spear-phishing attacks, bribing, or blackmailing government software engineers with access to highly classified information. The enemy had become increasingly adept at identifying high-value targets and flipping them.

What he couldn't figure out was how they covered their tracks. His software's immutable audit logs were designed to record every event with redundant vectoring commands using multiple data centers, one in each quadrant of the mainland U.S. and two offshore in U.S. territories. Had someone possibly tampered with the audit data? Someone within one of the agencies? He didn't want to go there, but after over two decades in cybersecurity, tracking hackers, and designing software to prevent attacks, he knew insiders—the people you trusted the most—were more often the greatest threat.

I've got to go through the log files again. The answer has to be there.

The challenge was the sheer complexity of the investigative analysis. Paul's software created millions of log file entries every second, and analysis required isolation filters to pinpoint a person or a time of day. That was the dilemma—an ocean of data to sift through, software logic to review, personnel with access to question; he knew the answer was there—who had initiated the breach? Whoever it was would lead him to the Thanksgiving Day attackers.

He had to figure it out—and soon, before they attacked again.

He considered calling Emma, but they hadn't spoken in over a year. Since Sara's funeral, he had retreated from the world, unintentionally neglecting the one person who needed him the most. He regretted not being there for her, acknowledging his absence had fractured their once unbreakable relationship.

Excelling in math and science from an early age, she achieved perfect scores on her college entrance exams and earned a coveted spot in MIT's prestigious mathematics-quantum physics program.

Now, as a mature young woman and graduate assistant at MIT's Computer Science and Artificial Intelligence Laboratory (CSAIL), Emma could take care of herself. She followed in her father's footsteps, yet surpassing him with her intellect while possessing what Paul didn't—her mother's compassion. She cared deeply for others, which made her truly special.

◆ ◆ ◆

The road to the airport was eerily quiet, a stark reflection of attacks that had shocked the nation. As the driver pulled up to the airport's passenger temporary drop-off area, Paul grabbed his leather backpack and stepped out of the car. His boot sank into the icy slush that coated the gravel walkway.

"Have a good day, sir," the driver said with a Somalian accent, his skin tone and elegant facial features confirming East African descent.

The TSA issued a new airport security policy prohibiting vehicles from directly approaching terminals. All airports were required to create pickup and drop-off areas at least five hundred yards away.

Paul lowered his head and leaned into the biting wind and sleet. The brutal lake effect weather resulted from the Canadian Arctic jet stream gathering energy and moisture as it moved eastward across the semi-frozen western basin of the Great Lakes.

To distract himself from the cold, Paul focused on how his software or audit data could have been compromised. It was theoretically possible for a hacker to break his code, but it was impractical with known methods, including unlimited computational power. The probability was infinitesimally low.

His mind switched to a more probable scenario—an enemy from within.

TRAIL OF TEARS

28 NOVEMBER, 0715 HRS — THANKSGIVING DAY
20 MILES NORTH OF CHICAGO, ILLINOIS

The operation called for one last stop to top off the SUV's fuel tank before the final approach to the target. Standard refueling procedures for operatives dictated that the Bridgeview Command Center would notify in-network petrol merchants when drivers arrived, signaling video surveillance devices to be disabled.

The Midwest supply network included fifty-three petrol refueling stations—west of the Pennsylvania-Ohio border, north of the Ohio River, and east of the Mississippi River. The Bridgeview Command managed all in-region operatives and coordinated operations, including recruiting, armament logistics, communications equipment, counterintelligence, and the Canadian-U.S. border crossing.

Hassan pulled off the highway and turned into the predesignated, operative-controlled Circle K.

The U.S. government had gone to great lengths to harden the southern border, shifting human asset entry to rural access points in Michigan, Minnesota, and North Dakota. The American Northern Border Control was slow to react, and Canada's liberal immigration policies aided in the effectiveness of the northern entry route.

Hassan shut off the engine and slowly exited the SUV. The Circle K was empty and dark except for a single fuel pump. He pressed the selector on the pump, staring at the digital display, which read all zeros. He thought about what his commander and mentor, Khalid Ghlam, had told him about the botched Trade Center bombing: *"Never deviate from the plan."*

Khalid had served multiple tours for ISIS in Syria, France, and now the United States. Earlier in his career, he acted as a communication runner for Ramzi Yousef during the 1993 World Trade Center bombing. Ramzi's plan had called for the detonation of a massive fifteen-hundred-pound urea nitrate-hydrogen truck bomb in the WTC garage, which would weaken the structure and topple WTC Tower One into WTC Tower Two, killing thousands. The plan relied on the precise placement of the truck under Tower One.

However, when security guards appeared unexpectedly, Ramzi had egregiously deviated from the prescribed plan. Unwilling to abort his mission, he made the unfortunate decision to place the truck three hundred feet from the prescribed location. The truck bomb detonated; however, Tower One remained standing because of the reinforced concrete that supported the roof.

Ramzi's second misjudgment was changing the execution time of the explosion. He lit the twenty-foot fuse at 12:17 p.m. rather than the 10:15 a.m. target time, which was chosen to ensure that both towers were filled to maximum capacity. However, at 12:17 p.m., over fifty percent of the occupants were outside the building during lunch hour. The mission was a complete failure, and Ramzi paid dearly for his misjudgment.

Following the WTC bombing, Ramzi boarded a flight to Pakistan. The following day, a tourist discovered his body in the Istanbul Airport bathroom stall. An assassin's bullet had entered through Ramzi's right eye and exited the back of his skull.

Hassan returned the fuel pump to its cradle, climbed back into the SUV, and looked up at the station's security camera through the frosted front window. The cameras would be powered off as dictated by operational refueling protocol. His visit would be known to no one.

After driving thirty minutes south, Hassan pulled over and grabbed his modified smartphone. All precautions had been taken to avoid tracking. Despite removing the GPS chip, authorities could trace a wireless device using cell-site triangulation. Hassan removed the phone's SIM card, broke it in half, and tossed it out the window.

He mentally reviewed his mission procedures, going over every step.

Disable phone.

Confirm timing.

The timing of his approach was critical to achieving maximum casualties.

The transportation roadway was jammed, bumper-to-bumper, with incoming and outgoing traffic. Hundreds of travelers scurried in and out of the baggage claim doors, pulling either roller bags or children. With their riders packed like sardines, giant, multi-purpose buses coughed plumes of spent diesel fuel into the air. Traffic police wore bright yellow safety vests, their faces red from continually blowing their whistles and shouting; their hands waved frantically in a feeble attempt to keep traffic moving.

Hassan's SUV approached, proceeding slowly, remaining patient, to the precise location predetermined by mission parameters. Deviation from the plan would not be tolerated.

A car pulled away from the curb, and Hassan stopped feet away from the large exit door as scores of travelers walked hurriedly across the crosswalk.

He tilted his head to the heavens. "Yousef, our time has come, my brother."

Hassan flipped the secondary safety switch on the electronic arming device. The status indicator changed from red to green. The detonator would fire if anyone tampered with the device from that moment forward. There was no turning back. No one could stop the glorious destiny that awaited.

He exited the weaponized SUV, locked the doors, and pulled his hood over his head. He walked unnoticed across the busy crosswalk, avoiding eye contact with the unsuspecting soon-to-be victims.

Hassan opened the black Escalade's rear passenger-side door and stepped in.

"Drive," he said in Russian.

LITTLE MOUNTAIN

> "These principles form the bright constellation which has gone before us and guided our steps through an age of revolution and reformation. The wisdom of our sages and blood of our heroes have been devoted to their attainment. They should be the creed of our political faith, the text of civil instruction, the touchstone by which to try the services of those we trust; and should we wander from them in moments of error or of alarm, let us hasten to retrace our steps and to regain the road which alone leads to peace, liberty, and safety."
> — Thomas Jefferson, 1784

JUNE 4, 1781
CHARLOTTESVILLE, VIRGINIA COLONY

Jack's legs had lost feeling after hours of what may have been the most grueling ride of his life. He could not dismiss from his mind the haunting vision of his father being escorted by the ghostly British soldiers. Was it a dream, exhaustion and his mind playing tricks, or could it have been a message from beyond the grave?

Celer slowed to a trot. Jack allowed himself a brief rest, sitting back in the saddle. The warmth of the rising sun provided some relief to his aching back. He removed his hat and pushed back his long, damp hair.

Droplets of dew glistened off the tall blades of grass while a delicate mist hovered gently over the meadow of lavender gayfeather and asters that lined the mountain's base. Glancing over his shoulder down Old Mountain Road, Jack spotted the ominous sign of the enemy approaching. In the distance, thick, black, billowing smoke rose above the pine forest. Time was running short; two, possibly three hours before Tarleton and his marauding soldiers would reach Charlottesville.

Jack gave his young colt a reassuring pat on the side of the neck. "I know, boy, I'm tired too. We're almost there. See, there's the house. Go on, get it!"

With a firm double-tap of Jack's boot heel, Celer surged forward, effortlessly leaping over a rustic wooden fence, galloping toward the governor's grand estate.

The weight of the moment began to enter Jack's mind. A mix of nervousness and anticipation swirled within him. What would he say to the governor? The great man who penned the Declaration of Independence and led Virginia's fight against the British.

"His new foals! I could ask the governor about his horses," he thought aloud.

Two weeks prior, Julius, a trusted friend, had overheard the governor had acquired a remarkable lineage of thoroughbred foals, arriving soon from France.

What am I thinking? The British would burn the stables to the ground. *I must warn him.*

Celer eased into a steady trot as they reached the top of the rise. The splendor and enormity of the governor's mansion was a sight that surpassed all his expectations. Glimmering sunlight reflected off the expansive front windows. Towering stark white columns supported the roof extending over the portico, and the reddish-brown brick of the mansion's façade created a striking contrast.

A low, friendly voice came from the direction of the stables. "May I hep ya, sir?"

A negro emerged from the side of the mansion—a giant of a man, a full hand taller than Jack, who, at over six feet two inches, was one of the tallest men in Amelia County.

"Yes, I must see the governor immediately," Jack said.

"He be in the stable. We musn't disturb the master."

"Yes, I must."

"With due respect, sir, he don't take visitors before his morn'n' ride."

"I am here to warn the governor that the British are marching on Charlottesville."

"Son, I appreciate your concern. Did you witness them with your own eyes?"

Jack turned toward the origin of the well-spoken voice. A tall, slender man with thick, graying red hair walked toward Jack from the stables. He was familiar. Jack had seen the governor speak with his father in Richmond numerous times.

"Yes, sir. I mean, yes, Governor, sir."

The governor nodded toward the servant standing on the porch. "Thank you, Caesar. Please take this young man's horse to the stable for water and feed." He turned back to Jack. "Son, those cuts on your face and arms. What, may I ask, happened?"

Jack felt the scratches on his face. He'd forgotten. "I rode from Louisa County through the night, following the backwood trails, sir. The redcoats are marching the main road. Over a hundred—Tarleton's Raiders."

"You must be weary and thirsty," the governor said calmly, dismissing the danger approaching.

Jack pleaded, "I must respectfully request that we gather your belongings and family and leave immediately. Tarleton and his legion will take no quarter."

"We have time, son," Jefferson said, remaining calm. "Please join me inside. I insist."

Jack had no choice but to comply with the governor's request.

The governor guided Jack into the opulent grand room, its walls lavishly decorated with indigenous tribal feathers, meticulously framed maps, various skins, and mounted antlers. Governor Jefferson promptly exchanged his riding boots for fur-lined moccasins. A stern look from his female servant caught Jack's attention; she gestured pointedly toward his mud-caked boots. Complying immediately, Jack removed them, unveiling his worn and dirty socks. The pungent odor swiftly permeated the mansion's hall, lingering like an unseen fog.

"Elizabeth, would you kindly bring this handsome young man a fresh pair of leggings? Also, fetch a bottle of Madeira—the fresh batch, please—the batch that arrived from my beloved Paris last week."

The governor wore a white blouse with dark brown leather breeches. Tall compared to common folk, though a few inches shorter than Jack. With measured strides, he led Jack into the sprawling east wing of the magnificent mansion. The sight left Jack breathless—never had he witnessed such grandeur.

As he walked, he marveled at the discovery of seven rooms before arriving at what appeared to be the library. Shelves lined the walls from floor to ceiling, housing an extensive collection of finely bound leather books. Volumes were scattered throughout the room. Neatly stacked piles flanked the governor's desk, occupying nearly every inch of available space.

Who could read this many books? It might take Jack three lifetimes just to read half of them.

An elegant mahogany writing desk with an angled top hinged in the front was positioned before a grand window that offered a sweeping view of sunflowers and orderly rows of grapevine fields. Stacks of parchment papers were piled upon the desk, overflowing onto the floor. The distinctive earthy scent of iron gall ink lofted in the air, mixed with the familiar aroma of aged tobacco.

Was this the desk?

"Sir, is this the writing desk? Where you wrote the splendid letter to the king?"

The governor slowly ran his hand across the top of the desk's polished edge as if caressing a beloved companion. "In a sense, yes. I drafted the First Rights at this desk, the forerunner to our Declaration. However, in the marvelous city of Philadelphia, I drafted the Declaration alongside my esteemed colleague, Ben Franklin, who lent his invaluable assistance."

The governor turned toward the picture window as the morning sun shined through the leaves of a large oak tree. "But time has passed, and many brave souls have died defending the words I penned. I am burdened with the thought and question if it was proper considering the innocent lives that have been lost."

"Sir, my dear father and brother died fighting for those very rights—that all men are created equal, that they are endowed by their Creator with certain unalienable Rights, that among these are Life, Liberty, and the pursuit of Happiness. And I will continue to honor those who have died; however, we must not forget that we also fight for those who will live and for their children's children."

The governor stared at Jack as if he was reaching into his soul. He turned to the desk, removed several long parchments, folded them, and slipped them into a finely stitched leather folio.

"I have toiled over these documents for many weeks. They hold the key to victory. Will you assist me, Jack? You have lost loved ones for the cause, and I trust you to be a man of honor."

Jack was eager to learn more about the governor's plans, yet he was acutely aware that time was of the essence. "Of course, sir. However, we must leave," he insisted.

"Now, now. The British are like that deciduous oak." Jefferson motioned to the window. "It is majestic and strong yet grows ever so slowly. The British possess a supreme and mighty fighting force. However, their generals are plodders and dawdlers. If, by chance, they venture this way, we will know. I built Monticello on Carter's Mountain because it affords the benefit of surveying the valley and beyond. We'll be fine, son," Jefferson said, his voice steady and calm.

"Sir, I must insist you gather your family and leave immediately. The servants can look after your home."

"Son, my father settled this land well before you were born. I have no intention of abandoning it. Also, Caesar, Elizabeth, and the other servants are my family. I could not and will not abandon them."

"Fine, sir. They may come with us."

"We will ride to Lookout Point and survey the valley with my new looking glass," Jefferson said with a smile. "I received this fascinating instrument from an old Austrian friend. He has been tinkering with spectacles and applying interesting light refraction techniques using small mirrors. Catherine the Great commissioned him to craft a long-range spectacle for her field generals. He has made splendid progress," he said as he handed the device to Jack. "On a clear day, you can see Sandy Hook with this amazing device."

With little interest, Jack held the heavy brass contraption and returned it to the governor. "A fine instrument, but please, may we go?"

Jefferson looked over Jack's shoulders as Elizabeth walked into the room holding a silver platter with two glasses filled with a light, amber-colored wine.

"Thank you, Elizabeth." The governor took a glass, handed it to Jack, lifted his high, and proudly proclaimed, "To General Washington's health and success. Long live the Republic!" He closed his eyes and slowly sipped the wine.

Jack lifted the glass to eye level. The crystal caught the light, illuminating the opaque crimson liquid. In one gulp, the wine disappeared. The distinct velvety taste of ripe, dark cherries lingered on his tongue. It was nothing like he had ever tasted. Certainly not like the harsh-biting, rock-gut whiskey old Abe poured at Cuckoo Tavern.

"Elizabeth, please ask Caesar to saddle Caractacus. We shall be going on a short excursion to Carter's Mountain," Jefferson said.

◆ ◆ ◆

Jack and the governor rode northeast for about half a mile before halting upon a majestic bluff that faced east. Jack looked out over the lush forest canopy, stretching as far as the eye could see. Cotton-white clouds slowly floated toward the sea high above the vast emerald-green forest. Shielding his eyes from the noonday sun, he focused on the Main Road, a thin, snaking line running westward from Richmond to Charlottesville, searching for signs of the approaching enemy.

"Ah, yes," the governor said with the bronzed spectacles held to his eyes.

"What is it, sir? What do you see?" Jack asked.

"As I suspected, there is no sign of those rotten scoundrels," Jefferson said.

Jack sighed and dropped his head. "Sir, you must trust me."

The governor's horse violently thrashed its head and let out loud snorts as it attempted to shoo an unwelcome bee. The governor lost his grip in the commotion, and the spectacles tumbled, disappearing into the lush, tall grass.

Quickly, Jack dismounted, located them, and respectfully handed them to Jefferson.

"Thank you," the governor said with a kind expression. "Please forgive my rudeness. I did not ask you your full name."

"John Jouett, Junior, sir, but my family and friends call me Jack so as not to confuse with my late father, John Jouett."

"A pleasure to meet you, Jack Jouett, if I may call you Jack."

"You may call me what you wish, sir," Jack said and smiled.

The governor raised the odd-looking spectacles again to his eyes, peering in all directions. He paused and turned the clicking dial on top, holding his stare for several seconds.

"Jack, I commend you for your persistence. We must return to the estate forthwith. Ten lines of British infantry soldiers, led by several dozen cavalrymen, are marching toward Charlottesville." He paused and then said, "Jack, did you hear me? There is no time for delay."

"Yes, sir," Jack said, noticing tension and urgency in the governor's voice for the first time.

GROUND ZERO

28 NOVEMBER, 0835 HRS
O'HARE INTERNATIONAL AIRPORT – CHICAGO, ILLINOIS

Chicago Police Sergeant Mike Johnson stood at his designated security station, methodically scanning the swirling mass of travelers that filled the maze of fourteen massive baggage claim conveyors. The crowd was more intense than usual due to the holiday weekend's surge. The boys of his unit had given him the nickname "Mack" for good reason—he was built like a truck, a giant of a man. With his yellow and white sergeant bars brightly displayed on his pressed black police uniform, he towered over those he swore to protect.

The constant rhythmic grinding of the baggage belts reverberated through the terminal. Working overtime, they spit out bag after bag.

A Japanese tour guide, impeccably dressed in her tailored blue suit pants and pink blouse, held up a small "Michigan Ave" tour sign. Her troop of foreign tourists followed in tight formation, weaving through the myriad of travelers, eager to locate their bags, friends, and family.

Mack coordinated incident response with Homeland Security, ATF, and local law enforcement for Chicago O'Hare International's Concourse B security. Yet, during his patrols in the lower concourse, he found himself dealing with people's travel issues or providing directions to the restroom rather than his primary security responsibilities. After sixteen years in the Marines—six deployed during the first Iraq war, where Mack reached Marine E-7 Gunnery Sargent—he had returned to civilian life and his job as a Chicago Police beat cop. Now, he protected one of the busiest airports in the world.

In rapid succession, explosive pops of firecrackers hit Mack's ears, quickly drowned out by the shrilling cascade of high-pitched screams. The eruption of fast-tempo discharges—the distinctive short-burst rhythm of an AR-15—was ominously familiar. He confirmed by the irregular spacing of the shots there were multiple attackers. A seasoned veteran, Mack trained his men to face the threat imposed by enhanced automatic weapons and the strategies to defend against them. However, reality seldom resembled those mock training scenarios.

As if time stood still, the clanking of the baggage carousels echoed. People once smiling, hugging, and calmly waiting on their bags stood motionless in stunned disbelief. Heads began turning, searching. Feet began to shuffle. Faces transformed, giving way to a mixture of wide-eyed panic and bewildered confusion.

Mack instantly found himself overrun and surrounded by a crowd of terrified travelers—innocent women and children frantically attempting to escape the relentless hail of bullets.

Mack's senses heightened, alert to the familiar echoes of fear, and the grim scent of death engaged his battle instincts. It was a spontaneous flashback to his days as a young corporal, fighting alongside his fellow Marines in the war-torn streets of Falluja.

Yet this was very different—Chicago was his home.

And now it was personal.

He assessed the scene, calculating the threat vectors and preparing the appropriate counterattack. The enemy's weapons were likely .223 caliber with the firing sears modified into an auto—similar to the Las Vegas and Sandy Hook shooters. Based on the rapid firing tempo, the shooters could crank out four hundred to six hundred rounds per minute. At that pace, the heat generated by the expelled energy would melt the barrel's gas tubing after one or two mags.

Triggered by instinct and experience, Mack's right hand

immediately dropped to his sidearm. He drew his SIG Sauer P226 Legion, instantly releasing the safety. His head swiveled to the right, then the left, his eyes and ears pinpointing the trajectory of the rounds.

From his left, another explosive burst of gunfire rang out.

Like a torrential river, high-pitched screams rushed down the cavernous corridor. Bodies tumbled and crashed upon one another, down the escalator and onto the floor. To Mack's left, terrified travelers ran in all directions, arms flailing, tripping, sliding, and falling.

"Move to the exit doors! Now!" Mack commanded the mass of humanity closing in around him.

The situation had two attack vectors: the left flank and the center.

"Mack to Command!" he yelled into his shoulder-mounted radio mic. "Two shooters, automatic rifles. Hot fire coming from the top of escalator A5. Second shooter on my left flank—near carousel three, exit door two. Double fast rounds. Send SWAT and AP tactical ASAP!"

He took a deep breath, thinking quickly through incident protocol.

"Execute Charlie Lockdown. I repeat, execute Charlie Lockdown."

In the incident response plan, Charlie stood for "Complete," but some of his team called it the "Chaos" scenario.

Mack recalibrated the threat vectors—the top of the escalator and his left flank. He chose to go left, toward the gunfire.

A rushing herd of bodies pushed and pulled; bags scattered. The panicked mass streamed toward the exit door. A woman crashed to the ground ten feet from Mack. She didn't trip and fall. Another woman next to her went down hard; her body slid toward him. Blood smeared on the polished white granite floor.

Terrified victims hid behind the carousel while others ran for cover. Parents dragged their children to safety. An elderly man fell, his blood splattering in a large leaf-shaped fan onto the tiles. The back of his head had been blown apart.

The shooter was within range, likely moving toward his position. Mack raised his SIG with a double overhand grip, searching for the target. The gunman came into sight with all-black clothing and mask, and the automatic rifle pointed at Mack.

In an instant, Mack calmed his mind and steadied his body. Decades of training, Middle Eastern wars, and, most recently, the gang battles of Chicago's South Side had prepared him for this moment.

Mack sighted the target below the center mass and rapidly discharged four rounds. The bullets leaped from his gun. The SIG's recoil was familiar and easily absorbed by his massive hands and forearms. He made slight adjustments as the barrel naturally elevated after each discharge. Each trigger pull was fast and smooth.

Mack had been diligent about his firearm certifications and practiced every Tuesday and Thursday at the officers' range in preparation for "The Day." He repeatedly told Chicago PD higher-ups, "We need more threat prevention and detection throughout the pre-screening and open areas." However, Chicago's budgets were tight due to the recession that had gripped the country, and the liberal mayor had redirected law enforcement funding to her pet social justice projects.

For over a decade, Homeland Security allocated the majority of the airport security budget to screening passengers, which, in effect, protected airplanes.

"What about the people and the common areas?" Mack would argue. "What about the masses of people outside of the TSA-protected areas?"

Yet, his warnings were ignored. While some might have recognized the risks, their failure to take decisive action spoke volumes—mired in politics. It wasn't until the crisis that the true cost became apparent. Now, all would bear the price of inaction, and everyone would pay.

Mack's bullets traveled thirty feet in the blink of an eye. Three shots struck the target's chest, violently throwing him to the ground. The fourth bullet sailed high, striking an electronic advertising display. The impact sent an explosive mix of bright white sparks and a cascade of shattered glass into the air.

Mack searched for the downed attacker, attempting to locate him in the chaos.

The masked shooter staggered to his feet.

Body armor.

Mack shuffled to his right to optimize his angle, elevated his sight several inches above the center mass, and pulled off four more rounds.

Two bullets ripped into the attacker's throat, and another displaced the jaw, sending the lifeless body to the ground.

Mack pulled a fresh load off his belt without taking his eyes off the frantic scene, released the partially spent mag, jammed it into his back pocket for safekeeping, and slammed in the fresh mag.

"Mack to Command. One threat neutralized, two more shooters—escalator two and near Claim Three."

Mack could feel the electrifying surge of adrenaline course through his veins, fueling him to push forward.

The chaotic scene had reached a crescendo. People screamed, and children cried. Terrified, they rushed for the exit doors, tripping over one another, many falling like rag dolls. Mack could see over the crowd surging toward him. Twenty feet to Mack's right, a man and a woman were hit from behind and went down hard.

A deafening blast sent shockwaves rippling through the corridor. Mack instinctively crouched low while others scrambled for cover or dove to the ground. A dark wave of smoke and billowing dust rolled down the corridor, engulfing everything in its wake.

Mack coughed, struggling to breathe. He stood and moved toward the rays of light breaking through the smoke.

In Iraq, he'd used concussion and fragment grenades to clear buildings, flush out the enemy, and repel overwhelming hostile fire.

Grenade!

"Get out! Move!"

Mack forced his way through the chaos, attempting to herd people out of the crammed exit door.

To his right, another grenade detonated, the force of the blast pushing him back into the crowd. Debris blew into his face; the light went dark. The constant screaming of those wounded and terrified fell silent, then slowly escalated again as the concussion from the explosion subsided. He coughed deep and wiped and opened his watering eyes. An overwhelming scene unfolded. Lifeless bodies littered the blood-stained floor, scattered like discarded, broken mannequins.

Those that could run crawled, pushed, and shoved through the exit doors to the covered arrival pickup area.

In an instant, Mack felt a searing bolt of pain pierce his left shoulder, rendering his arm limp. Warm, dark blood began to trickle from his hand, spattering the white granite floor.

With his other arm, he pointed his gun toward the exit and yelled, "That way, move!"

He had to choose—left or right, grenades or shooters? The gunman had started before the grenades, so Mack ran to his right. Like a red-hot poker shoved into bone, shocking pain radiated from his right hip. He fell hard to his knees. He threw his head back and yelled to expel the pain from his bullet-riddled body.

He torqued his upper body to the left, rolled, and found himself next to a trash can. He looked through the scores of people running toward him. The shooter, cloaked in black clothing and brandishing a high-powered rifle, fired a series of rounds from about twenty yards down the crowded corridor.

Blood pooling around him, Mack lay prone, sighted the shooter's right pelvic area, and squeezed off four shots in rapid succession. The shooter's leg was thrown out from under him. He went down, slamming his head into the baggage carousel's metal edge.

Mack grimaced as he pulled himself up and leaned against a shattered vending machine.

A small boy with blood on his shirt ran toward Mack, tripped, and fell. Mack hobbled to him, scooped up the boy, and helped guide people out the exit door into the covered transportation arrival area.

Pandemonium unfolded outside. People violently shoved and pulled their children like rag dolls, tripping over luggage and the fallen. Cars, vans, and buses were trapped. The drivers yelled and honked, unable to move.

Mack, dragging his dead leg, limped back inside to secure the scene and tend to the injured. The thick haze of dust and smoke slowly lifted, unveiling a scene difficult for Mack to comprehend. The toxic fumes stung his nostrils. The scent of melting plastic intermingled with the unmistakable charred aroma of destruction. But it was the burned, nameless bodies and the anguished cries of the wounded that would haunt him for the rest of his life. He'd witnessed death and destruction during the war, but this was different—this was his city, the place and people he loved.

A young girl, maybe five years old, sat sobbing uncontrollably over her mother or grandmother, who lay motionless, face down, with her once-pristine white blouse stained a dark crimson.

Mack knew what he would find, but his duty was to check.

He knelt next to the girl and made a hopeless attempt to find the woman's pulse.

9:11

28 NOVEMBER, 0905 HRS
O'HARE INTERNATIONAL AIRPORT — CHICAGO, ILLINOIS

"Stop here," Hassan said to the bald, muscle-bound driver from the back seat of the black Escalade.

The Russian obediently complied, pulling the vehicle over to the side of the airport service road. Hassan had explicitly requested a Russian from his Chicago Mafia associates, compensating them handsomely. The Russian driver had no connection to the operation and would lead the would-be investigators down the path he wanted them to go.

Hassan checked the time on his phone, then turned his attention to the billowing gray clouds of smoke rising from Terminal 3's arrival area. Lowering the tinted window of the Escalade, a symphony of sirens, alarms, and car horns from the airport flooded in.

"Brilliant," Hassan said, admiring the work of his suicide attack team—three Iranian men and one woman, smuggled into the U.S. six months prior. They'd been offered to Khalid by the IRGC. The brave fighters had told Hassan they'd "volunteered" for the glorious opportunity to sacrifice their lives in return for redemption and glory. However, Hassan understood that no one in Iran volunteered—Republican Guard soldiers followed the Ayatollah's orders and demanded unconditional compliance and sacrifice from his flock.

Hassan sat patiently awaiting Khalid's orders to initiate the mission's final phase. Precise execution timing was imperative to strike fear into the Americans. Deviation from the plan would have severe repercussions. The detonation device was to be triggered precisely at 0911 hours—a tribute to the heroic martyrs who sacrificed their lives for the cause. From this moment forward, forever, when their clocks struck 0911 hours, the Americans would remember this day and cower in fear of another attack.

Hassan glanced at the phone time display: 28 NOV 9:08.

The Telegram messaging app glowed and displayed a message.

EXEC CODE F26RH-EBNCH-HTYUB-BYJHH 28 11 0911

Hassan replied:

RCVD

He grabbed the trigger phone from his jacket pocket. The device was custom-built with software that contained unique cloaking technology designed to mask all NSA and TSA surveillance. Hassan keyed in his identity code and waited. He selected the preprogrammed IP address assigned to the detonation device that sat on the passenger seat of the explosive-laden SUV parked in front of the exit door of Terminal 3.

He typed *EXEC*, then *F-2-6-EBNCH-HTYUB-BYJHH*, and pressed *SEND*. Waited. He opened the window halfway. The cold air calmed his uncontrollable anticipation.

KEY ACCEPTED.
ENTER CONFIRMATION KEY:

He hesitated. A second confirmation key hadn't been part of the trial runs he performed over a dozen times with Khalid.

A flash of anxiety, followed by dread, pushed up from his chest into his throat. What was wrong? He checked the code. Had he entered it incorrectly?

Then, the phone went blank.

He pressed the power button, but it did not respond.

The escalating sound of sirens screamed, signaling the rapid approach of police cruisers from behind. Hassan's left hand instinctively moved to his chest-holstered Glock. As the wailing sirens drew nearer, he mentally prepared for the inevitable.

The Russian turned briefly toward Hassan. "We go now?" His head snapped back around, anxiously searching for the source of the sirens.

"No," Hassan ordered.

The police cruisers roared past, lights blazing and sirens wailing. A fire truck and two ambulances followed closely behind and sprayed ice and snow on the Escalade's front windows.

Hassan relaxed his gun hand and looked out at the terminal. Smoke continued to pour out from under the arrival tunnel. He glanced at the Escalade's digital clock: 9:11 a.m.

His phone vibrated in his hand and illuminated the message he had been anxiously anticipating:

CONFIRMATION KEY ACCEPTED
DETONATION SEQUENCE COMMENCING
05, 04, 03, 02, 01.

A bright white flash of light shot out from under the terminal tunnel, followed by a tremor reverberating through Hassan's leather car seat. Fire and debris rocketed into the air. Instantly, the terminal disappeared behind the thick curtain of smoke.

His phone vibrated again.

COMMAND EXECUTION SUCCESSFUL

The detonation of the SUV required confirmation by a second person. *Brilliant.* Khalid had thought of everything. He'd remotely completed the execution.

Hassan drew his Glock and pushed the gun's barrel into the back of the Russian's head. "Get out!"

He and the Russian exited the Escalade and walked over to the median. The service road was clear. There was a steep drop down the snow-covered embankment. At the bottom, a cement culvert filled with slow-flowing blackish water and ice stretched the length of the service road.

Hassan lowered his weapon. Both hands at his sides, he gave the Russian a slight nod. Hassan removed his finger from the trigger, further daring the Russian to pull his weapon. He waited for a five-count.

The Russian's eyes betrayed him—an unmistakable hint of reluctance flickered within, revealing the truth. A coward.

Hassan shook his head in disappointment, hoping to be tested on this glorious day.

The Russian slowly raised his hands into the air. "Why do this?" he asked.

"For the brave Syrian men, women, and children you bastard Russians killed. My family and brothers," Hassan said in fluent Russian. He wanted the man to understand his words clearly.

The Russian spat on Hassan's boots.

Hassan smiled, raised his Glock, and pointed it at the bridge of the Russian's nose. He pulled the trigger with determined force. His adrenaline-fueled arm and shoulder muscles absorbed the Glock's powerful .40 caliber recoil. The Russian's body crumpled with a violent burst of blood, brain, and bone matter splattering across the snow-covered service road.

Hassan took a deep, gratifying breath, content with the result. He rolled the body down the hill towards the ice-edged roadside ditch. As the corpse tumbled, a dark crimson trail marred the otherwise pristine, snow-white embankment.

The escalating roar of sirens signaled the high-speed approach of a potential threat. Hassan calmly holstered his weapon and made his way to the edge of the service road. The blaring sirens were abruptly silenced, and the ambulance skidded to a stop. The rear doors swung open.

Hassan stepped in, closing the ambulance doors behind him.

DISCOVERED

19 FEBRUARY, 0625 HRS — THREE MONTHS LATER
CLEVELAND, OHIO

Paul brushed the wet snow off his shoulders and backpack and walked toward the TSA security checkpoint. He caught a glimpse of his reflection in the polished floor-to-ceiling glass of the airport entrance ramp. His tired eyes met the image of a man with deep lines on his forehead, a two-week-old rough and scraggly beard, and shoulder-length peppered-gray hair.

Since his discharge and return from the tours in Iraq, Sara had begged him to grow his hair long. His hard-ass, by-the-book father would have demanded strict adherence to protocol—clean-shaven, hair neat and closely trimmed, neck tapered with military precision, never to touch the collar. But Paul was done conforming, and his father was long gone. Sara had loved it. So did he.

A handful of weary business travelers waited in line with worn shoes and old raincoats, each holding their morning fix of coffee. TSA pre-check lines and airline priority services were a thing of the past.

In the days before the Thanksgiving Day bombings, Paul could breeze through TSA pre-check without hassle. The TSA officers were cordial and, in most cases, friendly. Those days were gone. Airports were on lockdown.

Paul walked through the newly installed full-body detector after the TSA entry officer scanned his right hand. His backpack and phone emerged from the belt. He glanced at the incoming message.

United Flight 1307 Update: Gate B19, Cleveland (CLE) to Boston (BOS) ON-TIME boarding starts at 6:05 a.m.

Nearby, an armed female TSA officer patted down a man in his mid-seventies. Arms raised, the gentleman held his belt in one hand and his phone in the other. He struggled to hold his arms up as the officer made several passes up and down his legs. Another TSA officer wearing blue surgical gloves rummaged through the man's carry-on bag.

"Sir, come with me," an overweight TSA officer said to another man standing in line in front of Paul. The officer's light blue uniform with tight polyester black pants was two sizes too small. His bulk stress-tested the seams.

"What's the problem?" the dark-skinned man asked, frustrated that he'd been held. He appeared Hindu, likely from Western India.

"Come with me," the officer ordered.

Paul wasn't surprised the TSA had profiled the man. The officer escorted him to the secondary scanning area. The traveler followed as the officer plodded along, his shoulders hunched and knuckles appearing almost to scrape the ground.

Paul had been searched before, many times, but not today. A blue-eyed Caucasian didn't fit the target race profile.

The TSA had been scrambling to add security controls, and the latest was retinal scans for all travelers of color, while random scans were conducted on everyone else. Procedures were changed immediately following on the heels of the Thanksgiving Day attack, with more stringent security measures implemented after last month's downed flight over LA that killed one-hundred twenty-three onboard and fifty-four people on the ground when the plane struck a suburban office complex.

A controversial Presidential Executive Order had been issued, instructing the TSA to implement systematic profiling. The order was immediately followed by an overwhelming political outcry, violent demonstrations in D.C., LA, Seattle, and New York, criticism from the press, and ACLU lawsuits. However, public opinion polls supported the President's actions.

Paul advised NSA leadership against profiling, citing study after study that it wasn't effective because overwhelming false positives diverted valuable security resources away from more productive threat prevention. Not to mention the broader societal consequences—it simply wasn't right. Ultimately, politicians prioritized political expediency and party loyalty over the impact of their policies, which was why Paul had turned down offers to run for office. He simply couldn't allow a political party to challenge his integrity or core principles. While Paul didn't always see eye to eye with his father, there was complete agreement when it came to standing up for one's principles.

Paul watched the hefty TSA officer bark instructions at the man.

"Remove your glasses. Press your forehead against the plastic. Look into the machine and hold still. Or you'll do it again until you get it right."

The traveler obediently complied.

Paul had recently researched the new scanners, which analyzed dilation patterns and body temperature, correlating the data with predefined thresholds based on age, gender, and body type.

The light on top of the retinal scanning machine turned green.

"Okay, you can go," the TSA officer said.

Paul sat down and laced his boots. He then discretely pulled out his phone and quickly typed notes:

2-23-2022 5:57 am CLE to BOS Checkpoint 202A
Brent A Bernard, TSA ID Check Agent, 47372, 30
Dominic J Naples, TSA Retina Scan Agent, 56372, 35
Janice K Churchwell, TSA Bag Scan Agent, 37948 45

Years ago, Paul had started a personal TSA agent log. As he traveled through airports, he glanced at ID badges, committing names and ID numbers to memory—accumulating hundreds over the years. How long would it be before Homeland Security recognized they were exposing agents' identities? Paul was sure our enemies had already exploited this foolish weakness.

He would sit next to a TSA agent on a break and discreetly capture photos or videos of them to supplement his log. Subsequently, he would shadow the agent to the TSA office areas or locker rooms and observe as they entered their keypad combination. Paul had recorded every TSA keypad combination in the airport, often pondering why they hadn't upgraded to biometric readers. However, he had learned not to question government security procedures, no matter how much they defied common sense.

The first step was to obtain the personal identity facts of their target. Even a marginally skilled hacker, armed with a name and city, could simply gather a treasure trove of information about someone's personal life using Google and other public sources, such as court records, real estate sites, and sex offender databases. However, the reliable method of collecting personal data involved scouring social media platforms. Paul found what people shared, particularly on one of the most popular social networking sites, Lifeclip, astonishing.

Jason Anderson, the creator of Lifeclip and the former Facebook engineer who had followed in Zuckerberg's footsteps, was only twenty-two when he developed the app. Bill Gates had purchased Anderson's business for two billion dollars, making him one of the world's wealthiest twenty-somethings.

Lifeclip allowed people to stream video of their personal lives continuously, twenty-four hours a day, directly from their phones, home security cameras, GoPro glasses, and in-car video cams. The popularity of the site had exploded in just over a year. People had created thousands of personalized reality channels spawning the next generation of social influencers—"Life with the Smiths," or "Life with the Cominskis," and themed channels such as "Life as an Addict," "Life as a Single Mom," or "Life as a Tattoo Artist."

The most followed Lifeclip channels and influencers could earn hundreds of thousands per month in sponsorships and advertising. Big corporate brands such as Ford, Kraft, and Budweiser paid channel owners a few cents each time their products were featured in a Lifeclip reality feed, creating the next social media gold rush. Millions of hours of people's everyday lives were posted online for the world to see and hear.

The secret behind the app's success was Anderson's next-generation AI image recognition software, which deciphered, learned, and cataloged the videos' intricate color patterns and applied pixel-density computational models to tag each object in the stream of images.

Anonymity, privacy, and confidentiality had become relics of the past since the widespread adoption of Anderson's latest artificial intelligence technology, combined with Facebook's and Google's new government-sponsored surveillance and screening programs.

◆ ◆ ◆

The airport bars, newsstands, and souvenir shops were empty, and the restaurants had closed one by one. Recently, the TSA had placed India on the list of banned countries. Consequently, even the owners of the airport's coffee shops and other stores, run by accomplished immigrant entrepreneurs, were prohibited from overseeing their businesses.

Paul walked down the empty, dimly lit corridor to the departure gate. Three months ago, the same hallway teemed with people.

As he made his way to the gate, he casually scanned the crowd, his glance drifting left until it settled on a familiar face. Paul prided himself on his ability to remember every face, yet this one triggered a deep sense of unease within him.

Was it a connection from over a decade ago in Iraq or Kuwait? The guy looked familiar, no doubt about it. The question was: Did Paul recognize the bearded man seated by the window, or did the man recognize Paul?

The stranger maintained eye contact with Paul. His sunken, dark brown eyes radiated emotionless confidence, yet his stare carried a hint of weary tension.

Paul's heart began to pump faster, the warmth running from his chest to his neck.

The stranger looked away.

Overreacting? A coincidence?

Paul walked toward the newsstand, his mind racing to piece together the puzzle. The man appeared to be Mediterranean, likely in his late forties, and was dressed with an eye for detail—dark blue jeans neatly tucked into cowboy boots. His beard was jet-black, trimmed with precision. Ethnicity is likely Arabic or perhaps Greek. Clearly, he was not a local.

"In a moment, we'll begin boarding the flight to Boston," the solemn gate agent announced over the loudspeaker.

Paul's reaction and questioning of his instincts were out of character. He must have seen the man before. Over the years, Paul had groomed the trait of memorizing names and faces. He cataloged every encounter in his life. When he was a young boy, his father taught him that mental recognition and cataloging were valuable life skills.

Something was odd in this situation. Something about the man, a combination of things: his profile was consistent with the type of men Paul had encountered in Iraq and Kuwait. But over the years, there had been thousands of unsolicited glances. Why was this one triggering an internal alarm? There was an aura about the man Paul couldn't put his finger on—how he carried himself and dressed.

Paul had carefully managed every aspect of his life, cautious to avoid being targeted by criminals and nation-states he'd investigated on the dark web for all those years. His cyber-recon unit tracked the worst of the worst, and Paul had taken every precaution to conceal his unit's identity and movements. Had they stumbled into something or someone who didn't want to be found? Or was it paranoia triggered by the sleepless nights, the whiskey—or both? His gut told him this guy was bad news, and his gut was always right.

Always.

Paul felt his phone vibrate, signaling an incoming message. Glancing at the screen, he saw it was from Colonel Wilson's number, a contact he hadn't heard from in years.

GO TO A SECURE CONNECTION. EXIT INSTRUCTIONS WILL FOLLOW. C.W.

A wave of unease washed over Paul as he absorbed the message. Why now? The timing seemed too perfect to be a mere coincidence. It arrived just as he was wrestling with uncertainties about his intuition. Could there be a connection?

Paul looked up from his phone, glancing toward the stranger who stood with both hands in his jacket pocket. The man's face was dark, weathered by time and the elements. Paul noticed the scar on the side of his neck. The texture suggested it was the result of a severe burn.

The stranger pulled out mirrored aviator sunglasses from his pocket and slipped them on. With a subtle nod, he motioned for Paul to follow him toward the baggage claim area.

In response, Paul pivoted and walked in the opposite direction.

NARROW ESCAPE

> "Patriotism is as much a virtue as justice, and is as necessary for the support of societies as natural affection is for the support of families."
> — Benjamin Rush, 1776

JUNE 4, 1781
CARTER'S MOUNTAIN, VIRGINIA COLONY

Jack and the governor charged down Carter's Mountain, the warm summer wind pushing against Jack's face as they navigated the dense, overgrown brush. Jack urged Celer with his heel, maintaining pace without separating from the governor. A whirlwind of anxiety churned within him; he feared arriving too late to warn the others about the impending danger.

Celer's hooves pounded the dry, matted grass in a perfect rhythm as Jack considered the escape route options. He could outdistance the British by leading the governor northwest to meet up with the Overmountain men of the Appalachian territory. However, he feared there was little he could do for the members of the Virginia assembly meeting in nearby Charlottesville.

The main line of British appeared to be about a mile east of Keswick, marching along Millers Road. If they decided to pillage Charlottesville, many would die and be captured. Yet, Jack's immediate concern was that the enemy would send a raiding party to Monticello to capture the governor.

Celer led the way, galloping through the grassy clearing approaching the forest's edge. Jack leaned back on the reins to restrain Celer's natural ability to outpace the governor's horse. Celer slowed to a trot as they approached the tree line that marked the entrance to the expansive pine forest. The governor's horse pulled alongside and gently rubbed heads with Celer. Jack patted Celer, acknowledging his colt's calming spirit.

Jack felt the tremors rise through his saddle and glanced over his left shoulder. He tightened his gloved hands on the reins and straightened his back, recognizing the distinctive red jackets with white piping and bronze buttons. About two hundred yards to the east, two mounted British soldiers rode hard toward them, their long sabers jostling at their sides, mirror-polished blades flashing in the noonday sun.

"Advanced scouts approaching, sir. Please ride into the woods, remain hidden, and wait for my signal," Jack said firmly in a calm tone.

Jack reached down and unfastened his knife loop, tightly gripping the thick antler handle. He recalled the day the British soldiers rode away with his father, with hands tied behind his back like a petty thief.

Celer, sensing Jack's rising anger, shook his head, his long chestnut mane whipping from side to side in agitation.

"I've spotted them. We have the speed to outpace them back to Monticello," Jefferson said confidently.

Jack knew the odds were against them. He would prepare to make a stand. "Sir, I strongly request you move quickly and go deep into the woods toward Monticello. I will follow. I insist, sir. I shall deal with the soldiers. I must ensure your safety. Ride hard; waste no time," he insisted.

"Very well. Good luck, son." Jefferson turned his horse and disappeared behind the thick curtain of pines.

"Cel, I'll return shortly." Jack patted his friend on the neck, dismounted, and wrapped the harness around a low pine branch. He walked out into the open field and raised his hands, standing ready, prepared for a sudden charge.

The two approaching redcoats slowed to a steady gallop.

❖ ❖ ❖

Jefferson slowed his mare to a gentle pace, the soft, rhythmic crunch of her hooves on the carpet of dried pine needles delicately piercing the serene silence of the dense forest surrounding Monticello. Above, towering loblolly pines filtered the sun's rays, creating protective shelter beneath. This lush canopy provided a thriving sanctuary for the local wildlife, including deer, turkeys, and foxes.

He gazed up through the patchwork of branches to the open blue sky, his mind wandering as he watched a brown hawk comfortably nesting.

Freedom.

The governor firmly tugged the reins, gracefully dismounted, and secured his horse to a nearby low-hanging branch. Retrieving a small canteen, he indulged in a long, refreshing drink of water.

The tranquility of the moment was abruptly shattered by a sharp report of two musket shots, fired in rapid succession, less than a second apart. Jefferson was drawn to a brown mother hawk's sudden flurry as she burst from her nest. With her powerful wings, she soared gracefully westward, ascending high above the pines.

❖ ❖ ❖

The approaching soldiers were not members of Tarleton's ruthless Green Dragoons but low-ranking mounted British Legion infantrymen. They brandished short-barreled Brown Bess muskets; polished brass-handled sabers swung from their hips.

The muskets were of less concern to Jack. He concentrated on the lead rider's saber, a potent weapon wielded by a hard-charging rider. Acutely familiar with the damage a British saber could inflict, Jack recalled the heroic tale of Captain Stokes.

As the hard-charging Captain Stokes of North Carolina's First Rowan Artillery company led his men into battle, a hot musket ball ripped into the chest of his horse, and Stokes was thrown to the ground. Rushed by a mounted British Dragoon of Tarleton's 17th Cavalry Division, Stokes raised his saber to block the oncoming rider's blow; however, the razor-sharp blade cut straight through the bone, severing the captain's right hand at the mid-forearm. With defiance, Stokes refused to submit despite his horrendous wound. The Dragoon raised his saber. Captain Stokes raised his left arm to shield his head. The blade sliced through his arm from the elbow to the wrist.

Stokes glared with undeniable contempt. Fit with rage, the British soldier slashed Stokes across the head, and he fell face-down in the mud.

A British colonel had appeared and, in an act of rare battlefield humanity, prevented further assault. Miraculously, Captain Stokes survived but was taken prisoner and had become yet another victim of the floating prison.

Jack steadied his stance but maintained a nonthreatening position as he watched the redcoat scout dismount.

The soldier removed his helmet, pushed his long, slick hair back and carefully balanced the tall fur helmet on the saddle's pommel. He wiped his forehead with his coat sleeve before drawing his sword with a deliberate motion. Turning to Jack, he spoke with palpable contempt in his voice.

"Submit your possessions immediately, or you shall die."

"I have nothing of value, sir," Jack said.

"Your horse is now the property of the King's Legion," the mounted soldier said.

"Yes, your horse will do," the shorter soldier said in a sly, raspy voice. He turned away from Jack and walked toward Celer.

"I would recommend against that," Jack said.

"Quiet! Or you will feel my blade across your skull," the mounted rider commanded.

The redcoat sheathed his sword, and just as he reached for Celer's reins, Jack's young colt let out a piercing neigh, shook his head, and reared up, towering on his hind legs and kicking his forelegs.

Jack seized the moment, swiftly drawing his knife as he rushed the unsuspecting redcoat. With a forceful lunge, he drove the sharp blade into the man's throat, twisting it as the soldier's lifeless body collapsed to the ground. Jack pulled the fallen soldier's saber from his belt, drawing it swiftly. With his knife clutched firmly in his other hand, he tested the weight and balance of the sword with a swift slice through the air. Confident in the weapon's feel, he readied himself for the impending charge of the rider.

The mounted redcoat dug his boot heels into his horse. She responded by rising up on her hind legs and pulverizing the ground with each galloping stride. The redcoat wielded his saber high above his head, swiping down at Jack on his pass. Jack, anticipating the swing, tumbled to the grass and rolled. As he jumped to his feet, readying himself for the second charge, two booming musket shots rang out from behind.

The mounted redcoat fell backward as his horse reared up, throwing the rider and snagging one of his legs in the stirrup. With a sudden jolt, the horse sprinted forward, dragging the lifeless soldier behind.

Jack's head snapped toward the fading echo of the rifle shots. With relief, he smiled, pleased to see his best mates emerge from the edge of the tall pines, proudly brandishing their trusty long rifles.

Ben, his neatly kept beard resembling the fur of a beaver, flashed a smile brimming with confidence. With his broad shoulders and sturdy frame, he appeared to possess the strength necessary to conquer the entire British army. Julius, the youngest of the trio, walked tall, exuding an air of youthful enthusiasm with long strides propelled by his thin pine-board legs and well-worn leather boots that held his remarkably large feet.

"What took you so long?" Jack asked, slapping Ben on the shoulder.

"We reckon'd you could handle yourself, but decided to give ya a hand," Ben said, smiling with his long rifle propped on his shoulder and his favorite hatchet hanging from his saddle holster. "Where are the redcoat bastards? We'll show them," he said, swinging his long-handled hatchet around as if it were an extension of his arm.

Benjamin Greene—a master blacksmith regarded throughout the Virginia colony for the finest knives, hatchets, and bayonets—forged weapons when he was not shoeing horses or chasing the ladies of Richmond. He fashioned his hatchet design from the indigenous Virginia Indian tribes' tomahawk. Ben's "Greene Hatchet" featured a small hammer, one-inch square, with a thick mid-body tapering down from the center into a five-inch blade, resembling the traditional pipe tomahawk of the local chieftains. The brass-end cap on the extended, two-foot, cloth-wrapped handle provided the ideal counterbalance to the heavy metal hammer blade.

The Greene Hatchet was an all-purpose tool used for cutting wood, fence-mending, and other general works, yet Ben's true intent lay in its ability to kill British and Hessian soldiers. Crafted with meticulous detail, he fashioned the handle from American maple, renowned for its superior hardness and lighter weight than Caribbean walnut used in enemy muskets. He wrapped the lower portion of the handle with sand-tarred cowhide to ensure a secure grip.

As a solemn tribute to fallen patriots, he etched the mark "CH 80" onto the blade, commemorating the sacrifice of those lost during the Siege of Charlestown.

"Good to see ya, Jack. I reckon there're more Dragoons close by. Where's the gov?" Julius said as he reloaded his long rifle.

"Thanks, Jules. I sent Governor Jefferson ahead to warn the others," Jack said.

At eighteen, the generous and boy-spirited Julius Magnus held a special place in Jack's heart. Julius, the youngest of six brothers and two sisters, was kept in check by his strict Presbyterian father, Osgar Magnus, who governed the family with a firm hand and belt. However, Julius's life took a dramatic turn when he was thirteen, and his father went missing while on a logging expedition in the western Pennsylvania forests.

Julius's mother had moved the family to Richmond, fearing that her sons would follow in their father's footsteps into the dangerous logging trade. A skilled seamstress, she went to work for the wealthy Elston family. William and Margret Elston's only son had died of smallpox at age nine. While Julius's mother tended to the Elston family during the day and other wealthy merchants' wives in the evening, Mr. Elston, a prominent and esteemed lawyer, took a liking to young Julius. Recognizing something special within him, Mr. Elston surrounded Julius with a vast collection of books, taught him how to pen a letter with a quill, and trained him in the spoken art of lecture and debate.

◆ ◆ ◆

A friendship forged in battle, Jack, Ben, and Julius had fought side by side as members of Virginia's Amelia County Militia, pledging an unbreakable bond in the wake of the fiery aftermath during the British Siege of Charlestown.

In the spring of 1780, the British had sent a fleet of over ninety battleships and two hundred troop carriers that transported over fifteen thousand soldiers under General Cornwallis's command. The general had the fleet sail south of Charlestown, just out of reach of the artillery cannons that protected the city and disembarked his massive army on James Island. Cornwallis proceeded to encircle the town while, at the same time, he ordered his mounted Dragoons, led by Colonel Tarleton, into the countryside to cut off supply routes, pillage rebel munition stores, and burn sympathizers' dwellings.

The six thousand Continentals, including Jack's Amelia County Militia, were no match for the more powerful and experienced British force. After days of devastating bombardment by the British battleships and the army's artillery, combined with frontal attacks by Cornwallis's siege lines, the Continental commander, General Benjamin Lincoln, was forced to surrender.

During the two-day battle, Jack witnessed the ravages of war, including the deaths of many friends and fellow patriots. In the end, the rumor was that the British had killed over four thousand men and imprisoned hundreds more.

As the Continentals retreated, Ben, Julius, and Jack had escaped into the mosquito-infested swamps surrounding Sullivan Island. They hid for days, constantly on the lookout for the British Dragoon patrols, eventually making their way northwest through the densely wooded backcountry into central South Carolina and home to Richmond.

The harrowing experience had cemented their brotherhood, a sacred connection understood only by soldiers who have stared death in the face.

◆ ◆ ◆

Ben rested the butt of his rifle on the dead redcoat's back. "That was a mighty fine skirmish. I see that knife I made you served ya well."

"It certainly did," Jack said, wiping the blood from his knife on the soldier's pant leg. In the glare of the midday sun, the gleaming steel blade bore the unmistakable mark of Ben's forge—CH 80—a symbol of the trio's unbreakable bond.

Celer stood patiently at the edge of the forest and began

to swing his head from side to side, scraping his hoof against the ground, anticipating Jack's approach. Jack holstered his knife and stroked the smooth, fine hair on Celer's neck and his thick, coarse mane.

Off in the distance, the horse dragged the dead British soldier through the tall grass, galloping north toward Carter's Mountain. Jack pulled his rifle from the saddle holster and, with the tip of his knife, carved two X marks next to the dozen or so others. The markings etched a memorial to the family and friends, a reminder that they did not die in vain.

The boys turned in unison at the sound of cracking branches and leveled their long rifles at the rider emerging from the tree line.

"Men, don't stand there dilly-dallying," Jefferson said, looking down upon the British soldier's body and slowly shaking his head. "Life is fragile as a flower's petals and unforgiving as a wild dog's bite. How I hope this bloodshed will end soon."

"Sir, we must go before Tarleton's Dragoons arrive," Jack said.

"Yes, son. I will take my family to safety, westward to my old friend's estate. However, you will not be joining me."

"I must," Jack said, not understanding, as his duty was to protect the governor.

The governor reached into his saddlebag and pulled out the finely stitched leather folio Jack had first seen in the governor's library.

"My request is a matter of the utmost importance, and I must insist that you deliver a message to Washington's most trusted general. In the event I am captured or killed, the fight for liberty will live on. The contents of this brief will guide General Washington to victory. It must not be opened or leave your person."

"Sir, my foremost duty is to ensure your safe passage and then swiftly rejoin my men in Richmond," Jack said.

"Son, you and your men will ride north to the New York colony for an audience with General Washington's Chief of Artillery," Jefferson said.

Julius looked over to Jack, his grin beaming with boyish enthusiasm.

"Follow the Chesapeake's western shore, then travel east, following the mighty Delaware to Philadelphia. Near the city's center, you will find the City Tavern. In the fall of seventy-four, Mr. Franklin, Mr. Adams, and I discussed, well into the morning twilight, the parliamentary rules for the inaugural meeting of the Continental Congress." The governor laughed. "Oh, we consumed many a pint together."

Jack stared at the top of his boots and kicked a rock, contemplating, unsure of the path. After all, the governor was the Virginia militia commander, and Jack had sworn an oath to obey.

"Yes, sir. Please go on," Jack said, listening intently to each word.

"At the tavern, you will meet an impeccably dressed Frenchman. He shall remain anonymous to protect his identity. He will provide you with a guide and papers for your journey through the enemy territory of New Jersey and New York. The Frenchman will require you to confirm your authenticity. You will respond to his query by reciting this passage. Commit it to memory, for only a patriot will know its true meaning." The governor closed his eyes and recited:

"The sanctuary of Mary has five spires.
Those spires reach up to the highest heavens.
The roots of those spires reach down to the bottom of the ocean.
This new world is the time and period of our Creator."

Jefferson repeated the short passage. Jack listened intently but knew he would not recall the words. He turned to his friend, who could.

"Julius, did you hear the words?"

"This new world is the time and period of our Creator," Julius said. "Yeah, I will remember."

Jefferson then placed his hands on Jack's shoulder, infusing his touch with fatherly tenderness and unwavering conviction.

"Be cautious, Jack. The main roads are infested with British and loyalists apprehending our brave couriers. Evading capture is paramount. Your destination lies at the fort of West Point. There, you will find a large man..." Jefferson paused, subtly scratched his chin in thought before continuing, "a man of your stature but with considerable girth. Yes, that's more precise. General Washington's Artillery Chief awaits you there." Jefferson offered a reassuring smile and shook Jack's hand. "His name is Knox—Brigadier General Henry Knox."

Jack was familiar with the distinguished general's reputation. Richmond's newspapers had chronicled how Henry Knox, once a Boston bookseller, at the age of twenty-five, led a convoy of oxen and horses over hundreds of miles through harsh winter conditions, across frozen lakes and rivers, delivering crucial artillery from the conquered Fort Ticonderoga to the outskirts of Boston. Knox and General Washington strategically positioned the recovered cannons to expel the British forces from Boston, pushing them out to sea. This grand victory ignited the passions of the colony's patriots, including Jack's late father, lighting a fire in their hearts.

The governor reached into his riding jacket's small pocket. He opened his hand, revealing a splendid gold coin.

"Please accept this as a token of my gratitude."

Jack removed his riding glove, and the governor placed the coin in Jack's palm—a British guinea, with significant weight, glistening in the late-morning sun; however, its natural brilliance was muted by the engraving of the tyrant, King George III. Jack flipped it over, revealing the revolting royal crown and quartered shield of arms.

"That gold piece will serve as a reminder of the evil that shackles our countrymen and the prosperity that our great nation awaits," Jefferson said.

"Respectfully, sir, I do not require compensation, for I have vowed to fight until death. The king took my father, pillaged our lands, and killed my friends," Jack said.

"Very good, son. Revenge burns deep in your heart. Revenge can be a powerful elixir; beware, it must be consumed in small quantities. However, more relevant is that the gold piece authorizes you as my representative. Only a select group of men carry it, men whom the leaders of our cause trust undisputedly. It will grant you and your men safe passage and, if questioned, present this coin. He who possesses it is considered a friend and a true patriot."

Jack admired the coin, unsure of the appropriate words for such an honor. "I am humbled, sir. We shall not fail." He turned toward his Ben, who gave Jack a confident grin and reassuring nod.

Governor Jefferson tipped his hat and turned his horse toward the trail leading to his Monticello estate. "Keep the gold piece close. It will serve you well in times of need throughout your lifetime, which I pray will be long and prosperous."

AIRPORT EXIT

19 FEBRUARY, 0645 HRS
CLEVELAND, OHIO

Paul had spent nearly a decade wading through the muck of the dark web, cataloging and profiling the most dangerous cyber criminals, extremists, state-backed hacker groups, and child slave syndicates—who thrived in the depths of the hidden digital underworld. He trained his deep learning AI profiling software to detect the slightest anomalies, outliers, and anti-patterns, all to unearth terrorist threats buried within an immense sea of data.

He wondered if he had inadvertently tripped a security alert of one of the clandestine groups.

Glancing over his shoulder, a controlled shot of adrenaline coursed through his veins as he lengthened his strides, outpacing his adversary with each step. He focused on maintaining his composure, ready to act. The stranger trailed about one hundred feet behind—crew-style cut, hard jawline, and dark olive skin.

Paul mentally sized him up, wishing he had his Colt. The man was likely in his early forties, Syrian or Iraqi, wearing a weathered, black leather jacket and light brown square-toed boots. As Paul approached the guard station, his ankle popped, sending a familiar bolt of pain into his hip, as it did when pushed.

Paul reached for the coin hanging from the thin rope chain beneath his T-shirt. He rubbed the gold piece with his thumb and index finger, tracing the imprint on its surface. The coin's connection to his late father grounded him in the moment and resurfaced memories of his training.

22 YEARS AGO
CRATER LAKE, OREGON

Paul lay on his back amidst the towering Ponderosa pines and the weathered, gnarled white birch trees that flanked the secluded trail of Oregon's Crater Lake National Park. His eyes followed the pencil-thin contrail—a delicate white line cutting through the blue expanse—until they locked onto the distant speck of a commercial airliner cruising at thirty thousand feet. He let his mind wander, imagining himself aboard, far from the ground—anything to distract his mind from the mind-numbing pain in his ankle.

A competitive trail runner since the age of twelve, Paul was no stranger to the occasional rolled ankle. However, this time was alarmingly different. The searing pain felt as if a dull butter knife had punched through his skin, slicing through a tendon and lodging deep into his lower tibia. He shuddered in agony on the forest floor, blanketed by a layer of bark and pine needles, clinging on to hope that his father would arrive soon.

As the hours passed, nightfall descended on the forest, bringing a noticeable drop in temperature. In an attempt to relieve the pain, Paul elevated his foot up on a large stone, but the swelling had rendered his ankle unrecognizable.

Each year, following the last day of school, Paul and his father hit the road on a two-week camping trip to remote and untamed corners of the country. Paul learned to hunt, fish, and forage, giving him a glimpse into the raw beauty of nature and the splendor of America's national parks. However, these trips were far from typical family camping outings. Paul underwent training with the rigor and discipline reminiscent of his father's Army days, applying survival tactics honed in the jungle's heat during two tours in Vietnam.

That year's trip to Crater Lake was no different. Over the

past week, they hiked deep into Umpqua Park, trekking west from the Phantom Pillar's base, a spectacular rock formation marking the southernmost point of the world's third-deepest lake. Their path followed the crater's jagged rim at points ascending heights of eight thousand feet above sea level. Their pace at that altitude posed a challenge even for seasoned hikers and proved impossible for novices. Despite the grueling physical demands of these trips, Paul cherished the time spent with his father. However, this trip felt different—his father was all business, visibly on edge and short-tempered.

Now, at seventeen, Paul was old enough to sense the subtle changes in his father's demeanor. Unraveling the complexities of his battle-hardened father was a daunting challenge, as impossible as asking him to abandon his post. He shielded his emotions like impenetrable armor, never letting anyone glimpse the turmoil within.

Paul lay on the bed of dry pine needles, recalling his father's words before they had set out on the trip.

"Preparation separates leaders from victims and success from failure."

But at that moment, Paul's ankle hurt like hell, and he didn't give a damn about his father's words of wisdom. He attempted to stand and walk, but the slightest pressure sent shockwaves shooting through the left side of his body into his temple. He'd likely torn ligaments, or fractured bones, or both.

He made a splint of pine twigs, thick pine bark, and straps he cut off his backpack. Struggling at first, he forced the pain into a part of his brain that allowed him to focus on the task: walking. Walking at stints of ten to twenty steps, he made slow progress. Twelve hours later, exhausted, hungry, and dehydrated, he arrived back at base camp.

He remembered the conversation clearly as if it were yesterday.

"Pauly, what took you so long?" his father asked with a hint of sarcasm.

"Why didn't you come for me?" Paul said, even though

he knew the answer. His father was a cruel bastard, and this was another one of his damn lessons. "My ankle's killing me! I've been out there, lying in pain, cold and wet, while you sit around a cozy fire. Dad, I don't care about your life lessons anymore. I'm done."

Paul turned away when his father tried to put his hand on his shoulder. He couldn't stand the sight of him.

His father knelt next to Paul and squeezed the center of his ankle.

"Damn it! Stop!" Paul yelled and pushed his father's arm away with the back of his forearm.

His father retreated a couple of steps. "Yeah, it's bad, but you'll live. You sprained, maybe tore two peroneal tendons behind the ankle. The Achilles appears fine. Let's get it in ice and wrapped."

He helped Paul to his feet. Paul pulled away and limped over to the bench next to their tent.

"I know you're ticked off, but I don't give a damn. Life is unfair, and this is nothing compared to what you'll go through someday. Learn to live with it and block out the pain, anger, or anything else that will distract you. Weakness is the enemy's poison. There'll come a time when you'll be alone without anyone backing you up. Trust your instincts and training. Always. Mental toughness demands discipline, and last night, you proved your mettle. Not to me, but to yourself."

Paul heard the words but wasn't listening as the anger boiled over. At seventeen, and at that moment, he hated his father.

"Here." His father's voice broke through the dark cloud of pain. He unclasped the chain from around his neck and gently placed the slender gold-linked chain with the time-worn coin at the end over Paul's head. It was the first time Paul had seen his father without that chain.

"This was given to me by your grandfather when I was about your age, passed down from his father before him. It's been in our family for generations. Now it's yours. You've earned it, not simply because of what you did today, but for the person you've become and because you are my son. And one day, you'll pass it on to your son."

Paul had seen the coin dangling from his father's neck countless times, but now, holding it for the first time, he sensed the weight of its storied past. Its edges were worn, slightly larger and heavier than a quarter, the lettering and symbols faded yet recognizable.

"The coin dates back to our country's founding," his father said, tossing Paul a bottle of water. "Now, let's move. We've got a long hike back, and on that bad ankle, it's gonna take some time."

Paul stared at the coin, the stoic image of what appeared to be a Roman emperor surrounded by the inscription "*GEORGIVS III DEI GRATIA.*"

"What does it mean?"

"'By the Grace of God,'" his father said, his tone hinting reverence.

Paul flipped it over. Around its ragged edges, a Latin inscription framed an elaborate coat of arms, including the date—1773.

"Don't lose the damn thing. It'll save your ass someday," his father said, walking away and leaving Paul to stand on his own.

◆ ◆ ◆

Paul's father died a year later. At eighteen and preparing to go off to college, Paul was devastated. He shut down everything around him and erected a wall, shielding his emotions from the pain of loss. No one was allowed to get close—that is, until he met Sara. She was determined, committed, and strong—she broke down his invisible wall.

And he'd lost her, too.

Focus!

Paul glanced over his shoulder. The stranger, sporting mirrored sunglasses and cowboy boots, had narrowed the gap, now just twenty feet away. Swiftly, Paul pivoted around the corner, making his way toward the security guard station just outside the TSA entry checkpoint. He spotted the officer on duty there—a burly guy with a crew cut and bold yellow sergeant stripes on his shoulders. He sat slouched behind a chest-high podium, staring at his phone. As Paul approached, the officer looked up with an expression of silent anticipation of Paul's imminent question.

"Where can I find the nearest restroom?" Paul asked, knowing the answer. He again glanced back. The Middle Eastern cowboy was gone.

The officer, clearly irritated, likely having fielded the question countless times, pointed dismissively. "Down there," he said.

Paul wasted no time. He hurried down the escalator into the restroom, where he knew it would be free of surveillance cameras, at least legal ones.

He checked under the stall doors. No one.

Paul reached into his go-bag for his phone. He keyed in his passcode and launched the hidden "wipe" app. He had code-named his creation Cleaver. Using jailbreaking techniques, the app gained root access and bypassed the handset manufacturer's software-imposed restrictions that prevented unauthorized access to the non-volatile memory pages. It rapidly erased all traces of data—obliterating the operating system, apps, flash drive data, RAM, contacts, text messages, and emails. The phone powered down, its screen fading from gray to black, leaving no digital footprint behind.

Paul spun his head toward the entranceway. He listened as the lower-level escalator clacked in a steady rhythm. He breathed deeply to slow his heartbeat to match the escalator's cadence.

He slipped on his baseball cap and a dark blue hoodie from his go-bag, pulled out a six-inch tablet, and launched the modified Telegram messaging app. The tablet had a customized interface with a cell number randomizer and VPN to cloak the network routing. Combined with a custom encryption-enabled plug-in, the messages he sent and received were invisible to the outside world.

He paused. Was he overreacting?

Trust your instincts.

He typed the code Colonel Wilson had given him years ago. The colonel referred to it as the "break glass" scenario.

EXIT64

Paul waited, staring at the graffiti tagged with thick black marker on the stall's door. His tablet vibrated with a message.

LOT LOCATION 145

Paul understood the directive. He shoved the tablet back into his go-bag and listened for movement in the bathroom before going toward the baggage claim and down the escalator.

There was no sign of the cowboy stranger or anyone else. The lower-level underground tunnel connecting the terminal to the parking structure was eerily deserted. Overhead, a woman's prerecorded voice droned on, monotonously announcing safety messages. The passage, once bustling with travelers, now was like a tomb—a hollow concrete cavern—a stark reminder of how the world had changed in the wake of the terrorist bombings.

The electronic eye detected Paul's approach, prompting the heavy orange exit doors to swing open. A blast of dry, frigid air cut through his clothes, invigorating his senses. He located the parking row marked "100" just as the doors slammed shut behind him.

Parked in location "145" was his car. But that was impossible. Puzzled, Paul moved in for a better look. It was his Tesla Plaid, matte midnight silver with distinctive blue brake calipers.

As Paul's eyes adjusted to the dim light, a figure in the driver's seat gradually came into focus—a silhouette of a woman, barely visible. He approached and noticed her confident smile. He didn't recognize her. How had she managed to get into his car?

She smoothly lowered the passenger-side window, and Paul cautiously leaned in. He'd mentally cataloged every personal encounter, rarely forgetting a face. Hers was certainly one he would have undoubtedly remembered.

"Hey, Paul. Your old man sent me to find you. Get in."

LIBERTY UNIT

> *"Unless this is done, we shall be liable to be ruled by an arbitrary and capricious armed tyranny, whose word and will must be law."*
> — Henry Knox, 1778

MAY 25, 1781
DOBBS FERRY, NEW YORK COLONY

The smoldering embers of the campfire crackled, casting a warm, amber glow that sent shadows dancing across the meticulously arranged rows of canvas tents. Bright orange cinders ascended like fireflies against the clear, star-filled New England night.

A motley crowd of Continental soldiers gathered, encircling the two combatants. Pumping their fists and rifles into the air, they chanted in unison, "Knox! Knox! Knox!" urging Henry to rise up.

After knocking Henry to the ground for the third time, the burly Hessian confidently smoothed his bushy mustache, raising his arms above his head in a defiant victory celebration. The raucous crowd of Continentals quieted, then fell silent. The men exchanged their wagers, the losers hanging their heads in dismay.

As Henry's eyes adjusted to the flickering campfire light, the ground seemed to sway and slowly spin beneath him. The sensation was all too familiar—many times during his youth, brawling with rival gangs on the docks of Boston Harbor. He shook his head, willing the world to cease its spinning.

The encouraging cheers of his soldiers began to swell in intensity until they reached a fervent crescendo. Drawing on his reserve of determination, Henry pulled himself up. A wave of pain surged through his battered body as he rose onto one knee and then to his feet, his breath heavy, laboring to regain his strength. After one last shake of his head, he wiped the blood from his lip with the purple scarf—a treasured keepsake from his beloved wife, Lucy. Now, it was wrapped around the hand that bore the scars of war, missing two fingers. The pain vanished at the sight of the silk scarf, which brought back cherished memories of home, his wife, and his children.

With a determined gesture, Henry drew back his broad shoulders, placed his left foot forward, crouched, and raised his fists into an orthodox boxing position. He motioned with his unwrapped hand, inviting the Hessian to resume his frontal assault.

The crowd of soldiers erupted in a wild, euphoric cheer.

Appearing bewildered by Henry's ability to weather the devastating onslaught of blows, the Hessian took two steps back, shot a foreboding glare, and readied himself with clenched fists raised to his face.

Taller and stouter than every man in the camp, Henry had endured the Hessian's powerful blows as he had throughout his entire life. Whether with his fists or a howitzer, Henry embodied the spirit of a determined fighter, a trait he had honed since childhood.

Born into a once-prosperous Boston shipbuilding family, Henry's world turned upside down in the spring of 1759. His father, faced with the collapse of the family business, abruptly abandoned it and sailed to the West Indies, never returning. At just nine years old, without means, Henry was thrust into caring for his dear mother, Mary, who was bedridden and battling tuberculosis, and his three-year-old brother, William.

Henry's hopes of attending the newly founded Harvard College were dashed when he was forced to trade the classroom for the grueling work at the shipyards. There, he labored alongside orphans and impoverished children from dawn until dusk, six days a week, loading and unloading cargo.

Yet, it was the rough-and-tumble world of those shipyards where Henry had found a semblance of belonging. He quickly earned the respect of the ruffian street gangs that roamed the yards and alleys, rising through the ranks by instigating brawls with the older boys, demonstrating his unnatural strength, and honing his boxing skills.

However, Mr. Bowes, the esteemed proprietor of the popular London Book Shop on the south side, rescued Henry from the clutches of street poverty and the perilous path of life as a merchant seaman. Graciously, he took Henry under his wing, teaching the young apprentice mathematics, Greek, and Latin.

Yet, it was the allure of books—the textured feel of the old parchment between his fingertips and the burnt, earthy smell of the ink—that ignited Henry's imagination. They transported him from the unforgiving toil of the Boston shipyards to splendid and wondrous faraway lands. Henry became a voracious reader, devouring classics by Shakespeare and Voltaire. In his scarce leisure time, he enjoyed reading the adventure stories of Swift's *Gulliver's Travels* and Defoe's *Robinson Crusoe*, often aloud to his younger brother and the neighborhood boys.

As the winds of change swept through Boston, marked by growing tensions and surging patriotic fervor, Henry's focus shifted to the thick, voluminous European military manuals. The intricate details of weapon designs, battle formations, and tactical positioning, as devised by the great masters of artillery warfare, captured his imagination. Henry had diligently committed these strategies to memory, and his inquisitive fascination transformed into a profound understanding of the art of military combat.

Now, Henry sized up his overly confident Hessian opponent. The moment had arrived to conclude the contest and buoy the hearts of his battle-weary men.

The Hessian soldier charged, fists leading the attack.

Henry readied himself and quickly stepped forward, leading with a powerful right-handed roundhouse. His opponent bought the clever feint and instinctively ducked, unwittingly leaning his chin into Henry's punishing left uppercut. Henry's grapefruit-sized fist connected squarely with the Hessian's jaw, sending him reeling. With an awkward spin, the Hessian's knees buckled, sending him crashing to the ground.

The soldiers' whooping cheers fell silent as the circle of men converged to inspect the condition of the downed Hessian, fearing Henry's mighty blow had killed the man.

Henry's demeanor transitioned to solemn concern as he stood over his fallen adversary. Though his opponent was a foreign mercenary under British command, Henry deeply respected his bravery and discipline.

The Hessian twitched, drawing in several weak breaths, and shook his head as he struggled to regain his senses. He rolled onto his back, his eyes meeting a gaggle of curious faces hovering over him.

Henry helped the defeated man to his feet by extending a hand of camaraderie. Their eyes met, and Henry smiled, showing his fellow soldier the respect he deserved. The Hessian, still groggy, grimaced and nodded back. In a gesture of sportsmanship, Henry gave him a hearty bear hug, lifting him off the ground.

The American soldiers erupted in applause, pounding their musket butts on the hard ground, their voices rising once more in a unified chant of "Knox! Knox! Knox!" They patted Henry and the Hessian on the back, exchanged their wagers, and gradually dispersed.

A young corporal approached, extending Henry's thick blue woolen Continental field coat. His eyes lingered on the two silver stars adorning each gold-laced epaulette before handing it over.

"Thank you," Henry said, glancing down at the corporal's blood-encrusted feet, marred by scars of war and harsh winters, with several toes missing due to the dreaded frostbite.

Henry concealed his disappointment in the soldier's lack

of proper uniform etiquette, realizing that it wasn't the boy's fault. Despite Henry's repeated requests, Congress neglected to supply his men with the most basic supplies and clothing. He buttoned his coat, checked for blood on his white ruffled shirt, and combed his hair with his fingers.

Suddenly, Lieutenant Colonel John Lillie, Henry's trusted aide-de-camp, hurried toward him, his long coat flailing behind. "General! Sir, come immediately. They have arrived," John said, breathing heavily with excitement. Henry knew him well; a former copper and a member of Boston's Ancient and Honorable Artillery Company, John had fought alongside Henry since their days in the Boston Grenadier Corps, directing cannon fire together at the Battle of Bunker Hill.

"Slower, please, John," Henry said with a smile.

"My apologies, sir," John said, his tone respectful. Despite their cordial relationship, he snapped to attention, squaring his shoulders and bringing his heels together. "The French fleet has been sighted off the coast of New Port, Rhode Island. General Washington has just received a dispatch from the French General Rochambeau. He's requesting formal authorization to land his army."

Henry slapped John on the shoulder. "Now, that is truly exceptional news," he said, barely able to contain his joy. "We must conference with His Excellency at once to discuss his perspective on this development. I have no doubt he will be equally pleased."

"Yes, General Washington has requested your immediate presence."

As they made their way through the camp toward the main command tent, Henry surveyed his brave yet weary men sprawled on makeshift beds of hay and leaves. Contemplating their forthcoming march into battle, he hoped with all his being that the tide of the war might finally turn with the arrival of French reinforcements.

◆ ◆ ◆

The next morning, before Henry could finish breakfast, he was again summoned to General Washington's command tent. Approaching it, he paused momentarily, as was his tradition, and saluted the commander's standard flag that fluttered in the gentle breeze. The flag bore thirteen six-pointed white stars, each symbolizing a colony, intricately embroidered on a sea-blue silk backing.

Pulling away the heavy canvas flap of the entrance, he was greeted by a familiar, comforting aroma of burning tallow. Inside, a half-spent candle flickered on General Washington's unoccupied mahogany writing desk.

Stepping into the tent, Henry prepared himself to salute; however, the tent was unexpectedly empty. Puzzled, he wondered if perhaps he had misinterpreted the meeting time.

"Good morning," came a raspy yet unrecognizable voice from behind.

Startled, Henry turned around.

The stranger standing before him was slender, his deep-set eyes peering through rectangular spectacles. He was dressed in civilian attire, including a long charcoal overcoat that draped down to the tops of his polished black riding boots. In the tent's dimly lit shadow, Henry's attention was drawn to the ghastly scar on the side of the man's jaw.

"We have much to discuss, and time is of the essence," the stranger said. "My name is Mr. Pebbley. I'm pleased to make your acquaintance, General." The stranger's tone was solemn, and he made no move to extend his hand in greeting.

"I was expecting His Excellency," Henry said, slightly taken aback.

"Yes, sir. General Washington requested—beg my pardon—*ordered* me to relay a matter of utmost importance to our cause."

Mr. Pebbley's voice carried a sense of urgency as he began to describe the situation at hand. He revealed he had obtained intelligence from a reliable source indicating that Cornwallis had dispatched Colonel Tarleton, the notorious Green Dragoon commander, to capture General Washington at his Mount Vernon estate. Henry was all too familiar with Tarleton's reputation as "The Butcher" of Cowpens. He welcomed the day his men could direct artillery at the man or tighten a noose around his neck, whichever came first.

Moreover, Mr. Pebbley disclosed suspicions of a mole within the Continental or Congressional ranks aiding the British. The revelation stirred in Henry a bitter recollection of Benedict Arnold's betrayal—his dishonorable surrender of the fort at West Point. Now, it seemed, another traitor had conspired with the enemy, threatening General Washington's life.

"His Excellency has requested I offer you my services in formulating a plan to deal with this precarious situation," Mr. Pebbley said.

Henry understood all the sacrifices he and his fellow patriots made could be for naught if the traitor succeeded. Seven long years of fighting had kept him away from his beloved wife, Lucy, and their four children, including his newborn daughter. The mere notion of their great struggle amounting to nothing was unbearable.

"And what exactly would your services entail?" Henry said, evaluating the man who appeared, by nature, to be elusive and enigmatic.

"I operate discreetly, obtaining information by unconventional means. The kind of information our adversaries would prefer we not obtain."

"A spy, then?" Henry asked, confirming his suspicions about the man's role.

"I prefer to think of myself as a purveyor of intelligence. I serve at the pleasure of General Washington."

Henry listened intently as Mr. Pebbley explained that his sources had uncovered a small but influential faction within Congress scrupulously scheming to end the war. Rogue members had recently convened an unauthorized diplomatic conference with representatives of the British Crown. The delegation had agreed to remove all obstacles to a peaceful surrender, including General Washington.

"Dare they threaten the one man who can bring us victory!" Henry said, anger surging within him. His face warmed, and he became aware his voice carried beyond the tent's walls. He gathered his composure, lowered his tone, and continued with a passion born by seven years of unending sacrifice. "Are the delegates aware that the French fleet has arrived and our hopes of victory have been rekindled?"

"Conspirators within Congress are seeking power and wealth, not victory, liberty, or justice," Mr. Pebbley said. He removed his hat and peeled back the inner lining, removing a small piece of parchment. "The Crown's agents have bought these delegates' allegiance. These men are believed to be involved, and the French fleet's arrival is anticipated to prompt the conspirators to initiate a most devious plan."

"We must expose these traitors, arrest them, and send them to the gallows," Henry said.

"Agreed. However, these men have powerful allies within our ranks. And considering the scant evidence of a crime, a court would surely acquit."

"What would General Washington wish of me?" Henry said.

"His Excellency has requested you select men—those embodying bravery, skill, and honor. These men will be granted authority to employ unconventional methods to safeguard the founders and our cause," Mr. Pebbley said.

"Unconventional?" Henry inquired with a hint of unease at the nature of the request.

"You may use your imagination—the rules of engagement no longer apply. Our enemy is unapologetically plotting to assassinate our leader, and we must respond with decisive, lethal force, sending a clear message that such actions will not be tolerated," Mr. Pebbley said in a firm tone.

"This mission demands the strictest discretion. Additionally, General Washington requests that you expand the Fort at West Point in New York to train, develop, and produce advanced weaponry and soldiers. Through a special bargain with influential men in Philadelphia, funding has been secured to properly equip an elite group of patriots," Mr. Pebbley said.

Pacing the length of the tent, Henry absorbed the magnitude of his orders. The prospect of finally having the funds necessary to build what was required for victory was something he had long envisioned.

"Lack of financial support has burdened this army for years. How has he remedied this?"

"A unique bargain has been struck. The French and our most wealthy New England merchants and Southern landowners have contributed a significant sum."

"In return for?"

Mr. Pebbley glanced behind him and took a step closer. "Access to the newly formed government. Access to give them first rights to contracts and influence upon defining future laws and treaties."

Henry was taken aback by what he just heard.

"Yes, this bargain will have long-lived ramifications; however, these are perilous times, which require unconventional bargains," Mr. Pebbley said. "And, if support cannot be obtained or the Continental Congress concedes to the British, General Washington is determined to fight on. Governor Jefferson has drafted a plan to form an American Outlands army, including lands to occupy until the general can marshal the resources to return to battle."

"Retreat to the wilderness?" Henry said, understanding full well that meant abandoning his wife Lucy and living in exile. He had sacrificed so much, but Lucy and the children were everything, and he could not fathom life without them.

"Yes, the remnants of the Continental army would retreat,

yet never surrender."

Questions swirled in Henry's mind, chief among them the legitimacy of the general's orders. Military protocol demanded that orders of such significance be conveyed through a letter of instruction, penned either by the general himself or his secretary, complete with signature and the commander's official insignia stamp.

"How can I be certain this is authorized? I require an official order from the general himself," Henry said.

From the pocket of his long overcoat, the stranger retrieved an item. "This coin, presented on behalf of the general, symbolizes your unwavering dedication to the cause. It serves as His Excellency's endorsement of your mission. He was certain you, of all men, would recognize its profound significance."

A gold coin rested in the palm of Mr. Pebbley's worn black riding glove. Henry accepted it, examining it closely—the stern image of King George III, eyes exuding wickedness, encircled by the Latin inscription *"DEI GRATIA,"* and a spade-shaped, crowned, quartered shield of arms on the other side. The guinea, a '73, was unmistakably one of the Fort Ticonderoga pieces, a token Henry had presented to General Washington six years ago upon returning to Boston with the noble train of artillery.

"This coin conjures memories of the reason we endure and fight on. I understand what I must do," Henry said, acknowledging the significance of this moment.

"General, your skills are most highly regarded. Your leadership in the crossing of the Delaware, the victory at Trenton, and the retrieval of artillery from Fort Ticonderoga speaks volumes. For these reasons, General Washington entrusts you with safeguarding our cause and his life."

Henry's mind was already at work, considering the right man to lead this new unit—a man of honor who would go to extraordinary lengths with physical prowess, knowledge of weaponry, and unparalleled mental acuity.

As Mr. Pebbley prepared to leave, he offered a final piece of advice. "Discretion is of the utmost importance. A formal written order does not exist. General Washington must remain unaffiliated with this operation. He grants you the unprecedented authority to employ unorthodox methods and the necessary lethal protocols. Methods that diverge from the prescribed laws of war."

"I understand and accept this responsibility. I will face whatever consequences God has in store for me in the service of our great general," Henry said, a newfound sense of purpose invigorating him.

"General, proceed with caution. Deception abounds, and evil lurks. What appears to be is not," Mr. Pebbley cautioned.

"Thank you," Henry said, turning to shake Mr. Pebbley's hand, only to find that the mysterious stranger was gone.

The tent's canvas flap was closed and motionless.

JERSEY GIRL

19 FEBRUARY, 0655 HRS
CLEVELAND, OHIO

"Get in. He won't be too far behind," the young woman said, her voice carrying a serious yet friendly tone, unmistakably tinged with an East Coast Jersey Shore accent.

The woman looked like she belonged behind the wheel of Paul's car. Her jet-black hair was swept back into a sleek high ponytail, and her age was hard to place, somewhere between her late twenties and early thirties. She wore a dark, collarless jacket accentuating her broad, athletic shoulders. Oddly enough, Paul found himself not minding that she'd stolen his car.

"Come on, we've gotta move. I'll fill you in on the way," she said.

Paul hesitated. "I should drive," he said, eyeing her cautiously.

"We don't have time for that. Trust me on this," she said with a quick, confident smile. "And by the way, I love your car."

Paul weighed his limited options. Colonel Wilson's instructions had been clear—follow orders. Reluctantly, he opened the passenger side door, tossed his go-bag into the back seat, and slid in. The passenger seat felt unfamiliar. It was, after all, his car, yet he couldn't remember ever sitting there. He was always the one in control. Always.

"Hand me your phone," she said, extending her hand. Paul noticed a distinctive tattoo on her wrist—"*CH 80*" in light green ink, just below a rugged, ocean-blue Omega Seamaster dive watch with a vibrant red NATO band. Her wrist was slender, her forearms showed muscular definition, and her fingers were long.

"I wiped and dumped my phone," Paul said.

"Good. They're tracking you, and that's how they found you at the airport."

"No one can track that device," Paul said.

"Well, they did. Seems like they hacked into the NSA's secure comms."

Paul's curiosity piqued. "Wait a minute, who are you, and which agency are you with?" he asked, intentionally raising his voice.

"Sorry 'bout that. I'm Lia, and I'm not with any agency. I know you've got a lot of questions. Cap will brief you at the safe house. We'll be there in about forty minutes, maybe twenty in this car," she said with a hint of a smile, her hands gripping the steering wheel at a perfect ten-and-two position.

"And who's Cap?"

"He's the station chief—a real badass. Just do as he says. Now buckle up," Lia said.

Paul's attention turned toward the mechanical sound of the orange parking garage doors opening. The stranger stood with the mirrored aviators, his jeans neatly tucked into those tall cowboy boots.

"We need to leave now!" Paul said.

"Yep, that's him. Hold on," Lia said. She treated the accelerator with respect born of experience, backing out smooth and fast. Simultaneously, she spun the steering wheel hard to the right using one hand, the car's left front bumper narrowly missing the sedan in the adjacent space. She was precise.

Paul glanced back, and a sudden crash jolted him, causing him to duck.

"Damn it!" Lia shouted. "Keep your head down!"

Bullet holes appeared, spiderwebbing the center of the windshield just below the rearview mirror. Lia reached under the seat, pulled out a handgun, and lowered her window. She then spun the wheel to the right and slammed on the brakes, causing the seatbelt to tighten across Paul's chest.

She leaned out and fired four quick shots down the empty parking ramp, then hit the accelerator again, snapping Paul's head back against the seat.

"Here, take this," Lia said, offering Paul the handgun, grip first. His hand wrapped around the compact pistol's well-worn, textured grip. The barrel had deep scratches and scars, each telling a story about the owner's battles fought and the lives taken. "I know you're a pro with one of these. It may be a bit small, but it does the job."

Paul nodded, impressed with her choice of firearm—the XD Elite, Springfield's compact 10mm. He ejected the magazine, noting it was a double-column with an eleven-round, nine-millimeter capacity, eight rounds still loaded. Pulling back the slide released the acrid scent of spent gunpowder. He moved his finger to the trigger guard, settled the gun on his leg, and glanced back at the target, spotting three tightly grouped bullet holes in the rear window.

"I don't see him," Paul said.

Lia made a sharp, quick turn, the tires chirping as they spun before gripping the pavement. "I like the upgrades. The spectrum delimiter adds a nice kick of extra torque. And I think you must have added strut tower brace, not to mention you've done something special with the suspension," she said with an appreciative smile, her eyes locked on the exit ramp ahead.

Lia took another sharp turn, and the car's high-performance computer processors and advanced software algorithms sent commands to the regenerative braking system to compensate for the slick concrete. Its dual neural network accelerators allowed the vehicle's built-in computer to perform an astonishing thirty-six trillion operations per second. Power from its three engines delivered precise torque to the front and rear drive trains to counteract any potential wheel spin.

She straightened her line, and both motors surged into action. The Tesla leaped forward, acceleration smooth yet forceful, propelling them down the ramp toward the exit gate.

"Here, take this," Lia said, handing Paul a sleek, ultra-thin phone with a matte black casing. "It's configured for our private network, completely isolated from the standard channels. Neither the NSA nor the FBI can tap into this one."

Paul examined the phone. He unfolded it, noting a seamless full-screen display without any visible hinges at the fold.

"From here on, trust no one," Lia said gravely. "That guy back there is part of the same group that attacked O'Hare. They're after you and other NSA cyber engineers. We had a tail on you and planned to extract you earlier, but we've had our hands full."

"Was it your team in the van outside my house, or was it them?" Paul asked.

"Ya, it was one of my guys. They had someone waiting for you. But when we showed up, he took off. A lower-level guy."

"Who exactly are 'they'?"

"We don't know. But what we do know is that other NSA engineers connected to the special cyber ops network have been killed or have gone dark. And your name is on their list."

"What? Assassinations?" Paul said in disbelief.

"Yeah, they're eliminating our best cybersecurity minds. And, given your involvement with the Sixteenth and Colonel Wilson's unit, you are a target." She glanced at him; her deep brown eyes were striking and conveyed a hint of concern. "There's something they want from you, or they'd have killed you by now. That's why I'm here—to get you out."

Lia rounded the parking garage corner tight and fast. Sensing the sudden urgency, Paul quickly glanced in the sideview mirror before looking out the back window. A dark gray Chevy Impala with tinted windows was tailing them.

"Do we have a problem?" Paul said.

She peered into the side-view mirror, assessing the situation with a calm, calculated look. "Possibly."

"Where are we going?"

"To the safe house, about twenty miles southeast," Lia said. "But first, we need to lose that tail." She drove through the gate and took a sharp left turn onto the airport exit ramp and over the highway overpass.

In the side-view mirror, Paul kept a close watch on the Impala. It was still there, trailing by about a hundred feet.

Lia shot a calculating glance into the rearview mirror before hitting the accelerator. The high-performance Yokohamas struggled against the slick mixture of salt, snow, and ice but quickly found their grip, propelling the car with smooth, assertive force. Lia's hands were firm on the wheel, her arms slightly bent, and her shoulders braced against the seatback. She skillfully navigated the curving onramp; the car responded, hitting ninety miles per hour within two seconds and accelerating to one hundred as they entered the long straightaway I-480 East, effortlessly passing a semi-truck as though it were standing still.

The Impala was gone. Lia eased up on the accelerator and relaxed her grip.

"Who sent you to pick me up?" Paul asked.

"Don't freak out when I tell you. Okay?" She met his eyes with a serious look.

"Who?" Paul said, now agitated.

She kept her eyes on the road. "Your old man."

Paul suddenly felt his headache return on the back right side of his head, as if someone were pressing their thumb into a deep bruise. "My father died twenty years ago," he said, his voice strained.

"Nope, he went dark. Disappeared off the grid. Left everything, including you," she said, glancing at him. "That must've been tough. My dad died, too, for real. It's probably easier that way."

Paul sank back into the contoured seat, his mind reeling, unsure how to respond. He remembered the day his mother broke the news of his father's death, the devastating details of the car accident splashed across the newspapers. The body burned beyond recognition. Kneeling in front of a closed casket, saying goodbye, for the last time, to his father.

"My father's still alive?" Paul's voice wavered. "I don't even know you. And now you tell me this? What's next—that my mother's alive?"

"She never knew. She died not knowing the truth," Lia said, her tone softening. "It's a lot to process. Cap will brief you and get you set up at the safe house. Your gun case is right under the seat."

Paul reached under the seat, his hand finding the familiar shape of the case handle. "How did you manage to get this?"

"I got it when I picked up your car. You'll need it," Lia said.

"You broke into my house?"

"Not personally. My guy handled it. He was discreet."

Paul's mind flashed back to the van he had spotted from his bedroom window. He'd sensed something wasn't right about that van but had been preoccupied or careless. Carelessness was unacceptable and, in his line of work, usually fatal.

He entered his passcode on the case's front LED keypad, and the internal lock clicked open. Fixated on his Colt 1911 Competition SS resting inside, memories flooded back of his father's classic Army-issue single-action Colt 1911 with its checkered wooden grips, patinated by the oils and grit of his father's hand. The battle-worn scratches on the barrel made him wonder how many souls it had killed. He'd never asked.

Paul smoothly ejected the magazine from his Colt Competition, a modern variant of his father's classic 1911. The stainless-steel barrel construction not only added a striking visual appeal but also provided the necessary heft to reduce recoil, a key factor in maintaining accuracy during rapid-fire sequences. The advanced model differed from the classic by featuring an extended sight radius for remarkably precise targeting, combined with the finely adjustable rear sight and the high-visibility fiber optic front sight.

He quickly checked the load—eight .45 ACP rounds—before slapping the magazine back into the magwell and racking the slide to chamber a round, relishing the familiar and satisfying metallic sound.

Lia glanced over, took another sharp turn, and veered toward the exit ramp. "Impressive piece. Looks like it's seen its fair share of action," she said.

Paul nodded, his hand instinctively rubbing the worn, checkered blue G10 grip, admiring the heat-induced scarring on the muzzle and chamber area caused by countless rounds and hours spent honing his craft.

"And I hear you're an amazing shot," Lia said with a smile.

"Decent," Paul said with understated humility.

Lia raised an eyebrow. "Decent? Air Force's Advanced Marksman designation. Right," she said with a hint of sarcasm.

Paul reached back and pulled out his backpack. It was all going too fast. His mind was racing with too many questions and no damn answers.

She elbowed Paul in the arm. "Are you ready? I know you're not sure what end's up. But you're a part of something bigger. I'm taking you to Station 64. You'll get your orders there."

The word "orders" caught his attention. Years ago, Colonel Wilson had said this day would come, but the details had been vague.

For some reason, Paul's thoughts drifted to his last visit to the hospital—the sterile smell, the bright lights, and the sympathetic nurses. It could be that Lia's presence was stirring memories of Sara.

"What's the tattoo on your wrist?" Paul asked, wanting to learn more about her.

"It's something we earn. It'll make sense soon, trust me,"

she said, merging onto the freeway.

Paul examined the phone she'd given him. *Scan Ready*, the screen prompted.

"Go ahead. Activate it," she said.

He centered his eye on the scanner. The device instantly recognized him. Paul knew this wasn't the standard facial rec that was commonplace in consumer-grade devices. It was a highly advanced, secure retina scan with a biosignature iris sensor. Hackers had developed AI deep fakes to bypass the facial recognition pattern-matching sensors. Within the agencies, the iris had replaced all other identity-matching methods. His department was responsible for the encryption key vault, which stored all federal employee pattern keys. But how did they get his iris pattern?

"Your profile's in our database," Lia said, anticipating his question. "I know you want to know the how, where, and why. It's who you are. You're a problem solver. And a good one at that. What you did in Kuwait was impressive, and those questions in your complex mind will be answered soon. But for now, know you are part of something important."

Kuwait? Lia seemed to have extensive knowledge of Paul's past, even classified work for Colonel Wilson. Paul had been a key member of the covert team responsible for hacking into Saddam Hussein's military network. Back then, Saddam's computer systems were comparatively primitive, making them vulnerable to exploitation. Yet, the stakes were high; Saddam had repurposed Russian technology to build programs designed to disperse chemical agents into water and food processing facilities. While Saddam might not have had weapons of mass destruction, he planned to kill thousands of innocent people.

Driving down the slick, semi-frozen road, Lia slowed as they approached the highway underpass. "All clear. This is as far as I go—you walk from here," she said. "Down the road about a quarter of a mile. You'll find a dirt path leading north toward an old farmhouse."

"Where are you going?" Paul asked with reluctance in his voice.

"I've got other business to attend to. We'll meet up again soon."

Paul stepped out of the car into the cold.

Lia rolled down the passenger window, leaning over with a parting glance. "Thanks for trusting me," she said, a glint of sincerity in her eyes.

"You're leaving me here and taking my car?" Paul said, feeling an unexpected pull toward her magnetic presence. Maybe it was his reluctance to face whatever was waiting in that farmhouse, or he genuinely wanted her to stay.

"You need to do this on your own, Mr. Knox," she said seriously.

Mr. Knox?

"And my car?"

"I like it." Lia smiled, pulling up her jacket's zipper.

Was it more than a typical, friendly smile?

Wishful thinking, old man.

He watched her hands return to the wheel, and she hit the accelerator. The Tesla responded as no fossil-fuel power vehicle could ever dream. The tires spun on the icy road, desperately searching for traction. The car darted forward, reaching a hundred miles per hour in seconds.

Paul stood there for a moment, watching her drive away, feeling something he hadn't felt in years.

Focus! he reminded himself.

◆ ◆ ◆

The biting February wind of Ohio's farm country was relentless, yet Paul found himself oddly detached from the cold.

His thoughts drifted to the stranger in the airport. Those boots, the aviators—either a pro or a guy with a bad sense of style.

The farmhouses were spaced out about a half-mile apart. The cornfields stretched as far as the eye could see, row after row, remnants of the fall's harvest reduced to dried, bent, knee-high stalks.

Paul marveled at how the land had produced healthy crops for generations. How could the soil have any nutrients left? The next-generation fertilizers and pesticides were so advanced that they restored the soil in weeks, but how did those chemicals affect the food supply?

His mind was wandering. Paul checked himself.

Focus!

He concentrated on his immediate surroundings. The area was desolate—no cars or signs of life. The dead of winter in Midwest farm country was a quiet and lonely time. People, animals, birds, insects, and other living creatures either hibernated or migrated south.

The darkening winter clouds cast shadows across the endless fields of frozen dirt. The trees, strategically placed decades ago, were tired and old, with crooked trunks and barren branches. They'd weathered dozens of seasons, standing alone, unprotected, surrounded by corn, soybeans, and winter wheat.

Paul approached the top of a hill and a dirt road. A rusted mailbox rested on a weathered wooden post. The wind picked up, lashing his face with the icy remnants of the last snowfall. He pulled up his coat collar, lowered his head to shield himself from the freezing wind, and continued toward the old, two-story farmhouse.

He needed answers to the questions swirling in his mind.

EPSILON

20 FEBRUARY, 1300 HRS
DEARBORN, MICHIGAN — U.S. CONGRESSIONAL DISTRICT 13

In the fortified lower level of GloMink headquarters, Hassan stood stoic in the back of the room, staring forward as Khalid addressed their twelve chosen men. All were in their mid-twenties, freshly shaven, sitting attentively on prayer rugs with their eyes locked on Khalid. A large, unmarked map was spread across a wooden table, dotted with red, yellow, and green plastic pieces—circles, stars, and squares—each signifying a target location and Hassan's covert infiltration units.

Under Khalid's directive, Hassan meticulously prepared the map for tactical review. The map was devoid of explicit markings, and digital evidence of the target locations did not exist. Hassan's men were hand-selected, deeply trusted, and the only individuals privy to the operational details. Organized in two-man units, they were assigned to the six target locations represented by the coded pieces on the map.

Hassan was well-versed in the unforgiving law of tactical probabilities. He understood the stark reality: statistically, two units would likely fail, one might achieve partial success, and three would accomplish their mission objectives.

Khalid stood before them, wearing his traditional loose tan hemp pants paired with an untucked, long white linen shirt. His cotton-knit prayer cap, snug against his head, created a striking contrast against his bronze skin and immaculately groomed coal-black beard. He exuded confidence, purpose, and, above all, iron-clad determination. His command of the English language was equally impressive, a skill he consistently employed while addressing his operatives. Adhering to their in-country infiltration protocol, Khalid insisted his commanders enforce linguistic assimilation, reserving Arabic solely for places of worship.

As he paced behind the table, Khalid looked intently into the anticipating eyes of each man, reaching into their hearts, lifting them beyond doubt, above fear. With each carefully chosen word, he transformed their apprehension into unwavering confidence and conviction, preparing them for the task ahead.

"Loyal and brave brothers, our moment of action draws near. It is time for you to demonstrate your skills and fulfill the mission entrusted to you. We stand at a pivotal time in our historic struggle against the Western unbelievers," Khalid said, his voice escalating in tempo and tenor. "Remember, you walk not in solitude but in the revered path laid by generations of our martyred brethren, whose honor and sacrifice light our way."

Hassan could feel a growing confidence radiating from each man. With every word Khalid spoke, their focus and intensity sharpened as if they were blades being honed for battle. Khalid paced back and forth with purposeful, graceful strides. This group was his elite, chosen ones, his soldiers, witnessing their master conduct a fine concerto, inspiring them with impassioned words.

A wave of pride washed over Hassan, cherishing the opportunity to serve alongside his mentor and supreme leader of men. Anyone with the good fortune to be in Khalid's presence found themselves irresistibly drawn to his magnetic charisma, ready to follow him unconditionally to the ends of the earth.

"Over two decades ago, before many of you were even born, our esteemed leader's unrelenting truth blessed us with our monumental victory. Your brothers, under the guidance of the great Osama, piloted the jetliners into their towers—symbolic daggers driven into the very heart of Western greed and corruption. Those brave warriors of our cause unleashed havoc, sending thousands of unbelievers to an eternity of hellfire." Khalid's voice thundered through the room.

Even though Hassan had heard these words numerous times, each retelling reignited a fire within him. His muscles tensed in anticipation, and his focus sharpened on Khalid's unwavering conviction.

"Our fallen brothers, martyred in combat against the western invaders, were blessed and now revel in their divine reward. Soon, you will be chosen to embrace such a glorious fate." Khalid raised his arms, palms open toward the heavens. "Rise now and heed your final orders."

Hassan approached Khalid, standing rigid and back straight, with a stern expression. His hands were clasped behind his back.

"Commander Hassan will now review your mission," Khalid said. "Pay close attention. Under his leadership, we struck a devastating blow to the infidels' transport network. Commander Hassan, a brave warrior of our cause, will guide you toward victory."

Buoyed by Khalid's words, Hassan stepped forward and stared deep into the souls of each of his men. "Thank you for your wisdom, General," Hassan said. "Brothers, this map you have committed to memory represents your designated mission targets. You were briefed on the mission procedures tailored to each site. Adhere strictly to your assigned tasks. There must be no deviation from your prescribed orders.

"Do you understand?" Hassan said with a stern, commanding tone.

Heads nodded in silent unison.

"Do you understand?" Hassan shouted, his fists slamming down on the table. The plastic pieces shot into the air, scattering onto the floor. Each man stood, snapped to attention, staring ahead.

"Yes, Brother," they responded in resolute unison.

"Do you understand?" Hassan repeated forcefully, demanding obedience.

"Yes, Brother!" the men shouted, their faces filled with intense passion.

"Very well. You will remain in this facility until the time to deploy to your forward operating locations. Remember, any deviation from orders will have dire consequences. You are not to speak amongst yourselves until your base commander provides final instructions. Go now to your rooms, seek strength in prayer, and prepare for the glorious victory."

One by one, the men filed out of the room, each prepared to sacrifice their life.

"Excellent. The men are ready," Khalid said as he left the room.

Alone, Hassan collected the scattered plastic pieces and carefully rolled up the map, representing the only tangible trace of their impending strike.

◆ ◆ ◆

Hassan waited patiently for Khalid to change his clothes. When Khalid emerged, he had transformed into his capitalist alias, the epitome of Western affluence: dressed in a finely tailored three-piece charcoal Brunico wool pinstripe suit, a crisp white Egyptian cotton spread collar shirt, and polished chocolate calfskin Salvatore Ferragamo loafers.

Silently, Hassan followed him along the basement's dimly lit corridor. At the antiquated freight elevator, Khalid paused. With an obedient nod, Hassan opened the creaking outer wood doors, his actions a subtle yet significant demonstration of respect for his elder. Once Khalid stepped inside, Hassan closed the wooden doors and pressed the aged analog button. The elevator lurched into motion with a jarring knock and high-pitched screech, its metal pulleys groaning under the weight as they ascended to the GloMink Research and Development Facility on the fourth floor.

A remnant of Detroit's industrial glory, Hassan had purchased the building three years prior. The former Leeson

Brothers Die Casting Company headquarters—once a bustling hub for manufacturing engine blocks and other cast aluminum parts for automotive for Ford, Chrysler, and General Motors—had been a victim of the recent financial crisis. Leeson Brothers epitomized Detroit's prosperity for over half a century, offering well-paying jobs that fueled the city's economy.

The company's sudden bankruptcy signaled the end of an era, symbolizing Detroit's descent into economic despair. Skilled jobs vanished, replaced by low-wage service work, resulting in widespread blight, homelessness, and the downfall of a once-great city. Corrupt politicians and labor union leaders clinging to power betrayed the people, sending Detroit spiraling further into decline. Khalid often referenced Detroit in his teachings, citing it as a symbol of Western capitalistic failures—a mixture of greed, corruption, and moral decay.

Decades prior, Dearborn was chosen by ISIS central command for its covert operations center. With nearly thirty percent of its population being of Arab descent, Dearborn provided ideal cover and a recruiting magnet. The area served as a focal point for radicalization programs, further fueled by the influx of asylum seekers from Libya, Syria, Iraq, Iran and Yemen.

Khalid had received community awards and praise for revitalizing the old factory building. Outfitted with cutting-edge technology, the facility was a symbol of urban renewal. The city, eager to support this supposed economic rejuvenation, funded the construction of new roads and high-speed internet and provided generous tax incentives to support his telemarketing business.

In his carefully crafted persona, Allessio Urbani, Khalid's in-country alias, led the GloMink Group (مِنْكَ). This e-commerce apparel company catered to America's nearly four million Arab Americans, offering Western clothing that adhered to orthodox traditions yet allowed for a degree of self-expression that was strictly prohibited in their native lands.

The GloMink campus featured three renovated office buildings, a massive, five-hundred-seat call center, and a distribution warehouse. The crown jewel, however, was the Research and Development Technology Center. Guarded around the clock and equipped with state-of-the-art security surveillance, it housed a fortified, tier-three data center. Over a hundred software developers and operations staff worked there, supporting a façade of commercial enterprise while concealing a more nefarious agenda.

GloMink's patented product matching and search engine optimization algorithm led to meteoric sales growth. This remarkable growth earned Allessio Urbani the prestigious Entrepreneur of the Year Award and secured him a feature in *Forbes Magazine*, marking him as a rising star in the business world.

Yet, beneath the veneer of GloMink's corporate success lay Hassan's covert cyberattack unit, the dark heart driving the company's financial success. Masterminding sophisticated ransomware extortion schemes, this shadowy division funneled millions into the coffers each month, bankrolling the group's paramilitary operations with ruthless efficiency.

◆ ◆ ◆

"Brother, the men stand ready. Our embedded bot listeners monitor NSA and FBI email and messaging traffic, tracking every move. The Americans have taken the bait—redirecting their troops to guard their nuclear facilities, fully convinced that's where we'll strike next. Your brilliant foresight in this diversion was nothing short of genius, sir," Hassan said, commending his superior's cunning plan.

Khalid's stare was fixed on the immense ninety-eight-inch OLED wall TV on his office's rear wall. The screen was alive with vibrant blues and reds as giant talking heads of so-called economic experts debated the recession's impact on the ongoing Middle East war. Below them, the stock market ticker scrolled, painting a grim picture with stock symbols flashing red.

Hassan watched silently as the screen shifted to a chart showing the dramatic plunge, an almost vertical, roller-coaster descent. The NASDAQ and DOW plummeted, declining ten percent for the day and fifty percent since the fateful Thanksgiving Day attacks.

"Where is the market's bottom, and how long will this recession last?" asked the business channel's host.

One analyst weighed in. "The Feds are out of stimulus options. Interest rates are negative for the first time in our history, and continuous stimulus injections failed to stabilize the economy. The other consideration no one talks about is the massive federal debt, now exceeding our GDP and largely held by foreign governments. Japan and China, once steady buyers of U.S. Treasuries, are divesting at an alarming rate. This sell-off has put pressure on the Treasury Department's ability to attract new investors, driving up interest rates. The U.S. government's ability to pay debt obligations is now in jeopardy."

"For our viewers who aren't financial experts, can you sum up what this means for the average investors?" the host moderator asked.

Khalid broke his silence, abruptly interjecting, "That question is pointless. We know the effect. The fate awaiting the U.S. economy is akin to the fall of ancient Rome, hastened by our Chinese allies." He swiveled his chair toward Hassan. "But first, we must bring the infidels to their knees." The bright blue light from the screen cast a glow in Khalid's eyes, reminiscent of a propane flame.

"Yes, Brother," Hassan said with an elevated tone of enthusiasm.

The analyst on the screen continued, "It means the U.S. is paying for the sins of our past. As some would say, we have been living beyond our means, and now we are on the brink of default."

"But isn't this an overly pessimistic view?" the host said. "The U.S. economy has recently weathered two historic recessions. What makes this one different?"

"The difference," the analyst explained, "is that the U.S. has crossed a fiscal point of no return. For the first time, the government lacks the revenue to cover interest on its foreign debt. Moreover, countries like China have recognized our economic vulnerability and ceased buying bonds, especially as we continue to put money into endless wars and to expand social welfare programs."

Khalid's response was a slow, deliberate clap. "The time has arrived. Hassan, our efforts are bearing fruit," he said, turning back to the TV.

The guest analyst continued, outlining a dire financial situation. "As these countries dump U.S. Treasuries, the current crisis only deepens. Investors are waking up to the harsh reality, retreating from U.S. equities and flocking to assets like gold, silver, and alternative financial instruments, such as cryptocurrencies. This explains Bitcoin's unprecedented surge in recent weeks. Amidst governmental and economic instability, decentralized currencies have emerged as a safe haven."

Khalid abruptly silenced the television with the remote and approached Hassan. He placed his hands firmly on Hassan's shoulders and locked eyes with him in a moment of intense connection.

"*Alhamdulillah*," Khalid whispered with a gratified smile. "My friend, our plan is proceeding as envisioned. We have been blessed with divine wisdom and heavenly strength to strike the Western infidels. But be forever mindful that a wounded dog is unpredictable and can be most dangerous. You must now apply pressure on the adversary's throat. Never relent. Understood?"

"Yes, General," Hassan said with a resolute voice.

Khalid returned to his desk, sinking into the plush leather chair. He lifted a piece of paper from the glass desktop. "Do you recognize this?"

Hassan stepped closer. "I do not."

Khalid carefully held the aged paper in his hands. Its edges were slightly frayed, and the once-crisp texture had softened into a delicate parchment-like quality. For Khalid, this paper was not just a relic of the past; it was a treasured symbol of a defining moment in his cause, with both historical significance and deep personal meaning.

"This," Khalid said, "is the very message my father received from Brother Osama twenty-five years ago. It was sent to Al-Qaeda field commanders in the aftermath of 9/11. Listen to his prophetic words."

With that, Khalid began to read aloud, his voice carrying a mix of reverence and exuberance.

"'The enemy can be described as a wicked tree. The trunk of that tree is fifty centimeters wide. The tree has many branches, which vary in length and size. The trunk of the tree represents America. The branches of the tree represent countries such as NATO members and their Arab allies. On the other hand, we represent a person who wants to cut down that tree. Our abilities and resources, however, are limited, thus we cannot do the job quickly enough. Our only option is to cut that tree down slowly using a saw. Our intention is to saw the trunk of that tree, and never to stop until that tree falls down.

"'Assume that we have cut up thirty centimeters of the trunk of that tree. We then see an opportunity to cut into one of the branches using our saw. Say a branch that represents the United Kingdom. We should ignore that opportunity and go back to sawing the trunk of the tree. If we are to allow ourselves to be distracted by sawing this or that branch, we could never finish the job at hand. We will also lose momentum and, most importantly, waste our jihad efforts. We want to saw until the wicked tree is down. Once the tree is down, its branches will die thereof. You saw what happened to the Russians in Afghanistan when the Mujahidin focused on sawing the trunk of their wicked tree. Their tree fell, and its branches died out, from South Yemen to Eastern Europe. We must aim every bow and arrow and every landmine at the Americans. Only the Americans, but no one else.'"

Khalid paused, letting a deliberate silence envelop the room, giving weight to Osama bin Laden's words. Hassan listened intently, feeling history echo with each syllable.

"Our brothers have tirelessly chipped away the tree for many years, and now its trunk is weak," Khalid said. "Colonel Hassan, you have never asked about the axe."

Mounted prominently behind Khalid's desk, the ancient axe was displayed against a backdrop of supple red velvet, encased in a thick, clear glass display that appeared to float in midair.

Khalid unlocked the case and carefully lifted the axe from its brass mountings. He grasped the long wooden handle, wrapped in an aged, tattered cloth. "This is an ancient epsilon, a relic from our Persian ancestors who repelled the invading Mongol hordes. Its design and craftsmanship are truly magnificent. The warrior can skillfully wield it with one or two hands, adapting to the needs of battle."

Demonstrating its grip, Khalid approached Hassan. "The extended handle balances the weight of the brass blade head," he said, raising the axe over his head and bringing it down with precise ferocity, halting it millimeters from Hassan's shoulder.

Hassan did not flinch, feeling the air brush against his face.

Khalid grinned at Hassan's disciplined composure. "You and your warriors are akin to this razor-sharp blade. With these hands..." Khalid gestured with the axe. "...I will hack into the tree trunk. Our brothers will remember forever the epsilon that toppled the infidels."

"The men stand ready, sir. At sunset, they will depart to their designated positions, as per your orders," Hassan said.

RISING SUN

JUNE 5, 1781
FREDERICKSBURG, VIRGINIA COLONY

Jack jumped from his horse and stretched his arms high up into the air, happy to be out of the saddle. He removed his hat and wiped his face with the front of his shirt. A gentle breeze provided a brief respite from the sun's searing heat and the thick air familiar to the northern Virginia summers.

Exhausted, the boys welcomed the chance to rest. They had endured six grueling hours in the saddle, riding from Governor Jefferson's estate across the hilly terrain, northeast past the upper reaches of Lake Anna.

"I'm famished," Julius said, swinging his long, lanky leg and hopping down from his horse.

"Julius, you're always hungry," Ben said. "But so am I."

"Let's see if Charles can board us for the evening. We need to rest before we make our way to Philadelphia," Jack said, hopeful that his father's longtime friend could provide information about the British whereabouts before they traveled from Fredericksburg north toward Alexandria.

Charles, the general's younger brother, had been a close friend of Jack's late father. They'd crossed paths over the years, trading fur, riding equipment, and other sundries. On many occasions, Charles had been a frequent guest at Jack's father's Cuckoo Tavern in Richmond.

Jack walked up the weathered wooden steps of the modest white clapboard home. As he reached the porch, the door swung open, and a long musket barrel pointed directly at his chest. A petite, slender woman with long, braided blonde hair, a flowing linen dress, and riding boots held the rifle with the confidence of a skilled hunter. Twin boys—barefoot, shirtless, and in calfskin knee breeches—clutched her legs, looking up at Jack with curious blue eyes that peeked out from under their curly sand-colored hair.

"If you're loyalists, ride back to where you come from," she said boldly, raising the barrel toward Jack's head.

Jack could think of better ways to start his morning than being shot, so he slowly raised his hands and smiled. "Good morning, ma'am. We mean no harm. We're friends. I'm Captain Jack Jouett of the Amelia County Militia. Is Charles home? He and my father are acquainted, and we hoped you could provide us with boarding. We've traveled for the past two days on our way north to Philadelphia."

She loosened her grip on the rifle but turned the barrel toward Ben and Julius.

"These are my friends, Ben and Julius. They fought bravely alongside me at Charlestown. We are friends of the cause and are traveling north on orders from Governor Jefferson."

The little ones tugged on her dress, looking up at their mother. She lowered the rifle and patted each of them on the head. "I reckon you boys are hungry. Come in, and I'll fix you breakfast. My name's Mildred, Mildred Washington. These are my boys, Charlie and Willie. You can take your horses on back. There, you'll find water and feed."

"Thank you, ma'am," Jack said and gave Ben and Julius a nod to care for the horses.

The little ones ran inside, playfully pushing each other. Jack followed. The welcoming aroma of bacon, bread, and smoked wood filled the room. A steaming kettle warmed over a smoldering fire in the large stone fireplace. At the rear of the room, two large paned glass windows flanked a block wood cutting table and a gray stone washbasin. A finely made cotton quilt hung over a dark hardwood rocking chair in the opposite corner.

"Please sit," she said, motioning to the long, weathered

gray oak table that filled the center of the room. She took down a pewter mug hanging from a wall peg and filled it with water from a large, fluted tin pitcher.

Jack pulled out the sturdy bench, sat down, and raised the mug to her. "Thank you, ma'am." The cool water refreshed his dry throat as he finished the mug in several large gulps. She reached across and refilled his drink.

"Captain Jouett. My…"

"No, please call me Jack."

"Okay, Jack, my husband has spoken highly of your family. I was saddened to hear your oldest brother was killed in battle a few years back."

"Yes, ma'am, at Brandywine," Jack said as the memory of his older brother came rushing back.

"I'm so sorry for your loss. I do hope your father is well?"

"He also passed, ma'am," Jack said, attempting to restrain the intense emotion welling in his chest.

"I'm truly sorry to hear that," she said. "I pray he didn't suffer."

Jack stood silent and still, wavering ever so slightly. His attention drifted to the young boys staring up at him. "It's okay, boys. I reckon my father and brother died so you could one day be free. And while my heart is heavy, I will do what I must to drive the tyrants from our land."

"I'm sorry, but Charles left for the Carolinas a fortnight ago. He'd want me to tend to you properly, so please, come in and make ya'selves comfortable," Mildred said, turning to the little ones, "Go fetch them plates." Charlie and Willie heeded their mother's instruction and ran, pushing each other in a race to reach the cupboard first. "I've warmed Pease Porridge and cornbread. My apologies, meat's scarce in these parts cuz of loyalist pillagin'."

"Thank ya, ma'am, that's mighty kind," Jack said.

He pulled out Governor Jefferson's folio from his carry satchel. Inside was a bundle of letters, each folded crisply, wrapped in cotton twine.

Pushing and shoving, Ben and Julius came crashing through the rear door and stomped the dirt and dew off their boots. Julius patted the young ones on the head and leaned his musket against the wall.

"Ma'am, it sure smells mighty good," Julius said, always thinking about his belly.

"I'll fix ya up some breakfast. Make yourself at home," Mildred said.

"Yes, thanks, ma'am." Ben elbowed Julius hard in the ribs. "Where are your manners, you idiot?"

"Uh, thanks, ma'am," Julius said and punched Ben in the arm.

Ben didn't budge or seem to notice. "What's in the letters?" he asked, excited to see what all the fuss was about.

"Julius, take a gander at these. You're more sharp-witted than us ordinary folk," Jack said, smiling and winking at Ben.

Julius promptly shoved Ben aside, unfolded the letters, and arranged them neatly on the table. "These have been written recently on fresh cloth parchment." He picked up the first letter and held it to the light. "Hemp and cotton, I reckon. Not from around these parts. But this…" He examined larger parchments, studying the maps of the colonies and unfamiliar lands with keen interest. "This appears to be young sheepskin," Julius said.

Julius traced the route with his finger. "Interestin'. It's the western lands—Pennsylvania, Connecticut-Ohio territories—marked with symbols and numbers, but I ain't sure what they mean. What's this star and writin'—Fort Clinton, West Point? It's where the governor ordered us to deliver these documents, somewhere in New York. Remember, it's the fort from which that turncoat Arnold fled."

"And now he's a general in the British army, marching his marauders through Virginia," Jack said.

"God will make him pay for his treachery." Ben patted his

hatchet. A stout Presbyterian, Ben often called upon God to vanquish the enemy for the cause.

Julius studied the map. "There's also this." He pointed. "It looks to be a cannon near Boston at the intersection of these three rivers. '*Springfield*' is scribed underneath the cannon. Must be the name of the village and possibly an armaments store."

"What 'bout the letters, Julius?" Jack inquired.

Julius picked up the first and read it. "This one is to Mr. Adams. Oh, that would be the Boston Mr. Adams. The lawyer I read about who served as counsel to the Boston Massacre redcoats," Julius said. "The letter's dated three weeks ago. Let me see here." He mumbled as he read the letter. "It's 'bout the weather, crops, grape yields, phases of the moon, and temperatures for colonial towns—Philadelphia, Boston, New York, Richmond, Savannah, and Baltimore—signed '*Th-Jefferson.*'"

Jack looked at the third and final letter. "To make Brunswick stew," he said.

"A recipe?" Ben said.

"May I?" Julius asked. "Hum, Brunswick stew, written in what appears to be the governor's hand—season two pheasants with salt and pepper, equal parts onions, tomatoes, and one hand of parsley—"

Jack stopped Julius. "Awe, that's enough. Why have we been ordered to courier these?"

Julius continued reading. "Add a layer of potatoes and butter. That sounds real good," he said.

"You're always thinking about food," Ben said and punched him in the arm.

"Stop!" Julius said, rubbing his shoulder. He turned over the parchment. "To grow herbs—parsley, sage, rosemary, and thyme. It's a cipher."

"Huh?" Ben said.

"Spies and couriers use a code to avoid prying eyes. It requires know-how to decipher—a key, to read the hidden message."

"Put it back. It's not our place. Our orders are to deliver the package, not read them," Jack said.

Mildred brought over two plates of a mild green porridge while the little ones carried tin cups full of milk. As they set them down, one cup spilled. The milk sloshed across the table. Jack snatched the letters just as the milk splashed on one of them and soaked the cloth parchment. The ink lettering bled together.

"Uh-oh!" Julius said.

Young Charlie began crying, and Willie followed.

Julius patted them on the head and bent down, looking into their swollen eyes. "It's okay, boys. It was my fault." He used his shirt to dab at the letter.

"I'm so sorry," Mildred said.

"I think I can make out most of the words," Julius said.

Sniffling, Charlie and Willie jumped up on the bench on each side of him.

"Please eat," Mildred said, placing the plates before Julius and Ben.

"Thank you, ma'am. I'm famished," Julius said. He grabbed his fork and knife and dug in.

"Me too," Willie said with a brilliant smile.

"Yeah. Me too…" Charlie parroted.

Jack heard the sound of heavy boots climbing the front porch steps. His hand fell onto the handle of his knife. Ben pulled his short axe from his belt, and Julius looked up but continued eating. Ben shoved Julius, who reached for his musket.

A fist pounded on the door, shaking the wooden hinges.

"Who's there?" Mildred said and put her finger to her lips to shush the boys.

"Miss Washington, it's Constable Jones. I hope I'm not disturbing you."

"How may I be of service, Constable?"

"There's word strangers are roaming through these parts,

and I wanted to check up on you and the boys. You know, considering your husband's away."

"He's a Tory," she whispered. "Take this." She handed Ben a loaf of bread and a large chunk of salt pork. "Git out back. Hurry."

"Did you say something?" the constable asked.

"One moment. Just cleaning up," Mildred said.

Jack motioned to Ben to go to the rear door. "Be good, boys, and take care of your mother," he whispered. He bent down and gave Willie and Charlie a hug. "Many thanks, ma'am."

With the governor's satchel slung over his shoulder, he trailed closely behind Ben and Julius through the back door, his mind consumed by curiosity about the secret meaning concealed within its contents.

STATION #64

19 FEBRUARY, 0815 HRS
HIRAM, OHIO

Paul scanned the perimeter from the east side of the house. Twin red brick chimneys stood tall on each side of the nineteenth-century, whitewashed, two-story Victorian. Laced half-curtains hung from the dark windows that ran the length of the wide wraparound porch. An old, rusted, four-foot-high chain link fence cordoned off the house's backyard. Two empty dog bowls sat near the side steps.

All was quiet.

Where is it? Every farm has a dog.

Paul rubbed the dark purple, three-inch scar on his right hand. He couldn't stand dogs. He hated them. Sure, domesticated puppies were cute, but then some dogs took a wrong turn, deciding they wouldn't be man's best friend. The wild Kuchi dogs of Afghanistan taught him to respect canines. The Afghan herd guard dogs, or "Dogs of the Nomad," had been displaced by decades of war and unrest. In the remote outskirts of Afghan cities, the once-obedient and trusting breed had devolved into menacing, untamed beasts. With their large bear-like skulls, they roamed freely, capable of taking down a full-grown man if they were in the mood. In Paul's case, he nearly lost his hand as a vicious Kuchi clamped down with unrelenting force. It took a bullet through the dog's eye to finally force it to release its grip.

Where is that dog?

A cement path led from the house through the backyard—about fifty yards—to a towering two-story dark red corn crib barn. The four small windows at the barn's base and two double sliding entrance doors were trimmed in white. With an original stone foundation, it had likely been standing for a century. Massive barn doors faced north into the vast fields of last summer's harvested rows of corn and soybean. High above the doors, facing west, was a small eight-pane window under the medium-pitched tin roof.

Paul walked back to the front of the house. The blue-gray painted steps were chipped and worn, and a weathered porch swing with rusted chains hung still. He turned back and looked across the vast fields of frozen dirt and down the two-lane road. From the house, which sat elevated on a slight rise, he could see clearly for miles in both directions.

No signs of life.

As his eyes scanned, he caught a glimpse of something unexpected concealed in the lower front roof corners—surveillance cameras. These weren't the standard commercial-grade gadgets but high-end mirrored 360-degree eyes-in-the-sky pro models. Whoever lived in this place seemed acutely aware of Paul's presence.

He looked closely into one of the lead-panel glass windows flanking the thick mahogany-stained door. It was dark and quiet inside, and he listened for movement, footsteps, or the dog.

Nothing.

He turned away to see dark clouds slowly rolling in from the west. Snow was on its way. Why was he here? Who was chasing him? A woman with the tattoo claimed that his father was running an operation. He wanted answers.

The overcast sky provided just enough natural light to see between the gap in the curtains of the picture window in the center of the porch. On the living room's back wall was a dark maroon three-cushion couch with thick walnut wood legs and trim. On the opposite side of the couch were two petite brownish-yellow armchairs. An antique-style blue and red Persian rug blanketed the floor, and a large oval coffee table with a white and gray marble top sat in the middle of the rug. The room was designed for small after-dinner gatherings, conversation, and guests, but there was no sign of anyone.

His mind returned to the airport and the guy who shot out his car window.

Who was he?

Lia said the answers would be here.

Before he could knock, the latch disengaged, and the rusted hinges creaked. Standing in the doorway was a mid-sixties, stocky guy with a salt-and-peppered army-issue crew cut and a meticulously trimmed goatee. A Smith and Wesson .357 Magnum 38 Special hung from his belt holster—a left-handed draw with a well-worn wood grip.

"Appreciate you waiting. It takes me a few minutes to get up from that damn basement. Come on in, son. We've got a lot to cover," he said, with a Irish accent seasoned with a Midwestern twang.

Paul hesitated.

"Come on. I won't bite. My dog might, though."

Paul closed his eyes and shook his head.

He looked inside for the animal and proceeded through the living room and into the kitchen. It was simple, built for function, with old-style white appliances and a maple-colored oak wood table in the center with two aluminum chairs on each end. No sign of electronics, not even a clock. The classic Midwest farmhouse kitchen—utilitarian and neat.

Where's the clock? Every kitchen has a clock. That was the giveaway—this wasn't real. The antiseptic, metallic smell was another clear sign, reminding Paul of the hospital. The house was too clean.

"Paul, sit down. Make yourself goddamn comfortable."

"Who are you and what's going on?"

"We've got a lot to discuss. And you're gonna wanna sit for this."

Paul wasn't ready or in the mood to take orders. He stood tall, facing the man, eye to eye.

"Okay, suit yourself," the guy said, not backing down. "I'm Chanucey Mackay, but everyone calls me Cap."

Scottish. I was close.

"I know it's been a long morning, so I'll get to the point. Some really bad guys want you either dead or worse. But they also want to get their hands on your daughter."

Paul attempted to absorb what he had just heard. The word "daughter" lingered in the air. Emma was all he had left. "What are you talking about? Who? Why her?" he said, unwilling to stop until he got answers. His fists closed, and the skin on his knuckles tightened.

"No, don't blame me. I'm here to sort this out with you. It's because of her work at MIT. The techie network stuff. It's way over my head, but I'm sure you know more about it."

Paul hadn't talked to Emma about her work in a while. However, it was cutting-edge and likely funded by DARPA.

"But there's another problem. A bigger effin' problem," Cap said.

"What the hell could be more important than my daughter?"

"We monitor all communications, including local, state, and federal. We know when anything out of the ordinary happens as it relates to our people. And you have a problem. We suspect you've been under surveillance for some time. Someone disconnected your security and comms at O-seven hundred and broke into your home. Shortly after, we intercepted the police dispatch, which corresponded to the time of the breach. Someone notified police that shots had been fired in the local proximity of your home," Cap said.

"What? That doesn't make sense."

Cap handed Paul his phone with a news page open.

```
CLEVELAND — A woman was found shot to death
in a home on Fairmount Boulevard on Tuesday
morning, Cleveland Heights Police announced.
    At about 7:35 a.m., police were dis-
patched to a home on Fairmount Boulevard
```

responding to a 911 call reporting a domestic situation. Responding officers heard shots fired near the intersection of Coventry and Fairmount Boulevard at that time.

"While dispatchers were on the phone with the female caller, they heard multiple shots fired," said Cleveland Heights Detective Sam Powell.

When officers arrived, they found a 23-year-old woman with multiple gunshot wounds. The woman was pronounced dead on the scene. No other persons were at the scene.

The identity of the woman has yet to be released.

"Mr. Paul Knox, the owner of the property, is a person of interest. We're requesting the public's assistance for any information pertaining to his whereabouts," said Detective Powell.

"What the hell?" Paul went to the kitchen window and leaned on the chipped white ceramic sink.

"Yep, they've got ya by the balls," Cap said. "I figure it was their way of silencing your ass. Unless you *did* kill her?"

Paul turned his head and shot the man a look. "Hell no."

"I know you didn't do it. But the police don't."

Paul's frustration had reached a point beyond anything he could deal with. He wanted answers. "Enough. Who are you, and what's this all about?"

"Okay, here's the story—I shared a foxhole with your old man in Nam. He saved my life, and we've been close ever since," Cap said.

"My father?" It was simply too much to take in. How could it be?

"Yes, son. Remember when your father took you fishing in

the Wilds? You'd hike, camp, and fish them old quarry lakes." Cap grinned. "Me and the colonel used to deer hunt in the Wilds before you were born, well before the utility company bought the land."

Paul drifted in and out of the conversation, remembering those trips with his father. Together, they'd haul the heavy aluminum canoe from one small lake to another. His father had taught him to fly fish for monster bass on those quarry lakes.

"Did ya hear me?" Cap asked.

"Yeah. I heard you." Paul relaxed his hands and sat down at the table.

"So, these terrorist bastards think they've got you in a box, but little do they know they picked a fight with the wrong folks," Cap said.

Paul's headache returned to the back of his head. He rubbed it, pressing hard with his fingers into the bone and muscle, but as always, it didn't help to alleviate the dull pain. Cap went to the kitchen counter and pulled two glasses and the unmistakable green bottle of Glenlivet 12 from the cupboard. With practiced ease, Cap used the palm of his hand to spin the top off the bottle, then carefully poured two fingers of the light honey-yellow single malt into each glass. "Here you go. This'll help."

Paul focused on the golden light shimmering through the thin crystal-cut highball glass, silently acknowledging the deep inner conflict it represented. Without hesitation, he took two large gulps. The scotch slid down Paul's throat, carrying a smooth warmth punctuated by a subtle burn, a vivid reminder of its potency.

Cap poured him another.

A familiar warmth spread through Paul's chest.

Cap threw his back and shook his head. "Ah... A good way to take the edge off. Anyway. They fabricated the crime scene to pin it on you. The locals and FBI are out looking for you.

It's all happening fast. The Feds pulled your security clearance and disabled your NSA network access. They're tracking your comms. Your passport's been flagged. Your financial transactions, phone, and internet accounts are all monitored. Fortunately for you, Lia made it to the airport in time."

"Hold on, before you go there—how did they bypass my security system? It's hardwired into redundant backup systems, one wired and one wireless. It's also linked to my secure network—the basement's sealed with block glass and cement. I would've known if the house were compromised, and it would have been obvious to police if there was a break-in," Paul said.

"They're good. Sophisticated," Cap said. "Now it gets even more intense." He walked around, sat at the table, and offered Paul the bottle.

Paul poured them both another. "Are they connected to the attacks?" he asked.

"Bingo." Cap nodded. "These are the bastards that lit up O'Hare, planted the IADs on the turnpike, and mined the Port of Louisiana and Los Angeles. All strategic hits to our transportation system. And yet, the Feds don't have anyone in custody. Don't you find that odd?"

The scotch had started to set in, but Paul hung on the words "the Feds." If this Cap guy wasn't with the Feds, who was he with?

Paul stood, checked his balance, and walked over to the sink. "What agency are you with?"

"No agency."

"Then what branch?"

"We're a special ops group, and you've just been activated."

"Activated?"

"Colonel Wilson has been your handler since your MIT days. As for your father, he commands our unit. He's in D.C. at the moment dealing with bureaucratic crap."

Feeling the tension in his shoulders ease, Paul entertained the possibility. Somewhere deep down, he had always doubted the story about his father taking his own life.

"You can choose what you want to believe, but the fact is your father reports directly to the President, and we follow his orders," Cap said. "You know better than anyone that even the President can't trust his own cabinet members. That's nothing new. It's been that way forever. The President's the one person elected by all the people, so his interests are what matter. Congress does not allocate our funding, and we don't officially exist."

"You're saying standard rules of engagement don't apply?"

Everyone assumed a paramilitary group existed outside the purview of the Pentagon, the Director of National Intelligence (DNI), or the Justice Department. That was no secret. However, reporting to the President meant the group was independent of his cabinet and the eight other intelligence agencies.

"We don't have rules other than those dictated by the President or our mission parameters. Membership lasts a lifetime. However long or short that may be." Cap paused and stared at Paul.

"Lifetime? What kind of membership?"

"We've been committed for generations. The Founding Fathers and successive Presidents have called upon our forefathers when needed. Our oath demands the ultimate sacrifice, yet it also carries a tradition unparalleled in the annals of history. We protect an ideal created over two and a half centuries ago by brave men and women willing to lay down their lives for the many. And you, my friend, are a card-carrying member, as is your old man and his father before him."

"Bullshit!" The scotch had loosened Paul up, yet he wasn't buying it.

"Yeah, I felt the same way when I was activated after I returned from Nam." Cap stood and walked over to look out the window. "I know you're thinking I'm full of crap, but that's okay."

How could all of this be true? Is his father alive? Emma, a target? No way. But Paul had no choice; this Cap guy knew too much about him.

"That's enough for now. Your head must be spinning. You've gotta get some rest. You'll leave at nightfall. I can't afford to have you on the road in broad daylight. Bring your bag. I'll take you downstairs, and you can get somethin' to eat and then rest for a few hours." Cap turned toward the open basement door next to the empty pantry.

"This is too much. I need more answers before I'm doing anything," Paul said.

Cap got right in Paul's face and raised his voice. "Look, soldier, we're under attack, and they're about to hit us again. You've been called up. You're now part of the unit that flies under the radar and takes care of business for the President of the United States. Like me, Colonel Wilson, your father, you disappear, off the grid—you've officially gone dark. And if you don't like it, too bad, you have no choice. Otherwise, you're going to jail for that body that was found in your house."

Paul looked down at the empty highball glass, then glanced out the window over the sink. Winter-gray storm clouds were rolling in from the northwest.

Sara was gone. All he had left was Emma. He had to trust his gut, and right now, those instincts told him this guy was legit—nuts, but legit.

"Where's Emma? She's my priority," Paul said.

"That's where you're going. But in a few hours. You need to eat and catch some Zs first."

"I have to call her," Paul demanded.

"Not possible. Her comms and apartment are being monitored. You'll tip them off, and we can't allow that. So, let's get you set up and on your way to Boston."

LIGHTS OUT

21 FEBRUARY, 0230 HRS
DEARBORN, MICHIGAN

Hassan walked with purpose and anticipation, eyes forward, navigating the expanse of GloMink's customer service center. He weaved through the maze of cubicles. Each step brought him closer to his Cyber Command Center—the nerve center of his operation.

As he walked, he couldn't help but marvel at Khalid's flourishing empire. Yet, beneath the surface, the true lifeblood of the GloMink enterprise pulsed—HALIBRA, the ransomware hacker unit Hassan masterfully created. This covert unit kept the wheels of the operation turning, siphoning millions in cryptocurrency and extorting vulnerable targets—businesses, hospitals, universities, and government entities.

Hassan paused midstride, a wave of envy and jealousy washing over him, exposing a moment of weakness. He had taken immense personal risks, laboring day and night to bring Khalid's ambitious vision to life. Yet, Khalid reaped the rewards—a life of opulence, women, sports cars, and public adulation. Despite Hassan's unwavering loyalty, including the ultimate sacrifice—Yousef's life—Khalid received the accolades.

Hassan had pleaded with Khalid to spare Yousef. Still, Khalid was unyielding, insisting that their cause demanded such sacrifices and that Hassan, his devoted soldier, must obey or face grave consequences.

With a heavy heart, Hassan pushed tumultuous emotions into the dark corners of his soul. After all, Khalid was more than a commander; he was a mentor and surrogate father.

Hassan owed him a life debt for leading his family to safety from the war-torn chaos of Syria.

He passed row after row of obedient workers. Over a thousand low-skilled order-takers busily answering phone calls and chatting online with customers and suppliers, confined in their broken-down office chairs. The vast call center was a sea of drab, light brown cubicles, each barely providing space for a computer and its occupant.

Like cattle in a pen.

Khalid, in his relentless pursuit of profit, had squeezed as many bodies into the facility as the fire regulations would permit and then some. Every item in the facility was cheap and second-hand, from worn furniture to coin-operated coffee machines and outdated computers, yet not a single worker dared to complain. In a city ravaged by a three-decades-long recession, work was scarce. GloMink stood as one of the few companies that hadn't experienced the massive layoffs that had decimated Detroit's workforce.

The obedient workers at GloMink understood that Khalid micromanaged every aspect of the company, unilaterally approving expenditures, new hires, and signing off on employee leave. Those who dared to question his authority were demoted, terminated, or simply disappeared.

GloMink's employees harbored deep resentment toward Khalid, but open dissent was unthinkable. His handpicked managers emulated Khalid's dictatorial management style, further perpetuating a repressive culture that stifled independent thinking while enforcing blind obedience as the highest form of loyalty.

Hassan removed his glove, scanned his thumbprint, and keyed in his eight-digit code, granting him entry into HALIBRA's high-security command center. He stepped into the cool, oxygenated room bathed in soft yellow LED light, a deliberate choice to reduce monitor glare and lessen long-term exposure to reflective light.

The anechoic chamber, which spanned three thousand square feet, represented Khalid's grand vision and Hassan's meticulous oversight. Constructed two years ago, it served as the nerve center for HALIBRA's cyber operations.

Every inch of the space was engineered for maximum security and isolation. Its walls—a formidable three feet of concrete reinforced with an inner steel core—were impenetrable to all forms of energy waves. The outer surfaces were covered with layers of energy-absorbent material, rendering the chamber a dead zone for cell phones, Wi-Fi, and other wireless transmitting devices.

At the heart of the facility was the network core, connected to a dedicated fiber line by a combination of randomized proxy servers, VPNs, and TOR nodes, anonymizing all internet traffic in and out of the facility, making it virtually untraceable. Data was stored temporarily on local servers, with all logs and communication deleted every fifteen minutes. The most sensitive assets—the hacker unit's source code, scripts, and advanced engineering tools—were dispersed to remote servers located in Yemen, Venezuela, and North Korea.

To any external scan by federal agencies and local authorities, GloMink's network traffic appeared innocuous, just another e-commerce call center. But within these walls, Hassan commanded a cyberattack operation center, a digital fortress invisible from the outside world and cloaked in secrecy and security.

◆ ◆ ◆

Hassan's handpicked team of soldier hackers diligently monitored the network traffic on the six wall-mounted seventy-five-inch OLED monitors. He approached a small group of men seated at a circular pod of connected desks divided by head-height partition walls. These were no ordinary programmers; they were elite hackers, all male, in their early twenties, rigorously trained in Russia and Iran to penetrate the most secure American data centers.

Each hacker was equipped with a black gaming headset, the attached microphone curling from ear to mouth, and in front of them, four large computer monitors emitted a steady glow. They communicated in unison using the microphones, and their fingers danced on the keyboards as if they were playing an intense first-person shooter game, watching instructions register across the screens' black, red, and green command lines.

But the stakes were far from that of a video game. The HALIBRA unit was in the process of infiltrating four high-valued targets. Data centers were recently fortified with state-of-the-art cyber defense software developed by Dark Network Technologies. Their meticulously crafted plan hinged on exploiting the source code of Dark Network's advanced algorithm, obtained through two sympathetic engineers who had access to Dark Network's GitHub software repository. Skillfully, Hassan's team reverse-engineered the algorithm, finding loopholes to simulate network traffic and rendering their movements invisible to Dark Network's automated security tripwires.

Hassan picked up a headset from an empty cubicle and held it to his ear, tuning in to his men's conversations. Glancing at his watch, he was pleased. However, his expression remained stoic, concealing any outward sign of emotion from his men.

As planned, the team executed the final modification precisely. In unison, the men stopped typing and placed their hands in their laps.

The virus was ready.

One soldier looked up without making eye contact. "We are ready," he said, speaking in Russian. Hassan acknowledged the team leader with a subtle nod. Hassan despised the Russians, but there had to be exceptions in his line of business. He placed a portable key vault, no larger than a thumb drive, on the Russian hacker's desk. Inserting it into his computer activated the virus, which required an encrypted passcode to unlock the sleeper units in the DMZ.

Hassan authenticated the launch with his thumbprint and a voice command: "Zeta-Alpha-one-four-seven-eight." The device instantly synthesized the inputs into a single encryption key, checked against the device's internal authorization key and unlocked full operational access.

His eyes were fixed on the small key vault as the red light changed to pulsating green, signifying a match and triggering the virus's launch. Hassan focused on the young man's screen, carefully scanning the output for anomalies.

"Commander, phase two is complete," the Russian hacker reported with a smile that promptly vanished. "The web server sleeper units are active and have successfully penetrated the enemy's DMZs. You now have access, sir."

"Men, you are dismissed," Hassan said.

The men silently removed their headsets and filed out, each receiving a subtle nod of acknowledgment from Hassan. He consciously suppressed any visible sign of gratitude. Such emotions were a sign of weakness for a man in his position.

Moving to his desk, he quickly began to type, his fingers dancing across the keyboard. His gaze was locked on the string of commands appearing on the input line.

He logged into a remote-access session established by the RAGINGOWL Trojan virus that his men had previously planted months prior. He dumped the breached terminal server credentials and moved laterally through the data center's segregated network until he found his target—a domain controller that stored the company's critical usernames and passwords.

He stared at the first screen, executed the commands he had memorized, and waited for the power company's system to respond.

Seconds felt like hours as he waited for the system's response.

He caught himself holding his breath and drew a deep, steadying breath. The weight of the moment was all-consuming, his hope to be Khalid's choice as the North American Islamic State Commander hanging in the balance.

The computer screen burst to life, displaying a torrent of the priceless information he had painstakingly worked for months to obtain—hundreds of usernames streamed out of the hacked server. With these credentials in hand, he then executed an attack designed to impersonate a superuser administrator, granting him unrestricted access to the system and, ultimately, the power grid.

"*Alhamdulillah*," he whispered, his heart racing with the thrill of success. Khalid's master plan was on the brink of becoming a reality, and Hassan had been the architect of this pivotal moment. He had simultaneously breached four of the largest power generation stations on the East Coast.

Fueled by a surge of adrenaline, Hassan anxiously initiated the final stage. His fingers danced on the keyboard as he navigated through SCADA, the power company's central nervous system. With an intricate network of computers, display units, and specialized software, SCADA linked hundreds of substations, transmitting real-time data to control circuit breakers, relays, and capacitors. The system regulated power distribution based on the ever-changing demands of millions of households, factories, hospitals, water pumping stations, and other critical infrastructure connected to the grid.

Hassan was pressed for time, aware that he might have triggered the power company's cybersecurity alarms. He allotted six minutes to pinpoint the target user credentials and passwords, eight minutes to navigate laterally to the devices storing the integrated control system data, and three minutes to infiltrate each server, implant the ransomware and remote-access trojans, and then make his exit without being detected.

He scanned the list of names, titles, departments, and

access parameters of every user who worked in the dozens of facilities—company executives, attorneys, accountants, field maintenance personnel, engineers, and, most importantly, server administrators. Letters and symbols beside each name signified users with access to specific systems and their corresponding authorization levels.

He moved to the second screen and executed the identical commands. All four screens listed usernames and passwords for the users within the breached data centers. He repeated the commands with a slight modification to the parameters, reducing the list of names to those administrators with superuser access. Names were irrelevant. However, their elevated privileges would provide Hassan access to the heavy turbine control equipment.

His hands trembled ever so slightly as he focused his attention on the objective. His power was unmatched by anything attempted in history. Even the Chinese state-operated APT10 had not accomplished such an ambitious breach.

The Americans were so naïve to think they were invincible. Arrogance would be their downfall. For decades, the U.S. had occupied Hassan's homeland without meaningful repercussions. Yes, Osama had wounded the beast with his glorious attack; however, Hassan would inflict lasting damage on their economy and society, bringing the infidels to their knees.

The time had come.

He paused a moment to steady his hand and pressed enter.

The system responded immediately. A waterfall of emerald light cascaded across the midnight-black computer screen; letters, numbers, and symbols scrolled by line after line.

Scanning the output for keywords embedded in the pages of green text, Hassan smiled with childlike enthusiasm as the virus's bash script rapidly executed the lethal commands. The virus marched on, burrowing deep into the power company's data storage devices on a search-and-destroy mission, seeking the critical backup files.

Hassan momentarily closed his eyes as if his thoughts could guide the virus to its target.

The two most precious words a hacker treasured appeared on the screen.

‹ *Access Granted*

Containing his excitement, he noticed the delete command and hit the space bar to stop the scrolling.

‹ *rm -rf *.**

He pressed the space bar to resume the scrolling.

After about sixty seconds, the scrolling ceased, and a message appeared.

‹ *files deleted: 120,403,301*

Hassan laughed out loud, his first outward sign of emotion since Yousef's sacrifice.

The power company's backup files were gone forever.

No one could recover the files, not even Hassan. The power company would parachute in teams of cyber experts, data storage engineers, and forensic specialists. They wouldn't find a way. There wasn't one. They didn't have any other online copies of the data. For months, Hassan's hackers had used the virus to remotely scan all segments of the network and all data centers, inventorying every data storage device and backup system.

The power company would recall backup tapes from their off-site storage facilities, but that would not save them. Theoretically, tape backups had the data required to bring the systems and power back online; however, it would take weeks, or more likely months, to restore the data. And this would prove to be a fatal weakness. Backup tapes were notoriously unreliable and, worse yet, painfully slow. Computer tape backups had not changed materially since the late 1970s. Like the old music cassette tapes of the distant past, they were made of a fragile polyester-type plastic film with a magnetic coating.

Hassan smiled because even more satisfying was that the power company would be utterly oblivious to what had happened to their data.

He watched the emerald-colored text resume scrolling faster and faster. The virus searched for its next and primary target—the power company's central generator control system. Once deleted, the generation plant managers would shut down circuits manually, triggering a downstream surge overload.

Electricity would cease to flow throughout the entire East Coast of America.

He watched as the seconds ticked away on his G-Shock. In moments, his unequivocal sacrifice and obedience would be rewarded.

15, 14, 13...

He listened carefully for the sound.

3, 2, 1...

He waited.

A loud bang echoed throughout the control room as the freight-container-sized twin CAT 3521 diesel generator fired up, signaling Detroit Edison's main power feed into the GloMink facility was down. A low, rhythmic hum reverberated through the building. The overhead lights flickered, and his computer screen went dark and came back on as the backup generator took over, providing power to the building.

He visualized the chaos unfolding across the eastern grid: computer operators scrambling to switch substation relays into "safe mode" to prevent the turbines and distribution capacitors from overheating; however, their actions would be futile because the virus had taken out their ability to do so.

Hassan had estimated that the initial damage would take

at least forty to fifty generators offline. The eastern grid would destabilize, triggering frequency response events and the regional power plant protection systems to engage and disconnect from the grid, causing a massive, unstoppable cascading wave of outages across the country's east coast.

The wave just hit Detroit, which meant Philadelphia, New York, and Boston would also be offline.

He stood triumphant amid orchestrated darkness. Cities plunged into chaos, and the fabric of American society was torn apart. He instinctively reached back and traced the scar on his neck across his shoulder. Smooth nerves dulled, a reminder of his unwavering purpose. Yet for Hassan, this was just the beginning—the first strike in a relentless campaign to bring America to its knees.

Now was the time for the decisive blow, the moment to wield the axe with unyielding force, striking the heart of a weakened and vulnerable enemy. The hour had come for their plan's next, even deadlier phase.

RABBIT HOLE

19 FEBRUARY, 0845 HRS
HIRAM, OHIO

Paul followed Cap down a dimly lit basement stairwell, descending into what appeared to be the original cellar of an old farmhouse. At the end of the corridor, Cap approached a large, matte black steel door. With a push, the door opened, revealing a narrow passageway lit by harsh white fluorescent lights. Its walls were lined with cement block, and overhead, raw wood beams ran low across the ceiling. Twenty feet ahead, a gray steel dome-shaped hatch lay elevated a foot and a half off the dirt floor.

Cap entered a passcode into a keypad on the wall, triggering the release of the hatch's locks, their metal components spinning and clicking. He pulled the large handle on the top of the thick hatch, and with a hiss of air, the door swung open, its automated hydraulic hinges moving smoothly and silently.

The hole was pitch-black.

"No elevator?" Paul said.

"Son, this ain't goddamn *Men in Black*. This bunker was dug at the onset of World War Two," Cap said, pausing and shaking his head. "I know what you're thinking. No, I wasn't there—before my time. But the facility's been upgraded, as you'll see." Cap climbed into the hatch with one foot on the ladder, lowering himself one rung, then another.

Paul looked down onto the top of Cap's bald head and followed behind. They descended into blackness, dimly illuminated by small white lights mounted on each metal step. The air was cold and dry with a new paint smell. He could hear an HVAC unit humming in the distance below. After descending about fifty feet, they reached the cement floor, and a bright fluorescent glow filled the room.

Cap reached to his right and placed his hand on a flat black panel. Above his hand, a small clock on the panel counted down *13, 12, 11...* The clock stopped at five.

"Place your hand on the scanner," Cap said.

Paul did as he was told. Did he have a choice? The panel turned from red to green.

"To exit the bunker, you scan your hand here."

As Cap finished his sentence, Paul heard the hatch at the top of the ladder close. His ears sensed the change in air pressure.

"This area is completely sealed from the outside. It has dedicated water, air, and power. It can sustain operations for six months without external access. Refueling units are kept in strategic sites throughout the area, so sustainable power is not an issue."

Sensing motion, the room's electronics came to life. Mounted on the cement block wall, the glow of five large monitors illuminated the room, each one displaying a live satellite map of key metropolitan locations: New York, Miami, Los Angeles, Washington, D.C., and the fifth with their current location. The maps had dozens of pins labeled with five-digit numbers and were color-coded red, green, and yellow.

Cap went to the lockers on the wall adjacent to the large desk below the monitors. In the first locker was a large gray lockbox. "Here," he said and handed Paul a mini-USB stick. "To access our secure devices, you use this."

Paul recognized the device—an authentication key with an integrated hardware security module wallet. As it illuminated, a sixteen-digit encryption code appeared. Inputting the code into the lockbox keypad, he could hear the smooth hum of the locking mechanism disengaging. He opened the case to reveal an assortment of ID cards, passports, cash, and a white letter-sized envelope.

He flipped through several ID cards, each with his photo—one with a beard, another clean-shaven, and yet another sported glasses, a goatee, and a mustache.

"Pretty good deep fakes, huh?" Cap said, smiling. "The USB key also has one hundred thousand worth of crypto in ten thousand private-key increments. You'll need it where you're going. Let's sit down and review the game plan. Follow me."

Cap led Paul down a narrow hallway. The room looked like a police interview room with the faint smell of a spent cigar. Four metal chairs and a square table were crowded in the tight space. On the table was a used ashtray—this meant there was decent ventilation, but Paul didn't see the vents. Then he looked more carefully and noticed it was a drop ceiling with dark metal grates. He took note of the metal conduit: meticulously organized, running horizontally. It housed ethernet or fiber cables—a lot of them. That meant serious computing power down there.

How'd he get that kind of bandwidth routed out here?

Cap sat, pulled a cigar from the case in his shirt pocket, and offered one to Paul.

"No thanks."

Paul enjoyed a good cigar, but now wasn't the time.

Cap took several drags, spinning the cigar between his fingers as the match's flame danced up and down until the cigar glowed bright orange. He leaned back in his chair and blew the smoke into the ventilated drop ceiling. The smoke instantly dissipated from the room.

Paul wanted to get on with it. "Who are these guys, and why was I targeted?"

"Here's what we know. Your security monitoring software worked. It worked too well. It identified the IP source and routes of the Thanksgiving Day attacks."

"How can that be? I went over the logs personally a dozen times. There weren't any anomalies. I ran correlations to all cataloged threat vectors. Nothing turned up," Paul said.

"That's the problem. You were looking for anomalies. We analyzed the data and are confident we know where these guys are. But it's a bit more complex than that because they're distributed. Also, we have a working theory about how they bypassed your software's tracking protocols." Cap took another drag from his fat cigar.

"That makes no sense. I would've seen it by now. I've analyzed the packet traces with timeframes before, during, and after each attack. There's nothing there. And why are they after Emma?" Paul said, standing and starting to pace.

"These guys are sophisticated. You didn't spot it because they cloaked their signals and transformed the signaling into NSA, FBI, and TSA protocols. In effect, their communications disguise themselves as 'friendly' messages. They encrypted the payloads and used the Feds' network as authorized communications."

Cap smiled. "You can't ID a bad guy if they look, act, and respond like a good guy."

Encryption was Paul's specialty. He knew precisely how the protocols were established and the egress points that must be breached to do as Cap described.

"The only way that can be true is if they cracked our encryption algorithms, and that's impossible with today's computing power," Paul said, pacing the room, looking at the floor as he processed this information.

"Exactly. So, that leaves only one possible source of the breach..."

"...from the inside," Paul finished for him. "Damn it! Someone within one of the agencies has compromised the network and is working with these guys?"

"Bingo! We have a rat scurrying around inside the agency. But it gets worse," Cap said. "Our running theory is it's not one fuckin' rat. It's a lot of them. The Feds' network has been compromised, but not from an external hacker group; it's internal, and they let the bad guys through the front door to do as they please."

Cap stamped out his cigar in the ashtray. "That means it's beyond our internal agency personnel. We had to vet tens of thousands of people inside the U.S. and other countries, including those with authorized access to the Feds' secure comms network."

"Okay. I get it. But why me?"

"Because you have the monitoring software to unmask their communications, which would lead to the rats in our government and then the bad guys behind this whole thing. They know you're the one person who can expose them. The issue is someone on the inside gave you up and put you on the 'list,'" Cap said.

"A list? Why?"

"Aye, we're confident there's a 'list.' Over the past four months, computer scientists and analysts in the NSA, FBI, and CIA have disappeared. No bodies have been found; they simply disappeared. Whether they went to work, to pick up kids, to the store, you name it, they went somewhere and were never heard from again. We're sure you're on that list. It appears they are systematically eliminating our most brilliant computer engineering minds."

Cap's demeanor changed—tense, serious. He stood and planted both hands on the table, hovering over Paul, who started to sense the magnitude of his situation. "But you were different. They decided to frame you for murder. Think of it as insurance. The bastards knew, based on your military background and the fact that you're a trained marksman, that you wouldn't go without a fight," Cap said. "So, if you didn't go with them, they'd make sure the police picked you up, and you'd be out of the game—threat neutralized."

"But why not just shoot me in the head on my way to the airport?"

"The only thing we can guess is they want you alive. But that's enough for now. You need to get some rest before you take off." Cap said and walked out of the room.

REGROUP

19 FEBRUARY, 1040 HRS
HIRAM, OHIO

Paul lay still in the darkness, the uneven metal coil springs of the thin utilitarian mattress pressing into his lower back, reminiscent of the unforgiving cots from his basic training days at the 320th Squadron Base in San Antonio. He was much younger then and didn't care where he slept. This was different. The recent events had taken a mental toll.

He stared at the green glow emanating from the smoke alarm's indicator light suspended above, its faint illumination casting elongated shadows across the edges of the room. The steady hum of the generator reminded him of his fragile connection to the outside world. A frigid draft flowed over him from an overhead air vent, carrying a dampness that seemed to seep into his bones.

Is this all a dream?

A covert military unit reporting to the President? Terrorists wanted him dead or alive—he wasn't sure which. A high-tech bunker in the middle of farm country, an old soldier pal of his late father, and his father, alive, running the op?

The scotch's effect had worn off, and the damp recycled air made his eyelids heavy. So much had happened. He slowly began to piece it all together. He thought through what Cap had told him. But what was he missing or not being told?

The attacks were a prelude to something bigger. Cap detailed that there was a high probability the enemy was preparing for an even larger strike. In response, the Department of Energy placed all power generation facilities on lockdown. Meanwhile, the governors of twenty-nine states mobilized the

National Guard with orders to safeguard the nation's fifty-nine nuclear power plants and ninety-seven nuclear reactors.

The FBI's Laboratory Division DNA testing could not confirm the identities of the Thanksgiving Day attackers. Despite tattoos consistent with the Western affiliate of the Taliban, potentially ISIS-K, no definitive links could be established. Moreover, an extensive twenty-four-month look-back assessment of the intelligence databases failed to match the assailants with known terrorist groups.

The Feds were chasing ghosts.

Paul's thoughts shifted from Cap's record of events to the bunker's monitoring room. He had to figure out his next move and decide whether to trust him. What about the half-dozen computer screens displaying the live camera feeds of the safe house's property, rooms throughout the house, the perimeter, the barn, and the entry points to the property? Why such sophisticated security way out here? What was Cap protecting?

Paul didn't notice signs of other people in the facility; however, the design of the interrogation room, bunk beds, and computer monitoring facility clearly indicated that the complex was designed to be manned by multiple operators.

Where were the others?

Was this Cap guy legit?

Paul had worked alongside government intelligence agency personnel for years. If a group acted independently of the other agencies, it had to be sophisticated to stay under the radar. And then there was the question of how his father fit into the picture.

It was a lot to process.

Paul needed to get to the bottom of it all—that's what he did. He solved problems. All his life, he'd been the one others counted on to figure things out when no one else could. The complexity was off the charts when he developed the surveillance data algorithm and correlation database. He'd spent years working with senior computer engineers, pushing the hardware that ran the software to the limit.

He had to do the same thing, but rather than working in the virtual world of programming and databases, he had to deal with reality. This time, the problem was right in front of him, in the real world. He had to get to Boston and figure out who was behind it all.

For now, he'd have to trust Cap.

Cap had explained that Paul would depart the facility at one a.m. and drive a pickup truck stored in the barn. The vehicle had been sanitized—the serial number, registration, and plates wouldn't raise suspicions. He would drive straight through to Waltham, Massachusetts, via the northern State Route 20 east, following the Lake Erie shoreline through Erie, Pennsylvania, and across New York State. The route would avoid all major highways, federal turnpikes, and the recently implemented TSA-mandated highway patrol checkpoints.

Once he arrived in Waltham, he was to park the truck at the Waltham subway terminal, about fifteen miles west of Boston. Then, he would take the "T" to Harvard Square. Lia would meet him outside the home of the Harvard Lampoon on Bow Street.

Paul knew the area well. It was about a block from the Square.

Cap had stressed that Paul would be on his own until he reached Harvard Square and that he wasn't to deviate from the designated route.

Until they identified the agency leak, all forms of electronic communication were off-limits. Paul should assume he was being monitored. He must stay off the radar—no access to the internet or contact with anyone, including Emma. No one. Cap had emphasized it repeatedly—NO ONE!

Paul was on his own.

He stared into the darkness. His eyelids became heavy as the emerald glow of the smoke detector's indicator light faded.

What would Sara want him to do?

Find Emma.

DARK KNIGHT

21 FEBRUARY, 0345 HRS
DEARBORN, MICHIGAN

Hassan knocked on the door, prepared to provide Khalid with the glorious news of the momentous power facility breach.

"Come," Khalid said in a solemn tone.

Hassan stepped into Khalid's expansive office, bathed in light from the wall-to-wall OLED screen. Khalid stood with hands clasped behind his back, staring out the one-way glass that ran the length of the room. The mirrored glass enabled Khalid to discreetly observe the sea of workers confined to their cage-like cubicles.

Hassan stood at attention with his shoulders squarely leveled and arms rigid at his sides. He cleared his throat. "Sir, the second phase of the mission is complete. Power is down across the eastern seaboard, as you ordered."

Khalid remained still, seemingly unaware of Hassan's presence. Expecting some form of recognition for successfully bringing down the Americans' power facilities, Hassan instead sensed tension emanating from Khalid, who stared motionless through the one-way glass at the workers as they furiously typed away, oblivious to the soldiers' true purpose and cyber-attack capability hidden away in the GloMink facility.

As if a trance had been broken, Khalid turned and sat behind the oversized glass-topped walnut desk, appearing agitated, uncharacteristic of a man who exuded supreme confidence.

Hassan reiterated the successful status. "Sir, the power station control systems and safety monitor alarms have been disabled. All according to plan."

Khalid turned toward the paper-thin monitor on the far wall, seemingly oblivious to the information Hassan had conveyed or his presence. Al Jazeera's reporting of the U.S. military's nighttime bombing raids scrolled across the screen—"*BREAKING NEWS: U.S. Launches Airstrike on Tehran Government and Power Generation Facilities.*" Bright yellow bursts of Iranian anti-aircraft cannon fire streaked high into the midnight-black sky, searching for enemy targets. On the ground, large fireballs and plumes of thick, gray smoke erupted from the exploding buildings.

Hassan watched and wondered aloud. "Why are they not reporting our drone strikes in Riyadh or the damage we are inflicting on Tel Aviv?"

Khalid turned to look at Hassan, anger radiating from his eyes. He pointed to the monitor, his hand quivering with rage. "Remember those images. What we do to their homeland will send the infidels a message that their bombs and missiles cannot protect them. Our brothers back home are fighting valiantly, and it is up to you now, Hassan, to fulfill your mission."

"Yes, sir," Hassan said, noting the tension on Khalid's face. "Is there information coming from our brothers in the homeland?"

"Our attacks are proceeding as anticipated, and the Americans' bombs are having minimal impact, unable to penetrate the fortified underground command facilities," Khalid said. "As anticipated, they refuse to attack the mosques, schools, and hospitals. As a result of their weakness, our communication systems remain operational. Voice and data communications are transmitting via our low-orbit satellite network into our comms servers within each of our embedded affiliates in Europe, Asia, Australia, and our North American facilities—including this location."

"*Alhumdulillah.* Excellent news, Brother," Hassan said. He sensed that his commander was not being entirely truthful.

"I have new orders for you," Khalid said.

Altering the plan this late into the mission was unusual. It increased the probability of errors and had unknown ramifications.

"The American computer scientist is proving unreliable and unstable. We need a contingency," Khalid said. "If something happens to him, his assistant can provide us access to the network. And if she does not provide it voluntarily, you will persuade her."

Hassan didn't ask clarifying questions. He'd been Dr. Clark's handler for two years and understood the situation's magnitude.

Khalid walked to the office window and stared out into the blackness of the Detroit skyline. "The ransom will fund our global operation for a generation." He pointed out the window. "We have demonstrated our capabilities to the Americans, and darkness has befallen their so-called great country. Our brave soldiers will now begin their attacks, and like a great monsoon, rioting will soon wash through the streets of every American city. They will pay."

Hassan took a position next to Khalid, peering out the darkened floor-to-ceiling window. The power outage had rendered the Detroit-Canada Ambassador Bridge—North America's largest suspension bridge—invisible. The headlights from hundreds of cars and trucks appeared to float in midair above the semi-frozen Detroit River.

"There," Khalid said, motioning with a nod.

Hassan turned his attention northeast toward downtown Detroit. The brightly lit Motor City and MGM Grand casinos were barely visible. Flashes of red, white, blue, and yellow emergency vehicles glimmered in the darkness throughout Detroit's business district and suburbs.

"Cities throughout the East Coast are in chaos," said Hassan, standing straight, prideful of his accomplishment, waiting for Khalid to show some form of gratitude.

Khalid remained stoic, staring out into the night. "It is

now time for the Americans to transfer the ransom payment," he said, returning to his desk. "I have provided the congressman the ransom payment instructions. When the professor establishes the new network connection, the U.S. Treasury secretary will transfer the crypto to our accounts."

"What if they do not pay?" Hassan asked, accidentally verbalizing his thoughts. Questioning his superior—directly or indirectly—was strictly forbidden.

Khalid turned abruptly, walked over, and stood toe-to-toe with Hassan, so close that Hassan could smell his aftershave.

"Do you question my judgment?" Khalid said.

Hassan stared ahead, avoiding direct eye contact, respecting Khalid's aggressive move.

Khalid, satisfied with Hassan's submission, stepped back. "Our man inside the government has guaranteed it with his life. Like all their government officials, he's weak with fetishes and compulsive urges that enabled our agents to turn him easily. He knows the fate that awaits him if he doesn't comply. Do you understand your orders?"

"Yes, sir. I understand. I will see to it personally." Hassan understood the connection. Following the next phase of the operation, the professor would enable the transfer of the U.S. government's crypto to Khalid's overseas accounts.

"I've ordered Faras to accompany you to Boston. He will help persuade the professor and his assistant to comply."

It was unusual for Khalid to send Hassan with an escort. Faras was a thug, good for killing and maiming but not for thinking. Khalid had likely ordered Faras to eliminate any witnesses, including the professor and his female assistant.

Khalid turned his attention to his laptop screen and began typing. "Now leave—and close the door."

SOUTHERN ADVANCE

JUNE 7, 1781
HAVRE DE GRACE, MARYLAND — NORTH OF BALTIMORE

Guided by Jack's firm hold of the reins, Celer fast trotted along the narrow forest path that bordered the western bank of the Chesapeake. Their course carried them northward toward Philadelphia. Jack led the way, constantly looking for the enemy, while Ben and Julius followed, maintaining a close presence.

As the day waned, shadows began to engulf the last rays of sunlight that filtered through the dense tree canopy. The forest's character had transformed into a lush green and brown leaf-filled tapestry dominated by towering white oaks, starkly contrasting the familiar Virginia hickory and loblolly pines. Uncharted territory for Jack, he was in awe of the ancient oaks' massive, moss-draped trunks.

His mind drifted to his days on the docks in Charlestown, where loggers delivered giant stripped oak timbers to the local shipbuilders, who prized the oaks for their strength and stamina.

"These are fine timbers. Wouldn't you say, Ben?" Jack said.

Ben slowed his horse to examine one of the oaks. "Mighty fine. Old man Pritchard would pay a handsome bounty for these. He'd been building that two-hundred-ton packet since last autumn, but that was before the redcoats destroyed the Hobcaw Creek shipyard. Back then, Pritchard contracted my father to outfit the masts and booms for his big ships. Remember the *Heart of Oak*?"

"Yeah, the fine ship with the big dog painted on the mainsail," Jack said.

"That's the one—a greyhound. The fastest dog there is. A greyhound can outrun your boy Celer," Ben said.

"No," Jack argued.

"Yep. Trust me. But the damn British stole that ship, and I heard she was lost off the coast of the West Indies."

"That ain't right," Julius said.

"Nothin' right about them redcoats. That's why we must deliver these documents to General Knox," Jack said. "Stay alert. Those fool loyalists are thick in these parts. Julius, keep a sharp eye out on our rear. We don't need them bastards sneaking up on us."

Despite leaving Cornwallis's men far behind in Virginia, the main road wasn't safe to travel. The British paid loyalists handsome bounties for couriers and spies. But deep down, Jack hoped to run into loyalist traitors in these woods. He'd make them pay dearly for choosing to side with the Crown.

"How much farther?" Julius asked.

Celer's hooves sank into the soft mat of dead forest debris. The footing was damp.

"I reckon the river is near," Jack said, listening carefully for approaching riders. He pulled up on the reins and raised his hand, signaling to Ben and Julius as Celer came to an abrupt halt. Jack listened for movement. He swore he'd heard something, his hunter instincts finely tuned.

He felt eyes upon him. The birds were silent.

He turned his head and looked through the maze of trees as a gentle breeze rustled the leaves. A mixture of shadows and light danced on the trunks of the giant oaks.

At about thirty yards, the dark black eyes of a ten-point mule deer stared right at Jack. The stag's large ears fanned out under his impressive rack. Ever so slowly, he shuffled his hind legs and lowered his antlers slightly into an offensive position but kept his eyes locked on Jack.

Jack would have reached for his rifle if it were any other time, but the gunfire would give them away.

"It's your lucky day, old boy." His voice broke the tense standoff.

The stag's large spoon-shaped ears twitched forward toward Jack's voice, and with a big sweep of its head, it turned and bolted in the opposite direction. The animal's abrupt departure echoed through the forest.

"What a beaut," Julius said. "We mus' be close. He was likely heading to the river's edge."

◆ ◆ ◆

After half an hour of traveling, the woodland gave way to the river's sloping sand and rock shoreline. Jack pulled down the brim of his hat to shield his eyes from the sun's reflection but could barely see across to the opposite bank. The water flowed bold and swift, racing toward the Chesapeake, and the opaque stone-gray color warned of significant depth.

"There'll be no crossing here. This mus' be the Susquehanna River," Julius said while his horse drank from the river's edge. "It's named after the Delaware tribe, which still frequents these parts. But most have moved northwest over the Blue Mountains."

"What does Sus-catch-na mean?" Ben struggled to pronounce the strange word.

"Oyster River," Julius said. "Yeah, filled with oysters."

"How do ya know that?" Ben asked.

"I read 'bout it."

"Stop bragging, Julius. You're too intelligent to spend your days with us common folk." Jack smiled proudly at his young friend. "Let's head downriver to the ferryman, old man Gunn. He operates Harmer's ferry on the banks of the Susquehanna River and will show us safe travel northward to Philadelphia."

◆ ◆ ◆

Julius motioned toward the distant clamor, punctuated by the rhythmic splashing of oars. "What's going on?"

"Let's work our way around the bend to get a better look," Jack said, leading the way.

The ferry dock came into view, bustling with activity. Flatboats loaded with horses, barrels, sacks, wooden boxes, and artillery struggled to remain above the waterline. Hundreds of Continental soldiers, in their traditional blues with red and white piping, were ferrying from the northern shore, unloading supplies as they disembarked.

"They must be Washington's men," Ben said.

"I wonder why they're this far south? Rumor was they were marshaling troops for a campaign on Clinton in New York," Julius said.

"Let's move in closer," Jack said.

The men maintained a steady gallop along the shoreline, with Jack in the lead and Ben and Julius riding on either side, flanking him. Ben's hatchet hung from his belt, and all three men had their Virginia flintlocks slung across their shoulders.

Six soldiers in blue uniforms with white piping rode hard and fast to intercept them. The Continentals' arrival was a welcome sight.

"Halt! Identify yourself," the taller lead soldier said.

"Sir, we're traveling to the Fort at West Point on orders from Governor Jefferson," Jack said.

"Let me see your papers," the soldier said.

"Captain, we don't have papers, but I have this." Jack jumped down from Celer and approached the officer, extending his hand to present the coin entrusted to him by Jefferson.

Years of war and sacrifice were evident in the captain's uniform, its fabric worn down to his undergarments at the elbow and knees.

"Let me see that," the Continental captain said as he removed his riding gloves.

The rider to his left lowered his musket. The meticulously

polished brass on the French-made Charleville gleamed in the morning sun.

"Governor Jefferson said it would provide safe passage," Jack said.

"Don't give me that malarkey. You don't know Jefferson." The officer examined one side and the other. "This is nothing more than a common guinea. Come with me. You men remain here," the soldier said to Ben and Julius. "Private, watch these men while I take the tall one to the general."

Jack handed Celer's reins to Ben. "I'll return shortly. Water the horses, and don't get into mischief while I'm gone."

"Bring me back something to eat," Julius said.

"Get moving," one of the soldiers said, shoving Jack in the back.

Jack turned with fists tight and locked eyes with the soldier.

The captain quickly stepped between the two men. "I'll have none of this!"

Jack relented and continued toward the dock. He passed men unloading the ferry along the river's edge while another group stood guard, muskets ready.

A senior officer, distinguished with flowing white hair and neatly trimmed sideburns extending to his jawline, barked orders to the men unloading barrels and sacks of grain from the ferry. "Onward, lads, move those provisions this way, promptly! Five more crossings await us before dusk settles in."

"Sir." The captain saluted. "We captured three men spying on us upriver."

"What do we have here? A robust, strapping one," the senior officer said, exuding an air of dignified authority befitting his rank of brigadier general. A pink sash draped over his right shoulder, strikingly contrasting the crisp blue Continental uniform. However, Jack was drawn to the gleaming gold lace epaulets, each with a finely embroidered silver star, a sign of esteemed rank and testament to military achievement.

"They had no official papers on them. A satchel with correspondence and this." The captain handed Jack's coin to the general. "He claims Governor Jefferson gave it to him, but it's more likely he's a thief."

Jack quickly turned toward the captain, infuriated by the accusation. Restraining himself and following protocol, he removed his hat and saluted the general. "Captain Jack Jouett, sir. Virginia Amelia County Militia. At your service."

The general looked Jack up and down, appearing to assess his credibility. Jack stood respectfully and at stiff attention.

"Ah, a '73 Guinea," the general said, examining the coin. "How did this fine gold piece come into your possession?"

"Governor Jefferson, sir. We're on a courier mission per his direct orders."

Jack recounted to the general his encounter with Tarleton and the British raiders at the Cuckoo Tavern, detailing his urgent ride to alert Jefferson and the events at the governor's mansion, highlighting the skirmish with the Lobsterbacks, emphasizing that he and his mates had killed them.

"That's a mighty tall tale," the general said, offering Jack an outstretched hand. "General Anthony Wayne, commanding officer of the Pennsylvania Line. My friends call me Mad Anthony." He winked at the officer who escorted Jack. "Isn't that right, Captain?"

The young Continental captain straightened his back and pressed his chest forward. "Yes, General."

Suddenly, a mixture of anger and remorse overcame Jack. The name Anthony Wayne conjured memories of the autumn day four years prior when word came that Jack's oldest brother Arthur had died in a great northern battle—the Battle of Brandywine Creek, where a thousand or more men were wounded, captured or had died. The man himself—the man standing before Jack, the infamous General Wayne—had lost the battle.

Jack remembered the dark day that his father lost the

will to fight and his passion for the cause. Jack watched as his father cursed Wayne and the northern generals for allowing the British to take his oldest son.

Jack stared at the general, yet to decide if he would shake the hand of the man responsible for his brother's death.

The general pulled back his hand, and Jack saluted him rather than complimenting him with a handshake.

"Son, what offends you?"

Jack fought the urge to criticize the general for his failure to protect his brother and the other brave men who perished at Brandywine Creek but recognized harsh consequences awaited any man who dared disrespect a field general in the presence of his men.

Jack steadied his nerves and channeled his hatred in the direction of the true foe—the king and Parliament, who sent soldiers to pacify, kill and mame their own countrymen.

Jack noticed over the general's shoulder dozens of Continental soldiers in their ragged uniforms, holding their rifles high with both hands, struggling to wade across the turbulent river, while others marched south toward Jack's beloved Virginia to join the fight and risk their lives for the cause of freedom and liberty.

He knew it was improper to place the weight of blame on the man standing before him.

"Sir, I am familiar with the Battle of Brandywine, where my brother, Captain Arthur Jouett, lost his life. So please pardon me for my rudeness. My dear brother was a brave soldier and fine man."

Appearing to gather his thoughts, the general took a deep breath, removed his hat, and stared upriver. "Son, your brother's death and the sacrifice of the men under my command weigh heavy on my heart and mind. I lay awake each night and contemplate my decisions and critique my actions. Ultimately, when my final day arrives, I shall stand at the Gates and be judged harshly by our Creator."

Jack heard the pain in the general's words. To be responsible for thousands of men and their families would be a burden like no other.

"However, I take great solace in knowing we will be victorious. The British are superior in every conceivable way—better trained, supplied, and with superior numbers. However, it is not the number of soldiers or the caliber of guns that win battles; it is the passion in men's hearts." The general patted his captain's chest with an open hand. "A man's spirit will win the day."

The general returned his sullen yet powerful gaze to Jack and continued with what appeared to be genuine sincerity. "You and these fine men will bring us victory, and our fallen countrymen—men like your brother Arthur, who we fight to avenge—will be remembered as heroes for generations to come."

Jack wondered at the general's humility and compassion and understood why he deserved to wear the silver star on his uniform.

He reached out his hand, unsure if the general would reciprocate. "Thank you, sir," Jack said.

The general firmly grasped Jack's hand and put his other hand on top, holding it momentarily before releasing. "Son, kindly tell me about Governor Jefferson. I have not met the man."

"What would you like to know, sir? He's a fine Virginia gentleman, for starters."

"What about him impressed you?" the general asked.

"Impressed me? Well, his estate, for one."

"Yes, I've heard he designed the mansion himself, modeling it after the ancient temples of Europe," the general said, focused intently.

"Yes, sir. The estate is unlike anything I have ever seen. Just a short ride from Charlottesville and perched atop a mountain overlooking the sprawling valley below. To the west, the Blue

Ridge stretches as far as the eye can see, and on a fine day, the eastern horizon almost seems to touch the Chesapeake. The grounds have gardens with an astonishing variety of strange vegetables and remarkably beautiful flowers. And there are slaves, sir, dozens of them, who tend to the tobacco and wheat fields, servicing governor's household," Jack described.

"Indeed. The reliance on indentured servants troubles me deeply. I've voiced my concerns loudly, even though those views are met with disdain in the South."

"Truly, sir, to bind men, women and children into servitude goes against the grain of divine intent," Jack said, sensing his anger rising. He highly regarded the servants' ability to work the land with fortitude and vigor, but above all, he admired their commitment to family. He wished to have no part in the slave trade and was resolved to one day advocate for their safe return to their homelands.

The general returned the coin to Jack. "Hold on to this with care, son. It represents the unyielding spirit of liberty that fuels the hearts of men. Upon his return from Ticonderoga, General Knox presented it to General Washington, and now, it's in your hands. Your service has not gone unnoticed; I am truly grateful for that. We are marching south, by order of General Washington, to join forces with General Lafayette," he explained, his gaze shifting from Jack's mud-caked boots to the well-worn deerskin cap atop his head. "I'm in need of a guide well-acquainted with the Virginia territory, one who can spot the southern Loyalists and lead my men through enemy territory. Would you and your companions join us?"

"With all due respect, General, my orders are to deliver this package to General Knox, and I must fulfill my duty to the governor."

"I understand your position, son, yet the circumstances dictate that my command must take precedence. Despite his stature, Jefferson remains a civilian, and my orders override his. We find ourselves in a dire situation, and I require an experienced guide."

"Sir, I must refuse."

"Refuse? You are an obstinate one. No one disobeys my orders." The general raised his voice, and his eyes glared. "I could have you stripped bare, flogged, and dragged by boat downriver. Does that sound appealing, son?"

Jack now understood why the general had the nickname "Mad Anthony."

"Sir, may I offer a compromise?" he said.

"Go on."

"I must deliver the governor's package; however, my good friend Ben knows the southern territory better than I do. Ben will join you while Julius and I continue to Philadelphia."

The general paused and exchanged glances with the captain, who nodded ever so slightly.

"That appears to be acceptable," the general said. "However, beware as you travel north. British scouting parties are roaming the backwoods, rounding up couriers, and hanging spies. Captain, see these men to Gunn's ferry and ensure they are escorted safely and discretely to the northbound trail. There are spies amongst us, and they will be keenly interested in the messages you carry."

"Yes, sir." The captain saluted.

"Thank you kindly, sir," Jack said. "I'll inform Ben of his new orders. He will join you, and we'll be on our way."

Ben would not be pleased but would comply for the good of the cause.

"Godspeed, son."

DISCONNECTED

20 FEBRUARY, 0310 HRS
ERIE, PENNSYLVANIA

Paul glanced at the analog clock above the ashtray at the center of the old pickup truck's console. The red second hand ticked methodically across the black dial as the white hands pointed to ten minutes past three in the early morning. Having driven the back roads for about half an hour, he bounced and swerved, navigating the deep potholes torn up by giant snowplows, wrestling with the late-model F-150's loose suspension and oversteer.

The illuminated yellow divider lines passed by, one by one, blurred by the sheets of blowing snow. It had started to fall more steadily, and the temperature dropped from the low twenties into the teens, making driving conditions terrible.

Residual numbness from the previous day's events gripped his thoughts. Or was it the scotch? He wasn't sure. Probably both. Concentration on the road was secondary because his mind was focused on Emma and getting to Boston.

He approached Erie on the far northwest corner of Pennsylvania, just south of Toronto and Niagara Falls. Winter in that region was famous for lake-effect snow, and it was not uncommon to gain over a foot of accumulation every hour.

Cap's instructions were clear—drive northeast for two hours before stopping to refuel, avoiding the highways, specifically I-90 East, the more direct route to Boston. Instead, Paul was to take rural State Route 20 through the small towns along Ohio's Lake Erie coastline, east into Pennsylvania and the northern end of New York's Finger Lakes.

The windblown snow streaked across the truck's headlights and contrasted sharply with the night's impenetrable blackness. Periodically, the blowing snow and darkness were interrupted by the bright lights of an oncoming snowplow. At that hour, there weren't many vehicles on the remote rural two-lane road in the middle of a snowstorm, which was Cap's plan—stay off the radar.

The wind chill had dropped below zero, rendering the road salt ineffective. The truck's tires lost traction as if on cue, sending the F-150 skidding toward the guardrail. Paul pumped the brake pedal and eased off the gas. Gradually, the truck regained control and straightened out. He slammed the wheel, frustrated with the pace. Patience has never been Paul's forte, a stark contrast with Sara, who had always been the anchor.

The truck was stripped of all modern electronics—no built-in GPS and cell connectivity. Rarely before had Paul been this disconnected. He was cut off from the outside world. At first, it seemed paralyzing, but it was quickly replaced by a sense of peace. There was no digital trail for authorities to follow. The only way to locate him was possibly by satellite, camera surveillance, or, of course, highway checkpoints. While satellite tech had improved, it still had difficulty identifying moving objects in a snowstorm. Neither the FBI nor State Highway Patrol's camera surveillance software could correlate the F-150 and its plates to his identity. Nonetheless, anything was possible. He had to be prepared.

Paul reached under his seat, retrieved his loaded Colt, and set it on the seat beside him.

His thoughts and concern turned to Emma. Would she ever forgive him? Enough was enough—he had to get back online to try to contact her.

He could barely make out a tall, illuminated yellow truck stop sign through the blowing snow.

Perfect.

He needed a cell phone, but Cap had given explicit instructions—no comms. Any deviation would breach the Unit's protocol and risk discovery by the enemy or law enforcement.

Paul didn't care at this point. He knew precisely how to get what he needed while staying off the radar.

The video cameras were the main problem. The truck stop would unlikely have sophisticated monitoring cameras unless DHS had installed their recently developed VR-12 cameras, designed to relay video imaging to DHS's central process center and apply AI-enabled facial recognition and gait analysis correlation to flag persons of interest.

And what about the security guards, cashiers, and police? They could recognize him from the bulletins.

Paul didn't care. He had to contact Emma.

He eased the truck onto the roadside shoulder, and in an instant, snow blanketed the truck, rendering the vehicle invisible. Leaning over, he unzipped his backpack and grabbed the thick-rimmed glasses and baseball cap. Though the disguise wouldn't fool the VR-12's recognition software, it would sufficiently alter his facial profile to dip below its detection threshold.

Pulling his Colt, Paul checked the chamber for a round. He retrieved a double mag pouch from the backpack's rear compartment, chest-holstered the Colt, and clipped the mag pouch to his belt.

As he opened the door, a blast of icy wind hit him flush in the face, slicing through his jacket and hoodie. He zipped his coat to his neck, dropped his head, and began walking toward the truck stop's lot. The crisp smell of the fresh snow brought back memories of his honeymoon with Sara on the snow-draped slopes of New Zealand's South Island. She loved to ski.

Focus!

The blinding snow flurry blurred the truck stop's bright orange and yellow sign. The lamp posts illuminated the parking lot as the light receded into the darkness of the early winter morning. A half-dozen large tractor-trailers were parked in the lot, and three cars were in front of the truck stop's restaurant entrance. A red semi was refueling under the bright lights of the pumping station.

Paul walked toward the entrance and scanned the area for security or cops. Through the windows, the store appeared empty, only the cashier in sight.

Two cameras were mounted on each building corner and one above the entrance. The corner cameras covered the parking lot. The cameras weren't of concern because the heavy snowfall would diminish the image quality and render the facial or gait match ineffective. However, the store entrance camera was a problem.

Next would be the indoor cameras, specifically the one positioned above the cashier, and he couldn't risk a direct, front-facing image capture.

He needed a bit of help.

The hoodie and ball cap shielded Paul's face from the entrance door camera, and with his head down, he exaggerated a fake limp into the restroom and past the row of stalls—five were empty and one occupied. He slipped into the stall at the end of the row and waited.

It didn't take long before the man in the occupied stall flushed the toilet and washed his hands.

Paul came out of the stall and buckled his belt. "How's it go'n?"

The man wore a red Freightliner ball cap, snow boots, a thick beard, and a healthy beer belly.

"Not bad, but this damn snow won't let up. I thought it would've by now," he replied.

"Yeah, tell me about it. I just walked about a mile in it. My pickup hit a patch of ice and went straight into a ditch. I think the axle is bent. So even if I get it out, it isn't going anywhere soon," Paul said. "I'm on my way to my mother's in Buffalo. It's her birthday tomorrow, and I was stupid thinking I could drive through the night to surprise her."

The trucker walked over to the hand dryer.

"You wouldn't happen to be headin' east, would you?" Paul said.

The man didn't turn around. "Sorry, I don't take riders."

"I can pay you," Paul said.

"Sorry. I've got rules, and one of them's no riders unless she's six feet, blonde, and has long legs. And clearly, that ain't you."

"I understand. Rules are rules." Paul walked over to the hand dryer. "Can I ask you for one more favor that hopefully won't break another rule?"

"You can ask anything. But it doesn't guarantee an answer."

"Fair enough. Can you buy me a phone? I've got the cash."

"Why can't you buy it yourself?"

"I'm in...what you'd call a situation," Paul said.

"You're on the lam, are ya?" the trucker said. "I feel ya. I earned a nickel from burglary when I was young and stupid."

Lam? Who says that? He should be hanging out with Cap and his bingo.

"Yeah, it's something like that, but a bit more complicated," Paul said.

The trucker stepped towards Paul and reached out his hand. "I'm Wayne."

"Nice to meet you, Wayne. My name's James. My friends call me Jimmy."

"Okay, Jimmy, give me your cash, and I'll get ya what you need. Meet me out by my truck. It's the red rig," Wayne said.

"I appreciate the assist, Wayne." Paul opened his jacket and pulled out his wallet. He looked up and saw that Wayne was looking at his chest-holstered Colt. He waited for a second to see how Wayne would react.

Calmly, with a flash of excitement in his voice, Wayne asked, "Is that a Colt 1911?"

"You know your pistols," Paul said.

"You better believe it. In this profession, you never know who you're gonna run up against." Wayne smiled and lifted his jacket, proudly unveiling his sidearm. "My Ruger 45. I know it's small, but it does the job. Packs a punch. Best gun I've ever owned."

"Cool. Is that a Randall on your hip?" Paul asked, recognizing the knife's custom brass handle.

"Yep." Wayne unsheathed it and proudly handed the medium-length curved blade to Paul. "Not many people recognize a Randall."

"A Trout and Bird knife," Paul said, admiring the polished smoothness of the deer stag handle. The thick brass hilt fit perfectly under his index finger. "Awesome knife." He flipped it and handed it back to Wayne, grip first.

"Okay, enough show and tell. You got the cash?" Wayne asked.

Paul counted out two hundred. "Keep the difference. I'll meet you at the truck," he said, drew his tight hoodie over his head and exited the restroom with a fake limp, weaving his way through an aisle lined with chips and beef jerky. As he approached, the double glass doors opened, ushering in a blast of wind and snow. To his left, parked at the end of the row, a gray cargo van with tinted windows caught his eye.

With his head down, Paul unzipped his coat, pulled his Colt, slipped it in the front of his pants under his belt, and zipped up his coat. He walked fast through the icy slush to the refueling station where the red tractor-trailer idled. Standing beside the pump, shielding himself from the blowing snow, he kept an eye on the suspicious gray van, his hand resting on his weapon.

"Stop right there. Hands on your head, sir. Do it slowly."

Startled, Paul pivoted toward the voice.

A tall, young man stood in an oversized security uniform that hung loosely on his pencil-thin frame. His hesitant grip on the firearm was an obvious tell. A cap fit snugly on his head, and his shiny boots were barely broken in.

"You need to come back inside with me," the young guard said, his voice striving for an authority that seemed just out of reach.

Soft grip, finger not on the trigger, safety still on. He shouldn't be a problem.

Paul held his gun hand steady by his side, not wanting to provoke him, much less kill him. "What's the problem? Is that necessary?" he said calmly. His training taught him first to diffuse tension when the adversary had a superior offensive position.

"You heard me. Hands on head."

Paul stepped toward the guard to better understand what he was up against.

"Don't come any closer."

A familiar voice broke the tension. "Eddie, put the gun down," Wayne said, walking out of the store with a plastic bag in his right hand.

"Do you know this guy?" the guard asked Wayne.

"Yep, he's cool. I'll vouch for him. I'm giving him a lift to Buffalo," Wayne said.

Eddie relaxed and holstered his gun.

"Okay, if you vouch for him, I'll let him go," Eddie said.

"I'll catch ya on my way back to Detroit in two days."

"Okay, Wayne." Eddie turned and shuffled back to the truck stop's entrance.

Paul took his hand off his gun. "Thanks, man. It would've been a shame to hurt the kid."

"Yeah, Eddie's harmless. I wasn't too concerned about him shooting you. I was more worried he'd miss and shoot my rig or the pump and blow us all to hell."

"Were you serious about giving me a ride?" Paul said.

"Why not? I can sense something's going on with you. I've been there before. I got out of the joint, and no one was there to help me. It's not outta my way." Wayne handed Paul the bag.

Paul looked inside—a phone and a tablet. "Awesome, I appreciate it."

Suddenly, what sounded like gunfire rang out.

Paul ducked, swiveled his head, and dove under the trailer of Wayne's truck. He rolled onto his back, pulled his gun from his belt, and held it in a firing position close to his chest.

Did Eddie shoot? Why would he do that?

Wayne was lying face down on the ground.

"Wayne!" Paul yelled. The blast reminded Paul of Afghanistan when a rifle shot rang out, and the Taliban sniper's bullet tore through his friend Stan's neck.

Wayne didn't move.

Paul looked toward the store entrance and saw Eddie come out with his gun drawn.

Two shots rang out, and the large glass window next to Eddie exploded. Glass rained down on the store's floor.

Eddie fell to his knees, then onto his chest.

The shots had come from the east, the overnight parking lot with about a half-dozen snow-covered rigs, all with their lights off.

The gray van parked near the entrance was gone.

"Eddie, get back in the store," Paul yelled.

Eddie got to his knees, slipped, and fell forward onto his stomach. He got up, crouched low, and scurried back into the store.

Paul scanned the parking lot for a sign of a shooter. Nothing.

"Wayne?" Paul said.

Wayne didn't move.

Paul looked closer. Wayne's lifeless eyes stared back at him. The snow around his head had turned ink-black with the dark, oozing blood.

Paul stayed low, grabbed Wayne by the belt, and tried to pull him closer. He was too heavy. Paul crawled over and felt for a pulse. Nothing. He yanked the keys to his truck from Wayne's coat pocket and slid back under the truck to the other side, putting the truck between him and the origin of the gunfire. He unlocked the cab and climbed in the passenger side, staying low.

He made his way over to the driver's seat and, with a firm grip on the cold metal gearshift, put the truck in drive, the engine growling to life. He located the headlight switch, and with a quick flick, the truck sent bright beams cascading off the pristine layer of snow that blanketed the frozen parking lot.

Against the reflective white backdrop, a striking figure emerged, purposefully walking into the headlights' glow—a tall woman draped in a long, coal-black coat that fluttered in the wind. In her gloved hands, she cradled a bolt-action sniper rifle equipped with a long-range tactical scope. With a slow, deliberate motion, she raised the rifle above her head and smiled.

How'd she find me?

Lia walked over to the passenger side of the truck. "Come with me," she said, looking over her shoulder in anticipation of trouble.

Paul rolled down the window as he raised his right hand, pointing his Colt at her.

"Really?" Lia asked. "After I just saved your life for the second time. That's the thanks I get?"

Paul felt that something again. Maybe it was her smile or her unshakeable confidence.

"Come on, we've gotta go. I'll explain later. He left me no choice, and I don't feel one bit bad about it. He was one of them, one of their agents. Sent to pick you up."

RUSH

**21 FEBRUARY, 0645 HRS
DEARBORN, MICHIGAN**

Mack moved forward with deliberate steps, weapon poised, his grip tightening as he approached the sleek glass entrance doors of the GloMink office complex. A contingent of heavily armed FBI Special Weapons and Tactics agents followed close behind, mirroring his every move. High above beat the powerful rotors of the FBI's Midwest Tactical Aviation unit's support aircraft—a converted Sikorsky UH-60 Black Hawk and an enhanced Bell 429, each relaying live feed video surveillance to ground units.

The automatic doors opened, and with cautious determination, Mack stepped through, his senses heightened, focused on the task at hand—apprehending Hassan Hamadei, the ISIS leader suspected of planning the Thanksgiving Day terrorist attacks. The months of paralyzing pain in his surgically mended hip, a relentless reminder of the attack at O'Hare airport, had vanished, replaced by adrenaline-fueled alertness.

Mack scanned the cavernous lobby, searching for any sign of movement. Large LED fixtures suspended above the cavernous entranceway cast a pure white glow onto the lobby's polished brown-speck granite floor. Light gray walls were adorned with colorful modern art.

He had spent seventy-two hours planning the predawn raid with the FBI special agent in charge of Detroit's Joint Terrorism Task Force. But Mack had been told he couldn't refer to it as a "raid." Revised FBI protocol had recently replaced "raid" with the more politically correct term "Enforcement Action."

Bureaucrats.

The "enforcement action" plan began with disabling the facility's surveillance network, followed minutes later by subduing the front desk security guards. However, the polished marble security desk was abandoned.

The guards were nowhere to be found.

This was going to be tougher than Mack thought. He motioned with two sharp chops of his right arm to direct strike teams Alpha and Bravo toward the stairwells.

The agents fanned out, Alpha team agents to the left and Bravo to the right, moving fast but methodically with guns drawn down the hallways of GloMink's Dearborn five-story office complex.

Two weeks ago, a local Detroit gang informant had tipped off the Feds that Hassan Hamadei, GloMink's head of security, ran an illicit drug and extortion operation from the confines of GloMink's headquarters. The FBI proceeded to build a thorough profile on Hamadei—a Syrian with ties to ISIS and likely part of Iran's external Red Army network. Somehow, he had entered the country and flown under the radar for an undisclosed period. The last known report of his whereabouts was Iraq, ten years ago. There, he had been linked to a series of IED attacks that killed eight U.S. servicemen and wounded dozens of civilians.

What concerned Mack and the bigwigs in the FBI was Hamadei's willingness and, some would argue, eagerness to die for the ISIS cause. Hamadei would resort to extreme measures to avoid capture. Therefore, the best men were selected from the FBI's Detroit field office, augmented by Detroit PD. For that reason, Mack had a Hostage Rescue Team at his disposal, which remained stationed in the main lobby.

Charlie team followed Mack to the upper floor, which housed the executive offices and the operational command center. His confidence was high—the FBI strike teams were the best in the world. But he knew, despite meticulous planning and surveillance, that anything could happen. Army Ranger training taught him an important lesson—no battle plan survives first contact with the enemy.

It had been twenty years since his last battlefield test, not counting O'Hare on Thanksgiving Day, but like riding a bike, he was ready. Another adrenaline rush coursed through his veins like jet fuel, igniting a high-powered fighter engine. Each turn, each door passed, brought him closer to his target. The tension escalated with every step. Mack readied to engage the enemy.

The heads of GloMink employees popped out of their offices while others ran down the stairs toward the exit doors. Mack and the agents ignored them, irrelevant as they were to the mission's objective. The agents and local police stationed outside would round them up.

Flanked by strike team Charlie, Mack climbed the main entranceway staircase, holding his FBI-modified Remington 870 Express Tactical Magpul 12-gauge shotgun. His trigger finger was set firmly, ready for any sign of resistance.

These mutts didn't deserve the luxury of a warning. At O'Hare on Thanksgiving Day, Mack witnessed their disregard for human life firsthand—why not pay back the favor?

He reached the top of the stairs, turned his head left, then right, on the lookout for shooters.

"All clear!" Mack yelled and relaxed his grip.

Back in the field again, he was rejuvenated, even though his body had been through so much. After all, it had been thirty years since his 82nd Airborne days in Fallujah, Operation Vigilant Resolve, and the "lightning raids." Mack's platoon had cleared the bastards out, and thousands of enemy fighters were killed or captured. Street by street, domicile by domicile, the brutal three-week operation cost over one hundred and ninety-five American lives. A time he would never forget.

"Fan out and locate Hamadei and his crew. You men, come with me, and you…" Mack pointed the butt of his shotgun in the direction of the stairway. "...go to the next floor and search the conference rooms. Remember your orders—we're authorized to fire on first contact."

They had entered the dragon's lair.

Mack's mind was sharp, his senses heightened, and he felt a renewed purpose with each step. He knew exactly how it would go down. They'd resist and would die. Of course, they were brainwashed to think that death was an on-ramp to a pleasure party.

Damn fools.

Over his in-ear RF comms, Mack heard the unit commanders directing the raid.

"Sir, we have secured the offices on the second and third floors," an FBI agent said.

"Roger. Continue your sweep and proceed as planned to disable their comms network. Be on the lookout for Ghlam's men. Shoot on sight. We know they're armed."

FBI intelligence had briefed Mack, and he clearly understood they were stepping into the lion's den. GloMink's CEO, Allessio Urbani, was cover for Khalid Ahmed Ghlam, a former ISIS commander who had disappeared from the CIA's radar seven years ago. Ghlam had been captured and held in a U.S. Coalition prison located in the northeastern Syrian city of Al-Hasakah. The prison facility had been run by the Kurdish Syrian Democratic Forces, a CIA-funded Assyrian militia used by the U.S. in the fight against ISIS in North and East Syria. However, Ghlam and other captured ISIS commanders had instigated a prison riot, surprised and overwhelmed the SDF soldiers, and fled the facility. Following U.S.-led aerial drone surveillance of the escapees, most of the ISIS prisoners were either killed or recaptured; however, Ghlam and roughly a dozen others had managed to escape.

Loud pops, the familiar cascading of gunfire, filled Mack's radio earpiece—automatic weapon fire, but not the FBI-issued M4 Carbine.

It was on! His finger dropped to the Remington's trigger, his legs tensed to steady his stance, and he prepared to fire on sight.

Tactical status came in loud and fast over the comms.

"Bravo team is taking heavy fire and requesting immediate backup. Hostiles in storage rooms and offices. Men down! Medical assistance required immediately!" The voice of Lieutenant Armstrong, seasoned and composed, cut through the chaos. With two decades with the Bureau and a senior member of the anti-terrorist task force, Mack knew Armstrong would handle the situation and move his men to defensive positions.

Return fire roared, a blend of M4 bursts and the pulsating staccato of submachine gun fire, possibly from HKs or Uzis. Several shotgun rounds boomed, followed by the twin blast of M84 stun grenades.

Armstrong wasted no time releasing the full force of his unit's firepower on the enemy's position.

"Send in the tactical backup. Enemy engaged," Mack commanded into his RF radio mic. "Bravo team. Confirm status." He paused and focused his combat senses, waiting for an all-too-familiar silence.

In Fallujah, when his strike team breached a door, an unnerving silence immediately followed. Moments following the breach, it was typical that enemy automatic rifle fire would bark into Mack's headset. ComBloc battlefield weaponry the imported Syrian fighters utilized had a distinctive sound, crisper, with lower bass tones than his M16 or the British SA80. The familiar rapid-fire bursts of the AK47 on full auto had been etched into Mack's memory and echoed every night in his dreams.

The AK could lay waste to those on the receiving end at six hundred rounds per minute. Mack and the strike teams were prepared, but he had to act—and quickly.

"Bravo team, Alpha team, fall back to the rendezvous point

and take defensive positions," Mack said, tapping his sidearm for reassurance.

"Command Central, send in the heavy armor—rally point Whiskey."

ON THE ROAD AGAIN

20 FEBRUARY, 0330 HRS
ERIE, PENNSYLVANIA

Paul glanced down at the dashboard and acclimated himself to the big rig's instrument panel. The mosaic of buttons, switches, and gauges seemed to blur together, carrying him back to a vivid memory—seated in the simulated cockpit of a F/A-18 Hornet during pilot training at the Armed Forces Reserve Center at Austin-Bergstrom Airbase. The memory included the controls' tactile sensation, the indicators' flicker, and the Hornet engines' hum and vibration.

As his fingers brushed against the controls of the big rig, Paul crossed the past and present; whether it was the skies or the road, the essence was the same—a purposeful journey. A journey that began two decades ago when the tall, affable Colonel Wilson had approached Paul on MIT's campus that cold, sunny winter day at the beginning of his third year of undergraduate studies.

"Excuse me, young man, may I bother you?" Colonel Wilson had said as he intercepted Paul, waiting for the stoplight to change.

Paul had just finished his daily five-mile run along the Charles, through Harvard's campus, across the Anderson Memorial Bridge into Soldier Stadium, ten rounds of bleacher climbs, and then back to the dorm.

Colonel Wilson wore dark blue running pants, a light, all-weather shell with a turtleneck underneath, and black Gore-Tex trail shoes. A runner—long, lean—and a former baseball player, maybe a pitcher.

"This is forward of me, but I was wondering if you had a

few minutes to talk," Colonel Wilson said.

"Thanks, but I'm not interested," Paul said, turning his attention to the crosswalk light, hoping it would turn. He was eager to get back to his dorm and wasn't buying whatever the guy was selling.

"Paul, I'm not here to waste your time. Just hear me out."

"Do I know you?" Paul studied the man's face. His blue eyes radiated with intensity, and a confident grin exuded sincere authenticity. Paul considered facial memory recall one of his "special" traits. If he'd met this man before, he'd remember.

"Technically, we don't know each other. Dr. Clark speaks highly of you, and that, as you know, is rare. That is, to speak highly of anyone other than maybe himself."

The stranger had Paul's attention. Dr. Clark was the influential chair of MIT's Applied Mathematics program. Paul had worked for Dr. Clark that past semester as an undergrad assistant, and the two had formed a somewhat respectful relationship, which was unheard of for Clark. He had a reputation for being aloof, often condescending to his students, and losing his temper when someone misrepresented essential lesson concepts, which often happened.

MIT's administration tolerated Clark's lack of decorum because of his impressive résumé and ability to attract corporate donors. He held a dozen patents, was an advisory board member for AMD, NVIDIA, and Cisco Systems, a founding member of the International Network Working Group, and had co-designed the first modern internet gateway router. He'd earned a reputation throughout Silicon Valley and the East Coast venture capital circles as the father of modern network design. Clark was a rockstar on MIT's campus—and he knew it.

If it was true and Dr. Clark and this ex-jock were friends, Paul needed to hear what he had to say.

"I read your project paper on linear stability analysis.

Impressive decomposition of the Optimal Velocity Curve—when a particle moves in one dimension, at Mach ten, in dry air, at twenty degrees Celsius, then rotates by more than forty-five degrees, the system undergoes pitchfork bifurcation. Few, if any, have the analytical ability to solve that problem. Dr. Clark was also impressed. However, I'm sure he didn't tell you that."

"Definitely not," Paul said.

The hook was set. Paul listened intently as the retired Air Force colonel explained that he was recruiting the "best and brightest" to build the next-generation cyber defense system.

Colonel Wilson, a natural salesman—persistent with a non-threatening tenacity—relentlessly pitched the elite Air Force cyber program to his eager, ambitious, and impressionable recruits.

Paul had investigated Colonel Wilson's background and searched the internet for anything he could find. But he found nothing. He pressed the colonel, who explained that his role required complete anonymity.

So, to prove he was on the up-and-up, the colonel had invited Paul to Hanscom Air Force Base's Operational Command Center. Hanscom, located in Bedford, Massachusetts, was just a few miles west of Concord. Hanscom, a non-flying technical support base, was one of six bases within the Air Force's Materiel Command Center.

AFMC managed the Air Force's weapons systems, including research, development, evaluation, testing, and logistical systems support. The colonel had explained that the new Cyber Defense Unit would build the software to protect the Air Force's most sophisticated weapons, specifically the strategic fighter flight control systems.

Curiosity had always been part of Paul's DNA, and the sophistication of Hanscom's weapons technology combined with the mission of the cyber defense unit sparked something inside of him. The awesome power of the Air Force's weapons program captured his imagination.

Just one year prior, Paul had witnessed the 9/11 attacks. Thousands were killed, and thousands more were scarred, both physically and mentally, forever. The horrific images replayed in his mind, over and over—the Trade Center buildings collapsing in massive clouds of debris and dust; people jumping to their deaths; first responders heroically climbing the skyscrapers' stairwells; innocent onlookers on the ground, their faces covered with dust from charred bodies, smoke, and debris, suffocating in the clouds of toxic smoke, running for their lives.

Paul then decided to dedicate himself to finding those behind the attacks before they struck again. His friends were enlisting and being sent to the battlefield to hunt bin Laden. The visit to Hanscom Air Force Base had shown him the way, igniting a fire deep inside. The next day, Paul enlisted in the Sixteenth Air Force, Colonel Wilson's newly formed cyber weapons unit.

The pieces started to click together. The training trips, Hanscom, and even his enlistment into the Air Force were elements of an orchestrated plan. Paul realized his life had been meticulously scripted—an elaborate program for membership into his father's clandestine unit.

◆ ◆ ◆

The interior of the big rig glowed red-orange from the illuminated dashboard instrument displays as Paul's eyes adjusted to the bright fluorescent parking lot lights. The lifeless body sprawled face-down next to the gas pump brought the reality of the situation into perspective.

How could I be so stupid?

His father's lessons came flowing back.

Trust your instincts. When a situation becomes unpredictable, your first choice is the right one—instinct guided by experience.

Paul laid his gun on the center console and turned to Lia standing outside the truck. She looked in both directions, then at Paul. Her stare was deliberate, without a hint of sympathy for the dead man lying on the frozen pavement.

His instincts told him trusting her was the right move.

Paul pulled the keys from the ignition, grabbed his Colt and the bag, and jumped out of the truck. A strong gust of wind blew the snow across the parking lot, making it difficult to see. He holstered his gun and looked down at the dead body.

"No one's gonna miss that guy. Trust me. Let's get outta here," Lia said.

She walked over to the body, careful to avoid stepping in the pool of bloodred slush, and pulled the knife and clip off the corpse's hip. She flipped it, holding the blade, and handed it to Paul.

"My father had one—a Randall," Paul said.

Lia smiled. "I know. Randalls are standard issue for the unit. Come on, we gotta go. My van's over there." She pointed to the side lot, and they ran toward the gray cargo van and jumped in. The van's tires spun on the icy pavement and fishtailed. She straightened it out and took the eastbound entrance ramp toward Buffalo.

"Who was he?" Paul asked.

"One of their agents. I had no choice—and I saved your butt again. Ya owe me."

"But how did you know?"

"We've been tracking him for some time. Then we noticed you stopped. Cap sent me to make sure you got to where you needed to go. But you went off the reservation, as you were ordered not to." She stayed focused on the road. "I told you once. This time, you'd better listen. Stopping at that truck stop was stupid. You were ordered to stay on the designated route. And what do ya do? You don't follow orders too good, do ya?"

"Better at giving them. But I hear you."

Still unsure, Paul listened to her every word. She had earned his attention. After all, the woman could handle a rifle and wasn't afraid to use it.

"I disabled the cameras and the network while you were doing whatever you were doing in the bathroom. So, the camera's video feed and alarms won't be a problem. But that security guard and the cashier for sure called 911," Lia said.

Paul pulled out the phone the dead guy had bought him.

"Are you crazy?" she said and grabbed it from him. She rolled down the window and tossed it. "My orders are to get ya to Boston and to locate Emma. You need to get online and ID these guys before they hit their next target. By the way, it's going down in the Middle East," she added.

"I figured the President would use it as an opportunity to pull the trigger on the Iranians. The Thanksgiving Day forensics pointed to Tehran with assistance from the Russians," Paul said.

Lia worked to keep the van in its lane. The road conditions had deteriorated. The plows had difficulty keeping pace, and deep ruts of ice and snow caused the van to slide from side to side.

On the horizon, thick gray bands of winter clouds had become visible as the night's blackness surrendered to dawn.

"Yep. '47 ordered full-on retaliation after the FBI concluded Iran was behind the Thanksgiving Day terrorists," Lia said.

"How did they figure that out?"

"DNA. Bastards were smuggled in through the Southern border. Russia's involved, but we're not sure how. They did find a Russian dead at the scene, dumped near the airport. FBI thinks he could have been the triggerman," Lia said.

"Or a decoy," Paul said. "Iranians backed by the Russians. Seems too obvious. But the decades of sanctions may have forced the Red Guard's hand."

She nodded and pulled off her knit cap, allowing her long

raven-black hair to drape over her shoulders. "Cap sent me a detailed briefing about the offensive—the U.S.S. Virginia launched TLAM-Es from the Arabian, and the newly commissioned B-21 Raiders hit several strategic Iranian sites with JDAMs. But Iran had been fortifying for years and was prepared."

"Yeah, I'm sure those Raiders hit them hard and were out of enemy airspace before the Iranians knew what hit them. Or they launched the long-range standoff missiles from well beyond the reach of the SAMs," Paul said, thinking about the B-21's impressive stealth technology advances compared to the B-2 Spirit predecessor.

"The offensive was effective; however, the Iranians relocated their F-14, HESA, and F1-Mirage fighters from Isfahan, Mehrabad, and Soga airbases. The satellites have located them," Lia explained.

"Let me guess, Russia?"

"Yep, the Russians allowed access to southern airbases in Armenia and Gyumri. And in no uncertain terms, Russia warned NATO they'd shoot down any unauthorized aircraft that entered Russian airspace. So, we can't touch the Iranian planes unless we want Russians involved. Which is more than likely, regardless," she said.

"And there's more," Lia said, turning toward Paul. "Iran countered, launching twenty-three Qiam-2 missiles at our air bases in Iraq and Kuwait, in addition to population centers in Tel Aviv and Riyadh."

"The Qiam-2s are their new mid-range missiles. I knew they were upgrading the Q-1 but didn't know the Q-2 was ready for prime time," Paul said.

"Yep. And like the Q-1, the Q-2 is road-mobile but can also be launched from protected, underground silos. However, the Q-2 has increased payload capacity and has a more accurate navigational targeting system," Lia said.

Paul was impressed. She wasn't only good with a gun and car—smart too.

They passed a semi-tractor, and she looked intently into the rearview mirror.

"Are we being followed?" Paul asked.

"I don't think so."

"How successful were Iran's missiles?"

"Damage assessments haven't come in yet, but Cap's sources indicate they hit Aramco's Ras Tanura and Jazan refineries. If they're disabled, which is likely the case, that's one-third of Saudi's output. And I checked the markets after I read the briefing. Crude has broken three hundred dollars a barrel for the first time, and I expected it to continue to rise based on everything else."

"What else?" Paul said.

"The Israelis didn't hesitate."

"Not surprising. They've been preparing for decades for this day."

"Yeah, the IAF wasted no time and hit Tehran, Shiraz, and Tabriz as soon as they detected the Iranian missile launches," Lia said. "And hit them hard. Israeli F-15 Ra'ams didn't discriminate, hitting military, government, oil processing, and civilian targets. Iran claims to have downed half a dozen Israeli F35-Lightning fighters; however, we know not to trust their propaganda. And at this point, everything in the press is unverified. My sources tell me Iran was ready with their Khordad-15 and Mersad SAMs."

"Despite the Iranian's defensive build-up, the Israelis unleashed holy hell on Tehran."

"Good for them," Paul said, having had the good fortune of training alongside men and women from the IAF. He respected their capabilities and conviction.

"But there's news: Iran launched fleets of long-range Shahed-191 stealth loitering drones from their southern bases and short-range Shahed-136 kamikaze drones from Yemen. They're like swarms of African killer bees attacking Riyad, hitting the crown princess's palace and other densely populated civilian targets. The Saudi's C3I Peace Shield is knocking them down one by one, but there are too damn many."

"So, it's on?" Paul asked, staring at the windshield wipers throwing the blowing snow and ice off the glass. What were his friends and colleagues doing right this minute? Those in the Air Force reserves had been called up right after the Thanksgiving Day bombings and were now likely on forward bases.

Paul realized all too well that the U.S. military was exponentially more powerful than Iran's and prepared for what would transpire. However, that didn't matter; young men, his friends, would die on the frontlines. And it was the unknown unknowns that concerned him. How is Russia, North Korea, or China going to act? Would they be opportunistic? War planning could anticipate the enemy's capabilities and likely targets, but all bets were off when the bullets started to fly.

"Israel is being hit hard on all fronts," Lia said. "A faction of the Egyptian military high command launched SCUD-Bs on Tel Aviv from their Cairo missile base. And from the northern Lebanese border, Hezbollah launched a ground offensive led by Syria's Russian-made T72 tanks and the advanced T-90s. Fortunately, the Israels had evacuated the border villages months before."

Lia glanced again into the rearview mirror and held her stare.

"What is it?" Paul said.

Bright blue lights lit up the side-view mirror. A state trooper's car approached from a distance.

Paul felt his chest warm as his blood pressure rose, and his heartbeat became noticeable. He slid the Colt under his seat.

"We've got a problem," Lia said. She didn't slow down. "Someone pinned that murder on you. Not to mention, there's a dead body a few miles back. That security guard probably called it in." Lia pulled out her phone and hit a preprogrammed number.

"What can I do for you, princess?" a friendly female voice

said over the van's Bluetooth.

"Hi, Crystal. Say hello to Paul. He's been a bad boy. Not following orders."

"Well, you're in good hands. Lia'll take real good care of ya. Enjoy the ride," Crystal said.

"Thanks. I think," Paul said.

"Do ya see that cruiser about a klick behind me?" Lia asked.

"Sure do. Give me one sec."

"That's about how long we've got." Lia watched the cruiser close in on them in the rearview.

"Rerouting now," Crystal said.

"You're the best," Lia said.

"Anything for you, princess."

The call disconnected.

The cruiser's blinding blue lights became larger and brighter in the side mirror. The sirens grew louder.

Lia took her foot off the gas, and the van decelerated.

The police cruiser raced up and trailed a few yards behind.

Paul stared into the side-view mirror. He couldn't be taken in. Why had he trusted her?

"He's being rerouted now by central dispatch. We have hooks into the State Highway Patrol system," Lia said.

The cruiser abruptly changed lanes, accelerated, and roared past, spraying snow and ice on the windshield of Lia's van.

"How'd you do that, Princess?" Paul said with a hint of humor and a smile—the first lighthearted comment he'd made in days.

"My superpower," she said and returned the smile. "Someday, I'll show ya how it's done. Right now, we've gotta get to Boston and find your daughter."

CITADEL

21 FEBRUARY, 0650 HRS
DEARBORN, MICHIGAN

Hassan checked his laptop connection. A red X was displayed on each network link symbol. He quickly launched the command prompt, initiating a ping to a distant host server in an attempt to diagnose the issue.

"*Request Timed Out*" appeared.

In a state of dismay, he stared at the glow of the blinking cursor. The network's failure was inconceivable. He meticulously architected the GloMink building's network infrastructure and power generation systems, ensuring maximum redundancy. He designed the network to maintain uninterrupted connectivity even during prolonged power failures or telecom circuit disruptions. This unexpected breakdown defied his every expectation.

Above his head, the wireless receiver's power indicator light was off. Behind the thick bulletproof glass, the array of flashing green, yellow, and blue computer server lights was absent, dark, and lifeless.

He dropped his head, closed his eyes, and rubbed his wet palms together, taking short, uneven breaths.

What was happening? Fear was a foreign feeling. He had controlled every situation from the time he set foot on American soil, meticulously planning all aspects of the operation and preparing for every contingency.

He took a deep breath and rubbed the scar on his neck. He rubbed it again and again. The touch of the glasslike skin steadied his breathing.

Hassan stared up at the ceiling's fluorescent lighting. How

could the lights be on, but the servers be down? He could hear the steady hum of the diesel generators. Someone had cut the power to the distribution units in the server room, taking the internet circuits and wireless connectivity offline.

There was no way to contact Khalid or his men from inside the computer room.

Hassan jumped as a high-pitched electronic horn screamed, and the blinding white strobe light flashed. His interior guard had triggered the panic alarm.

Hassan pushed open the door leading to the hallway. Automatic weapon fire erupted from the north side of the building. He fell back quickly into the Ops room, pulled his Glock, and prepared himself for the inevitable.

Another set of rapid-fire shots echoed through the door. However, this time, the gunfire had come from the southern corridor. It was not the familiar bark of his men's AKs but American-made automatic weapons. They were under attack.

Hassan set the bolt lock. The door's reinforced steel would afford him the time he needed.

He closed his eyes to gather and prepare himself. The deafening, high-pitched, pulsating siren triggered a vivid memory from the ISIS-Syria war—the war that had molded Hassan into a warrior.

◆ ◆ ◆

The loud, rhythmic moan of the weather-beaten World War II air raid siren warned of incoming Russian attack helicopters. The people of Aleppo scattered and ran for the shelter of the Citadel, which had withstood countless battles for over three millennia and would be a place of refuge that day.

Hassan and his fellow freedom fighters rushed to their defensive positions within the medieval, war-torn fortress. Its massive block walls bore the scars of recent battles against Assad's army—marked by AK-47 rounds and the more extensive damage from RPG detonations.

The deep, reverberating roar of incoming attack aircraft propeller blades signaled they were out of time.

Russian-made Mi-8 helicopters unleashed a barrage of oil barrels rigged with explosives onto places of worship, commuter buses, schools, and a hospital, killing scores of men, women, and children that day.

The Citadel's ancient, crumbling limestone walls afforded Hassan and his men protection from the blasts' fury. Nevertheless, the siege on Aleppo lasted two days, culminating in the death or capture of hundreds from the ISIS Free State ranks.

Hassan and his men used the Citadel's age-old tunnels to escape, carefully avoiding the PMN "Black Widow" land mines they had strategically placed the days prior.

However, Assad's pursuing government troops would not be as fortunate. Hassan found a dark satisfaction inући irony that these Russian-backed fighters would fall victim to the lethal Soviet-era mines.

◆ ◆ ◆

The roar of an explosion triggered Hassan's combat instincts.

He urgently needed situational awareness—details of the activity inside and outside the GloMink facility. Though the parking garage, exits, and entrances were monitored by ultra-high-definition video surveillance, the security monitors near the data center entrance door remained dark.

Hassan pulled up the console and typed commands to check the security system's status. All twenty-four cameras on the monitoring dashboard bore ominous red Xs, indicating they were offline and disconnected from the network. Now rendered blind, he had no way of ascertaining the enemy's positions or transmitting a request for reinforcements to units stationed throughout Detroit.

The floor shook beneath him as a series of intense vibrations reverberated through his body. His men had engaged the enemy with their GP-34 under-barrel mounted grenade launchers, unleashing forty-millimeter fragmentation grenades—a modern version of the weaponry Hassan had wielded in Aleppo to repel Assad's forces.

Hassan ran to the opposite side of the room, flipped his Glock to his right hand, and slammed a red emergency button concealed under his desk. Two large floor tiles opened, revealing the control room's emergency escape ladder, which descended into the facility's lower level. He climbed down and closed the hatch door.

Hassan supervised the construction of the underground escape tunnel, which connected the GloMink headquarters with one of Detroit's many abandoned auto parts warehouses.

If Khalid had escaped, he would be there. However, there would be no escape for Hassan's men. They would fight to the death, avenging their brothers and sisters who had fought and died in Syria and Iraq.

Hassan felt no remorse. The men were expendable and necessary to achieve victory.

Anger filled his heart. The enemy now occupied the very place he had labored all those years to build and protect, and he'd taken every conceivable precaution.

How did they get past his entry guards? How did they breach his network?

No, he could not allow self-doubt to prevail. He must escape and find Khalid.

Hassan moved quickly down the damp, dimly lit connection tunnel, cautiously avoiding the explosive detonators buried in the tightly packed gravel floor. He reached the end and turned to look back; the dark tunnel was deathly still, lying in wait, quietly anticipating the prey about to enter.

Next to the decades-old black steel warehouse entry door, he unlocked an electrical panel and pulled the lever to the "ON" position, arming the tunnel munitions.

He turned, calmly inhaled the tunnel's cool, recirculated

air, and thought back to his escape from the Aleppo Citadel tunnels. That night, the buried IEDs had protected him and his men. They would again this day.

Hassan entered the key code to unlock the steel warehouse entry door. The keypad indicator switched from red to green, and the electronic cylinder mechanism slowly opened the dual deadbolt lock. Hassan pulled, straining to break the stubborn rust clinging to the old door's hinges. With a sharp crack, the rust gave way, revealing a cavernous warehouse where dim gray light filtered through frost-covered windows, casting long shadows over the grimy cement floor.

He quickly walked past a dozen rows of ten-meter-high stacks of old wooden shipping pallets. Behind several empty steel oil drums, his car was covered in a blue plastic tarp. He yanked the tarp away, stepped back, and admired his stunning vehicle—a matte silver Dodge Charger SRT. It symbolized power, speed, and beauty, the one indulgence he had afforded himself in anticipation of this day.

Hassan slid into the Charger's snug, contoured, two-tone graphite leather seat. Appreciating the new leather smell, he slowly pressed the illuminated ignition button. The Hemi 6.2L V-8 roared to life, and the deep bass of the custom MagnaFlow dual exhaust echoed through the warehouse and reverberated into the seats and his back. He had to give the Americans credit—they built fast and beautiful cars.

Hassan pulled his phone from his jacket pocket. No messages. No signal. The cellular network throughout Detroit was down. Detroit was no longer safe. He had no time to waste; the FBI would soon arrive. He stepped out of the car and pulled the garage door's rusted chain, hand over hand. He dropped his head as the frigid wind hit him, blowing snow into the warehouse. He stepped out and looked in both directions down the dark alley.

The streetlights were out. The sound of sirens wailed, warning him the authorities were nearby.

A familiar voice called out over the baritone idle of the Charger's engine. "I did not think you would make it out alive. Your resourcefulness is to be commended," Khalid said.

Relieved, Hassan turned to look around the warehouse. "Where are you, sir? I am pleased you are well."

Khalid emerged from behind a large cement support beam about fifteen meters away. Hassan's sense of relief immediately evaporated and was replaced with dread.

Aiming his Glock squarely at Hassan's chest, Khalid stood relaxed with a half-smile and dressed in his designer jeans, a custom-made white dress shirt, and a black cashmere suit jacket.

Hassan had witnessed Khalid kill men from much farther distances and knew that he could instantly end Hassan's life with a simple pull of the trigger.

"Khalid?" Hassan slowly raised his hands. "Why?"

"Your time has come to join your brothers and reap the rewards I promised you. You've been a brave and obedient soldier," Khalid said, taking a couple of steps closer, his finger clearly on the trigger.

"Why do this? Did the FBI raid of our facility cause you to lose faith in me?"

"Have you learned nothing? I gave the FBI our location," Khalid said.

"I don't understand," Hassan said, thinking through his escape options.

"No, Hassan, you are right; you do not understand. To achieve true greatness, you must be willing to sacrifice what and who you love. I have loved you as my son, but you have served your purpose."

Hassan's dread had slowly transformed into rage. His fists clenched. He felt the blood racing to his forearms, the veins expanding under the pressure.

"Don't be afraid. Death waits for us all."

"No, Khalid, it is you who should be afraid. I live a life

absent of fear, knowing that the greatness of our Creator will protect me," Hassan said.

"You think you know greatness? Greatness is having the power to end a man's life and feel nothing. Greatness is having the wealth that other men can dream only of. Greatness is knowing that men fear you when you enter a room. Greatness is watching men kneel in your presence. That is greatness. I made you the man you are. And now only I have the power to choose whether you live or die," Khalid said.

Hassan now clearly understood. He had known the truth but chose not to believe it.

"Everything we have done is not for the homeland, our families, or fallen brothers. The sacrifice was for your personal gain?" The memory of Yousef's body lying at the bottom of the steps consumed Hassan's thoughts and fueled his rage. He looked above Khalid, then to his right, searching for a way out.

Khalid raised his weapon, pointing it at Hassan's head. "No, you cannot prolong your destiny. No one will save you. Your fate has been decided. Not by Him, but by me."

"No, Khalid, please, you have been like a father to me," Hassan pleaded, stalling for time.

Khalid was not a father figure and cared only about one thing—Khalid. Over the years, while living in America, Khalid had been seduced by the very materialistic and heathen life that Hassan labored to destroy.

"I will explain. I owe you that much, for you will appreciate my genius as you leave this world," Khalid said. He moved his finger off the trigger but kept the gun leveled on Hassan. "While the GloMink operation was exceedingly profitable, it was merely a means to greater personal wealth. I found a partner with compatible ambitions, and in return for my contribution, I will earn an unbelievable sum and a seat at the table. Riches and power that are impossible for you to comprehend."

"Contribution?" Hassan said, not interested in the answer.

But with his options limited, he had to keep Khalid talking.

"You, Hassan, have done everything for your righteous cause: the Thanksgiving Day bombings, the power station cyberattacks, and now the last and final installment of my contribution to wielding control over the internet. I am only hours away from realizing immortal greatness, and unfortunately, you will not be present to witness it."

"Wait. You would have me kill my only brother. For what? Money?"

"Yes. How do they say it in the American movies? Yousef was expendable."

Hassan closed his eyes and was met with the image of Yousef smiling and laughing as the two brothers played football in the street with the other orphaned boys of Damascus. He opened his eyes and stared intensely at Khalid, prepared to draw his weapon.

Khalid moved his finger back onto the trigger. "Can you now appreciate my genius?"

"Did your partner provide the information to access the NSA systems?" Hassan asked, wanting to see if Khalid would reveal his contact.

"Of course, you would like to know, wouldn't you? Considering your life is about to end, I will grant your wish. It will further enlighten you to my greatness. Corrupt politicians. People high in the American government. Entrepreneurs like myself. They have been assisting our cause for years. They brought the idea of the ransom to me. It was divine. Riches beyond our imagination."

Hassan looked out the warehouse windows into the darkness, listening to the man he had once worshipped. He took a deep breath of the cold air to calm his anger.

"Do you now appreciate my brilliance? Your botnets have yielded a stranglehold on the internet. The Americans have no choice but to pay the ransom. Without the internet, their drones, tanks, fighter jets, and ships will be rendered useless.

Their people, obsessed with social media, as opium addicts, are desperate for yet another fix. Banks will collapse, the financial markets will cease to exist, and that is when America's enemies will attack. China and Russia are poised to pounce like hyenas encircling their prey. The Americans are wounded and vulnerable."

For years, Hassan had trusted Khalid, followed his orders, bled and killed for him. For what? Greed. He had fought all his life against the greed of the Western imperialist, and now his commander had betrayed him for that very thing.

"You see, you were a brave warrior and now...expendable."

Hassan heard Khalid talking but was no longer listening.

Suddenly, an explosion erupted from deep inside the tunnel, sending birds scattering, their wings frantically beating, reverberating through the expanse of the old warehouse. A thick wave of dust and debris blasted through the door as Hassan covered his nose and mouth with his coat sleeve moments before the wave consumed him. He could hear Khalid violently coughing. Hassan squinted and wiped his watering eyes with his shirt. Khalid's hunched-over silhouette stumbled back toward the large cement support pillar.

Without hesitating, Hassan moved behind the tower of empty wooden pallets stacked along the exposed brick wall. He could see his Charger about twenty meters away.

Two gunshots rang out, and wood shrapnel from the pallets hit Hassan in the face. He wiped his cheek. Blood was smeared on the back of his hand.

He slid to the other side of the pallet and returned fire. Three powerful .40 caliber bullets leaped from his Glock, exploding into the pillar inches away from Khalid's position, ripping grapefruit-sized craters in the concrete.

Hassan ran to the second stack of pallets and stopped, ready to unload the remaining rounds if Khalid moved out from behind the pillar.

"Hassan, this is strictly business," Khalid yelled.

"No, Khalid, this is personal!" Hassan yelled back. He dove to the ground in a prone position and fired three rounds. Two rounds hit a concrete pillar, and he did not hear the last round hit a target.

He waited. The cavernous warehouse echoed with the low hum of the Charger's engine.

Was Khalid down?

He listened carefully, looked toward the Charger, and readied to run for it.

A booming shotgun blast erupted.

Startled, Hassan's muscles tensed and released in an instant. He looked back at the warehouse's door from behind the stack of pallets.

Out of the swirling gray haze of dust and debris, an imposing figure emerged, wearing black fatigues, goggles, and a military-grade helmet. His movements were measured and cautious, a hunter's poise in every step. With his shotgun steadily aimed, he advanced with caution toward Khalid, who lay motionless, curled up in a fetal position against the blood-stained concrete column.

FIFTY FEET DOWN

21 FEBRUARY, 0715 HRS
DEARBORN, MICHIGAN

Mack's radio headset filled with Lieutenant Armstrong's commanding voice. He marshaled his team with urgency to evacuate the wounded to safety and return to the designated secure zone.

Gripping his Remington tightly, his finger poised on the trigger, Mack led his five-man squad through the dark maze of office corridors toward the far west wing of the GloMink facility.

Suddenly, the sharp, staccato bursts of automatic rifle fire burst into his comms earpiece. Light flashed in the distance. Mack raised a gloved fist without hesitation, signaling his team to halt their advance.

Mack and Armstrong had planned for resistance; however, the enemy fighters were likely tipped off, more heavily armed and tactically effective than anticipated. Mack's battlefield awareness signaled that they were dealing with an unpredictable and irrational enemy and that more of his men would die. He uneasily checked his forward and rear positions, wondering if there was a way out. His confidence wavered, but his experience in Iraq had taught a critical lesson: hesitation in battle is fatal.

He shook his head and tightened his grip on his shotgun.

"Breach!" Mack called out to the agent trailing closely behind with the Stinger door ram.

Mack checked the hinges, door casing, and locking mechanism—a class-two reinforced steel door with a multi-bracketed locking mechanism. Something important was on the other side, and he wondered if the ram would be effective. He couldn't take the risk.

"Wait," Mack said, placing his hand on the ram. "Get up here, Sam! We need to take this door out, fast."

Sam, an FBI breaching expert, immediately moved, pulled the hydrogel adhesive backing from the rubber explosive strip, attached it to the door—running it from the top to the bottom hinge locations—and connected the detonator cord.

"Clear!" Sam shouted and backed away to the side of the doorframe.

Mack and the other men crouched and covered their heads.

A bright yellow flash and low-pitched explosion rang out, followed by the sound of the steel door crashing to the floor. A cloud of dark gray smoke and a burnt tar odor filled the hallway.

Mack, leading with his trigger finger poised, pivoted around the mangled doorframe. Sam and two other agents flanked Mack, their weapons primed to fire on first contact. The remaining two agents guarded the rear.

No one was inside what appeared to be a computer operations room. A half-dozen workstations were all powered on, and banks of computers lined the other side of a wall-to-wall, framed glass window.

"Sir, I found something," said Sam on the far side of the room, pointing his rifle down an open hatch in the raised floor.

"Marcus, Sam. Cover us," Mack said. "Jensen, Hank. Come with me."

"All clear, sir." Sam pointed a flashlight into the opening. "Leads to a tunnel about fifty feet down."

Mack stared down the long shaft that led to a lower level. A metal ladder was attached to the mason block, dimly lit by what looked like three white light bulbs. He could barely make out the floor below.

He hated tunnels and confined spaces. He was too damn big for cramped quarters, his aching hip hurt like hell, and his size-fourteen boots would spell trouble for the narrow rungs of the ladder, yet most concerning was the fact that he was the least coordinated man of the squad. He knew that taking the lead would only slow down the younger, more agile men.

"Let's move. Jensen, you take the lead," Mack said firmly. "Remember, once you're down, shoot first, ask questions later. I'll be right behind you."

"Yes, sir," Jensen said, who was fearless in his compact, stocky frame. Standing five-foot-seven, he possessed cobra-like reflexes, a trait honed from his days as an NCAA championship wrestler at the University of Iowa.

Mack watched as Jensen reacted without hesitation. He moved to the open hatch, threw his rifle over his shoulder, and stepped in. Hand over hand, he lowered himself down the ladder smoothly, as if he'd done it a thousand times.

Mack motioned to the other two men to follow. One by one, they descended into the hole. He took a deep breath and stepped onto the round metal foothold, balancing as he placed his hands on the floor and lowered himself into the hatch.

The debilitating back and hip pain, a remnant of the O'Hare Airport bombing, returned and shot up from his tailbone to his temple. In a futile attempt to ease the pain, he shifted his weight off his right foot, lost his footing, fell backward, and slammed the back of his head on the rear of the hatch door. If it weren't for his Kevlar helmet, it would've been lights out—not to mention a very embarrassing moment.

He gathered his senses, firmed his grip, took another deep breath, and began down the ladder, one careful step after another. After about twenty steps, he paused and looked down between his legs. His men were already on the lower level.

A thunderous blast echoed deep inside the tunnel, and damp, cold air rushed into Mack's face, bringing the pungent smell of oil-laden fumes. He coughed as the dust and smoke enveloped the stairwell. He lifted his feet off the ladder's steps and let gravity do the rest. Like a falling brick, his body slammed into the hard gravel floor of the tunnel. A lightning bolt of pain shot from his hip and continued for what felt like minutes. Dirt rained down on his helmet as he slowly picked himself up, fighting through the agonizing pain.

A row of candescent bulbs lined the plywood ceiling, casting a dim yellowish hue against the cement block walls. Jensen's agonized moans called out from deep inside the tunnel. As Mack ran, the stench of smoldering debris grew stronger, and the moans intensified.

Mack came to a sudden breathless halt, his mind paralyzed by what lay before his disbelieving eyes. Jensen sat propped against the wall, his face unrecognizable, littered with bone-deep cuts, flesh from his jaw dangling and dripping blood. The explosion had severed his leg from the kneecap down. Dark blood pooled on the dirt floor.

A three-square-foot crater was carved out in the center of the tunnel floor.

IEDs!

"Stop! Do not move!" Mack yelled to the trailing agents.

He scanned the area, noticing the floor had transitioned from dirt to cement about twenty feet farther into the tunnel. He yelled into his comms, "Get medics down here! Now! Send in the bomb squad and the dogs."

"Jensen, help's on the way," Mack said, putting his hand on Jensen's shoulder as another agent applied a tourniquet to his femur. "Hang in there. We got you."

He felt responsible and angry at himself for not leading the way. He should have been the one lying there, not Jensen.

He felt a rush of fresh air from the far end of the tunnel. A light glowed brightly, illuminating the cloud of smoke and debris.

Those animals were close, within reach—the men behind the attacks that had killed and maimed so many. But it may as well have been miles away. Who knew how many IEDs lined the path?

Who am I kidding?

In the winter of his life—his wife had passed two years ago; his kids were grown and busy with their own lives—Mack was alone. The decision was a simple one.

The monsters at the other end of the tunnel had killed hundreds and would kill more if Mack didn't stop them.

"Men, take care of Jensen and wait here until medics arrive. That's an order."

He took a deep breath and began walking slowly, searching for signs of disturbance on the dirt floor.

"Sir, stop! Don't move," an agent yelled. Mack froze. "See the red beams, sir? Your left foot is six inches from one, and there are more. If you break a beam, you're done, sir."

The dust and smoke particles illuminated the previously invisible infrared beams that crisscrossed the cement path. They were spaced two feet apart and elevated twelve inches off the ground.

"I see them," Mack said, not moving a muscle, willing himself to hold his balance. "Thank you, son. I owe you. Beers are on me when I get back."

Mack slowly stepped over the first beam, then the next, straining to shift his weight from one leg to another without dropping any part of this leg into the beam's path.

Three more steps.

Two rapid-fire gunshots echoed from deep down in the tunnel.

Mack realized he was out of time.

"Screw it!" he said and lifted his right foot, hopped over the beam, then the next, and threw himself over the last, landing hard on the cement floor.

"Way to go, Sarge!" one agent yelled, and another clapped.

Mack picked himself off the ground and rushed toward an open door.

Shots rang out, louder this time. Closer, just off his right flank, from inside what appeared to be an empty, abandoned warehouse.

He stepped away from the wall and, with a swift twist of his shoulders, flung the shotgun around from his back. The rifle's barrel landed perfectly in his left hand and felt like an extension of his body as he flicked the safety release. He slid his index finger down the glossy black trigger guard, landing it firmly on the gold-plated trigger.

Charging through the open door, he pivoted to his right and aimed at the dark silhouette standing upright next to a support beam.

As he'd done countless times during mock assault training drills, he mounted the weapon and sighted the target with his dominant eye. He paused, holding his fire to confirm the threat.

However, the target decided its fate by pointing a weapon at Mack.

Mack's trigger finger responded instantly, releasing the full power of the Remington. The shotgun's projectiles hit the man in the chest, throwing him violently against the cement beam. The body slid down, resting in a heap at its base. A thick, dark trail of blood coated the beam above the crumpled body. Mack kicked the gun away from the dead man's hand.

Mack had faced the harsh realities of combat before, killing men without a flicker of remorse or empathy. It was the nature of war, and he was a Marine; it was what he was trained to do. And he did it well. However, this was different. He was no longer in the dusty streets of Fallujah, dressed in his battle fatigues, gripping an M-15. This was Detroit, in the heart of the USA, and these bastards had brought war to his doorstep. He stared at the lifeless face, the man's eyes frozen open in a final, astonished stare, his clothes soaked in blood.

Mack's thoughts went to Jensen, lying in agony back in the tunnel, and then to the haunting Thanksgiving Day carnage at Chicago O'Hare, where men, women, and children lay strewn across the blood-smeared tiles. It was clear now—the emotion coursing through him was a deep-seated anger.

Suddenly, he felt reinvigorated, twenty years younger. The persistent pain in his back and hip had vanished. His job was not done. There were more of them out there.

Crouching low, he racked the shotgun, chambering another round, his eyes sweeping the area. The low hum of an idling car nearby caught his attention.

A car door slammed, followed by the growl of a powerful engine roaring to life. Tires screeched against the warehouse's concrete floor, echoing in the empty space.

Mack looked cautiously from behind the large cement support beam. A vehicle burst out of the open garage door, too fast in the darkness to distinguish make or model—perhaps white, yellow, or gray. No plate.

He charged toward the sound and the open garage door. The bitter February wind hit him flush in the face. Holding the Remington tightly in both hands, finger tense on the trigger, he stepped out into the dark alleyway.

Yet, he didn't bother to raise his gun. Deep down, he knew what he'd find.

The streetlights and buildings around were dark, the only movement being the dead leaves and trash whipping across the frozen pavement.

The alley was empty.

BROTHERLY LOVE

JUNE 10, 1781
PHILADELPHIA, PENNSYLVANIA COLONY

Jack recalled Governor Jefferson's cautionary words as Philadelphia came into view: a city teeming with spies, Tories, and thieves. Down the main street, as far as the eye could see, were brick and wooden buildings, taverns, and stables. Excitement and anticipation welled within him as he approached the heart of the city.

"Never seen anything like it," Jack said.

"I reckon there're more people in this city than all of Virginia," Julius said.

On horseback, the townsfolk were busy going here and there, others riding splendid carriages with velvet piping and large gold and black wheel spokes. Men walked briskly, dressed in formal black suits with knee-high white stockings and adorned with tall, short-brimmed hats. The ladies were dressed elegantly in their delicate silk and cotton dresses, shading themselves from the summer sun with fancy embroidered white parasols.

Celer's hooves clipped and clacked down the newly laid brick road. Jack gazed at the brilliant white spire and bell tower as he passed a grand, red-brick structure. It could only be the Pennsylvania State House, the meeting place of the Continental Congress.

"That's the place," Julius said, pointing to the State House. "The home to the Continental Congress and the birthplace of Governor Jefferson's Declaration of Independence."

Jack recalled that momentous day five years ago when Julius barged into the stable waving the *Virginia Gazette* containing a broadside of the Declaration sent to King George III declaring "all men are created equal, that they are endowed by their Creator with certain unalienable Rights, that among these are Life, Liberty and the pursuit of Happiness." Those words, penned by Virginia's own Thomas Jefferson, had inspired Jack and the boys to join the Richmond militia that day to fight against tyranny.

Jack turned, startled by the door slamming shut. A bare-chested, olive-skinned native stormed down the front steps of the City Tavern wearing a red-dyed buckskin cap decorated with white feathers and red and blue beadwork. Trailing a step or two behind were two taller and younger natives, their faces filled with fury, wearing deerskin pants, their naked chests adorned with black and white strands of beads that matched the paint encircling their eyes. Their heads were cleanly shaven except for a round tuft of hair tied with two or three white and black feathers.

Jack met the old warrior's glance and sensed willful pride cloaked in intense anger.

Julius and Jack stepped aside, allowing the natives to pass.

One of the younger braves took a step toward Julius, shook his head violently, and screamed. Julius held his ground.

Jack stepped in and shoved the young brave with two hands to the chest, sending him hard to the ground. The Indian sprang to his feet like a cat, pulled his tomahawk, and spun to flank Jack.

Jack drew his knife, pointing the tip of the blade at the throat of the savage.

The older Indian stepped in front of Jack's blade, raised his hand, and, in his native tongue, uttered a stern command to the others, who yielded and obediently lowered their weapons. The old Indian moved closer. Jack took a breath, noticing the strong scent of tobacco and sweat. Two long, thick scars crisscrossed the old man's chest. The whites of his eyes gleamed against bronzed, sun-aged skin and gunpowder-smeared cheeks.

"Forgive them, for they know not the white man's ways."

The old man's words reminded Jack of his father's forceful and wise tone, which commanded respect. Jack nodded and slid his knife into its sheath.

The warrior turned, and the three natives walked away, rounding the street corner.

Julius removed his hat and wiped his forehead. "Them some wild injuns. Did ya notice the silver rings in their noses and ears? Mus' be Shawnee."

"Those were warriors. That's for sure. Luckily, the older one was there to calm the others down," Jack said.

"Let's go. I'd like an ale—my stomach's achin'. I can't look at dried venison and beans ever again," Julius said.

"The tavern should have beef and potatoes. But stay alert and don't speak with anyone. Tory spies will be as thick as bees on molasses," Jack said.

"You bet." Julius nodded and patted the long rifle cradled in his arms.

Jack smiled. "Keep that close."

The men bounded up the short pyramid of brick steps and through the large white oak door of the grand three-story structure. The beautiful smell of freshly baked bread mixed with the aroma of smoked meats made Jack's mouth water as his eyes adjusted to the dim candlelight provided by a half-dozen tin wall lamps hanging throughout the spacious dining room.

"Hey, what's this?" Julius ran his hand over the colorful wall. "The walls are made of fancy cloth. Ah, so smooth. Nothin' like the old Cuckoo's shabby timber and stone walls. Wait 'til I tell Ben about this place. He's likely up to his knees in mud or sitting on a wet log with that angry General Wayne barking at him."

"Keep your eyes sharp, Julius. We need to find the Frenchman," Jack said, surveying the unfamiliar faces that crowded around the large round tables.

Men gathered near the unlit fireplace, smoking pipes, resting their pewter pints on the gray wood-plank mantel. Nearing twilight, travelers from all parts had come to the tavern for an early evening meal and ale: boisterous laughing, the occasional yell, and spirited debate echoed through the dining room.

The tavernkeeper greeted them, wearing a crimson vest and a bright white shirt with sleeves rolled up to his elbows. "Pardon me. The City Tavern's a gentleman's establishment. Weapons are not permitted. May I hold them for you?"

Jack unfastened his soft-leathered long blade sheath, kneeled, pulled his buck knife from his boot, handed it to the tavernkeeper, then removed his powder sack and hung it on the tavernkeeper's shoulder.

Julius hesitated. Jack gave him a confident nod, and Julius reluctantly handed over his long rifle and trusted friend. The tavernkeeper grasped the barrel, but Julius wouldn't let go. The tavernkeeper pulled to no avail.

"Let go, Julius," Jack said, and Julius relented.

The tavernkeeper clumsily walked to the coat closet, dropped Jack's buck knife, and picked it up.

Jack and Julius followed the tavernkeeper through the main room into a smaller room with three empty, stained walnut oval dining tables. The pungent smell of burnt whale oil overwhelmed the remnants of sweet tobacco as they passed a tin lamp hanging on the paper wall above one of the tables.

"Will this do?"

"Outstanding," Julius said. "Could you be so kind as to bring us a pint of ale and your standard evening fare? I assume you have beef on the menu?"

"Unfortunately, sir, we haven't had beef in months. The damn redcoats have raided the countryside of cattle and other fine livestock."

Julius's shoulders dropped, and he sighed. "Venison, I presume?"

"Yes, we have a lovely roasted venison garnished with kidney beans and turnips."

Julius looked at Jack and rolled his eyes.

"Something wrong?" the tavernkeeper asked.

"No, that'll be fine. Two pints as well," Jack said. "One last request, sir. Do you know where I could locate a Frenchman named Lublue?"

"A Frenchman?" Jack's question elicited a puzzled look. "No, I don't know a Frenchman of that name," he said, his tone tinged with suspicion. Without waiting for a response, the man swiftly turned toward the kitchen doorway. He leaned in close and whispered into the ear of an old, heavyset woman, her wrinkled face etched with years of drudgery.

She shot Jack a sharp, stern glare, wiped her hands on her stained apron, and retreated into the kitchen, closing the door behind her.

CAMBRIDGE

22 FEBRUARY, 0700 HRS
CONCORD, MASSACHUSETTS

Startled, Paul shook his head and sat up as a Concord Township fire truck roared past, its red and white lights flashing and sirens blazing.

"What's happening?" Paul said, turning his head slowly, trying to orient himself to his surroundings. He felt a stiffness in his neck, a reminder of sleeping in an awkward position against the van's door.

"Good morning. You were out cold," Lia said softly.

Ahead, sunlight broke through the gray cloud cover. The snow had stopped falling, and the snowplows had cleared the accumulated snow and ice ruts, making driving conditions much better. Paul watched as the emergency vehicles turned off and headed south. He didn't see any signs of smoke.

"How long have I been out?" Paul asked, turning his head to look in the back of the van, where wool blankets, red plastic fuel containers, and an olive-green rifle hard case were piled on the seat.

"We've been driving for about three hours. You dozed off right after that state trooper went on his merry way."

They passed the entrance sign for Minute Man National Park. Paul knew the area well. "We're about a mile from Hanscom Air Force Base, where I was stationed after undergrad, twenty years ago before I deployed," he said. It seemed like a lifetime ago—the year he'd proposed to Sara.

"We're just outside Boston, about thirty minutes from Cambridge and Emma's apartment," Lia said.

"What's the latest?" Paul asked, wondering if there had

been another attack.

"Cap sent me an update before the cellular service went out."

"Why's the cell network down? Forget to pay your bill?" He realized it was the most lighthearted comment he'd made in days.

"Ya' do have a sense of humor. I knew it. You've been so darn serious since we met. But I get it. A lots been thrown at you," Lia said, smiling. Her dark brown eyes, focused on the road, flickered repeatedly to the rearview mirror. "The power's out along the entire East Coast. Cell phones won't connect. Everything is down. It's a mess. Oh, and it gets better. The governor has deployed the National Guard and closed the interstate to allow the transport of military vehicles. Since the power is out for millions throughout the East Coast, they're preparing for riots and looting. The country is going into lockdown."

Paul turned on the radio and scanned the stations—the hiss of static reverberated through the van.

"I tried that. Before everything went down, I received an update. There's no restore ETA. The Feds are involved, working with the power companies. But I'm not sure they will help or hurt the situation," Lia said.

"They'll just get in the way. A hack, or was it an attack?" Paul said.

"Still assessing the details. Likely a combination of both. The utility companies are scrambling to triage and restore, but based on what Cap briefed, transformer stations throughout the network overloaded before manual braking systems kicked in."

"Not surprised. Infrastructure has been a prime target for decades. The last administration convened a task force after the Russian hackers crippled the natural gas pipeline. Yet nothing was done. The task force was merely a political response, not a practical one," Paul said.

"Yep. And it could be weeks before the power's restored."

Paul looked out the window. It was still early. Dark. There weren't many cars on the road.

"Without power, that means a lot of people and facilities are vulnerable," he said.

"Yep. I'd expect looting and potentially more attacks," Lia said.

Paul's immediate concern turned to Emma. Where was she, and was she okay?

"Have you heard anything from Emma?"

"Nothing yet."

Paul could hear the trepidation in her voice. The dull pain in the back of his head returned.

"We'll be at her apartment soon. I'm sure she's fine," Lia said and put her hand on his knee for a brief moment.

Paul looked at her. Her tough veneer had been replaced by warmth and kindness—something he welcomed.

"Let's go find her," Paul said with a less-than-authentic smile and a weak attempt to disguise his concern.

Lia took the off-ramp and pulled over. She turned to him, her eyes locked on his. "Paul, I've got your back. And Emma's, too. I'm here to make sure nothing happens to you guys. Your father has big plans for you, and our enemies will not let up. Our job is to protect and serve. And based on what I know about you, the kind of person you are, and now that I know you much better, you will be a great unit leader."

Her eyes radiated with compassion, and Paul could feel the sincerity in her tone. He had so many questions, but they would have to wait.

"You'll need this where we're going." Holding the barrel, Lia handed Paul his Colt 1911.

The well-worn, custom-contoured grip slipped perfectly into the curve of his palm. With meticulous precision, he drew back the slide. The barrel, milled smooth to perfection, sent a spark of vitality up his arm as the cold steel met his skin. The metallic click broke the silence as he checked the chambered round.

"Let's go find Emma," Paul said.

◆ ◆ ◆

At seven a.m., the quaint East Cambridge neighborhood was dark and quiet. But that morning, it was exceptionally dark. The streetlights were out, as were the lights in the surrounding homes and apartment buildings. Candles and other random light sources were visible in a handful of windows.

Paul led the way toward the entrance, his Colt held at his side, safety off, index finger above the trigger guard.

The apartment complex's side door was ajar, and the electronic locking mechanism was open. In the shadows cast by the emergency lights, dark red stains, which looked ominously like blood, marred the yellow stucco wall of the apartment building and spilled onto the walkway. A surge of fear as powerful as a locomotive barreling down the track shot through Paul's nervous system.

Compelled, he traced the grim trail of blood toward a row of bushes.

"I can't," he said to himself. The very thought of finding Emma lying there sent a wave of nausea through him.

Lia put her hand on his shoulder and cautiously walked past him into the tall row of shrubs. "It's not her."

Paul inhaled deeply and exhaled.

A young man, twenty-something, laid face up, eyes wide open, with a bullet entry wound in his chest. Blood stained his yellow ski coat.

"Let's go—nothing we can do for him now," Paul said.

They quickly made their way up the unlit stairwell to the third floor. At the door, Paul listened for sounds within the apartment—footsteps, music, anything to signal she was okay.

Silence.

Lia stood at the side of the door, her weapon drawn close to her chest, and looked in both directions down the hallway.

Paul closed his eyes momentarily and prayed Emma was out on her morning run. Like her father, she was an early riser, running the Charles trail virtually every day.

He turned the knob, expecting it to be locked. It wasn't. He pushed it open, not realizing the force he'd used on the door. It swung open and slammed against the doorstop. Paul raised his Colt, holding it with a steady two-hand grip, and aimed down the apartment's short hallway that led to the living room. The room's floor-to-ceiling windows overlooked the park, letting in the early morning light and revealing Paul's worst fear: the place was completely trashed.

"Damn it!" Paul said. The pain immediately returned to the base of his skull. He winced, closed his eyes, and turned his head, hoping to loosen it up.

The couch and chair cushions were knifed open. Emma's books had been thrown off the desk and bookshelf and scattered on the floor. The kitchen cabinet doors were thrown open, their contents strewn across the floor.

Lia put her index finger to her lips.

Paul sighted his weapon down the hallway and walked toward Emma's bedroom. The anxiety of finding her dead was overwhelming.

Her roommate's bathroom and bedroom had been turned upside down, and cosmetics, jewelry, and broken mirror glass littered the floor. The mattress had been knifed, and the dresser and side table drawers were pulled out, with clothes, books, and towels scattered throughout the room.

He listened carefully for any movement. All was quiet.

He paused before checking Emma's bedroom, terrified about what he might find.

The room was a disaster, searched like the others—no sign of Emma and no blood on the bed and carpet. He took a deep breath, relaxing. The tension in his shoulders and arms dissipated.

Paul picked up a broken picture frame on the floor next to the couch. Sara had given it to Emma as a high school graduation present. As if it was yesterday, he remembered the turquoise-blue sky on that beautiful June day. The towering oak trees shaded the yard with the fresh bloom of spring foliage. Yellow and red tulips lined the backyard flower beds. Dozens of friends and family mingled as they celebrated Emma's high school graduation. They'd come to wish her well as she was about to spread her wings and venture off to begin her undergraduate studies at MIT in Cambridge.

Emma radiated enthusiasm, ready to conquer the world. Both Paul and Sara were so proud of her. Sara had told Emma that, though she was heading to college, the photograph would remind Emma of their love for her. Whenever she felt sad, lonely, or homesick, it would reassure her that she always had a place in their hearts.

Turning the broken frame over, Paul noticed the photo was missing.

"What is it?" Lia asked.

He showed her the empty frame and tossed it onto the couch.

"They're searching for her," Paul said, walking toward the door. "I need to get to her lab."

"Here," Lia said, tossing him the keys to the van. "I've got someone I need to contact. You go and make sure she's safe. Remember, stay away from cameras and no cell phones. They'll be monitoring public traffic. And be careful."

The usual confidence in Lia's voice gave way to a hint of apprehension as though she knew something Paul didn't.

SEARCHING

21 FEBRUARY, 0600 HRS – ONE HOUR EARLIER
CAMBRIDGE, MASSACHUSETTS

Hassan had spent twelve grueling hours behind the wheel of his Dodge Charger, skillfully navigating the lesser-known back roads, carefully evading highway patrol checkpoints and speed traps. His route took him south from Detroit to Toledo, then east along Old Route 2, tracing the frozen shores of Lake Erie.

In Pittsburgh, a covert stop at a nondescript Circle K allowed for a calculated change of identity. An operator there swapped his plates and handed Hassan a fresh set of counterfeit documents, including a driver's license and registration, designating the alias Michael Stephanopoulos, a second-generation Greek American and a concrete mason from Waltham, Massachusetts. In-country agent protocol mandated the I.D. changeover when crossing state lines.

As the Dodge turned onto John F. Kennedy Street in Cambridge, Hassan scanned the century-old colonial brick buildings lining the Charles River. The windows were dark, a result of the power outage crippling the eastern seaboard—a situation that would last for weeks, if not months.

He glanced in the rearview mirror and ahead at the upcoming cross street, on the lookout for police or unmarked government vehicles.

Across the river, the DoubleTree hotel's entrance and windows stood out, glowing defiantly against the darkness, with its powerful diesel generators providing power to the building.

Suddenly, a car shot into Hassan's peripheral view. Reacting instantly, he wrenched the wheel and slammed the brakes, narrowly missing the red Honda Civic, which sped off through the intersection and disappeared. The Dodge skidded, its momentum sending it careening into the curb. Furious, Hassan cursed loudly and punched the steering wheel with his fist. In his line of work, even a momentary lapse of focus could prove fatal.

Taking a moment to calm his mind, he watched the wind whip across the river, the waves frothing wildly. Gulls floated back and forth in their endless search for a meal. The presence of water brought him a sense of peace, a gift He provided to His flock. He who'd created life on the basis of water that gave life rebirth. Hassan's dream for his homeland and a return to greatness.

Jolted back to reality by a car horn, he backed into the intersection and turned onto John F. Kennedy. He pulled into the Charles Hotel's parking garage and descended two levels to the dimly lit underground. The emergency lights cast a circular white light on the floor near the entrance.

Finding a secluded spot, Hassan backed the Dodge into the shadows. With his vehicle concealed, he pulled out his Ruger, resting it on his leg as he waited. In close quarters, he preferred his compact Ruger over the Glock. The thought of killing Faras was appealing, but he reminded himself that Faras's unique skills would prove useful when it came time to deal with the young woman.

News of Khalid's death would inevitably reach the leader of the Islamic State, setting into motion a chain of events. In the interim, Hassan assumed command over all North American in-country agents. Time was not a luxury he could afford; his destiny and mission hung in the balance.

He must locate the female researcher, the key to accessing the network required to facilitate the transfer of the U.S. government's ransom payment. She was the crucial link in the plan, yet to Hassan, she was expendable. Once her purpose was served, he intended to let Faras do as he wished with her.

"Finally," Hassan whispered as the tall, muscle-bound man approached the vehicle.

Dressed in a tight-fitting light gray leather jacket, black jeans and high-ankle gloss-black tactical boots, Faras opened the passenger door and climbed in.

In an overt display of dominance, Hassan slid his Ruger into the open, ensuring Faras was acutely aware of the peril involved with any attempt at betrayal.

Without uttering a word, Faras drew his Glock from the chest holster beneath his coat and placed the gun on his thigh, his finger poised on the trigger.

Hassan, sensing the testosterone-fueled tension, readied himself for a close-quarters gunfight. However, Faras gradually lifted his finger off the trigger and gave Hassan a sharp nod, wisely avoiding what would have been a certain death.

Hassan pulled slowly out of the garage without saying a word or acknowledging Faras's presence. In this line of work, words were unnecessary—Faras was neither a friend nor a confidant, merely a tool to be used and discarded when no longer useful.

Outside, the city was plunged into darkness, and chaos had spilled into the streets. Gangs and vandals had taken over, wreaking havoc, hurling rocks at storefronts, igniting fires in dumpsters, and smashing car windows.

Hassan eased off the accelerator, slowing the Dodge to avoid a swelling crowd of masked rioters engaged in a tense standoff with a line of police officers, all clad in heavy riot gear.

He was satisfied to see the years of sacrifice and labor yielding results. America, once a symbol of democratic ideals, had regressed into a militarized state at war with itself. Its precious principles of democracy had evaporated, much like raindrops disappearing under the heat of the desert sun.

Hassan parked in clear view of the apartment complex, reconfirming the address on his phone. He subtly glanced over to Faras, who was prepared to use extreme measures to convince the young woman to comply.

With tactical precision, both men slipped on leather gloves, unscrewed their weapons' thread protectors, and attached titanium can suppressors to their modified Glocks. They continually scanned the area as they made their way to the rear entrance of the apartment complex. The building was dark, with no sign of power, and the surveillance cameras, one above the door and another overlooking the parking lot, were inoperable.

A car door closed, instantly drawing Hassan's attention. A young man with a backpack headed toward the door. Hassan turned, concealing his weapon behind his back and signaled to Faras with a subtle nod.

"Hey guys," the young man said, oblivious to the impending danger.

"Mornin'. We're here to see a friend," Hassan said smoothly in his best American voice.

Before the young man could react, Faras struck him with full force on the side of the head. Hassan sidestepped swiftly, avoiding the blood splatter.

Faras dragged the limp body by the boots behind tall bushes. A muffled gunshot broke the silence. Hassan immediately scanned the parking lot for witnesses. When Faras returned, he handed Hassan a key.

With a nod, Hassan took the lead, eager to locate the woman researcher.

♦ ♦ ♦

Faras took three minutes to bypass the apartment's lock. He quickly spoofed the tag's signature with his modified RFID reader, successfully deactivating the magnetic locking mechanism.

With weapons drawn, they began a systematic search. The young woman was nowhere to be found, so they methodically dismantled each room in search of any device—a tablet, computer, or phone that could connect to the lab's central processing system.

Hacking into her devices was the least of Hassan's concerns. He had beaten the best, and in the unlikely event he couldn't, he knew several dark web hackers who could for the right price.

His attention was drawn to a framed picture on the floor. Flipping it over, he stared at the image of a man with his daughter and wife—the NSA analyst from the airport.

Glancing out the window, Hassan's eyes focused as he observed a gray van pulling into the parking lot. A man and woman stepped out. Hassan looked down at the photograph and back to the man outside. He couldn't believe his luck.

But it wasn't luck; it was divine providence. God willed it to be. It was the girl's father, and he would unknowingly lead them to her and the lab.

The woman accompanying him caught Hassan's attention. Her confident stride and focus were familiar to him. Who was she? In Syria, he had crossed paths with this type of woman. *A black scorpion*—possibly KGB or Mossad—known for their cunning and lethal skills.

"We must go. Use the side exit," Hassan said to Faras as he pulled the slide on his Glock and checked the load.

"It's done," Faras said upon returning to the car.

"Good." Hassan nodded.

Faras had attached a GPS tracker to the van's rear bumper. They watched as the father and the female agent hurriedly left the complex. Time was of the essence. The next phase of the attack would commence in three hours.

Hassan reminded himself patience was key.

As the pair exited the complex, the woman paused, scanning the area with the poise of a seasoned professional with her weapon drawn. Hassan remained concealed behind the Dodge's blackout windows. If there were to be a confrontation, he would enjoy the opportunity.

The van pulled out of the parking lot.

Patience.

He pressed the ignition button, and the supercharged V-8 engine roared to life. He found pleasure in the low rumble of its power. He eased the car out of the parking lot, glancing at Faras, who was tracking the van's movement on his phone. The next phase of their operation would now begin.

STATA LAB

22 FEBRUARY, 0850 HRS
MIT STATA TECHNOLOGY CENTER — CAMBRIDGE, MASSACHUSETTS

Paul drummed his fingers on the steering wheel of the cargo van; his knee bounced with anticipation as he sat parked in the early morning shade of the imposing five-story, red-brick Metropolitan Moving and Storage building. On the corner of Vassar and Massachusetts Avenue, a block from the Stata Lab, the Metropolitan resembled a medieval fortress with its commanding corner watchtowers and four smaller square towers adorning the façade and the giant curtain walls.

The traffic lights and crosswalk signals were dark. Cars honked, and students scurried about, gripping their precious coffee cups, oblivious to the events swirling around them.

Paul struggled to remember when he'd last visited Emma. The three years since Sara's death had been a blur, and Emma had made it clear her need for space and time to process the loss of her mother and best friend. Sara and Emma had shared everything—joy or sorrow, good times and bad. Sara had always been there for her, and then, like the flick of a light switch, she was gone.

Paul regretted not being there for Emma. Instead, he allowed Sara's death to consume him. Why hadn't he been stronger?

However, that was behind him now, and he held onto the hope that it wasn't too late to restore their once-cherished relationship.

Now was the time to focus—get to the lab and find Emma.

He scanned the cars parked outside the lab, searching for anyone who didn't belong and for those searching for him.

A student sat on a bench with her boyfriend east of the lab's rear door entrance. They laughed while watching something on his phone. On the sidewalk, a tourist took pictures, turned, crossed the street, and walked away from the lab before jumping on a tourist bus.

A sudden double knock on the van's passenger window startled Paul. His heart raced as he straightened up in his seat, his left hand instinctually moving to the Colt holstered beneath his leather jacket.

A stocky man wearing a dark blue knit cap emblazoned with bold yellow "POLICE" leaned into the window. He gave a stern nod and motioned for Paul to lower the window.

Subtly, Paul slid his hands to the steering wheel to draw the officer's attention from the concealed firearm.

"You can't park here. It's a restricted area," the officer said, looking into the rear of the van.

"Sorry, Officer, I've got a delivery across the street. I'll move."

"Do it now. With the power outage, we can't have anyone loitering," the officer said.

"Yes, sir. Any idea when the power may come back?" Paul asked, curious to hear what he knew.

"Maybe days. Some are saying weeks. All hell is breaking loose, so I'd suggest you get out of the city while you can."

Paul started the van, flipped on the turn signal, and pulled onto Cambridge Avenue. In the side mirror, he watched the officer walk down the street.

As Paul eased into the busy intersection, he glanced in the rearview mirror. A sleek silver Dodge Charger came into view, carrying two middle-aged men. Their facial expressions were solemn and business-like. Paul's hands tightened on the steering wheel as unease settled into his gut. Was he being overly paranoid? Who knew about the van? Lia had said it was clean and free of tracking electronics, radios, or GPS sensors.

With the traffic lights out, the intersections were treated

like four-way stops. He waited and turned left to circle the block.

The Dodge followed.

He tested the tail and made a sharp right turn. The Dodge continued straight, passing through the intersection. Paul relaxed his grip and pulled the car over at the corner of Vassar and Main. Yes, he was paranoid.

The brushed gray steel of the Stata Lab reflected in the sunlight, casting a striking image on the van's front windshield. The post-modern facility was the renowned home to MIT's Computer Science & Artificial Intelligence Lab. The visionary architect Frank Gehry, celebrated for his unique geometric creations, designed the iconic building. His uniquely whimsical designs included the Guggenheim in Bilbao, Spain, and the stunning Walt Disney Concert Hall in his hometown of Los Angeles.

Gehry's work near Paul and Sara's home was indelibly etched in his memory. Their Sunday walks through University Circle, passing Case Western Reserve, boasted another of Gehry's spectacular modernist creations. Its gleaming aluminum curves starkly contrasted the traditional designs of the nearby Art Museum and Symphony Hall.

Paul drove along the Charles River and then circled back to the MIT Stata Center lab entrance.

He glanced into the side-view mirror. A wave of anxiety jolted him.

No, he wasn't being paranoid. The unmistakable gray Dodge charger was lurking two cars behind.

Without hesitation, he hit the gas and spun the wheel with a tight right-hand grip. The cargo van lurched around the corner. The rear slid hard and fast into the intersection. He let up on the gas, and the van straightened out.

He punched the accelerator again and sped down Main Street, turning and weaving to avoid bicyclers and slower-moving cars. He approached a four-way intersection, hit the brakes, and turned right down Cambridge Avenue.

He slowed and followed closely behind a bread delivery truck. The Dodge appeared in the side-view mirror.

Damn it!

Paul had no choice. He had to ditch the van and make his way back to the Stata Center. The Stata required security clearance and was manned by armed security personnel. The men in the Dodge wouldn't follow him into that building. Or would they? Not knowing who they were, he wasn't sure of anything.

Paul had clearance authorization to the Stata Lab. At least, he hoped he still did. Or did they revoke it after the Feds' APB?

The van couldn't outrun or outmaneuver the Dodge. He remembered one of his father's lessons: *When confronted by a superior foe, nature's surroundings are your friend.*

It was probable that they weren't familiar with the area, and Paul knew well the Boston maze of one-way streets and tunnels. That would be the advantage he needed. The Charles River was flanked by winding, congested one-way roads and narrow bridges connecting the Back Bay and Cambridge. He'd lead the Dodge away from the Stata Lab, away from Emma, toward the city, east along Memorial Drive, then across Longfellow Bridge into the heart of Boston—and find his way back on foot.

◆ ◆ ◆

Paul gathered his composure, slowed his breathing, and wiped the sweat off his forehead. He had dumped the van in a downtown alley and made the long jog back to MIT's campus, crossing the Charles at the Harvard Bridge.

There was no sign of the Dodge or the men chasing him, but he knew it wouldn't be long before they realized he doubled back. He pushed open the heavy glass door of the Stata building, his carry bag slung over his shoulder. Finally, he had caught a break.

A familiar face welcomed Paul. "Good afternoon, Mr. Knox. It's been a long time. What brings you to campus?"

"It's great to see you again, William. I'm here to surprise Emma," Paul said, happy to see his old friend.

Since Paul's days as a grad assistant, Big Will has been a steadfast presence at MIT. An imposing figure, he diligently guarded the Stata Center as if it were his own home. For two decades, he had become the gentle giant protector of MIT's high-tech computing center.

The toll of time had painted streaks of gray into his beard, yet William remained an imposing physical force, tipping the scales at three hundred pounds, with legs like tree trunks and a head that seemed to sit directly atop his broad shoulders. To students and faculty alike, Big Will was more than just a security guard—he was a campus legend, affectionately described as half-man, half-Alaskan grizzly bear.

Would his badge trigger an alert? Big Will scanned it, and the indicator light changed from red to green. Paul relaxed his clenched fists.

"I'm sure Emma will be happy to see you. She's up in the networking lab. Been there all night, working on somethin' important with the professor."

"Excellent!" Paul said as a wave of relief washed over him as he learned his daughter was safe and secure.

"Please place your bag through the scanner," said Big Will.

Paul hesitated, acutely aware that concealed Colt would set off the scanner alarm.

THE FANCY FRENCHMAN

JUNE 11, 1781
PHILADELPHIA, PENNSYLVANIA COLONY

Jack moved with caution through the bustling streets of Philadelphia, acutely aware that his capture was not an option. Governor Jefferson's solemn warning rang in his ears— the city was now teeming with British spies and loyalist sympathizers. Amid the throngs of unfamiliar faces, each one potentially the enemy, the daunting task loomed: how was he to locate the Frenchman in a place entangled in secrecy and deception?

A gentle morning rain fell as a well-matched pair of mules tugged a wooden cart stacked full of fresh vegetables and sacks of grain. The clapping of hooves against the brick and cobblestones drew Jack and Julius's attention as the cart lumbered by the front steps of the City Tavern. Jack paused, marveling at the sight of a dapper gentleman striding past, his fashionable waistcoat adorned with exquisite brass buttons and a pristine white shirt with long wrist cuffs. With graceful precision, he sidestepped the mud puddles that dotted the walkway.

"Jack, what do we do now?" Julius said.

"Don't know." Jack shook his head, questioning if he'd misunderstood Jefferson's orders.

Julius slapped Jack's arm, motioning with his head toward the stables. A large man pulled on Celer's reins, and a shorter man in a fancy suit stroked the neck of Julius's mare.

Jack curled his lip and emitted a high-pitched, short whistle. On cue, Celer reared back, raised his forequarters high into the air, and shook his head, tearing the reins from the hands of his startled captor. The two men quickly backed away from the horses.

Jack slapped his thigh two times, and both horses settled and trotted to their masters.

Julius leveled his rifle on the larger of the two men.

"How may I be of service, gentlemen?" Jack said with a hint of sarcasm, his hand resting on his knife handle.

"Pardon us, gents, we mean no harm," said the shorter man, spoken with a refined French accent. As he stepped toward Jack, his white-gloved fingers twisted his tightly curled mustache. He wore an extravagant green waistcoat adorned with intricate gold thread patterns. His mustard-colored breeches clung tightly to his slender legs, and a black flat-brimmed hat tilted at an angle, casting a shadow over his pale, round face.

"I've been informed you are inquiring about a Monsieur Lublue."

Jack stared into the eyes of the Frenchman, recalling Governor Jefferson's instructions. Jack carefully read aloud the secret passage:

"*The sanctuary of Mary has five spires; those spires reach up to the highest heavens.*"

The fancy Frenchman smiled and replied with a stately tone, "*The roots of those spires reach down to the bottom of the ocean.*"

Jack carefully replied, "*This new world is the time and period of God.*"

"*Bonjour je suis Francious Lublue.* And this is my able friend, Monsieur Rapp," said the Frenchman.

The tall, robust man politely raised his hat, revealing his gleaming, freshly-shaven head.

"*Bonjour, le Monsieur Lublue,*" Jack said.

Julius lowered his rifle. Rapp relaxed his stance.

"*Oh là là!* You are a tall one. And you are Monsieur Jouett?"

"*Oui,*" Jack said.

"I am the brother-in-law of Gilbert du Motier. You may know him by Marquis de Lafayette, presently in the service of General Washington," Lublue said, speaking in French. He looked left and right. "The city has ears. Come, let us conference."

Jack patted Celer on the head, stroked his neck, and led him back into the stable.

"We mustn't loiter," said the Frenchman. "Tories are on the lookout for you and your friend. The British have issued a bounty for information pertaining to the killing of Tarleton's scouts and those responsible for aiding Governor Jefferson's escape."

"How did the news find its way to Philadelphia so quickly?" Jack asked.

"The redcoats run spy couriers on clippers on the Delaware and Chesapeake. However, General Washington has also employed his agents." Lublue smiled and twirled his fancy mustache.

Julius turned, walked toward the stable door, and stood guard, watching for lurking strangers.

"After your departure, Tarleton's men captured several of the Virginia assembly meeting in Charlottesville, including Colonel Boone. My sources tell me you fought alongside the captain."

"Yes. He's the best shot I know," Jack said.

"Huh?" Julius said.

"Besides you, of course, Julius."

"The British detained Colonel Boone for two days in a coal cellar at the Lewis Plantation before they released him," Lublue said.

"And the governor?"

"Thanks to your bravery, the governor and his family escaped into the western mountains."

"Excellent. The governor is vital to our cause," Jack said.

"Yes, we must thank our heavenly father," said the Frenchman as he stepped closer to Jack. "General Washington has asked me to pass his appreciation to you and your friends for your patriotism," Lublue said.

"The general knows my name?" Julius asked.

"His Excellency ordered safe passage north. There, you will conference with General Knox, Washington's Master of Arms. He's anticipating your arrival in a fortnight," Lublue said, his eyes shifting upon noticing something over Jack's shoulder.

Jack pulled his knife and turned. Two Indian braves drew their tomahawks and held them high over their heads.

Julius wheeled around and leveled his rifle on the older Indian.

"*Bonjour*, my Shawnee friends," Lublue said, raising his hands. "Gentleman, lower your weapons, *s'il vous plait*."

"Not friends. Shawnee no friends with white man," the old Indian said and shot a glance toward the two bare-chested braves, who obediently lowered their tomahawks.

Jack flipped his knife in the air, grabbed the antler handle, and slapped it back into its sheath.

"The great bluecoat general ordered guide," the old Indian said.

"General Washington has commissioned these Shawnee gentlemen to escort you north," Lublue said. "May I introduce Chief Black Hoof? He and your great blue coat general, as the chief refers to him, have known one another for many years, dating back to the French Indian War. Unbeknownst to the British, he has enlisted two western Virginia tribes to aid the cause in return for future land rights in the new United Colonies."

"We don't need an escort." Jack had seen firsthand what the natives could do with a blade and didn't trust them.

"Chief Black Hoof knows the whereabouts of the British checkpoints littered throughout New York and New Jersey. You'd have little hope of navigating through enemy territory without a guide," Lublue said.

"Very well," Jack said begrudgingly. "However, it will end poorly if they do not hold true to the bargain."

The chief grunted and made a motion with his hand. One of the younger braves walked out of the stable.

Lublue extended his glove hand. "May I be permitted to peruse the package?"

"I'm afraid not. My orders do not permit me to do so," Jack said, placing his arm over the satchel.

Lublue smiled. "Splendid. It cannot fall into enemy hands. It contains information that will change the tide of the war. If it fails to reach its destination, I'm afraid all is lost."

"Lost?" Julius asked.

"Yes, the situation is dire. Washington's men have not been compensated in months and are defecting in large numbers. Word from my foreign agents is that surrender terms were presented to the king. If the king accepts, Washington will be forced to lay down his arms."

"No, that is not possible," Julius said.

"Yes, my friend, I'm afraid it is true; however, Marquis Layfette informs me that the general will never surrender. The marquis met with the governor at Monticello to develop a… what is the English word?"

"Contingency?" Julius offered.

"Yes, you are clever—a contingency plan. The general's inner circle is committed to continuing the fight. However, he does not have the money or men to continue," Lublue said.

"What's this plan?" Julius asked.

"I do not know," Lublue said.

"Must go!" The chief began walking away.

"Yes, we have lingered far too long," Lublue said.

Jacked turned toward a sudden muffled scream and scuffle. The younger brave returned, dragging a young boy kicking violently in the grip of a headlock.

"Must go!" the chief said, pointing toward the street.

"The loyalists are aware of our presence. You must be on your way. My colleague will deal with this young traitor. Chief Black Hoof will escort you to Trenton, and to the Fort at West

Point. I have sent a courier ahead to inform General Knox that you will arrive within the fortnight," Lublue said.

"Must go!" the chief said sternly.

Jack and Julius slung their rifles over their shoulders and mounted their horses.

Lublue pointed to the satchel draped across Jack's shoulder. "Protect that with your life. It contains the hopes and dreams of your fellow patriots."

"You have my word," Jack said, shaking the Frenchman's hand. "We will depart immediately."

For the first time in his life, he felt an overwhelming sense of purpose. He had always enjoyed adventure and fighting; however, this mission would avenge his father's death. He would deliver the satchel to General Knox or die trying.

"*Au revoir et bonne vitesse*," Lublue said to Jack.

"*Merci beaucoup*," Jack replied, nudging Celer to follow the Shawnee warriors to the main street.

"Julius, keep a watchful eye on those savages. I don't trust them."

REUNION

22 FEBRUARY, 1145 HRS
MIT STATA TECHNOLOGY CENTER — CAMBRIDGE, MASSACHUSETTS

A familiar female voice called out, jarring Paul from his thoughts. "Dad, what are you doing here?"

Her voice tinged with surprise, and a hint of disbelief filled him with a mixture of joy and relief. He hadn't missed his chance. The weight of fear and uncertainty he'd carried melted away. She was here, safe.

Paul wouldn't let her go again, ever.

He threw his backpack over his shoulder and looked past Big Will to see Emma standing with her hands on her hips, looking surprised and not entirely happy to see him. She wore a black, knee-length, puffy goose-down parka. Her long, sandy-brown hair was pulled back into a tight ponytail, the ends dropping onto her hood's fur ruff. A forest-green leather bag hung from her shoulders. Her sunglasses were propped up on her head, just as her mother had worn them.

Paul's little girl wasn't so little anymore; she had grown into a beautiful woman, filling him with immense pride.

He stretched out his arms, waiting for her to leap into them as she used to do when he returned from business trips. "I came to find you. It's so great to see you're okay."

"Why wouldn't I be?" She stood defiant, firmly planted to the ground.

Paul lowered his arms. No, it wasn't a surprised look; she was upset or probably angry. Sara would give him the same look when he walked through the door after midnight. She never approved of Paul's long work nights.

Paul had always known that Emma shared her mother's

features, but it had been almost two years since he'd last seen her. The resemblance was unbelievable.

"You look terrible. You look like you've been sleeping in your clothes. Are you drunk?" Emma asked.

After Sara's death, Paul numbed the pain with bourbon. Emma never understood why, but he had convinced himself it helped. He was wrong—dead wrong.

Paul rubbed his week-old beard and pushed back his hair. "No, I'm not. It's been a long few days. I tried to reach you, but with the power outage and everything else going on, I was worried," he said.

She walked toward him. She had her mother's eyes, a deep hazel. She also had her mother's instincts and wasn't buying it.

He tried one more time and opened his arms. He wasn't sure if she would accept his peace offering.

She walked into his arms and gave him a halfhearted embrace. Holding her tight, he realized how much he missed her. Then she backed away and looked into his eyes as if reading his mind.

"What's wrong?" Emma asked. "Why are you here?"

"Everything's fine now that I know you're all right," Paul said, forcing another smile.

"Why wouldn't I be fine? Other than the power is out everywhere, cell service is down, and the President is getting us into yet another war, I'm wonderful," she said with potent sarcasm.

She would continue to interrogate him until she got what she wanted. And she wanted facts. Her world was black and white—the computer scientist in her couldn't handle gray. There was only one right answer; nothing was ever partially correct. Subjectivity bothered her. No, it repulsed her.

"I'm fine," she said again. "But really, why are you here?"

Paul knew she would give it to him as soon as she put her hands on her hips for a second time.

"It's been two years since you visited, and suddenly you're

worried? What about all those times I called you? You never had time to talk. Too busy with work or whatever bottle you'd crawled into."

Ouch. He clearly deserved that.

At just eighteen years old, Emma had watched helplessly as Sara wasted away in the sterile hospital room, cancer gnawing at her ever so slowly until finally, she became a shadow of her former self and, in an abrupt, heart-wrenching moment, vanished from their lives. Paul hadn't coped as a father should, and Emma resented him for it.

"So why are you really here?" she said.

He had to try. "I'm here for you," he said finally. "Unlike before—when I wasn't."

Emma's eyes suddenly darted past him, over his shoulder, toward the door. Without hesitation, he followed her gaze, and his heart pounded as a thousand thoughts swept through his mind.

Paul steadied himself, controlling his emotions, something he had learned in combat. He turned back to meet Emma's stare, a promise etched in his eyes, determined to protect her at any cost.

ANSWERS

22 FEBRUARY, 1155 HRS
MIT STATA TECHNOLOGY CENTER – CAMBRIDGE, MASSACHUSETTS

Outside the Stata building, a wintery mixture of rain and snow fell, illuminated by the harsh glow of the incandescent emergency lights. Two men paced restlessly in front of the glass doors.

The first, a lean figure with a crisp crew cut and mirrored aviator glasses, wore dark jeans neatly tucked into brown, square-toed cowboy boots. He held a handgun in his left hand, barking orders to his companion—a taller, muscle-bound man.

Paul unzipped his go-bag, reached in, and wrapped his hand firmly around the Colt's G10 gunner grip. His thumb swiftly flicked the beavertail safety while his index finger rested with purposeful tension on the trigger.

He lowered his firearm to his side, and his stance shifted, feet planted shoulder-width apart, every muscle poised and ready.

"Go get Big Will," Paul said to Emma.

"What's wrong? What are you doing with that gun?"

"Please. Get Big Will. Now!" Paul raised his voice just enough to send Emma a clear message. She paused and then quickly walked to the other side of the entranceway.

Paul stared intently at the men. *If you come any closer, you won't leave upright.*

The urban cowboy paused as he was about to walk through the door and held the larger man back with his non-gun hand.

Without taking his eyes off the two men, Paul slid his Colt back into his bag but held on to it, the safety off.

"What's up, Mr. Knox?" Big Will said.

"Those two guys out there are carrying," Paul said.

"Carrying? Weapons?" Big Will asked, swiftly pressing the release on his holster and gripping the gun. He stared at the two men and pulled out his handheld radio. "Officer Yarbrough to central. Send backup to Building 20, front entrance. Two men, possibly armed."

Paul looked out toward the men. The leader measured up the bear-sized guard, exchanged words with the other man, turned, walked out of the light, and disappeared around the corner.

As Big Will cautiously moved towards the door, he drew his firearm. The distinctive squared-off barrel and matte black finish made the Glock unmistakable, even in his massive hands.

Paul's confidence had finally returned, spurred by the threat and the fact that his mission was clear—to protect Emma. To do so, he needed answers.

"Follow me," Paul said to Emma.

"Where?"

"Just trust me, please."

Paul recognized the manufacturer of the walk-through metal detector—a newer model with multiple zones; each had an independent transmitter and receiver coil positioned at designated heights. His Colt would certainly trip the detector's alarm circuit, so he slid his bag on the floor outside the machine, walked quickly through the metal detector, and grabbed his bag on the other side.

"What's going on?" Emma said as she walked through the metal detector and caught up with her father.

"I'll tell you everything soon. But right now, I need to get online." He looked back toward the entrance. Big Will was on his radio out in front of the building.

"Let's go," he said. "I need to talk to Professor Clark."

PATIENCE

22 FEBRUARY, 1230 HRS
MIT STATA TECHNOLOGY CENTER – CAMBRIDGE, MASSACHUSETTS

Hassan cursed under his breath, frustration simmering within. He berated himself for his lack of preparation. He vowed never to let such a careless oversight occur again. Such lapses were inexcusable in his line of work; success demanded unwavering clarity and meticulous planning.

He closed his eyes while his fingers pressed gently the back of his neck, focusing his mind. The scar tissue, smooth as glass, was a constant reminder of his lost family and homeland.

He opened his eyes and breathed deeply.

Through the Charger's tinted windshield, the blanket of dark winter clouds marched east toward the city, reminding him of the ferocious desert sandstorms that regularly engulfed his village.

Hassan turned to Faras, leaning against the car door, asleep with his mouth open. The man was good for only one task: killing. He could not think for himself. And with Khalid dead, Hassan would soon end the association. However, for the time being, he had to be patient.

He glanced down at his watch. The digital battlefield would erupt within minutes, and the outcome would define the new world order and Hassan's destiny. The first team of worm bots would breach the U.S. internet providers' servers from within, and an ISIS battalion of in-country hackers would unleash a relentless storm of Distributed Denial of Service attacks on critical infrastructure data centers. This two-pronged digital assault was meticulously designed to cripple the very backbone of communications that powered the internet.

Simultaneously, the embedded ISIS North America soldiers, aided by their Iranian and Syrian brothers, would initiate ground attacks on strategic governmental and civilian targets. However, it was necessary for Hassan to gain access to the MIT lab. The woman researcher's network access was required to complete the crypto transaction Khalid had orchestrated with the U.S. government.

Hassan's attention was suddenly drawn to movement in the rearview mirror. A man dressed in black, wearing a ski mask, and carrying a large metal club ran toward Hassan's car.

Hassan's finger rested lightly on the Glock's trigger, poised to counter any threat. Yet, he eased his grip as the man sprinted past him toward the central business district. The city was in the throes of looting and violent demonstrations.

Hassan continued monitoring the lab. His thoughts returned to the GloMink warehouse, and he was angry for not anticipating Khalid's final transformation and betrayal. The signs had been obvious, but he hadn't allowed himself to believe that his mentor would abandon him.

Greed.

Hassan had watched, over the years, the dreadful disease of capitalism that had infected the Western non-believers. Khalid had been inflicted with this disease and cared only for himself and what was best for Khalid. He wore a mask of contempt, concealing his reprehensible intentions and preaching the importance of serving the cause. However, when Khalid removed the mask and revealed his true self to Hassan in the warehouse that day, the Divine demonstrated His power, and Khalid paid the ultimate price for abandoning Him and His flock.

Hassan had remained faithful, disciplined, and patient. He would avenge his brother's death by destroying the Americans' way of life—damage that would last a generation.

Hassan spotted motion to his left. A tall Black man emerged, rounding the corner—a long-staggered stride, head turning side to side, sweeping the area. He stopped in front of the MIT lab building's entrance, turned, and scanned the area again, left, right, and then in Hassan's direction. From that distance, Hassan recognized a bulge on the stranger's left side. He was armed. A left-handed draw. Based on his movements, he was likely military, federal law enforcement, or both.

"Get up," Hassan said, shoving Faras hard in the arm with the butt of his Glock.

The tall stranger entered the computer lab facility. Hassan was out of time.

Speaking in Arabic, he said, "We must go."

Hassan stepped out of the car, scanned the area for threats, and pulled his secure phone from his jacket pocket. The cell network was down; however, the Dodge was equipped with a micro-cell transmitter to communicate with his field commanders. He typed quickly and sent a message requesting support from the local area. Located on the outskirts of Cambridge, the Islamic Center of Boston was within transmission range.

Hassan closed his eyes, raised his head toward the sky, and prayed. Then, he slowly reopened them, and a renewed power flowed within him, relishing the upcoming battle and the opportunity to demonstrate servitude. He would overwhelm the infidels with force and cunning, locate the woman researcher, and fulfill his mission.

His prayer included Yousef, who would be proud of the fruits of their labor. The power was out along the East Coast, and riots and looting had taken hold while the war raged in the Middle East. Soon, he would complete his mission. But he needed the girl and access to the network.

Hassan popped the trunk, revealing an array of equipment neatly arranged inside. Shedding his heavy leather coat, he put on a level three tactical vest over his white T-shirt, shifting the weight of it on his shoulders. He reached for another vest and handed it to Faras, their eyes locked in silent understanding as they prepared for the mission ahead.

Hassan pushed a duffel bag aside and unsnapped the metal buckles of the gun case, revealing the two midnight-black AR-15 Patrol Carbine rifles chambered in 5.56 NATO with select-fire capability. He pushed the rifle case out of the way and unbuckled a smaller molded plastic case. Inside were four camo-green M67 fragmentation grenades secured tightly in gray packing foam. He held one of the compact steel spheres in his palm, appreciating the raw power concealed within—six ounces of high-grade composite explosive. He clipped two potent orbs to his belt and handed two more to Faras.

"We must take the girl alive. You may do as you wish with the others."

Faras secured the grenades to his belt and checked his rifle's sight and the high-capacity magazine load.

Hassan pulled out his phone. Nothing. The local commanders had not acknowledged his message.

Had the transmission link been compromised?

He could wait no longer.

He slid his hands into the combat shooting gloves, relishing the snug, reassuring fit of the injection-molded knuckle protectors. The black balaclava mask followed, covering his face as he felt the cool fabric against his skin. He flipped the AR's safety to automatic fire, the metallic click signaling a prelude to the imminent chaos.

He reached into the trunk and retrieved two midnight-blue lightweight jackets, each with bold, reflective yellow lettering on the front and back:

F B I

TRENTON

JUNE 11, 1781
TRENTON, NEW JERSEY COLONY

Jack pulled back firmly on the reins and released the pressure, a silent command to his loyal friend.

"Hol'up, Cel."

Celer obediently responded, slowing to a steady trot, and gracefully stopped at the edge of the quiet village of Trenton. With a sigh of relief, Jack swung one leg over the saddle and jumped onto the dusty dirt road. The long hours spent in the saddle had taken their toll. He stretched his neck and back in an attempt to relieve the strain of navigating the unforgiving forest's dense overgrowth. Throughout the journey, the Shawnee scouts had led their party northward from Philadelphia, deep into enemy territory, proceeding cautiously and skirting the small New Jersey hamlets and trading posts that peppered the well-traveled Delaware River.

As the sun dipped below the tree line, the fading light cast a yellow reflective glow over the rippling river's surface. The wind rustled the fresh spring leaves of the massive oaks while the towering white pine branches danced high above. The occasional bird chirped a steady and slow cadence, and a dog howled in the distance.

Julius and the three Shawnee scouts trailed on horseback as Jack walked Celer into the quaint village of Trenton. Candles flickered in the windows of the dozen or so wood and stone houses that lined the eerily empty main street. At the far end of the village, the glow of two lanterns flanked the doors of what appeared to be a church.

"Where's everyone?" Julius asked.

"Not sure. Strange," Jack said and swung his rifle around into his hands. He placed his finger on the trigger and pulled back the flintlock. His intuition told him something was afoot. Had the townspeople abandoned the city, or were they hiding?

The old Shawnee chief stared into the giant pines, which stood like colossal guardians protecting the village. He muttered in his native tongue to the taller Indian scout, who nodded and walked toward the river's edge with his horse's reins in one hand and his tomahawk firmly grasped in the other.

Jack kicked a stone with the toe of his boot, recalling the day he'd first learned of the Battle for Trenton. *The Richmond Gazette* had reported the harrowing story of Washington's three-thousand-man army's daring nighttime crossing of the Delaware. Jack recalled the overwhelming pride he'd felt when he and his mates read about Washington's army's rout of the Hessians, capturing over eight hundred men and killing eighty, including Colonel Rall, the Hessian's commander. The town of Richmond had erupted in joy, inciting a day-long celebration with militia parades and cannonade salutes.

"Jack, are you with us?" Julius said.

"Yeah. I was thinking about the men who fought and died here."

The old Shawnee interrupted, muttering something, and abruptly raised his hand. With his eyes closed, he bobbed his head and chanted with a haunting, solemn voice.

"Chief, what are you doing?" Jack asked, sliding his knife out of its sheath.

The chief stopped, turned toward Jack and Julius, and with intense fear radiating from his dark eyes, cried out, "*Tianuwa, Tianuwa!*"

"*Tee-u-wa?*" Jack made a futile attempt to pronounce the word.

"*Tee-a-an-u-wa,*" the chief said, enunciating each syllable and pointing to the tops of the trees. "Evil spirit from below earth." With a raised arm and a long, thin finger, he motioned from the treetops to the rooftop of a two-story stone house at the far end of the village.

Jack searched the moonless night sky but saw nothing except the faint outline of storm clouds drifting toward town.

"Giant hawk creature. Feathers of iron. Steals children and dogs to feed young in caves. Must go!" the chief said and turned to mount his horse.

"Nonsense," Jack said. "I don't see anything."

"I don't know, Jack," Julius said. "Something's not right. Let's get off the main road and head back to the river trail. I've read natives have ways to communicate with the spirit world, and I don't think we want to stick around to see this hawk creature."

Jack stood motionless, listening and scanning the dark sky for a devilish, winged beast. The birds had stopped chirping, dogs no longer barked, and the air was still. Nightfall had enveloped the town, making it impossible to see into the windows of the houses that lined the abandoned street. The only sign of life was the solitary candle in the window of a dry goods store.

"Yeah, let's get outta here," Jack agreed, rarely afraid of anything or anyone.

Like a cannon exploding, a thunderous blast broke the unearthly silence. Jack threw himself to the ground, his mind racing to catch up with his body. The sound was all too familiar —a rifle discharged from mid-distance.

He laid low, lifting his face from the rocky dirt road, and strained to locate the origin of the shot. To his left, the chief lay on his back, grasping his shoulder. Blood oozed through his fingers. His face was wrenched in pain.

Jack remained on the ground, waiting for a sign of other riflemen. "Julius, stay down!" he yelled. "A sniper. Over in one of the houses across the way."

The pounding of footsteps came from behind. Jack reached

for his knife when the younger Indian scout rushed to the aid of the chief. He grabbed his foot and dragged him behind a white picket fence.

A second blast rang out, and the musket ball exploded nearby, throwing dirt onto Jack's hat.

He had counted to fifteen between rifle blasts, which meant the shooter had outstanding reloading skills. He remained still, prepared to dash the fence.

"Julius?" Jack said in a low hush, not wanting to give away his position.

"I'm over here, behind the fence, ten paces from you," Julius said.

Jack could hear Julius priming his rifle.

Another blast erupted, echoing through the night's air. Dirt flew into Jack's face. He rubbed his eyes.

Julius's musket let out a vicious eruption and white plume. A window crashed in the distance.

Jack guessed the sniper was less than one hundred yards away based on the lapse between the blast of the powder and the ball striking the ground. A great distance for a musket but a modest distance for a grooved long-barreled rifle. Jack could hit a deer from over three hundred yards with his J.E. Brown forty-four-inch, and the British snipers, with their Fergusons, had a range of up to five hundred yards but were realistically accurate to three hundred.

Another blast echoed in the distance, and the fence plank sent shredded wood into the air.

Pinned down, Jack felt an overwhelming mixture of rage and fear, emotions he had learned to push down during the long years of war. With his cheek pressed firmly against the dirt road, he closed his eyes and searched for answers.

What brings a man to risk everything, including his life? Was it revenge for his father's death or the prospect of glory and gain?

The sniper's rifle unleashed another thunderous blast,

causing Jack to clench his eyes even tighter. A vivid memory emerged in the darkness as if he were transported back to that fateful October day two years prior. There he stood, side by side with his militia brothers, their bayonets glinting in the sunlight that had penetrated the tangled canopy of towering oaks and pines of King's Mountain. Two hundred frontiersmen, a gathering of fathers, sons, and brothers from the western lands of Virginia and the Carolinas. The roar of British muskets rumbled from above, shattering the anxious, low whispers and the shuffling of men's feet. The thunderous volleys tore through the dense foliage, sending leaves and branches cascading down like an unrelenting hailstorm.

Jack and the militiamen charged into the chaos, ascending King's Mountain's steep, rocky slope. Men and friends fell on either side of him, some succumbing to exhaustion while others met their fate under the hail of relentless musket fire. With each step, Jack climbed higher and higher, his heart pounding with the force of the musket blasts. He paused only to fire and reload his rifle. Beside him, his fellow riflemen unleashed a storm of lead, their shots finding their marks with chilling accuracy. Once concealed among the rocky outcroppings, the enemy lay exposed and vulnerable.

The air was thick with the pungent scent of gunpowder and the cries of the wounded. Jack and his men pressed on, a relentless force that finally overwhelmed the enemy, bringing them victory on the blood-soaked slopes of King's Mountain.

"Jack! You okay?" Julius's familiar voice broke Jack's trance, and he slowly opened his eyes, unveiling the gray, weather-beaten fence a few yards away.

Once more, Jack questioned why a man would willingly stake everything, including his own life. Then, with Julius's voice yelling out for Jack, the answer appeared. He understood now why he and countless others risked it all. It was not for glory, revenge, or gain. It was for the bonds forged among his militia brethren, for brave men like Julius and Ben whose sacrifice inspired every step up the mountain.

Jack called out, "I'm fine, Julius. How many are there?"

"One sniper in the stone house just beyond that large oak. Second floor, third window to the north. I'll draw his fire, and you make a run for it," Julius said.

"Go!" Jack yelled and heard the double click of Julius's rifle hammer, a silent pause, and the familiar sound of the flint striking the frizzen. Julius's rifle let out a booming crack, followed by the distant sound of crashing glass.

Jack sprang to his feet, instinctually hunched, and bolted for safety, his boots pounding the earth with each long stride. Another menacing sniper blast spurred him onward as he dove over the fence, his shoulder slamming onto the ground.

Breathing hard, Jack slapped Julius on the back.

"Good to see ya, my friend."

"A nine-count," Jack said.

"Yeah, I've never seen a reload that fast," Julius said, steadying himself on one knee. He calmly loaded his rifle and prepped the pan, readying to return fire. Jack's heart swelled with pride as he witnessed Julius transform from a mischievous young man into a fearless soldier.

The beating of hooves captured Jack's attention.

"Here comes an injun. With our horses," Julius said.

A brave ran toward the fence line, holding the reins of Celer and Julius's horse in each hand.

"Let's go," Jack said.

He sprinted toward Celer. As he reached his horse, he grasped the harness's crownpiece with a firm hand and, with a swift, practiced flick of his wrist, expertly turned Celer, the colt's powerful muscles responding to his command.

In one effortless motion, Jack set his foot in the stirrup and swung his leg over the saddle, the leather creaking softly under his weight.

Another deafening explosion reverberated through the air. The ball struck a rock and veered off course, finding its mark in the brave's leg and sending him crumpling to the ground, his anguished cry cutting through chaos. The remaining Indian ran to the fallen warrior's side. Together, they staggered and limped behind the protection of the fence.

Jack looked down at his chest as his heart pounded, realizing the satchel was gone.

He desperately scoured the ground around his horse and beyond the fence.

The earth quaked, vibrations reverberating through the saddle as the unmistakable sound of pounding hooves grew louder. Jack's muscles tensed with anticipation as he watched Julius aim toward the approaching riders, rifle steady in hand. Five horsemen charged from a distance, their figures blurred by the darkness that shrouded them.

Fearing an ambush, Jack squinted, straining to pierce the hazy blackness, desperate to identify the approaching riders thundering toward them.

INFINITE CORRIDOR

22 FEBRUARY, 1350 HRS
MIT STATA TECHNOLOGY CENTER – CAMBRIDGE, MASSACHUSETTS

Paul and Emma hurried down the Charles M. Vest main hallway, reaching the final stretch of MIT's Infinite Corridor. This architectural marvel, spanning through buildings numbered 7, 3, 10, 4, and 8, featured a virtual corridor that, during mid-November and late January, aligned perfectly with the plane of the ecliptic. On those days, sunlight would flood the corridor from end to end—a spectacle that had left a lasting impression, symbolizing the boundless possibilities and innovative spirit MIT epitomized.

Paul couldn't take his eyes off his daughter. Sara would have been so proud. She had always recognized something extraordinary in Emma—fierce independence and unwavering determination. How he wished Sara could see her now, transformed into the confident woman she had become.

The time had come for Paul to show Emma how much she meant to him, to rebuild the trust and restore the bond they once shared.

Emma stopped and turned, emotion filling her voice. "Why are you here? I just don't get it. Who were those men?"

Yes, now was the time. If he was going to earn her trust, he had to share everything with her. She'd never forgive him if he held back.

"There's something I have to tell you. Let me explain what's going on. Please sit."

Emma reluctantly sat down next to him at the hallway table. Paul rested his arms on the table, steadying himself, collecting his thoughts so he could somehow explain. But could he—or perhaps more importantly, *should* he? Would it put her in more danger?

"There's something big going on. It is too complicated to explain or even believe. I'm still trying to comprehend it," Paul said, looking into her eyes for a reaction to guide his next move.

"What is it?"

"I'm involved in something. You know how my job required me to keep some things secret at times from you and your mom and how I hated to do that?"

"Yeah, I got used to it," Emma said.

"Well, this is one of those times. In fact, it's more complicated than any other time." Paul looked at her and took in her expression. Somehow, she knew he was serious.

"Dad, I know your job involves really bad people who do terrible things. Mom and I knew. Does it have something to do with the terrorist bombings or the power outages?"

She was always one step ahead. She has that sense. A gift.

"Something serious is about to go down, and I've got to figure out who is behind these attacks. I was getting close to answers, and I think that's what triggered all of this," Paul said.

Emma seemed to be letting down her guard. "Professor Clark will be able to help us. He's in the lab working on our new network project. He's been working nonstop for weeks. No, it's been months," she said.

"What specifically is he working on?"

"He won't tell me. He said it needed his undivided attention and wouldn't tell me what it was. He's been writing code, and I haven't seen him write code in a long, long time. He's building something."

"Can you guess what it is?" Paul asked.

"No. He's kept to himself. You know how he gets. Totally stressed out. He's consumed with whatever project he's working on and blocks everyone out. But I've never seen him like this before. He even started smoking again. Maybe he'll open up to you. Do you think it could be related to what's going on?" Emma said.

"Maybe. He's typically oblivious to what's happening outside the MIT lab. But let's go find him," Paul said.

Emma's voice trembled with genuine emotion. "Oh, by the way, Dad, thanks," she said, wrapping her arms around him and resting her head on his chest. "I've missed you."

Paul held her tight, not wanting to let her go for fear that time—or someone—might once again pull them apart.

OVERMOUNTAIN MEN

JUNE 11, 1781
TRENTON, NEW JERSEY COLONY

The thunderous approach of the charging horsemen grew louder. Jack's heart raced, every instinct warning him that the British cavalry was bearing down on them along with the looming threat of being captured—or worse, cut down by the riders' deadly long blades.

With their long rifles clutched firmly, Jack and Julius sprinted for the cover of the nearest house, their boots hammering the cobblestone road.

Jack jumped the short steps of a white clapboard house and crashed through the door, landing hard on the broad wood-plank floor. A smoldering fire crackled in the fireplace behind a long table with chairs centered in the room and a small staircase leading to the upper floor. The house appeared abandoned.

Julius slammed the door and leaned over with his hands on his knees. "What now?"

Jack, working to catch his breath, dusted off his coat and picked his hat and rifle off the ground. "They'll be on us any second." He felt the tremors of hooves radiate through the floorboards. "We're boxed in like a raccoon in a cage trap. We have to make a stand. Load up," he said.

"Let's give 'em hell," Julius said, busily loading his rifle.

Jack pulled back the canvas covering the window. Five horsemen, all frontiersmen, galloped at a steady pace toward the house. He relaxed his grip on his rifle and walked toward the door.

"You won't believe this," Jack said with relief. "It's good ol' Ben."

Ben rode several horse-lengths ahead with his long-handled hatchet securely fastened to his saddle while his rifle hung over his shoulder. With a firm pull of the reins, his fine sand-colored colt let out a mighty exhale and snort. Jack reached out and stroked the smooth fur, tracing the ivory stripe that ran the length of the colt's broad nose.

He looked up and smiled, joyful to see his old friend. "How'd ya find us?"

"I reckoned you'd be in need of a hand," Ben said with a broad smile.

"Is that Jefferson's satchel?" Jack asked.

"Here." Ben tossed it to Jack and smiled. "You dropped this."

"You sure did save the day," Jack said.

"Ya, it's good to see you, Ben. You were the last person I was expectin' to see way out in these parts," Julius said as Ben jumped down and gave him a firm hug.

Jack turned as the other riders approached. Two peeled off, riding hard toward the sniper's location.

"Sir, what a pleasant surprise! We'd been told the redcoats captured you in Charlottesville," Jack said to his old friend, Colonel Daniel Boone, who was mounted on a brilliant, gray-speckled mare.

Boone, the territory's most accomplished marksman, wore his well-traveled hunting leathers: a wide-brimmed hat, a fringed and tanned leather jacket, and buckskin trousers.

Months had passed since Jack had last seen Colonel Boone. His white beard had grown long and wild, complementing the frontiersman's stark blue eyes. Yet, Jack's attention was drawn to the magnificent rifle held firmly in the colonel's hand, the one-of-a-kind Kentucky long rifle with intricate silver inlay. The same rifle he carried on the Wilderness Road, fighting Indians and shooting wild game from virtually any distance.

The colonel shook his head. "Not my finest hour. The bastards held me with the other assemblymen overnight in a makeshift stockade, yet by morning, they had abandoned Charlottesville to hunt for Governor Jefferson. However, with the assistance of our Overmountain friends, he vacated to the safety of the western lands, out of the reach of the British devil Dragoons."

Jack met the eyes of the two rugged Overmountain riders, passing a silent expression of appreciation and gratitude with a slight nod.

"You're lucky I didn't shoot you," Julius said and smiled.

Ben embraced Julius and lifted him high off the ground.

"Put me down," Julius yelled.

Ben laughed and dropped Julius, his boots slamming to the ground.

"How did you find us?" Jack asked.

"The Frenchman in Philadelphia told me where you'd be. He seemed to know much about your plans. One of Washington's agents, I suppose," Ben said.

"But you were guiding General Wayne's men back to Virginia? What happened?"

"We located Morgan's men shortly after I left you. General Wayne received a message from Major General Lafayette's courier stating that your mission was paramount and that Governor Jefferson's documents must reach their destination. General Wayne ordered me to locate Colonel Boone and escort you for the remainder of the journey north. So here I am," Ben said, slapping Julius on the shoulder.

"Have you seen our Indian friends?" Jack said.

"They're treating the old man down near the river's bank. He's in no condition to travel," Ben said.

From the east, two horsemen raced toward them at a fast gallop. Jack grabbed his rifle, but Boone placed his hand on the barrel.

"Those are my men. I sent them to locate the sniper."

The riders approached, pulling back hard on the reins. Their horses, a stout breed with muscular necks covered with pulsating veins and long, tousled manes, responded on cue. Jack stepped back as their hooves sprayed dust and dirt. Frontiersmen by the look of the craftwork of the saddles, well-worn moccasin boots, and coonskin caps.

The larger of the two men had a thick, fiery red beard. Crisscrossing his broad chest hung an oversized powder horn and a long rifle with what appeared to be an eagle or hawk carved on the hardwood stock. The second rider also carried a Kentucky long rifle and wore a full deerskin shirt and chaps. His menacing expression and well-weathered face, no doubt, were sculpted by many fierce battles and the unforgiving wilderness.

These were no ordinary men; they bore the unmistakable marks of Overmountain men, hailing from the wild and untamed Appalachia. Men that Boone had crossed paths with during his westward expeditions across the rugged mountains and into the uncharted Ohio territory. The Overmountain men were molded by the harshness of the frontier, possessing unrivaled hunting, sharpshooting, and tracking skills. Their hearts were filled with devotion to the land, God, and family. Their self-reliance was unparalleled, rejecting authority and harboring an utter disdain for the British monarch—a disdain that ran as deep as the rivers they crossed and as profound as the mountains they called home.

The large, red-bearded rider spoke with a low, commanding voice. "Whoever fired on you and your injun friends are gone. We found wading scraps near a broken window that looked toward the fence line. We tracked the rider to the eastern edge of the town." He pointed toward the river. "He crossed there, but we're unsure how. The river's deep, and the current too strong to cross on horseback. He must have had help."

"One man? Any sign of others?" Boone inquired.

"One. I found a shop owner hiding in the house. He said a platoon of British Dragoons raided the town, stole food and livestock, harshly questioned folk, and rode off several hours ago."

"That explains why the townsfolk are hiding," Jack said.

"What were they after?" Ben asked.

"Spies and messengers," Boone said and gave Jack a slight nod. "What direction did they head?" he asked the fire beard.

"North. The shop owner overheard the British captain say Princeton, a hard two-hour ride."

"Then why a lone sharpshooter?" Jack said.

"The tracks of the sharpshooter didn't follow the British Dragoons. Maybe a loyalist?"

"Fine work, men," Boone said to the mounted riders. "Let's be on our way. We must escort my friends northward to the fort in the New York colony." Boone removed his hat and ran his fingers through his thick white hair. "We'll head northwest, away from the Delaware and Princeton, toward Morristown, which I understand to be held by the Continentals. We have a long ride ahead. Find some grub, and let's be on our way."

"Agreed," Jack said, turning toward Julius, smiled, and gave Jefferson's satchel, strapped tightly across his chest, a reassuring pat.

"Don't lose that again," Julius said with a stern look and a good-natured tone.

Jack walked down the worn, creaking wooden steps and affectionately stroked Celer's neck. He guided Celer down the street as the townsfolk cautiously emerged from their homes like timid creatures venturing from burrows. The windows of the shops and houses began to shimmer with the light of candles being lit one by one. Each flame spread a golden glow into the evening darkness, breathing life back into the village of Trenton as it awoke once again.

KILL SWITCH

22 FEBRUARY, 1215 HRS
MIT STATA TECHNOLOGY CENTER – CAMBRIDGE, MASSACHUSETTS

With Emma close by his side, Paul quickly made his way up to the second floor of the MIT Networking Lab, eager to discuss with Professor Clark his theory on the origin of the power blackout. As they moved through the corridor, Paul glanced into empty glass-walled offices, each a testament to the unique style of their accomplished occupant. Thick, colorful textbooks lined office shelves, their spines worn from constant use. Photos hung from the corkboard walls, forming vibrant mosaics of family memories and adventures to distant lands.

Near the open office door, the air was thick with an overpowering mix of scents—a pungent blend of old socks and the bitter aroma of burnt coffee. Paul watched Professor Clark's fingers dance across the keyboard in rapid, powerful bursts, his mind channeling his thoughts in fixed-length computing segments. His head pivoted back and forth, tracking the cascading lines of glowing text as they materialized onto the dark canvas of his monitor.

Seemingly oblivious to Paul and Emma's presence, Professor Clark paused his relentless typing. Agitated and unsettled, he stared at the keyboard and ran both hands repeatedly through his long, thinning, snow-white hair. The professor's ragged, black-peppered beard had grown exceptionally wild. He wore his standard uniform consisting of knee-length, khaki cargo shorts, a Pink Floyd "Dark Side of the Moon" prism T-shirt, and Jimmy Buffett-style flip-flops. Famous for throwing himself into his work, he would go without sleep or showering for days to the detriment of his colleagues and students. Inside the cluttered office, a well-worn drip coffee maker, its glass pot marred by years of overuse, sat on a small round table next to an Army-style cot tucked away in the corner. Paul couldn't help but recall how the professor would work through the night, sending emails to Paul and other students well past midnight.

Extensive system diagrams were on the whiteboard next to Professor Clark's desk and extended onto the glass separator wall. The spaghetti-like, multi-colored data input and output lines, depicted with arrows connecting rectangular boxes, represented what appeared to be border gateway networking servers. Each border gateway server had been labeled with the abbreviation for a region of the U.S. and then a count indicating the number in that region.

"I'm sorry to bother you, Professor, but there's someone here to see you," Emma said.

Professor Clark's eyes remained fixated on the four computer monitors mounted on large, matte black graphite arms that extended from the wall. Random printouts, magazines, textbooks, and fast-food wrappers were strewn across his desk and the floor.

"Hello, Professor," Paul said.

Professor Clark continued but slowed the pace of his typing. "Paul Knox? Is that you?" He looked down at the keys and then back to the monitors, then repeated the motion—head down, eyes back up to the monitors. Paul watched as text scrolled by on the large screens, but he couldn't make out the commands.

"Yes, sir," Paul said. "Thank you for taking such good care of Emma."

"Nonsense. Emma can take care of herself."

Paul smiled in Emma's direction. Having her by his side gave him an incredible sense of pride.

"Professor, we need your help," he said.

"Can't. I'll come talk to you when I'm finished," Professor Clark said.

"Sir, we must talk. It can't wait."

"We need your help," Emma said.

"In a few minutes. Please," Professor Clark insisted.

It had been years since Paul had last heard the professor's voice, but he couldn't help but notice the unusually tense tone. The professor, known for his impatience bordering on unapologetic arrogance, had always treated Paul differently. Over time, they'd formed a rare connection built on mutual respect.

"What is it, Professor?" Emma said, moving closer to Professor Clark's monitors, straining to see what he was working on.

"I'm afraid it's too late."

"Too late for what? What is it?" Emma asked.

"I told you. I can't talk right now. I must finish this," Professor Clark said in a harsh and agitated tone.

Paul raised his voice to wrestle the professor's attention away from the mesmerizing glow of the monitors. "Sir! With all due respect, there are bad people outside the building. I just left Emma's apartment, and they had torn it apart, searching for her or something. We're here because we need your help. I need access to the NSA database and audit logs. I have reason to believe someone inside the U.S. government is assisting these guys. And the answer may be in those logs."

Emma turned with a surprised look. "My apartment? When were you going to tell me?"

"I didn't want you to worry," Paul said. "They were looking for something. Do you know what that might be?"

Emma turned toward the window. "I can't think of anything that important." She turned back around quickly. "The only thing I can think of is that I've been working on a network project with the professor and the corporate AI team. Could that be it?"

The professor stopped typing. His head dropped as if she'd hit a nerve.

"It's a new predictive analytical rules engine designed to route internet traffic more efficiently," Emma continued.

"New routing protocols leveraging machine learning algorithms? What type of ML model?" Paul said.

Professor Clark swiveled around in his worn-out chair. He put on his round wire-framed glasses and, in a failing attempt to look presentable, tucked in his T-shirt and slipped his bare feet into his flip-flops.

"It's a new neural network based on simulated biological attribution. They're likely after the new network designs," he said. "I was afraid this could happen."

Paul walked over to the whiteboard and studied the diagram.

"Someone's been attempting to hack my research and test lab for months. But I never thought they'd go this far," Professor Clark said, turning back to type as he talked. His fingers tapped the keyboard in a steady, fast rhythm. He spoke, but his fingers never paused or slowed. They continued their rhythmic dance.

"As you know, the Gates Foundation has long contributed to MIT and our work. Gates himself is involved. Also, DARPA's providing the project funding. We're in the final phase. We've spent months coding and testing the new neural network. All of it's classified. But I have other more pressing concerns right now."

"Does it have anything to do with this?" Paul asked, pointing to the diagram on the whiteboard.

"I'm afraid so. Maybe there's something you'll see that I may be missing. I doubt it, though."

The professor hadn't changed, always considering himself the smartest person in the room. But Paul respected him because, despite his arrogance, he'd mentored Emma and channeled her talent and stunning intellect into a meaningful scientific contribution.

"I've been hip-deep into this for over a week now, and I think I know what's about to happen." Professor Clark pulled himself out of his chair, walked to the whiteboard, and pointed to a red rectangle on the spaghetti diagram. "Someone hacked Verizon's and AT&T's primary network BGP servers."

"Wait, if the BGP servers are compromised, it could impact the routing of all internet traffic," Emma said.

Paul nodded. She did know her stuff.

"Yes, Emma, but that's not the half of it. It's not just Verizon and AT&T; that wouldn't be a problem. The border gateways for all the autonomous systems in the U.S.—Google, Microsoft, you name them—have been infected by malware. Specifically, a sophisticated botnet."

"Dad, aren't botnets your specialty?" Emma said.

"Yes, they've been used by the NSA and other agencies for decades to perform various intelligence counter-surveillance," Paul said. "But targeting the BGP servers is interesting. The Egyptian government built a program to modify their telcos' BGP routing parameters during the Arab Spring. It blocked all internet traffic in and out of the country, including X, Facebook, and Instagram. They wanted to block the videos of their military putting down the protests."

Paul was curious about the professor's involvement. The big telecoms would typically never disclose to an outsider other than the FCC or another government regulatory body.

"How'd you learn of the breach? And why can't Verizon simply block the outbound ports so the bots can't send IRC signals to the bot herder and the external command and control server?"

"An NSA friend messaged me for help about unusual network activity. He asked me to help him decipher the encryption signature of the malware Verizon had sent him. Fortunately, I was able to break the malware's encryption with the latest version of the Lincoln Laboratory's quantum operating system. I then could confirm the origin of the breach."

Paul was familiar with MIT's Lincoln Lab, where the DoD had funded advanced computer science security research for years. Encryption deciphering had been one of their main objectives.

The professor went on to explain his findings to Emma and Paul. "The botnet is multi-staged, communicating peer-to-peer, with no central command, **and it's** been mapping the national telecom network for some time, maybe years. AT&T and Verizon didn't know it was inside their networks. They completely missed it. The bots subverted their outer edge firewalls and cloaked themselves as normal, innocuous LINUX processes. Once the bots completed mapping the BGP servers, they **penetrated deep into the network infrastructure**."

He pointed to the other symbols on the whiteboard. "These networks enable communication with over two-thirds of the world's autonomous systems, routing trillions of data packets a second, from one region to another."

He walked toward the glass wall and, with the marker, pointed to the blue cylindrical database symbol labeled with the red letters *BGP*. A dozen smaller rectangles were connected to the larger rectangles with curving black lines.

Professor Clark circled the smaller rectangles. "We know these edge firewalls, which protect the ISPs' BGP servers, aren't impervious to these types of attacks, and both AT&T and Verizon had thought they'd designed their firewall rules to block this type of malicious traffic, as they've successfully done on countless occasions. Denial of service attacks are old hat to these guys, and the latest generation firewalls are excellent at defending against DDoS attacks.

"However, the hackers didn't have to deal with the edge firewalls. They infiltrated the servers from within," Professor Clark said. "I'm fairly sure the bots were cloaked as a trojan horse embedded into the server operating system. I'm quite impressed by the cloaking design. I'll show you. Each bot has a unique binary signature, which means I can easily identify them, but that's where the problem began for Verizon's security experts. They couldn't unpack the binaries—the source code was obfuscated, as was their peer-to-peer intra-bot communication. They've encrypted the bots using an algorithm I've yet to encounter in all my years."

He walked back to his desk and sat. "It's sophisticated stuff."

"Help me understand—exception patterns, file sizes, and extensions. Anything relevant," Paul said, examining the integration of the various system components on the whiteboard.

Professor Clark stood again and joined Paul. He pointed to the list of file names and locations written in the corner of the whiteboard. "These indicate the encryption technique is atypical. It's dynamic and controlled by some type of deep learning intelligence. It mutates, changing the filenames and extensions with each defensive interaction within the host server operating system, rendering it undecipherable. Every time I think I've cracked the encryption, the private key changes, and I'm forced to start all over again."

"I've heard about the dynamic key algorithms developed by the Chinese and North Koreans, but I have yet to see the technology deployed in the wild," Paul said.

"Well, they have it. It's now about to control the internet network. I suspect the Chinese are behind it. Likely a hardware implant targeting high-value corporate and government network access, similar to the **Supermicro hardware chip infiltration that hit Amazon and Apple**," Professor Clark said. "We know China's been targeting our telecom network for years, so it's safe to assume the networking hardware and software purchased by Verizon and AT&T is the source of the hack. My theory is that China hacked the networking gear and embedded code into the ISP's core network. Also, this explains why it's been difficult to identify the bot-herder. I don't think there is one because the botnets are acting as if they are self-aware."

"But there has to be a master bot-herder instructing them

unless the bots were programmed for this mission over a decade ago," Paul said.

"I believe their objective is to corrupt the ISPs' **BGP routing tables**. And as you know, if they accomplish that on a wide scale, then routing of all internet traffic will be disrupted until the routing tables can be rebuilt, which could take weeks," Professor Clark said.

"Wait, if AT&T and Verizon's core network servers were infiltrated, that would mean it's highly likely that any ISP utilizing that same hardware and operating system is also infected," Paul said, pacing back and forth.

"Exactly. If someone breached the primary BGP servers, the entire internet has been compromised."

"But how can that be?" Emma asked. "If it were true, the original BGP and routing software developed over decades ago had this malicious branch of code, hundreds of thousands of routers—no, more like millions—would be infected."

"Yes, I'm afraid so, Emma," Professor Clark said. "What makes the problem more interesting is that whoever created these bots has also figured out the attribution dilemma. Most viruses can be traced to the original author using various proven techniques because we know hackers love to sign their work to build their brand. They always leave behind a calling card. It's usually subtle, but you can find it if you know what you're looking for. I can't find it in this case, and the NSA can neither identify the nation of origin nor the author." He turned to Paul. "But now that you're here, maybe you can."

"The NSA has shared this information?" Paul inquired.

There was a long pause as the professor thought about his answer. "I'm sorry. I'm not thinking clearly. I know I shouldn't have disclosed classified sources, even to my close friends," he said.

Paul understood the magnitude of this breach. It was probably the most severe in U.S. history. And it wasn't a simple case of theft of trade secrets. This attack aimed to inflict lasting damage on the infrastructure that powered the nation's internet.

"The result will be a complete internet shutdown. Fixing it would mean propagating updates to thousands of BGP servers across the country and likely the world."

"Wait," Emma said. "How can that be, Professor? Your original internet routing design anticipated routing failures. We always knew the BGP routing was a weak link, but it would auto-correct because of the massive redundancy built into the network."

"That's correct," Professor Clark said.

"You've said countless times there's no 'core' for attackers to exploit, making the internet inherently survivable," Emma said. "Sure, someone could take down a specific facility, campus, or region, but not the entire internet."

Paul thought it through, analyzing the spaghetti diagram as Emma continued to pepper the professor with questions.

"DARPA commissioned Project Lightsaber with the express purpose of developing exactly what I've described—to shut down the internet—a **kill switch**. Over a dozen technology companies and several universities responded with proposals to DARPA to build the kill switch. Two companies were selected, but DARPA canceled the program due to lack of congressional support," Paul said.

"Yes, but the program was secretly approved," Professor Clark said. "DARPA never authorized the disclosure of the program because of the political ramifications. A kill switch would allow the U.S. government to shut down all internet sites and communications without checks or balances. Think of it as a new nuclear option—a 'red button' sitting on the President's desk. And considering who is currently in the White House, I wouldn't trust him—or any one person, for that matter—with that kind of power," he said and grimaced. "You know how I feel about that guy."

Emma nodded. "You've made it explicitly clear numerous times."

The professor swiveled his chair around and returned his attention to the four monitors. "Whoever developed this strain of botnets used DARPA's kill switch design. I'm positive. Someone who had access to Project Lightsaber. Pull up a chair. Look at this.

"When I compared the encryption signatures of that attack and these botnets, they're the same. It appears to be something they planned for years, maybe longer. See, right here," Professor Clark said. His fingers went to work, and with a few command-line instructions, a listing of binary files and the attribute parameters appeared. He split the screen. "The one on the right is a sample of the BGP botnet binaries extracted from Verizon's compromised servers, and this one is from the Baltimore Power Company's Operational Control system. Both have identical signatures," he said.

"So, the power outage and the internet BGP virus are linked," Emma said.

Professor Clark grimaced. "Right again."

Emma walked away to study the diagram on the whiteboard.

Paul could see that the professor hadn't slept in days. He was scared—not of the ramifications of a nationwide internet outage, though. It was something else. He was holding back. Paul could read people, and something wasn't right. Why hadn't the professor included other MIT networking experts? He hadn't mentioned AT&T or Verizon's security teams. Why not?

If the professor was right, the impact would be catastrophic: from financial institutions to water treatment plants, hospitals, police, fire departments, cell phones, credit card machines, GPS, and heart monitoring devices—everything. Society had become entirely dependent on the internet.

Emma stared at the diagram, walking back and forth. "I've

got an idea," she said. "What if we bring one of our new neural network service nodes online and introduce it into the live network? We can redirect traffic to our new internet routing gateway."

"It's possible," Professor Clark said. "But we need to figure out how to repopulate the BGP servers. There's more work to do. You can help me with that."

"I need a computer so I can figure out who's behind this," Paul said.

"Is that necessary? You can help us configure the new network?"

Paul pulled his Colt from his go-bag and placed it on the table with a resounding thud.

Professor Clark, startled, instinctively took a hesitant step backward, his eyes locked on the weapon.

"Professor, there're men right outside the building—bad guys. I need to figure this out before it's too late. I'm close, and this is the information I needed."

BEAR MOUNTAIN

JUNE 12, 1781
HANOVER, NEW JERSEY COLONY

Jack inhaled, savoring the scent of spring evergreen pollen mingled with the crisp, cool air of the northern forest. He gently pulled back on the reins, slowing Celer's spirited gallop to a steady pace as they traveled northward along the well-trodden, moonlit path of the Piscataway Trail. Like an honor guard escorting a revered general into battle, Jack rode flanked by Ben and Julius, with Colonel Boone leading the way and the Overmountain men forming a protective rear guard.

Before departing Trenton, the colonel and Jack charted the route northwest through the foothills of the New Jersey colony and into the thickets of enemy territory. Their destination, Fort Clinton, lay near the town of West Point, located on a sharp elbow bend of the mighty Hudson River.

Jack and his companions were keenly familiar with the notable Fort at West Point. Less than a year ago, General Washington himself had foiled Arnold's unspeakable betrayal and evil plot to concede West Point to the British. However, the despicable Arnold managed to escape downriver to an enemy vessel, the *HMS Vulture*. Jack harbored hope that one day, he would confront the traitor and be given the honor of fitting a noose around Arnold's treacherous neck.

The boom of cannon fire echoed far to the east. Jack recognized the familiar man-made thunder as twelve- or sixteen-pounders. The slow, rhythmic blasts were spaced roughly three or four minutes apart. The Continentals were likely probing the British perimeter defenses of New York, merely pestering the enemy occupiers.

The British commander Sir Henry Clinton held the town of New York, its port, and the surrounding countryside; however, according to Colonel Boone, General Washington was secretly preparing to push the redcoats back into the sea, and recently, the prospect of executing such a bold move had heightened. Several weeks prior, the French fleet made landfall along the shores of Rhode Island. Onboard were more than three thousand highly trained and heavily armed troops, prepared to unite with General Washington's forces for the impending offensive.

An Overmountain man galloped fast toward Jack and Colonel Boone, pulling up hard on the reins and coming to an abrupt halt. "Sir, I've spotted redcoat picket guards positioned two miles ahead. Three or four soldiers and a six-pounder."

"Fine work," Boone said. "Men, we shall drift westward. Keep a sharp eye. The enemy is near."

After Jack gave a brief nod, Boone abruptly raised his hand, signaling to hold in silence. He pivoted, eyes sweeping the dim forest path. Known as a legendary tracker, Boone had bonded with the forest, sensing what others could not.

Tremors rose through the hard-cured leather of Jack's saddle. Three, maybe four horses approached. Jack raised his rifle to sight the oncoming riders, then glanced at Julius with a silent command. Julius dismounted, slung his reins over a branch, and moved alongside a thick white pine. He leveled his rifle down the forward path, using the tree as a shield and brace to steady his aim.

Jack signaled to Ben, who drew his tomahawk axe, gripping it tightly in his powerful woodsman hands.

A voice called down the trail. "Watchword: Freedom!"

Jack closed his left eye, focusing, and aimed down the narrow trail. The last remnants of the night's rain fell on the barrel of his rifle.

Colonel Boone said in reply, "Countersign: Liberty!"

A rider emerged from the trail's darkness into the moon's

gray light wearing a dark uniform—Continental issue. Jack sighted his rifle on the second silver button of the soldier's coat—the British had been known to use confiscated Continental uniforms.

With one hand raised, the other gripping the reins, the rider approached on a stout dusty-brown mare. Three finely uniformed soldiers followed close behind, maintaining a disciplined formation.

"Stand down, men." Boone dismounted and, with his horse in tow, walked toward the Continental soldier.

Jack took a deep breath to slow his heart and lowered his rifle. Julius remounted and joined Jack and Ben.

The lead continental soldier straightened his back and saluted. "Colonel Boone. It's an honor, sir. Your reputation precedes you. Lieutenant Gresham, of General Knox's Guardsmen unit, at your service."

Boone returned the salute. "A pleasure to meet you, Lieutenant. We welcome the grace of His Excellency's men on this fine day."

Gresham turned to the four men on horseback spaced evenly behind him. Each had a straight back, broad shoulders, and eyes trained forward, all the marks of seasoned, well-trained soldiers.

"My men are the Highlands' finest. Brave riders from the Third Light Dragoons, hand-picked to ensure your party's safe passage to Fort Clinton," Gresham said.

Jack admired the soldiers' impeccable woolen uniforms and gleaming black leather riding boots, polished to a silvered mirror-like finish.

"Sir, General Knox has ordered me to escort you northward on the final leg of your journey. It's a half-day ride, but we must take the less-trodden western path to avoid redcoat scouts and raiding parties. However, before we proceed, there's a matter we must discuss," Gresham said. "My orders are to inspect the courier's package upon contact. I've been told a Virginian named Jouett is in your party."

Jack moved his hand to the satchel secured tight across his chest. Gresham spotted Jack's movement and with a gentle nudge with his boot, prompted his horse to advance. The mare, responsive to its master's touch, moved steadily toward Jack and Celer.

Jack applied firm pressure with his legs and pulled down gently on the reins. Celer responded, backing up.

"With all due respect, sir," Jack said. "Governor Jefferson's orders were clear and direct—to deliver this satchel to General Knox and no other."

Ben moved forward, holding his axe with two hands, and Julius raised his long rifle.

The Continental guards reached for their rifles as their horses let out forceful snorts and began scraping the ground with their front hooves.

"Steady, men!" Boone pulled his reins. His horse responded with obedience, moving gracefully to the left, blocking Gresham's forward progress. "Lieutenant. I vouch for Captain Jouett, his integrity, and the authenticity of his orders."

Gresham held his horse steady and stared intently at Jack, then at Ben and Julius. "Very well, Colonel. Your word is as good as gold in these parts."

Julius lowered his rifle, and Ben sheathed his axe. The Continental guards relaxed their stance.

"We shall ride toward Bear Mountain, then follow the Hudson River to Fort Clinton at West Point," Gresham said as he wheeled his horse around, leading the way. The trail ahead was illuminated in the soft glow of dawn. His men followed, each horse maintaining a disciplined interval of one length.

"Let's not delay, men," Colonel Boone urged, steering his horse to follow Gresham's men. "By nightfall, we will enjoy a hot meal and barrel of the Army's finest whiskey."

"Hopefully not venison and beans," Julius muttered to Jack. Jack, though famished, was eager to finally meet the renowned master artilleryman, General Henry Knox.

ERROR 404

22 FEBRUARY, 1400 HRS
MIT STATA TECHNOLOGY CENTER — CAMBRIDGE, MASSACHUSETTS

Paul settled into Emma's desk chair, scanning the neighboring cubicles, each warmly decorated with personal touches and photos of friends and family. In stark contrast, Emma's cubical was bare, devoid of any photos. To the left of her computer, two neat stacks of paper sat perfectly aligned. On the right side, a single pink mechanical pencil rested in a matching cylindrical cup, the only hint of color in her otherwise drab setup.

His attention was immediately drawn to Emma's screensaver and an image of her and Sara radiating beauty and happiness. He had taken that picture on a brilliant summer day by the lake. Emma was around fourteen—still his little girl. Sara's eyes sparkled. That was the year before her diagnosis and the last summer they shared together.

Paul couldn't afford to slip back into that solemn, dark place. Emma needed him in the here and now.

His fingers swept across the smooth matte surface of the laptop's trackpad. The touch of cold, machined aluminum brought his attention back to the task at hand. He launched an encrypted Tor browser and quickly scanned news sites, searching for clues linking the attacks to the men pursuing him. The President had issued an executive order to fast-track military recruitment, federalize the National Guard, and call up reserves to active duty. There were reports that he had initiated discussions with congressional leaders to authorize a draft, something not seen since 1973 when the Selective Service System legislation was last passed. Social media was exploding with reactions, devolving into outright threats against the President and members of Congress. Paul leaned back in his chair, astonished by the speed at which the situation was escalating.

Reportedly, for the **first time in U.S. history, three carrier strike groups** had been deployed to the Persian Gulf—a Nimitz class carrier, the *U.S.S. Ronald Reagan*, and two Ford-class: the *U.S.S. John F. Kennedy* and the newest and most powerful ship in the Navy's arsenal, the *U.S.S. Enterprise*. All three warships had begun launching fighter jet sorties against military targets in Iran, Egypt, Syria, Iraq and Yemen as part of a coordinated international coalition military action.

The Saudi oil refineries were offline following coordinated attacks from Iranian mid-range missiles and **Houthi** fighters storming the southern border. Syrian and Iranian anti-aircraft defenses had downed a U.S. F-22 Raptor and two Apache AH-64 helicopters.

Paul scanned the list of U.S. pilots—those killed and those presumed missing, likely captured, and being tortured by Hezbollah or the IRGC.

Inhaling deeply, he tried to steady himself against the imminent possibility of a third world war.

News agencies and pundits blamed the Russians for the power grid outage, citing their propensity for energy-related cyberattacks, specifically the gas pipeline breach, the New York Power Authority's Hydroelectric Power Station breach, and the California Solar Farm breach.

The Russians could likely be directing the botnet attack on the U.S. infrastructure; however, Russian state-sponsored hackers were typically more focused on politically motivated targets, and the oligarchs' underground cyber units in the Baltics and South America specialized in ransomware exploitation and copyright exfiltration, all with monetary gain as the goal, not military objectives.

While the evidence seemed to implicate Russia or Iran

as the likely culprits behind the cyberattacks on U.S. power companies, Paul's instincts raised red flags. Such overt aggression reeked of misdirection, a smokescreen to divert attention from the true perpetrators. He had no doubt the NSA analysts were already pursuing that conspicuous trail, but his gut warned him that the obvious was a carefully constructed ruse, concealing a far more insidious threat.

Paul continued his forensics analysis by cross-referencing profiles of notorious Russian hackers against known breach attack vectors. His instincts gnawed at him, warning that time was running out. Throughout his career, his ability to outmaneuver hacker adversaries had proven his best breach deterrent, always staying one step ahead of the cyber attacker.

Paul had modeled his technique after U.S. Air Force Colonel John Boyd's OODA Loop concept, which described a four-stage rapid decision cycle for military combat operations: Observe, Orient, Decide, and Act. Applying Boyd's theories to cyber defense, Paul's algorithms were designed to outpace opponents in the relentless cycle, the premise being that the combatant who could process information the fastest would ultimately prevail.

However, Paul was out of time. Once a hacker initiates an attack, they could obliterate their target within hours, rendering defensive systems or recovery efforts futile. He needed more intelligence before the window of opportunity slammed shut.

He continued to scan the newsfeeds, selectively speed-reading articles for clues.

Al Jazeera had reported that Iran had weathered twenty-four hours of U.S. bombing raids, and airfields, military bases, and government complexes had been rendered inoperable. However, the journalist defiantly reported that Tehran's IRGC's mobile Shahab missile attacks on both Saudis and Israelis had an equally devastating effect, killing thousands. The commander of the IRGC was quoted in the article, "Despite the western invaders' attempts to destroy us, our missiles remain fully operational and can launch at any place and any time, with precision and force."

Iran had launched attacks on Israel from newly constructed underground launch facilities in **Yemen**, Syria, and Sudan. Hezbollah simultaneously had launched a ground offensive that was raging on the northern Israel border.

Egypt had amassed troops on the southern Israeli border. The article had included satellite images of a hundred of Egypt's newly commissioned Russian-made T90 battle tanks, interspersed with M1 Abrams.

Al Jazeera quoted the Israeli Prime Minister, "Abraham was with his men and women bravely fighting to protect the Holy Land, and his government would prosecute the enemy to the extent the world had yet to witness in the history of humankind."

Paul scanned another article that detailed the alliances, specifically that the Egyptian Brotherhood had coalesced its military power with remnants of Hezbollah, Al-Qaeda, ISIS, and the Taliban, then aligned with Iran's Shia militia groups and their broader network, including Houthi rebels and Hamas, to form a coalition to battle the Israelis and their western allies.

The power had been out for thirteen hours, triggering widespread looting and destruction. Paul checked his social media feeds and read the President's latest tweet:

"I've authorized a nationwide curfew beginning at 8 am ET. I'm deploying the military to all major U.S. metropolitan cities. Federal highways are now closed for troop and tank deployments. RULE OF LAW WILL PREVAIL!"

The United States was now under Martial Law for the first time since the Japanese attack on Pearl Harbor. CNN and MSNBC were having a field day criticizing the President for his unscripted remarks and discriminatory executive orders.

In New York and D.C., violent clashes had broken out

between the militant units of the right-wing **Oath Keepers** and **Three Percenters** and the left-wing **Antifa** and BDS groups.

Paul had noticed in the video footage of the riots, particularly in D.C., that all groups, regardless of political affiliation, focused their attacks on municipal, state, and federal buildings, taking the opportunity to exploit the power outage and the absence of video surveillance. They were in the process of dismantling, defacing, and destroying all symbols of the U.S. government.

Paul watched live news reports describing the fires that were ravishing businesses and how the local police and fire response had been inadequate in quelling the riots. In response, the governors had begun deploying the National Guard.

The enemy's strategy was clear: to distract the U.S. military by engaging in yet another Middle Eastern war while destabilizing the government with widespread domestic civil unrest.

America was under attack, the likes of which had not been seen since the horrific events of 9/11. However, unlike that tragic day that united a nation, the objective of this new enemy was to tear apart the very fabric that bound a country together. The U.S. government was battling foreign adversaries abroad and terrorists within its borders but also, more ominously, finding itself in a battle against its own people.

Paul clicked on another link. The browser froze. He waited. The browser displayed:

404: Server Not Responding

He pounded the desk, knocking Emma's pink pencil holder to the ground.

Paul entered the commands to flush the cached DNS. That didn't work, and he knew it wouldn't. The next thing to do was to reset the local router, but he knew that would be pointless.

"Dad, we're too late," Emma's somber voice echoed in the silence.

Paul swiveled his chair and picked up her pencil holder.

"The lab's network won't connect, and my cell phone won't connect either. The internet and cellular networks are down," Emma said.

Paul considered the staggering ramifications and chilling realization that millions of homes and businesses nationwide were without internet access.

Chaos. Panic.

While people could begrudgingly endure without their cell phones, Netflix, and mindless social media scrolling, the internet had become society's central nervous system upon which vital functions depended.

Commerce, essential health services, transportation, food production—society's most essential functions were now offline. Lives hung in the balance. Visions of crippled hospitals, water pumping stations grinding to a halt, dams teetering on systemwide failures, and air traffic control blinded.

His mind raced until it pinpointed the most probable target—the U.S. military apparatus. All branches and operational assets relied on the internet for guidance systems, communication, logistics, and security. There were backup systems and manual contingency plans; however, without the internet, the most powerful military in the world would be vulnerable to an unrelenting offensive attack.

Emma waved her hand in front of Paul's face. "Dad, are you still here? We have to do something, and I have an idea." Her voice strained with urgency. "The only way to access a website now is by entering the specific IP address of the server. I've tested it. That tells me that domain name resolution has been disabled. The problem is nobody knows the IP address for websites and apps because they all rely on BGP routing. I'm getting ahead of myself..."

Paul stood up, realizing his daughter was onto something.

"You're right, so let's go find Professor Clark. If anyone knows what happened and how to fix it, it's him. But my gut tells me he's somehow involved in all this."

"That's just it, Dad," Emma said, a quiver of fear in her voice. "I can't find the professor anywhere."

FBI

22 FEBRUARY, 1415 HRS
MIT STATA TECHNOLOGY CENTER – CAMBRIDGE, MASSACHUSETTS

Emma's smile, usually bright and confident, faded into unease and worry. "He's not here, Dad," she said. "I've looked everywhere. It's not like Professor Clark to leave his computer like that, still logged in. This...this isn't normal. Something's wrong."

She had her mother's uncanny intuition, which meant one of two things: the professor was in some kind of danger—or they were.

Paul reached out and took her hand. "Let's go find him," he said. A sudden flash caught his attention, followed closely by another and another. Bright bursts of light streamed through the glass window, throwing shadows into the professor's dimly lit office.

"What's going on out there?" Emma asked, turning to the window, which lit up again.

Light flashed below as a car in the intersection detonated in a violent blast, sending a thick plume of smoke into the sky. Panic ensued; people scattered in every direction.

Paul tightened his fists. Without power and access to the internet, anarchy had taken hold.

Along the Charles River, towering columns of black smoke rose from homes and buildings along its northern shore. Entire blocks of retail and warehouse buildings were ablaze as emergency vehicles' red, blue, and white lights darted through the early evening darkness.

Boston, the city Paul loved, was burning.

He'd had enough. He'd been on the run for forty-eight

hours, chased by men likely involved with the attacks. He had to act.

But to do so, he needed help.

Paul reached into his carry bag and pulled out the phone Lia had given him.

"Damn!" No signal.

"Miss Knox," someone called out from down the hall.

Paul and Emma turned as a security guard and a tall stranger approached. His long raincoat swung open with each stride, revealing a holstered firearm and a gold-plated badge. He walked with a pronounced limp, but the determination etched on his face commanded attention.

"This man is with the FBI. He insisted I find you," the security guard said. "If it's okay with you, I'll leave him with you. The internet's down, and I need to help Big Will cover the entrance."

"Thank you," Emma said.

"Are you Emma Knox?" the man asked, glancing at Paul.

"Yes," she said.

"My name's Agent Mike Johnson." He pulled his wallet from his jacket and held up his ID with his FBI credentials. With a barrel chest and massive hands, the man's bald head glistened in the overhead lighting. He wore a tweed sport coat under his raincoat and a crisp blue dress shirt, notably without a tie. His shoes, polished to a mirror-like shine, were unmistakably those of a police officer, likely ex-military—a Marine if Paul had to bet.

"I don't have much time and need to ask you a few questions," Agent Johnson said.

"What's this about?" Paul asked.

"And you are?"

"I'm her father," Paul said.

"I'm looking for this man." He handed Paul a piece of paper with a grainy black-and-white photo. "We think he's nearby."

Emma took the photo, looked it over, and handed it to Paul.

Paul could sense the FBI agent sizing him up while he studied the picture.

If Agent Johnson knew this man, Paul wanted to learn more. But he also remembered Lia and Cap's final instructions:

Trust no one.

"No, she doesn't recognize him. Who is he?" Paul said.

Agent Johnson ignored Paul. "Are you sure, ma'am? Please take a close look."

Emma took the photo and shook her head.

It was a still image taken from video footage from a distance, magnified to the extent that it became pixelated on the cheap office paper. The man wore a dark jacket and sunglasses, his black hair cropped short.

"Don't recognize him," Emma said.

Agent Johnson shifted his weight and looked down at the ground, clearly frustrated. "Are you sure?" he asked.

"Who is he?" Paul asked, probing for more information.

"He's a prime suspect in the Thanksgiving Day bombing. We've reason to believe he's in the area."

"Sir," Emma jumped in. "Why do you think it has something to do with us?"

Agent Johnson took a step closer. The deep wrinkles on his forehead stretched as his tone turned serious. "Okay, let's drop the formalities. I'm tired and don't have time for this. You two aren't being frank with me." He took another step toward Paul and motioned to Emma. "I know she's somehow involved, and the FBI has evidence the bad guys were in communication with this lab facility."

Paul looked at Emma.

She shook her head and shrugged. "It wasn't me," Emma said.

The agent pointed to the man in the picture. "This mutt escaped an FBI raid in Dearborn, Michigan, yesterday, and we have satellite imagery of the suspect's vehicle here in Cambridge."

"They must be trying to get access to our new network," Emma said.

"Emma!" Paul said. She had always been a trusting soul, but Paul, too, sensed that this guy was legit.

"Why?" Johnson said.

"It's likely related to the internet outage," Emma said. She turned to Paul. "Dad, I trust him. I don't know why, but I do. And right now, we need his help."

Agent Johnson again pointed to the picture. "This guy's bad news. He'll be heavily armed when he shows up here."

"He already has," Paul said.

THE HIGHLANDS

JUNE 12, 1781
WEST POINT, NEW YORK COLONY

Resting silently in the saddle and flanked by Ben and Julius, Jack took in the breathtaking panorama unfurling below. High atop a sheer cliff, they had an unobstructed view of the mighty Hudson River, with the New England forest stretching eastward like a sprawling emerald blanket. The early morning air, cold and damp, swept in around them, carrying a rich scent of sea salt and pine.

The commanding vantage point offered a clear perspective on General Washington's strategic brilliance. Washington had established his main garrison in the Highlands, perched on the cliffs overlooking the Hudson's sharp elbow bend and framed by rugged bluffs and fortified redoubts. This natural fortress formed a formidable chokepoint, a defensive gauntlet that would thwart any British naval advance and secure vital supply lines that linked the northern and southern colonies.

On the horizon, storm clouds gathered like a dark ocean wave surging toward the men.

"A Nor'easter's headed this way," Boone said.

"We should move to shelter. General McDougal, the Fort's commander, ordered I accompany you and the package to Moore's House, situated on the northern perimeter of the encampment," Lieutenant Gresham said.

Ben pointed toward the base of the jagged rocks on the Hudson's edge. "What are those men doing?"

"That's a security detail on the lookout for raiding parties. They're inspecting the Great Chain, which crosses the river and is moored over there..." Gresham pointed. "...on

Constitution Island. The Chain and our guns prevent enemy ships from daring to venture upriver. Ever since the betrayal by Arnold, there have been reports of the British plan to dislodge the Chain and attack the Point. But I say let them try! Our commander will never permit it. They would pay dearly." His voice echoed with unwavering conviction.

Jack marveled at the colossal iron chain links. He had never seen anything of the sort. Each link was as large as a feed barrel and thick as a man's thigh.

"The storm will soon be upon us," Gresham said, turning to his men. "Take them to Sherburne's Redoubt. Ensure their horses are watered and fed and shelter these men in the officer's barracks."

"The commander has permitted the dispensing of ale to accompany your meal," Gresham said.

Ben and Julius grinned. Weary, they had been in the saddle since sundown the previous day.

"We'll continue down the trail and meet Commander McDougal and General Knox," Gresham said.

"My thanks, Lieutenant," Jack said.

◆ ◆ ◆

General Knox lifted his large pewter mug high, his hand wrapped in a crimson silk handkerchief.

"As my honorable friend Dr. Franklin said, 'Beer is living proof that God loves us and wants us to be happy,'" General Henry Knox said to Jack, Boone, and the other Continental commanders sitting around the old pitted and stained oak table.

"Kindly pass that bowl of potatoes and fill these fine men's cups with ale," Knox said.

Jack attempted to refrain from staring. The general's brilliant blue and yellow Continental officer's jacket decorated with red facings, was adorned with a gold lace epaulet on his right shoulder, signifying his rank as Brigadier General. Jack had never seen such a fine uniform nor been in the presence of a man with a reputation as exalted as his.

A stout, portly man, Knox was regarded as General Washington's most trusted and loyal commander. He appeared to be in his middle years with graying white, bristly hair, a boyish oval face, and rosy cheeks that appeared painted on his chalk-colored skin.

Knox took another gigantic gulp of his beer and reached for the plate of rare venison. Respectfully, Jack wondered whether the buttons would hold under the strain of his girth. The general clearly enjoyed and likely never missed a meal. It was a wonder that Knox had maintained his robust stature despite living for years through the harshest of New England winters on the slightest of army rations.

When dinner had ended, the general stood, buttoned his coat, and offered a toast. "We shall drink to His Excellency's health—all under his command would get drunk with pleasure to serve and protect him in perpetuity."

"Here, here. Here, here," the men chanted in reply.

"Thank you, men. Fill your bellies. You've traveled a far distance, risking life and limb. Your commitment to our honorable cause is profoundly appreciated," Knox said. "Mr. Jouett, kindly follow me, and of course, bring the satchel you so courageously guarded on your journey. The time has come for us to get down to the day's business."

The general led Jack through a narrow doorway into the sitting room adjacent to the dining parlor. The rich, smoky scent of tallow wax and charred firewood filled the modest parlor. A brilliantly cut glass bottle, filled to the neck with an amber spirit, flanked by two short-stemmed sipping glasses, rested in the center of the thick pot-marked oak table.

The general motioned to a chair. "Please sit."

Jack removed the satchel from across his chest and placed it on the table.

The general paced in front of the crackling fireplace, staring at the bright yellow flames and orange embers that glowed at its base. "It's extraordinary to imagine that it was less than a year ago," he said. "In this very same room, General Washington, by the hand of God, decided the fate of the captured British spy, Major John Andre. To end his life by the rope. His Excellency said that day, 'Traitors are the lowest form, concealing their motives in a cloak of lies, as do snakes that slither on their bellies in the mud.' General Washington believed Andre and his coconspirator, Benedict Arnold, should pay the ultimate price for their crimes. Unfortunately, as you know, Arnold escaped across the Hudson to an awaiting British vessel that day. But Andre, unfortunately, did not."

Turning and reaching across the table with his thick, meaty hand, the general handed Jack a short glass filled to the brim with whiskey. "Gratitude for your service. Let us drink this fine rye in honor of those who have fallen. Cheers."

"Sir, I pray Arnold's dark day will come soon," Jack said. "I've lost many friends at the hands of that traitor's men. I will never forget."

The general stood, walked behind Jack, and placed his colossal hands on Jack's shoulders, close to his neck. Jack attempted to turn, but the general held him firmly in place.

"Son, have you been forthright with me?" The general's tone transformed from spirited to terse. "Are you a spy sent by the British to kill me? You must be honest. I have ways of learning the truth."

It was difficult for Jack to remain calm. His heart began to race. He tried again to stand but was held firm in place.

After journeying hundreds of miles, braving enemy lines, enduring relentless rains, and crossing treacherous rivers, he had faithfully delivered Governor Jefferson's package. And now the general dare question his loyalty?

The door burst open, crashing against the wall. Gale winds from the storm blew in rain and scattered leaves across the floor. In the doorway stood a tall, slender man. His long, dark coat flapped, and his hat sat low, casting a shadow on his face. With a long-armed reach, he shut the door, walked to the fireplace, and leaned his distinctive rifle against the wall. Jack's eyes focused on the weapon—a Ferguson, a signature British sniper rifle.

Anger swelled as Jack resisted the urge to pull his knife.

The stranger turned and placed a revolver on the table near the satchel.

THE PATRIOT

JUNE 13, 1781
WEST POINT, NEW YORK COLONY

General Knox loosened his hold on Jack's shoulders and joined the tall stranger beside the smoldering fireplace. The general prodded the charred logs with an iron poker, sending flames and cinders spiraling into the air. The two men exchanged whispers, frequently glancing toward Jack.

"Outstanding to see you, Mr. Pebbley. Take off that coat and have a seat. There is someone I'd like you to meet," General Knox said in a curious tone. "Jack, this is Mr. Pebbley. Mr. Pebbley, this is Captain Jack Jouett."

The stranger didn't respond. He remained motionless, staring at Jack from under his low-brimmed hat. His eyes were shrouded in shadows.

Jack stood from his chair, readying himself for a fight. He sensed the interview with the general had transitioned into an inquisition.

"Jack, I employ Mr. Pebbley to perform special tasks. He has unique skills. Traitors are slithering among us, which is why I've asked him to join us. He's trained in the art of spy-craft and counter-deception, including rooting out those who would threaten His Excellency."

"Sir." Jack stood, clenching his fists. "Are you suggesting I am a spy?"

"I'm not suggesting anything of the sort other than to note that spies are lurking. I'll leave the suggesting to Mr. Pebbley."

Pebbley took a step toward Jack, revealing deep-set eyes, shadowed and recessed into his weathered face. A thin, jagged purple scar stretched from the corner of his mouth to his ear, stark against his milky complexion.

"Sir, this so-called militia captain is not who he claims," Pebbley said in a raspy voice. He leaned over the table with an aggressive posture, staring at Jack with a devilish smile.

"You are wrong! I have stood firm for the cause, faced down redcoats, and bled for this land! How dare you question my honor? My conscience is clear, and my resolve will not be shaken," Jack said, pushing away from the table and readying himself.

"Sit down," Knox said. "Now!"

Jack hesitated, took a breath, and sat. His heart pounded in his throat.

"Please explain, Mr. Pebbley."

"The British arrested this man's father two years ago."

"And he died on a prison ship at the hands of those ruthless bastards," Jack said, the anger welling again in his heart.

"Your father was not taken to a prison ship. He sailed off to England and joined the British intelligence service. You know that is true. Do not play coy with us."

Jack did not believe a word the hideous stranger was spewing. His father had died on a prison ship.

"And you, his offspring, are a traitor. Is that not true?"

In a blur of motion reminiscent of a snake striking a field mouse, Jack unsheathed his blade, poised to plunge it into the throat of the stranger. Fury surged within him and raced through his veins.

"No! That's a lie," Jack said, his voice carrying loudly through the room. "Present your evidence or be prepared to die."

Pebbley's eyes widened, and he stepped back.

Jack suddenly realized that the stranger, Pebbley, undoubtedly was the sharpshooter who had ambushed him and shot Chief Black Hoof in Trenton.

"It was you!" Jack said, leveling the point of his blade at Pebbley's throat. "You're the coward who sought to take my life in Trenton."

As Pebbley's hand reached for his pistol on the table, Jack thrust his blade deep into the oak, landing precisely between Pebbley's index finger and thumb. Startled, Pebbley pulled back his hand and turned toward his rifle.

"I wouldn't if I were you," came a familiar voice, steady and calm, from the parlor doorway. Ben held his tomahawk axe just over his head, poised to dismember the stranger if he made a wrong move.

Suddenly, a deafening blast rang out, spraying dust and wood splinters throughout the room. Jack shook his head to attempt to stop the stream of noise in his ears.

General Knox held his flintlock pistol pointed at the ceiling, smoke rising from its brass barrel. "Lower your weapons! Now! Summon the guards. And take these men to confinement."

Jack inhaled, then reached into his jacket pocket and removed Jefferson's coin. With a swift motion, he slammed it on the table, revealing the golden silhouette of King George III.

"General Knox, this coin was given to me by Governor Jefferson. He assured me it would serve as proof of my loyalty to the cause and in situations when my patriotism is in question. This appears to be one of those moments," Jack said.

"This means nothing," Pebbley barked and turned to the general.

The general paused and smiled. He reached into a small vest pocket, held the contents for a moment, and slapped his thick palm down on the table. Then, he lifted his hand slowly and stared at Jack and Pebbley.

The candlelight flickered in the reflection of the identical gold pieces.

The general picked up Jefferson's coin and tossed it into the air.

General Knox spoke with a reflective tone, "This coin was a gift from General Washington himself, a fine gold guinea I carried from Fort Ticonderoga in '75. It symbolizes the sacrifices made and the spirit of our fledgling nation. Possession of this coin is a testament to honor and patriotism." He then gently picked up Jefferson's coin, flipping it into the air with a flick of his thumb.

Jack caught it and tucked it safely into his jacket pocket. He stared down Pebbley, who promptly conceded and turned toward the fireplace.

"Mr. Pebbley, reveal your evidence of this conspiracy, or I shall dismiss the charge," Knox said.

Pebbley shook his head in submission.

"Very well, men. Sit, pour yourself a glass of rye as we unveil the contents of Mr. Jefferson's package."

The general filled his glass to the brim, downed the contents in a swift gulp, and passed the bottle to Jack.

ECHOES OF DECEPTION

22 FEBRUARY, 1425 HRS
MIT STATA TECHNOLOGY CENTER – CAMBRIDGE, MASSACHUSETTS

From behind, the slapping of flip-flops against the polished floor tiles caught Paul's attention as he turned away from Agent Johnson. Professor Clark looked as though he'd run a marathon—sweat dripped from his forehead, and he gasped for breath. His bold confidence—or what some would call sheer arrogance—had disappeared, replaced by a palpable sense of defeat infused with fear.

"Where were you? We were worried," Emma said.

"I apologize. I had to attend to an urgent matter," Professor Clark said, struggling to breathe.

Agent Johnson interrupted and moved toward the professor. "Sir, I'm FBI Agent Johnson. Have you seen this man?" He held up the grainy photo.

"No," Professor Clark said without even looking at the photo. Paul noticed his hands shaking and his eyes darting as if someone was chasing him.

"Professor, are you okay?" Paul asked.

Bang. Bang. Bang. Bang.

The sudden, staccato burst of gunfire echoed from down the lab's corridor. Paul threw himself over Emma without hesitation, every instinct driving him to protect her. He grabbed her arm, pulling her into the shadow of a support column. From the lab's lower level, rapid automatic rifle fire originated from the direction of the front entrance. The unmistakable deadly cadence of a dozen spent rounds of an AR-15 pierced the silence.

Paul tore open his go-bag, pulled his Colt, checked the load, and released the safety.

Retreating to the opposite side of the hallway, Agent Johnson drew his service pistol.

Four pistol-caliber shots rang out below.

Return fire.

Paul and Agent Johnson simultaneously directed their weapons toward the source of the incoming gunfire—the open stairwell. Paul's instincts urged him to charge forward toward the gunfire, yet he remained poised and steadied his aim. This was no active shooter simulation or an insurgent skirmish; the stakes were unspeakably high—with Emma's life hanging in the balance.

"We're too late! They're here," Professor Clark yelled, spinning around toward his office and stumbling to the ground.

"I'm sorry, Emma. It's all my fault," he cried out as he scrambled on his knees into his office.

"Come on, we have to move," Paul said to Emma, tightening his hold on her arm.

Gunfire erupted from the floor below, and the sharp, acidic scent of spent gunpowder filled the corridor.

"Go! Get her to safety. I'm not letting these guys escape again," Agent Johnson said, motioning for Paul to fall back.

Paul and Emma took cover in Professor Clark's office.

"Professor, we have to get out now!" Paul said.

Professor Clark rummaged through his desk drawer, frantically tossing paper and books on the floor. He found what he was searching for and tossed a USB key fob to Emma, who snatched it out of the air.

"You don't have much time. They'll transfer network control to their overseas command center if they gain access before you do. Don't let that happen."

Paul recognized the desperate look behind the distinctive calmness in the professor's voice.

"Professor, we can make this right," Paul said. "Whatever

you're involved with, we can deal with it."

But Professor Clark turned away. He had made his mind up, reached into the lower desk drawer and pulled out a compact stainless steel, snub-nosed revolver.

Paul raised his weapon, sliding his finger onto the trigger and sighting the professor's chest. "You don't need to do this," he said.

Emma attempted to pull away from Paul's grip on her arm but couldn't stop the inevitable.

Paul pulled her close to shield her eyes.

"No!" she screamed, struggling to pull away. "Let go!"

The professor pushed the revolver's short barrel into the soft tissue under his jaw and cocked the hammer with his thumb.

"Don't!" Emma yelled.

NO TURNING BACK

22 FEBRUARY, 1430 HRS
MIT STATA TECHNOLOGY CENTER – CAMBRIDGE, MASSACHUSETTS

Paul aimed the Professor's exposed forearm and smoothly squeezed the trigger of his Colt. The hammer fell, the shot rang out, and the professor's gun went flying. Collapsing, Professor Clark clutched his wounded arm, blood seeping into the carpet. Emma rushed to his side, her voice trembling with emotion. "Why?" Emma cried. "What were you thinking, professor?"

Paul realized the unfortunate truth. "He must have been involved with these guys. To what extent, I don't know, but whoever is behind this, they got to him," Paul said and stepped toward the elaborate diagram drawn on the professor's whiteboard. He pulled out his phone and compared the photo he'd taken earlier.

"Emma, look at this." Paul pointed to the whiteboard. She turned, but his words didn't seem to resonate—she was likely still processing what she'd witnessed. "Look. Look at this." He pointed at the top left area of the diagram.

Shots rang out on the ground floor but closer, near the stairwell.

The gunfire startled Emma as she quickly turned to the whiteboard and scanned left and right, focusing on the diagram's undisturbed upper section.

"Whatever you found, it'll have to wait," Agent Johnson said, aiming his gun toward the stairwell. "Go. That way. Now!" He pointed toward the service stairwell and elevator. "Take her with you. These guys are my problem. I'll deal with them."

The hallway was dim, the emergency lights at the exits

throwing dark shadows onto the stark white lab walls. The sporadic gunfire was closing in. Likely two, maybe three gunmen.

"Emma, let's go. We'll take the rear elevator to the basement."

"When they come up the stairs, I'll draw their fire," Agent Johnson said.

Gunfire erupted from the lower level. It was a different caliber than the automatic rifle fire. Someone was returning fire. An automatic rifle barked out a series of short blasts. Paul waited. Silence.

Whoever was firing the pistol had lost.

Paul ran into the professor's office, returned, and handed Agent Johnson the professor's revolver. "Six more rounds. Good luck."

Agent Johnson stuck it under his belt, gave Paul a quick nod, and readied his SIG Legion equipped with a pro sight.

Paul and Emma ran in the opposite direction, weaving through the cubicles and into the open hallway. He pressed the service elevator button multiple times.

From Agent Johnson's direction, fiery flashes lit up the corridor, followed immediately by the bark of his SIG auto.

The elevator doors slowly opened.

"Em, time to go."

She reluctantly stepped into the elevator while Paul waited. His life was now on a different path. Most importantly, he wasn't about to abandon a fellow soldier.

He reached inside the elevator and pressed the button.

"Em, go down to the basement, use the rear service exit, and go to Building 91. I'll meet you there."

Their eyes met, hers filled with determination. He took a mental picture as the elevator doors began to close.

"No, Dad!" Emma threw her arm between the doors.

"I'll be fine. Head to the data center and activate the network with the USB the professor gave you. I'll find you." He almost added, "I promise," but he stopped himself. He knew what to do and refused to make a promise he might not keep.

The doors began closing.

"You better show up," she said as tears welled up. "I need you."

It had been ages since he'd heard her say those three words.

"Trust me," he replied, his hand slipping from hers as the elevator doors closed.

Turning to rejoin Agent Johnson, a sudden blast sent tremors through the concrete floor. Filling the air with smoke and the pungent smell of burning plaster.

CROSSFIRE

22 FEBRUARY, 1435 HRS
MIT STATA TECHNOLOGY CENTER – CAMBRIDGE, MASSACHUSETTS

Mack shifted his shooting stance to find a better balance and brace his arm against a concrete support column. Twin infrared gun sight beams flickered through the haze of dust and smoke rising from the open stairwell.

Staring down the barrel of his SIG, Mack aligned the red dot of his fiber optic sight on the anticipated position of the approaching attackers. He drew in a steady breath and waited for a clear shot.

The smoke cleared momentarily, revealing two figures in black balaclavas and matching BDU cargo uniforms. Armed with AR-15s, they cautiously ascended the stairwell. Mack sighted the center mass of the lead gunman, firmed his grip, and began to put even pressure on the trigger. He held his fire for a split instant as protocol required inspection of the target. The men reached the top of the stairs and turned abruptly toward Mack's position, sweeping the area with their AR-15s held close to their faces.

Mack inhaled deeply, ready to unleash a volley into the torso of the lead target, when he noticed the bold yellow letters emblazoned across the chest:

F B I

His finger eased off the trigger, but uncertainty crept in. Why would the agents be wearing balaclavas without protective headgear?

Mack held his position, focusing intently on their next

move. He took a half step, remaining shielded behind the column, preparing to identify himself as a friendly. But before he could speak, the lead gunman unleashed a barrage of gunfire toward Mack's far left flank. The loud, rapid bursts echoed, followed by the hollow crash of pulverized steel, shattering the tense silence.

The second gunman reached the top of the stairwell. He turned and, without hesitation, fired, sending bullets whizzing down the hallway and crashing into glass and drywall, one immediately after another, hurling debris into the air.

"Hold your fire! I'm FBI! Hold your fire!" Mack yelled and raised his badge.

From behind, the roar of large-caliber gunfire rang out. Bullets struck the lead agent squarely in the chest, sending him sprawling to the ground. He rolled to his side, pressing up onto his knees.

"Hey, hold your fire. They're friendlies!" Mack yelled. "Hold your damn fire! I'm FBI!"

The gunmen ignored his warnings and unleashed half a dozen rounds. Mack dove for cover as the bullets slammed into the support column, sending debris into the air. The incessant roar of the automatic weapon fire, combined with the intense smell of gunpowder and plaster dust, brought back the stark memories of the Thanksgiving Day attack.

Several rounds crashed into the wall. He shook his head, trying to clear the high-pitched ring in his ears.

Mack caught a glimpse of the girl's father, Knox. He advanced with the precision of a pro, skillfully returning cover fire. After ejecting the spent magazine, he slammed in a fresh load. He confidently returned fire in the direction of the agent targeting Mack.

Nearby, the agent, stunned by a bullet absorbed by his Kevlar vest, took cover behind a support column.

Mack hit the magazine release, checked his remaining rounds and pulled a fresh magazine from his belt. He slammed it into his weapon and steadied his aim down the corridor.

"Put down your weapons!" Mack yelled.

He waited for a response. Silence. A temporary cease-fire had been reached.

Mack heard the faint voices of the two gunmen talking in what sounded like Arabic. A gunman stepped out and swung his arm in a softball pitch motion.

Mack's trigger finger responded on instinct, unleashing four rounds toward the gunman. He didn't wait to confirm a hit, as his attention focused on the grenade arcing toward him, rotating end over end as if in slow motion.

Out of the corner of his eye, he caught a sudden flash of motion. A forceful impact blindsided him, sending him crashing into an office. Mack's shoulder collided with the doorframe. A sharp pain streaked up his neck.

A powerful explosion rocked the hallway, its force reverberating through Mack's body. The concrete floor shook, and in the aftermath, all went silent, leaving only the gradual return of the escalating, high-pitched ringing.

Mack's eyes burned, blurring his vision as though he were looking through a dense, grainy fog. He lost all sense of time and place.

A pungent acidic odor and a metallic taste overwhelmed his senses.

He rolled over on his back, rubbed his eyes, sat up, and attempted to focus on the figure moving slowly next to him. The man—Knox—used the desk as a prop and rose to his feet.

He offered his hand to Mack. "Get up, big man. We gotta move," he said. "You okay?"

"I think so," Mack said, taking inventory of his body parts.

The conversation abruptly ceased as gunfire erupted from the main stairwell's direction—automatic rifle fire followed by a shotgun blast, followed by another.

Mack flanked the door, prepared to hold his ground until his last bullet.

Another shotgun blast echoed loudly in the open hallway, breaking the momentary silence, and was immediately followed by a short scream, stuttering groans, and fluid-choked gasps. Mack recognized the all too familiar pattern—a dying man.

A female voice called out, "Paul...you good? Hold your fire. Don't shoot me!"

A tall, slender woman appeared through a haze of fine settling debris and smoke, wearing yellow-lensed aviator glasses, dark olive fatigues, field boots, and a waist-length leather jacket. She stood over the attacker's motionless, dead body, resting the barrel of a matte black M27 Marine Combat rifle on her shoulder. A pair of holstered handguns hung from her hips.

"Lia?" Paul called out.

"What other girl do ya know who carries a shotgun for fun?" she said with a smile.

"None," he replied.

The second attacker had disappeared. Mack kept his finger on the trigger of his SIG and scanned the area for potential threats. He shook his head as the adrenaline began to wear off, replaced with shooting pain radiating from his injured shoulder.

"Who are you?" Mack asked, holstering his weapon and dusting off his pants.

"I'm Lia, special unit agent for the President. Welcome to the party. I'm here for the same reason as you and to help this guy." She nodded toward Paul. "What do ya say we go get the one that slithered away?" She motioned down the hallway with the business end of her rifle.

"The President?" Mack said.

"It's a long story. We can fill you in later. Right now, I have to find Emma. Are you okay?" Paul asked.

Mack lifted his arm to make sure his shoulder still functioned. He managed to lift it halfway before the pain became unbearable.

"You okay?" Lia asked.

"Never been better," Mack said, wincing as the pain played havoc on his brain. He checked his SIG, released the partially spent mag, and slipped it into his back pocket. He slapped in a fresh mag and pulled Professor Clark's revolver from under his belt. The gun looked like a child's toy in his bear paw-sized hand.

"That lil' gun is cute," Lia said.

Mack liked this gal. Humor after a gunfight—the mark of a real pro. He smiled and slid the revolver back under his belt. He thought about tossing it but had learned from experience never to waste a bullet during a battle.

Lia walked over to the dead man and pulled off the black balaclava. The shotgun blast had struck him above the vest, tearing into his neck. His face was smeared with blood, and his eyes looked glassy and distant. Blood dripped steadily from the open wounds on his neck, soaking the carpet in a dark, nearly black mixture of body fluids.

Lia unclipped a grenade from the dead guy's belt and clipped it to her ammo belt. "This may come in handy," she said, all business-like. She picked up the dead man's AR-15 and tossed it to Mack. She did the same with the spare mag cartridges strapped to his belt.

"That's a better look," she said with a clever smile.

Mack pulled the charging handle, ejecting the round. He pressed the magazine release, dropped the cartridge, and tossed it. Pulling the trigger multiple times, he tested the action and raised it to his eye, confirming sight alignment. He slammed a full magazine into the magwell and chambered a round.

"Much better," he said. Turning to Lia, he asked, "Which way did the gunman go?"

But she was gone.

The dim light faded into darkness as smoke spiraled down the long corridor.

Mack leaned over the stair railing, catching a glimpse of Paul as he sprinted toward the front entrance.

TRADECRAFT

JUNE 13, 1781
WEST POINT, NEW YORK COLONY

Jack stared intently through the fogged window, his heart racing in anticipation. General Knox was preparing to open the satchel that Jack had risked his life to deliver, unveiling the secrets hidden within Jefferson's letters.

Raindrops pelted the thick, steamy glass, blurring the world outside. Through the darkness, silhouettes of the giant northern pines swayed in a harmonic rhythm. The mighty nor'easter's fury tested the age-old trees' resolve to remain rooted to the earth. The storm's erratic gusts rattled the rear door like an unseen guest wishing to enter and join the clandestine gathering.

"Mr. Pebbley, you may proceed," General Knox said. "Let's examine the contents the governor entrusted to you, Captain Jouett."

For the first time, the general acknowledged Jack's militia rank. Having secured his respect, Jack joined the other men at the table and stood anxiously over his chair.

The yellow light of the lantern's flame shone on Mr. Pebbley's emotionless, scarred face. His slender, stick-like fingers carefully opened the satchel and lifted out the weathered cowhide folio.

Jack refrained from telling the general what he knew of the satchel's contents. Jefferson's orders precluded him from opening it before delivery to the general.

"There's a letter with a recipe for Brunswick stew," Julius said.

Jack turned and shot a glance toward Julius.

"Have these documents been tampered with?" General Knox asked sternly.

Jack felt the blood warm his ears. "Of course not. Sir."

Pebbley pulled out a map, laid it in the middle of the table, and placed the letter from Jefferson to Adams beside it.

The general pulled out his spectacles, leaned over the documents, and examined the map. He ran his huge index finger from New York harbor northwest along a prominent river until it reached a red-ink triangle symbol labeled *"Connecticut-Ohio Territory."* From there, he traced the route eastward to a black star symbol, where three rivers converged and a fair distance from the ocean and Boston's harbor.

The general leaned back and crossed his arms. "Ah, the town of Springfield, Massachusetts. Jefferson has approved my proposal to General Washington. Springfield shall be the location of our grand armory. Men, this is fine news." He stared at the map, puzzled. "Connecticut-Ohio lands? What is the significance of this location? Mr. Pebbley, the answer must lie in these documents."

"Sir, the letter to Adams appears inconsequential—a ruse, a decoy," Pebbley said. "Unless…"

"Unless what?" General Knox pressed, his voice carrying an authoritative urgency that left no room for hesitation.

"Sir. I suspect Jefferson has encoded these documents with a modified version of the Culper. Yes, the governor has taken exceptional measures to safeguard this message," Pebbley said and removed his hat, unveiling patches of coal-black hair matted on each side of his bald head. He peeled back the hat's inner lining, exposing several small pieces of folded parchment paper.

He spread the papers on the table and pulled a short metal object from his jacket pocket. Jack had never seen anything of the sort. Pebbley pressed the pointed end of the device to the cloth parchment. It produced a black ink line.

A metal writing quill?

Pebbley drew lines under the numbers in the Jefferson-Adams letter. Next, he repeated the line, drawing on the parchment containing the Brunswick stew recipe. In all, there were dozens of underlined numbers on both documents.

Pebbley barked orders to Julius. "Boy, fetch a piece of writing parchment."

Julius stood firm, immovable as a century oak rooted to the ground. His eyes turned to Jack, who gave him a nod before shifting his cold glare to Pebbley.

Julius left the room and returned promptly. Pebbley motioned with an outstretched hand, demanding the parchment. Julius turned away and placed the parchment in front of Jack. Pebbley grabbed it abruptly and scowled in Julius's direction.

"Enough, men!" The general slammed his giant hand on the table. The candle wobbled, fell over, and splashed wax across the table and the documents. "Get on with it, Mr. Pebbley," Knox said.

Pebbley wrote a word on the parchment, paused, moved to the next underlined number, matched the number to the corresponding number in the Culper book, wrote the word, paused, and moved to the next underlined number in Jefferson's message, wrote the matching word, and started over again, repeating the pattern for several minutes. The numbers in Jefferson's writings corresponded to a word, letter, or number in the Culper codebook. An ingenious method for shielding the message from the prying eyes of the enemy.

The general paced, his meaty hands clasped firmly behind his back. He muttered to himself as if he were thinking aloud. "Jefferson has been working for over a year on the grand plan at His Excellency's request. Our armies are in dire straits. We desperately require divine intervention, for without financial support, Congress will be forced to capitulate. What has Jefferson concocted?"

The unmistakable strain in his voice was a culmination of

years of fighting a bloody war against an adversary renowned for their battle-hardened experience and vast resources—resources well beyond anything the colonists could muster. Despite the general's imposing stature, Jack, for the first time, noticed weariness etched into his face, likely the result of the heavy burden he carried with him. Thousands of men had died under his command, and more would fall until a final resolution could be attained.

Pebbley put down his metal quill. "Sir, something is awry. The message has no meaning."

"You've clearly made a mistake," General Knox said, his fury directed at Pebbley.

Jack grinned, pleased to watch the spy squirm.

"With respect, sir, I checked and double-checked my work. There's no meaning. Random words, letters, and numbers," Pebbley said with a noticeable quiver.

The general examined Pebbley's notes and cross-referenced the letters to the Culper code. His anger subsided. "Why would Jefferson change the cipher?"

Jack thought back to the governor's final instructions:

"Protect the satchel with your life. My wife embroidered the leather binding with her blessed hand. Her fine stitch shall protect the future of our republic."

"May I, sir?" Jack said to the general. He picked up the leather folio, turned it to expose the binding, and closely examined the seam. Using the tip of his knife, he carefully cut the leather stitches.

"What are you doing?" Pebbley asked, alarmed.

Jack ignored him, gently tore back the binding, and pulled out a small, folded piece of parchment.

"Very interesting," Knox said with a nod of approval.

Jack read it out loud, "'*Divide by three and one plus. Life, Liberty, and the Pursuit of Happiness. Th. J.*' Sir, I believe the note refers to a revision to the Culper code."

Pebbley glared at Jack and went back to work with his

metal quill. He wrote a word on the blank parchment, paused, moved to the next underlined number, matched the number to the number in the Culper book, wrote a word on the parchment, paused, and moved to the next number.

"The Culper's likely been compromised by either the British or traitors. Jefferson must have known that. Brilliant. A very brilliant man," General Knox said.

Pebbley wrote furiously, deciphering John Adams's letter and recipe with the new cipher. Minutes later, he finished, read the note to himself, paused with astonishment, reread it, and handed the message to the general.

The general placed his spectacles on the bridge of his nose and read the message. His cheeks lost their rosy shine, and his expression turned dour.

"Interesting. Very interesting," Knox mumbled. "Men, pardon me, I must retire." He began to walk out of the room. "We shall meet in the morning."

"But, sir?" Jack said, anxious to know the contents of the message.

Pebbley stared at Jack with sunken, bloodshot eyes.

"Son, you and your men are to be commended. Our country owes you a debt of gratitude. However, I'm unable to divulge the contents at this time. I must confer with my officers. However, I can tell you that Governor Jefferson has provided valuable information regarding the whereabouts and plans of Lord Cornwallis and the British Southern Army. However, it also confirms a snake slithering in our midst and that General Washington's life may be at risk. We shall speak at sunrise. I must retire and assemble my thoughts."

The general placed his hand on Jack's shoulder. "Thank you, son." He exited the room.

Pebbley holstered his pistol, picked up his Ferguson, and made his way to the rear door.

Jack pushed back from the table and blocked Pebbley's exit. "I will never forget," he said in a low voice, his hand poised, resting on the top of the carved antler handle of his knife.

Pebbley, taken aback, took a deep breath and squared his shoulders, avoiding Jack's steely gaze, conceding his unspoken surrender.

Sensing the redemption of his honor, Jack stepped aside.

◆ ◆ ◆

The following day, General Knox's aide-de-camp summoned Jack to a conference in the officer's quarters adjacent to the artillery battery, which overlooked the southern section of the Hudson's elbow.

The morning sun began to make its appearance as Jack walked through the camp. Soldiers and Africans chopped fallen trees and stacked branches, remnants of the night's storm.

General Knox conveyed his heartfelt gratitude for safely transporting the governor's secret message on behalf of General Washington and Congress. He presented Jack with an esteemed opportunity to join the elite unit of guardsmen named "The Liberty Unit." Their explicit mission: safeguard General Washington, the army's cash, and official papers.

The guardsmen's identities remained secret, absent from official army rolls and unknown even to Congress, affording the guardsmen the freedom to employ unconventional methods.

General Knox extended an enticing proposition: timber-rich lands north of the mighty Ohio River as compensation. Jack and his mates were promised formal officer training at the Fort, including hand-to-hand combat techniques, mastery of the most advanced weaponry, and, most appealing, exemption from following the army's standard code of conduct.

For many years, Jack had experienced the freedom of a militia soldier. Transitioning to a professional soldier demanded the highest level of dedication. He was not inclined to follow orders or abide by the rules of others.

After a spirited evening of ale and cards, Jack, Julius, and Ben reached a unanimous conclusion: Governor Jefferson had foreseen their destiny, and without hesitation, they willingly accepted the general's proposition to join the esteemed ranks of Liberty Unit guardsmen.

Training would commence at the break of dawn under the command of General von Steuben.

BUILDING W91

22 FEBRUARY, 1440 HRS
MIT DATA CENTER, BUILDING W91 — CAMBRIDGE, MASSACHUSETTS

Hassan burst from the Stata Lab, doors shattering on impact with an echoing crash, scattering thousands of glass shards across the icy concrete. Each step reverberated up from the hard rubberized soles of his tactical boots, sending shockwaves of pain into his wounded hip. His intense weight training and long-distance runs had conditioned him for these moments, yet the biting cold made every breath a struggle. More than the cold, however, it was the sharp pain from his bruised, possibly fractured ribs that slowed his pace. His Kevlar vest had stopped the bullets, but their impact had left a painful reminder of his narrow escape from death.

The professor's assistant had a formidable head start, sprinting through the university's central circle toward the main road, parallel to the river.

Hassan hurdled a low brick fence, his trailing foot catching the top of the jagged stone. With an extended hand, he landed awkwardly, and like a bolt of electricity, pain shot up his ankle, through his leg and hip, and into his temple.

He stumbled forward, steadied himself against a tree, and shifted his weight to the other foot. He cursed himself for letting the girl escape.

Testing the injured ankle, he picked up his pace. He wouldn't let mere pain stop him now, not when he was this close to the prize of immortality. He had been in this place countless times in battle before; pain served as an excellent motivator.

Far ahead, the girl reached the main road. He pushed

himself to keep up, watching as she crossed the bridge that spanned the wind-swept, steel-gray river.

Hassan stopped and steadied himself on a signpost. His lungs burned, and his ankle throbbed in unison with his rapidly beating heart. He glanced down, feeling as if his swollen ankle might burst the seams of his boot.

The gusting wind blew a light sheet of freezing rain into Hassan's face. Shielding his eyes, he strained to locate her far in the distance. He'd sacrificed everything and was determined to continue on.

Oncoming traffic drove past Hassan, one car after another. The drivers, mostly men, had serious and curious expressions as they stared at him. Hassan had lived in the shadows for many years and was now exposed. His local operatives hadn't responded, and with Khalid and Faras dead, Hassan was on his own.

From a distance, he spotted the unmistakable silhouette of a military vehicle approaching at high speed. Its front radiator grill resembled a monster with teeth, hungry and charging toward him—the signature of the all-too-familiar HMMWV.

Hassan's muscles tensed as the sight of enemy soldiers brought back vivid memories of Syria and the damage these vehicles and the men they carried had inflicted on his homeland.

He anxiously searched for cover but found none. He was exposed.

The mud-colored beast came into full view, its engine roaring while its massive wheels pulverized the ice and debris beneath. He knew others would follow close behind—they always traveled in packs. Trailing the lead vehicle, he counted them as they approached...three, four, five.

The lead vehicle carried a shielded gun turret, atop which a soldier aimed at the horizon what appeared to be the powerful M2 .50-caliber machine gun. The gunner's eyes remained forward as the motorized beast passed, ignoring Hassan. Unlike in Syria, Hassan was not their prey.

On the horizon, dark black smoke rose high into the air. The city of Boston was ablaze. Hassan relished the sight, and his strength began to return.

The armored vehicles roared past—each hurling dirt and ice in its wake. Hassan stepped back and shielded his mouth and nose from the thick, oily smell of the spent diesel fuel. The trailing vehicle was larger—an armored personnel carrier filled with soldiers.

Hassan closed his eyes and momentarily transported himself back into the desert homeland. Clutching the heavy, weight-forward Soviet-made RPG-7, he dropped to one knee and positioned the launcher firmly on his shoulder. The crude metal crosshairs centered on the vehicle's rear. Silently, he prayed for guidance as he squeezed the trigger. The lethal OG-7V fragment grenade hurled toward its target, exploding in a spectacular burst that turned the truck into a blinding inferno of fire, smoke, and human debris.

A blaring horn startled him out of his dream. Hassan's eyes snapped open as an ambulance, lights flashing, rounded the corner, racing toward the city center in the same direction as the military caravan.

The unrest had escalated into violent riots, now consuming the city. Hassan prayed his men had engaged the enemy in the streets. He wished to be there, fighting shoulder-to-shoulder with his brave brothers.

The pedestrian crosswalk lights were dark, as were the stoplights and streetlights. Despite the pain radiating from his ankle, he managed a slight grin. The power company's computer engineers were scurrying like frantic schoolchildren, desperately trying to restart the grid. But the extensive damage inflicted by Hassan's virus was devastating, likely requiring weeks, if not months, to repair. America would remain shrouded in darkness, being torn apart by looting and riots. He lifted his head to the sky, savoring the moment. The bombings, power blackout, and crippling internet outage together marked the most prolific attack in U.S. history.

The pain had vanished as his dream of eternal glory reignited his resolve.

He would not fail.

The girl would not escape.

BUSINESS PARTNER

22 FEBRUARY 1616 HRS
MIT DATA CENTER, BUILDING W91 – CAMBRIDGE, MASSACHUSETTS

The shuffling of footsteps on damp pavement grew louder from Hassan's left flank. He paused, a knot of anxiety constricting his chest. His eyes swept over the street and adjacent office buildings, cursing under his breath. His IRGC intelligence training had mandated securing the perimeter before advancing into unknown territory. He recognized the oversight as a glaring lapse in judgment.

He stepped back, concealing himself in the shadow of the office building's entranceway. His instincts, honed by the back alleys and alcoves of the Old City of Aleppo, had never failed him. Someone was close. He pulled his holstered Glock and lowered it to his side.

The shuffling footsteps softly echoed again as a stranger advanced toward Hassan's position. He was a tall, slender man dressed in a knee-length tan raincoat and wingtips polished to a high shine. His face remained hidden beneath the brim of a sports cap.

There was no visible sign of a weapon, yet he was almost certainly carrying.

Hassan tightened his grip on his Glock, prepared to engage. He exited the shadow of the entranceway and slipped around the corner toward the rear of the building. If the stranger followed, he'd put him down.

The rhythmic rumble of an engine reverberated through the alley, accompanied by the smell of burnt fuel. The old CAT diesel generator expelled plumes of black smoke, providing power to the structure and the overhead emergency lights, which cast a neon glow on the empty loading docks. High above, surveillance cameras guarded the secured rear maintenance doors.

A calm voice spoke over the humming of the generator's pulsing engine.

"Hassan. I'm a friend of Khalid," the stranger said.

Hassan turned, pointed his weapon at the man's chest, and slowly exerted pressure on the trigger.

The man held his hands high in the air. His face was shrouded. "I'm here to help you."

Hassan contemplated ending the discussion; however, he used his discretion to spare the man's life, at least for the moment. "Who are you?" he said. "And I will not ask you a second time."

"I'm a friend," the man said, his voice calm and reassuring. "Who I am isn't important right now. I assure you there's no one else following you." As he spoke, he took deliberate, measured steps toward Hassan.

The stranger was either brave or foolish. Hassan couldn't decide which.

"Hassan, it's imperative we get inside this building before they arrive. Khalid is dead, and the Feds are taking out your network of agents. Most are either killed or arrested. The FBI not only raided your Detroit headquarters but cells in D.C., New York, and Chicago. And a few hours ago, they shut down the Boston ISB Mosque."

Hassan didn't want to believe him and strained to conceal the anger that began to consume him. "Why should I believe you?" he demanded.

"Check for yourself. Have you been able to contact your agents? I'm guessing not."

Hassan kept his eyes on the stranger and pulled his phone from his jacket. But he didn't have to look. He knew what he'd find. It was all unraveling.

He glanced down at the phone's display.

The stranger took another cautious step forward. "Now, lower your gun. Don't let your Yousef's death be in vain."

Startled by the man's recognition of his brother, Hassan lowered his gun and processed the stranger's words. Khalid was the only person who knew the fate of Hassan's younger brother.

"How do you know about my brother?"

"Khalid was my business partner. He kept me informed. I provided access to the government network and shielded you, Khalid, and your agents from the authorities for years. You see, we both have much to lose. For the past ten years, along with others from our government and like-minded entrepreneurs, I've provided Khalid and your brethren the support and intel required to execute the plan you've been skillfully carrying out."

The man inched closer, and his features gradually came into sharper view. Hassan recognized him.

"Now that Khalid is out of the picture, you're next in line. But first, we've got some important business to attend to inside," the New York congressman said.

TARLETON'S VISIT

AUGUST 15, 1781 – TWO MONTHS LATER
MOUNT VERNON, VIRGINIA COLONY – 300 MILES SOUTH OF WEST POINT

Jack had endured a grueling seven-week initiation into the rigor of army life at West Point—a perpetual cycle of drills, target practice, and close-quarters combat. Day and night, under the moon's glow and the sun's harsh glare, the tough old Prussian General von Steuben, a man whose tactics were honed by the old wars, imposed his iron will upon Jack and his fellow cadet guardsmen.

A battle-scarred warrior of the Seven Years' War, the general not only served as Frederick the Great's aide-de-camp but also earned the men's respect and the unwavering confidence of General Washington himself. His most notable contribution to the cause, *Blue Book*, detailed the Continental Army's manual, recognized by its signature ocean-blue cover.

On the five-day journey, Jack led Ben, Julius, and a pair of veteran guardsmen southward from New York to Alexandria, Virginia, constantly on the lookout for enemy pickets and loyalist bounty hunters. General Knox had entrusted Jack with the mission's command, recognizing his familiarity with the southern territory but, more importantly, his knowledge of the Green Dragoons' tactics—a strategic advantage the general held in high regard. General Knox's orders were clear—survey and secure Mount Vernon in preparation for General Washington's homecoming. However, the ultimate goal was to capture or kill the traitors who dared to threaten his life. The general issued orders with an ominous warning: evil lurked among them, and those who seemed loyal might not be as they appeared.

Jefferson's encoded message had brought to light a conspiracy that ran deep in the ranks of Congress. The evidence suggested that members had made the unconscionable decision to side with the king and had architected a scheme to end the war by facilitating the capture or the unthinkable—the assassination of General Washington.

Within hours, General Washington would arrive at his Mount Vernon home. General Knox had devised a plan for Jack and the guardsmen to encircle the estate and lie in wait.

Now, by the flickering campfire light, Jack turned the tattered pages of the *Blue Book*, each worn leaf containing combat-tested instructions that had shaped warriors before him. Jack readied himself for battle, the memories of his late father sharpening his resolve and fueling the fire burning in his heart.

◆ ◆ ◆

Under the cover of a clear and moonless night, Jack, Ben, and Julius secretly ferried across the wind-swept waters of the Potomac River, reaching landfall at the rear of General Washington's magnificent Mount Vernon estate.

At six horse-length intervals, precisely as General von Steuben had instructed, Jack positioned the guardsmen in a crescent formation on the edge of the woods bordering the estate.

Lying low, the tall grass and dense thickets concealed Jack and the guardsmen as the dawn's early light rose over the mansion, casting long shadows onto the sprawling and impeccably groomed front lawn and its meandering stone pathways.

With discreet caution, Jack lifted his hat and wiped the beads of sweat that dripped into his eyes. Confident the plantation's occupants had not spotted him, he remained motionless. He closed his left eye, staring down the rifle's long iron-forged barrel. He observed the servants performing their morning chores—carrying pails of milk and baskets filled with vegetables into the estate's southern entrance.

During the mission briefing, General Knox stated that the conspirators' identities remained unknown; however, suspicion based on eyewitness accounts showed that Lund Washington was involved. Lund, General Washington's cousin and long-time caretaker of Mount Vernon, was suspected of collaborating with the enemy. Specifics of the plot were unclear; however, information was gathered by Jefferson's spies that Lund had conferred with the British following a raid of the Mount Vernon estate in May of that year. Washington's spies discovered that a British raiding party had surveyed the estate and coerced or bribed Lund to aid in capturing or assassinating the general.

Ben whispered to Jack, "Would they do it? Assassinate General Washington?"

With his eyes fixed on the distant doorway, Jack replied in a low, steady voice, "The British will stop at nothing. Consider their collusion with the traitor Arnold. It was inconceivable —a general turning traitor against his own."

Jack shifted his rifle sight to the pathway that led through the kitchen garden to the eastern outbuilding.

The pounding of hooves reverberated through the ground, up into his chest. Many horses. More than a dozen. Jack quickly shot two short whistles, warning the guardsmen to prepare to engage the enemy.

The red uniforms were unmistakable, with their white and gold trim reflecting in the rising sun. Jack's head swiveled toward the sound of riders approaching from the opposite direction. A dozen more riders thundered into view.

"It's him—the Butcher," Julius whispered with excitement.

Flanked by a mixed cavalry and light infantry unit, the Green Dragoon commander, Banastre Tarleton, sat tall and straight-backed atop a shimmering, midnight-black stallion.

"Should I take the shot?" Julius asked.

Jack silently weighed his options. Firing a rifle shot meant exposing their position, potentially compromising the entire mission, yet the opportunity to end the life of "the Butcher" would be a prize like no other.

He reached over and gently placed his hand on Julius's rifle. Understanding the unspoken command, Julius slowly eased the hammer down and relaxed his aim.

From the estate's kitchen gardens, a short man wearing a wide-brimmed hat, cropped olive hemp leggings, and a loose white shirt hastily approached Tarleton.

"That's the traitor, Lund Washington," Julius said.

Tarleton dismounted, removed his battle helmet, and stood before the grand entrance doors. His stance was confident, almost predatory, as he waited with an air of aristocratic lineage.

The two men conferred, and Lund pointed north.

Tarleton's words appeared terse as he stripped off his riding gloves. Then, with a sudden, sharp movement that caught Lund off guard, Tarleton delivered a resounding slap across Lund's face. He drew his sword and pressed it to Lund's neck. Overwhelmed by fear, Lund dropped to his knees, begging for mercy.

"A coward," Jack said under his breath. He would die before kneeling to that British devil.

Tarleton lowered his blade and turned abruptly in Jack's direction, scanning the field.

Jack dropped his head, pushing his face into the matted grass. He held his breath, which seemed to stretch for minutes, before cautiously opening his eyes and raising his head.

Tarleton turned to his men, barked orders, and walked up the stone stairs into Washington's mansion with a commanding air of ownership. Lund followed, his demeanor reduced to that of a submissive servant.

General Knox's information was proving accurate. It seemed almost certain now that Lund had betrayed his kin and conspired to ambush Washington on his impending visit to Mount Vernon.

The British regulars dismounted and began unloading supplies in what appeared to be preparation for an extended stay. An officer paced back and forth, surveying the tall grass field.

Jack's heart quickened as he took a deep breath, steadying his aim on the officer's shining column of gold coat buttons. The officer turned north, continued scouting the estate's surroundings, and shouted orders to his men.

Jack gently nudged Julius with his elbow and motioned for him to follow. Crouched, Jack and Julius slowly retreated to the safety of the forest's edge.

Within the tree line, Jack held the bridle of Julius's sandy brown colt. "Head northeast," he said. "Find General Washington's traveling party. They should be near the Potomac Trail, south of Baltimore. Warn them of the enemy's strength and position."

"What about you and Ben?" Julius asked with obvious concern.

"We'll manage, my friend," Jack said, patting his long rifle. "Take care. Keep a sharp eye for redcoats and loyalists in sheep's clothing."

Julius led his horse eastward, disappearing into the thick foliage bordering the Potomac. He would soon warn General Washington that his "guests" had arrived.

The mission was proceeding just as General Knox had planned.

DISBELIEF

22 FEBRUARY, 1445 HRS
MIT DATA CENTER, BUILDING W91 – CAMBRIDGE, MASSACHUSETTS

Paul burst from the lab building, turning sharply around the corner and toward the riverwalk. In the distance, the wind whipped across the water's icy surface, pushing flocks of seagulls side to side.

Fueled by the adrenalin flooding his veins, Paul leaned into the biting wind, taking the familiar path along the river and across the Memorial Bridge. He lengthened his stride, his thoughts racing to Emma. She would make her way to the safety of MIT's data center—he had to believe she would.

He passed the towering Cambridge Hyatt, with its massive red marquee looming overhead. The entranceway and the windows were dark. Ahead, the data center building offices were well-lit. He took steps toward the front entrance; however, it was more likely Emma would have entered the rear delivery access to the data center.

He hadn't set foot inside in years. The building housed an extensive array of servers, networking gear, and data storage equipment that powered the computing infrastructures of both Harvard and MIT and, most importantly, Professor Clark's engineering lab.

Paul unzipped his backpack, his hand wrapping around the cool metal of his weapon. The custom grip slid firmly into his palm. A well-practiced thumb flicked the mag release, allowing him to check the load. He slammed the magazine in and racked the slide with a smooth, fluid motion. He approached the building's rear entrance and pressed his back against the cold, corrugated metal wall.

Gripping his weapon with both hands in a ready stance, he cautiously looked around the corner, scanning for any sign of movement.

The entrance door was propped open, with the security keycard swipe pad hanging by its wires. Shards of plastic and glass littered the ground.

Am I too late?

A flash of panic hit him, demanding he rush in and save her, yet he held back. Years of training called for a calculated response; a bullet might be waiting for him to step through that door.

The rumble of the generator's diesel engine masked any noises from inside the data center. Was the gunman waiting? It didn't matter. There was no choice. Emma was inside.

He approached the open door, keeping his gun in a low, ready position, and slid his index finger onto the trigger. He made quick, sharp peeks around the doorframe. The overhead fluorescent lighting cast a sterile glow down the long, deserted hallway.

From behind, tires screeched as a dark Yukon SUV barreled into the alleyway, skidding to a stop just yards from his position. Paul adjusted his stance, aligning the gun sights on the driver's side window.

The Yukon's tinted window gradually opened, and two hands slowly emerged.

"Can you not point that at me?" Lia said with her familiar Jersey accent. A mischievous smile played on her lips. Her dark ponytail fell onto her shoulders from beneath her black knit cap.

Paul eased his finger off the trigger, letting the gun's barrel drift lower. The passenger door slammed, and Paul's weapon was up again instantly. A man emerged: a burly guy wearing camos and a heavy tactical vest. His face was obscured behind dark, silver-rimmed glasses.

"Someone you know wanted to join us," Lia said and stepped out of the SUV. She walked around to the back as the trunk opened automatically.

The man approached, and as his face came fully into view, the shock nearly overwhelmed him. He stood silent, searching for words to verbalize his intense emotions. He took a deep breath, steadying himself.

Paul never forgot a face. It was his gift. But he'd buried this man's features deep into the recesses of his mind, believing they would remain there forever.

"Son, I know I've got a lot of explaining to do, but first, we've important business to take care of," his father said, his voice unchanged by a decades-long absence, a voice that carried weight and commanded attention. "I understand my granddaughter's inside."

Paul was drawn to the scar under his left eye as he spoke—a remnant of a training trip together through the Oregon wilderness. The years had worn deep lines on his once-firm cheekbones, now sunken by time. Yet, his eyes remained unchanged—as blue and intense as Paul remembered.

Paul was only sixteen when his father had died—which he now knew had been a lie. He'd worked hard over the years to push the memories of his father aside, and now, suddenly, those painful memories came flooding back.

He turned and pointed his weapon at his father. Paul's heart beat so hard he could feel it in his throat.

His father calmly walked over and put a firm hand on the gun barrel. Paul obeyed his father's silent command, letting the weapon dip toward the ground.

"I'll explain once we get this damn train back on the rails," his father said, speaking with a rough firmness, the same voice Paul remembered from all those years ago.

Paul couldn't simply surrender to the moment; he needed something more from his father. "You abandoned us, and now you just expect me to deal with it?" he said, anger about to boil over.

"Yes, and it was the hardest damn thing I've ever done. But it's your mother who deserves the apology, and she died before I could deliver it. I'll regret that for the rest of my life. You and I may still have time." He pointed the barrel of his M-15 rifle at the building. "But we have business to finish first."

Paul's mind immediately went to Emma. "Okay, we'll continue this conversation later."

Lia placed her hand on Paul's shoulder, steadying him. "You go. I'll cover you and take out the generator. You've got four minutes," Lia said, starting the timer on her watch, and Paul's father did the same.

Paul's father moved toward the data center's door with his rifle raised. Paul reached out, gripping his father's shoulder. "No, Emma's my responsibility. I'll take point."

He advanced cautiously and quickly down the corridor, which was awash in harsh fluorescent light, and forked at the far end. Paul froze and listened for any hint of movement.

Nothing.

He motioned to move right. Through the rifle's optical sight, his target aligned on a door with a glass window into what appeared to be a sophisticated mantrap, a security measure designed to guard the main control room.

Paul saw several figures with their backs to him through the thick, reinforced glass. Among them, Emma sat in front of a laptop, with a man holding a gun to her head.

Paul held his breath for a count of six, forcing himself to contain his anger and slow his heart rate. He sighted the target, prepared to send several rounds into the man's head. He let out a slow breath and relaxed his trigger finger. A slight deflection from the door's glass could send a bullet astray.

He signaled to his father, and they moved out of the direct line of sight. Paul tapped his watch and pointed toward the light above. His father produced a pair of lime-green chemlight sticks and handed one to Paul.

Paul was set. This was for Sara. He wouldn't let anyone harm the person who meant the world to him. *Nine, eight, seven...*

RANSOM

22 FEBRUARY 1525 HRS
MIT DATA CENTER, BUILDING W91 — CAMBRIDGE, MASSACHUSETTS

Hassan towered over the lab assistant, pressing the barrel of his Glock firmly against her temple. In his line of work, the cold steel touch of a gun's barrel was a powerful motivator.

Under the white glare of the data center's fluorescent lights, her hand trembled as she plugged the internet cable into her laptop. The blue cable snaked several meters down a row of servers and terminated into one of the data center's four network core routing devices.

"No mistakes or this will not end well for you," Hassan said and jabbed the gun's barrel hard against her temple, jolting her head to the side. He expected her to succumb to her fear and comply immediately. Instead, she turned slowly, her eyes ablaze with defiance that caught him off guard. Their eyes locked in a silent battle, her rage colliding with his ruthless determination.

"Don't toy with me, young lady. I will pull this trigger. Log in to the network, and you are free to go," Hassan said, lowering his weapon to demonstrate a temporary sign of hope. Of course, he had no intention of sparing her life.

A flash of concern passed through Hassan as the lights overhead flickered briefly. He looked down the row of tall server cabinets, each alive with a pulsating mixture of green, yellow, and red status lights. He strained to catch the reassuring hum of the diesel generator's engine, which provided the much-needed power to the network.

With a steady hand, the young woman inserted the USB stick into the side of the laptop. She waited for the screen prompt and began typing. Hassan watched with heightened anticipation. She typed another long string of commands, executed a ping test, and slowly removed her hands from the keyboard.

The green command prompt flashed on the black screen. She remained silent and still.

He was in, gaining full access to Clark's next-generation neural network. Confidence surged through him like a rushing river after a great monsoon, flooding from his heart to his biceps and hands. He squeezed the Glock tighter and tighter.

"Is it done?" the New York congressman asked, his condescending tone snapping Hassan's concentration. It was a harsh reminder that the man—an infidel—could not be trusted.

"Yes," Hassan said.

"Excellent."

Hassan could now access the internet, indicating the professor had successfully initialized the neural network. However, all other devices connected to the outdated public network remained offline.

He pushed the woman aside and keyed in commands to initiate the ransom exchange. He whispered a prayer under his breath and then gently pressed the enter key.

A sense of great elation swept through him as the screen emitted hundreds of lines of numbers and letters. The Ethereum cryptocurrency began transferring from the U.S. Treasury account onto the USB wallet connected to the laptop. The exchange of billions of dollars had taken a mere four seconds.

Hassan paused, savoring the gravity of his achievement. He had orchestrated the greatest ransomware exploit the world had ever seen. Now, an orphaned Syrian refugee wielded control over the global internet. He was the true architect of power, not the traitor Khalid Ghlam nor the treasonous congressman. This was more than a victory; it was a redemption for all the immense sacrifices Hassan had endured.

The congressman handed Hassan a business card. On the back was a sixteen-digit crypto wallet key.

"Transfer the ransom to that account. Quickly!" The congressman used a tone intended for a common housemaid.

"What are you doing?" the young woman said.

"Quiet! I did not give you permission to speak," Hassan said, raising his gun yet resisting the urge to strike.

She recoiled and shielded her head with her arms.

The congressman took measured steps toward Hassan. The man's eyes appeared to retreat into their sockets. His pale skin, unkempt beard, and rounded shoulders were signs of the man's false sense of power.

"Young lady, we have your Dr. Clark to thank for facilitating this transaction. He believed his new internet would save the world. It won't. But it will give our friends control. Control over what people perceive to be the truth. More control than ever before. And as a byproduct, he made me an extraordinarily rich man."

"Enough! Silence now." Hassan's patience had finally reached its limit. With a swift motion, he retrieved the USB drive, a small yet immensely valuable device containing thousands of untraceable crypto keys—the equivalent of billions of U.S. dollars. His other hand aimed the Glock at the fork-tongued politician.

The congressman stumbled backward and raised his hands in a half-hearted gesture to defend himself. "What does it matter, anyway?" he said, his voice a mix of fear and defiance. "Just like Khalid and your brother, she won't live to see another day."

Overcome by uncontrollable rage, Hassan seethed as the politician callously invoked Yousef's memory. His breath turned ragged, short and shallow, and his hand, clutching his gun, trembled. The haunting image of his brother's charred body lying at the base of the stairs flashed in his mind, igniting a fury he could not contain.

All a lie!

Hassan swiftly raised his Glock, centered the sight on the congressman's forehead, and, without hesitation, pulled the trigger. The gun blast reverberated through the room. The hum of the computers, generator, and air conditioning unit fell silent.

Blood sprayed in a wide arc across the white ceramic tiles as the congressman's lifeless body crumpled to the ground, his head smashing against the tile, splattering bone and red matter.

Hassan spat on the lifeless body, releasing the final remnants of his fury. He inhaled deeply, savoring the familiar scent of gunpowder that hung in the air.

The young woman sprang to her feet. Her face twisted in a silent scream—the room was devoid of all sound. He shook his head to clear the deafening quiet, but his eardrums were numb, muffled as if he were submerged underwater.

The floor shook, the lights flickered, and the room was plunged into darkness, a blackness so absolute that the world had ceased to exist.

Hassan searched for a glimmer of light or anything to anchor his senses. He reached out toward the girl, hands grasping air with each attempt. His panic intensified in the absolute silence and suffocating darkness.

He lunged forward toward the door. Suddenly, his face crashed into an immovable metal object. A sharp, searing pain exploded in his forehead as if he'd been struck with a rifle butt. The bitter taste of blood filled his mouth, and the throbbing pressure built as his broken nose began to swell.

Hassan frantically waved his weapon in all directions, slicing through the darkness, searching for a target. A profound sense of desperation had eclipsed his anger.

A sharp and sudden rush of air blew into his face, carrying with it the sting of burnt diesel fuel, a scent that reengaged his senses.

His eyes, struggling to pierce the darkness, registered a faint green glow. Instinctively, he swiveled toward the light source and unleashed a rapid, erratic burst. The bullets traced a wild path through the blackness, hurling toward the distant green light.

HOMECOMING

AUGUST 15, 1781
MOUNT VERNON, VIRGINIA COLONY

Jack surveyed the estate grounds from within the shadowed confines of the dense tree line, preparing to reposition the guardsmen for an impending assault. The sweltering heat baked the British soldiers as they milled about Washington's Mount Vernon estate courtyard. Many had discarded their helmets, while others had shed their heavy green woolen riding coats, seeking respite from the relentless grasp of the Virginia sun.

Jack wiped the sweat from his eyes and counted a dozen Dragoons in his line of sight. He observed two men leading their horses to the estate's rear while three others mingled with a small group of British regulars busily unloading crates of cannon ammunition and heavy sacks. Another group of regulars wheeled a pair of artillery pieces, likely three-pounders, toward the estate's entrance. The sunlight glistened off the polished brass barrels as the men methodically positioned the heavy cannons. The white-painted spoked wheels of the carriages turned slowly, aiming the guns down the road.

The remaining Dragoons were occupied near the watering trough, attending to their horses while they harassed two female slaves who were making a concerted effort to remove themselves from the fray.

Jack turned to the sound of leaves rustling as Ben walked toward him with his long rifle firmly grasped in both hands.

"The arrogance of the British to occupy General Washington's home. The people will not stand for it," Ben said, gritting his teeth and tightening his grip.

"Yes, I agree. They are preparing for the general's homecoming. And indeed, General Knox's information was accurate. Someone informed the British that General Washington was returning home."

"Who?" Ben asked.

Jack's voice took on an edge as he spoke, his anger simmering at the mere mention of the name. "The spy, Pebbley, has reason to believe that it is Lund Washington—the general's cousin and the long-standing caretaker of this estate."

"That's beyond belief. Such a cowardly act of treachery," Ben responded, his voice thick with anger as he vehemently shook his head in disbelief.

Dry sticks and brittle pine needles crunched softly a short distance away. Reacting swiftly, Jack and Ben quickly slipped behind a tree. Jack raised his rifle, braced himself, and readied to fire. But as the men came into view, he relaxed, lowered his rifle, and stepped out to greet Colonel Boone and his party of Overmountain men.

"It's a fine day to bag a scoundrel," Boone said, grasping Jack's hand with a firm shake.

The four Overmountain riders sat tall atop their mounts, each carrying a pair of rifles crisscrossed on their backs, prepared for the imminent skirmish.

"From General Knox's encampment, a courier brought word of your pressing need for aid, a matter of the gravest importance," Boone said.

"A pleasure to see you again, Colonel," Jack said, his eyes drawn to the splendor of Boone's Kentucky long rifle. The weapon boasted a curled tiger-striped maple stock, complemented by a gleaming brass patch box and matching brass trigger guard.

"Our uninvited guests have indeed arrived," Jack said, gesturing toward the main house. He crouched down, sweeping away a layer of pine needles, and sketched the estate in the dry soil. Carefully, he noted the position of the Dragoons, the regulars, and the twin three-pounders. "The British have superior strength; thus, our rifles must be unerringly precise. The bastard Tarleton arrived not an hour past with a score of raiders. And has since been bolstered by about twenty British regulars. They've positioned two three-pounders at the main entrance, fortifying their hold in anticipation of Washington's return, while Tarleton takes comfort within the mansion."

"Men." Boone addressed his band of Overmountain sharpshooters with a commanding tone. "This day shall indulge in a hunt for redcoats. Ready your rifles and sharpen your blades."

Jack glanced up at Ben and traced a path in the dirt using the tip of a stick. "Proceed with two of our stout friends and secure the western entry near the vegetable garden, just behind the servants' cabin."

Ben nodded with a confident grin. "And where will you be?"

Jack met his eyes with a determined look. "I'm heading in from the rear. But before I do, I will create a diversion to draw their attention."

A gentle shower of dry pine needles fell onto Jack's makeshift dirt map. He gazed up. The tops of the towering Virginia pines swayed gracefully in the breeze. High above, grand, luminous clouds floated eastward toward the sea, their white shapes stark against the blue sky.

"The winds are in our favor. The cornfield, here," Jack said as he drew a circle in the earth, "will burn nicely, especially with a sprinkling of gunpowder to aid it."

Boone nodded in agreement. "Indeed, surely that will draw them out. Meanwhile, I will lead my men in the opposite direction—toward the distillery. We'll engage them from there."

"With all due respect, Colonel, your rifle is required to clear those cannons." Jack gestured toward the location of the artillery. "The range is significant—my guess is at least two hundred yards, possibly farther."

Boone smiled, stood, and affectionately patted his rifle's

stock. He reached into a small pocket and retrieved six lead balls. "I poured these myself just last night, specifically for this occasion."

Jack took one, rolling its impressive weight in his palm before returning it to Boone. "Outstanding," he said. Then, refocusing on the plan, he pointed to the map and traced a curve representing the Potomac River. "Your other two sharpshooters will advance to the edge of the tree line. As for me, I will work my way around to the river's edge and approach from the rear of the estate."

Jack stood and turned to face the men. "Hold your positions until the smoke rises from the cornfield. That will be our signal to commence the assault," he ordered. "Colonel, with fortune on your side, your rifle will take out those manning the field cannon. And your sharpshooters can set their sights on the Dragoons and redcoats as they scatter, like scurrying rats."

"Me go with you," a strange voice said from behind.

In startled unison, the Overmountain men swung around and swiftly leveled their rifles at the unwelcome visitors. Standing before them were the old Shawnee chief and his two young warriors. They stood tall and proud, their long black hair adorned with crow feathers. Their faces were strikingly painted bloodred, accented with bold, contrasting streaks of white.

Colonel Boone raised his hands and stepped in the path of the rifles' aim. "Men, lower your guns. They're friends," he said.

The old Shawnee chief gingerly walked forward with an obvious limp and exchanged a firm forearm grip with Colonel Boone.

"I requested the services of the chief," Boone said. "He graciously agreed—repayment for saving his life at Trenton."

Jack silently nodded in acknowledgment to the chief and turned. He took a deep, purposeful breath before addressing the men.

"My fellow patriots, the notorious 'Butcher' Tarleton has taken occupancy of His Excellency's home. Our orders are to secure the estate and to take Tarleton—alive. General Washington has specific intentions for him. Remember, Tarleton and his Dragoons slaughtered our brethren at Waxhaws, raided our homes, and laid waste to our farms." Jack's gaze moved deliberately, meeting the eyes of each man. "I know the desire for revenge burns within us all, myself included, yet our orders are to capture him alive. Agreed?" His tone was firm yet underscored their deep-seated thirst for vengeance.

"We stand with you, Captain," Boone said, raising his rifle in solidarity, and his men promptly followed suit.

MAN DOWN

21 FEBRUARY, 1645 HRS
MIT DATA CENTER, BUILDING W91 — CAMBRIDGE, MASSACHUSETTS

The floor trembled, sending shivers up Paul's spine as the lights flashed and died, plunging the hallway into blackness. His heart pounded in his ears, his breath quickening as the visible surroundings vanished.

He cracked the inner glass tube of the glow stick with his thumbs, and inside, the hydrogen peroxide mixed with the diphenyl oxalate solution to form carbon dioxide. The electrons in the green dye molecules absorbed the fluid's energy, releasing a surreal fluorescent green glow.

His eyes adjusted and searched for his father.

The distinct sound of feet scuffling was followed by a loud crash from inside the data center room. With adrenaline surging through his body, Paul sprinted toward the door, his mind racing with possibilities of what he might find inside.

Through the dim, hazy light, his eyes locked on Emma as she ran toward him. Reacting instinctively, he grabbed her arm, pulling her away from the entrance. At that moment, his father shoved Emma into Paul's arms with such force they both tumbled to the ground.

Paul's father ran into the data center and slammed the door shut, leaving Paul and Emma outside looking in.

"Are you okay?" Paul asked, his voice filled with concern. He wrapped his arms around her tightly, her body trembling. He never wanted to let her go again, but he had no choice. Paul handed her the glow stick. "Take this. And get out."

"No, you're coming!" she said with intense, tear-filled eyes.

"I'll be fine. I have to do this," Paul said.

She paused and looked back down the dark hallway. He nodded a reassuring smile, silently signaling that it would be all right.

With reluctance, she turned away and sprinted toward the exit door. As it swung open, she vanished into a bright, smoky haze that filled the hallway.

At that moment, the anxiety and bone-deep exhaustion that had plagued him since Sara's death disappeared. Relief washed over him. Emma was finally safe.

He tightened his grip on his Colt 1911. Perfectly balanced, it felt like a natural extension of his body. His mind fired quick commands, and his hand responded with trained agility. Tightening his hold, he disengaged the grip safety. With an effortless flick, he released the thumb safety and slid his finger onto the trigger, applying measured pressure.

Suddenly, bright flashes and thunderous bursts of gunfire erupted from inside, shattering the tense silence. In shock, Paul watched his father crumple to the floor, his body contorting in pain.

Dropping into a crouch, Paul rushed to the dark entranceway and, with both hands, dragged his father out of the line of fire. He pivoted sharply into a low, balanced stance and unleashed six rounds in a rapid, scattered formation toward the source of the gunfire. The Colt's .45 caliber ACP rounds barked out, striking the metal racks with such force that shockwaves thundered through the data center.

His eyes, sharp and scanning, caught a glimpse of a shadowy figure darting across an aisle. Muscle memory and training took over as Paul adjusted his aim. Three rounds exploded from the Colt's barrel. Two bullets crashed into metal, their impact ringing out. The third, a muted thud, had found its mark.

Paul turned back to his father, pulled off his jacket, and carefully propped it under his head. He searched for the entry wound and found a wet, dark stain below his right collarbone, an inch above the protective vest.

Paul felt the slick liquid on his hand. His own father's blood. The man who had returned after being gone for more than half of Paul's life.

"Damn you. Don't you die on me now," Paul said, putting pressure on the wound and watching his father's chest gently rise and fall.

His father's eyes opened—the same eyes filled with wisdom and intensity Paul remembered from all those years ago.

"Go. Just go," Paul's father said, fighting to get the words out.

Paul looked back toward the data room and, for the first time in memory, was unsure of his next move.

"All...all those years...prepared you... Get him... Get the bastard..." his father said, each syllable a battle as he struggled for breath.

Paul nodded in silent acknowledgment.

Suddenly, sunlight swept down the hallway, illuminating the smoke that floated like a long line of cirrus clouds.

Paul aimed his Colt, ready to fire.

He lifted his finger off the trigger when he recognized it was Lia sprinting toward him.

Kneeling next to his father, she checked the wound. "He's still breathing. Let's get him outta here," she said.

"Where's Emma?" Paul asked.

"She's just outside—she's safe," Lia said. "Trust me. Nothing's going to happen to her. Our big FBI friend is with her. Let's get your father out."

"He's lost a lot of blood," Paul said. "Take him. I need to finish this."

"Go. I've got him," Lia said.

Paul helped her pick his father up, and with one arm around his shoulder, she dragged him toward the sunlight.

◆ ◆ ◆

The data center room was bathed in a dim, hazy green glow, casting shadows on the long row of computers that stood silent and dark. Paul's attention was drawn to a man's body, lying still, surrounded by a wet, dark stain. The blood, a stark crimson against the white ceramic floor tiles, pooled around the head.

Paul was stunned by the realization that he recognized the man: the outspoken congressman from New York, the Chairman of the Homeland Security Committee. The very politician who had led the high-profile hearings investigating the Thanksgiving Day bombings. Now, his body lay in an unsettling silence, a jarring contrast to the fiery politician who had once dominated the national stage.

The sudden shuffle of footsteps echoed down the hallway, causing Paul to tighten his grip on his Colt and pivot toward the sound. He advanced with cautious, measured steps, following a faint blood droplet trail leading to twin oversized service doors. Firmly, he pushed the exit bar. The mechanical click of the latch releasing broke the heavy silence. Every muscle in his body was coiled tight, prepared to fire his weapon at the slightest hint of movement.

He pushed the door open. Light flooded in. From a distance, a dark silhouette came into view. As the figure turned, a flash of recognition struck Paul. It was the same man from the airport, the very man who'd chased Emma.

Paul swiftly centered the rear sight and squeezed the trigger four times. Each round aimed precisely where he predicted the man would move to evade, a calculated guess based on instinct and experience. The bullets sliced through the air, racing toward their intended target.

The outer door slammed shut, plunging the hallway into an impenetrable darkness. The bullets tore into the steel door, their impact and the echo of the gunfire reverberating in the confined space.

Paul ran toward the sliver of light creeping in from beneath the exit door. In the faint light, blood splatter marks were visible on the floor and door casing.

He'd hit the target.

SMOKE SIGNALS

AUGUST 15, 1781
MOUNT VERNON, VIRGINIA COLONY

General Knox had been reluctant to disclose the reason for insisting on Tarleton's capture alive, hinting only that there were varying degrees to which "alive" might be interpreted. Jack understood that apprehending the infamous "Butcher" without resorting to lethal means would require both creativity and considerable restraint.

Moving cautiously, Jack made his way on foot toward the rear of Washington's estate. He stayed close to the protective shadow of the tree line along the edge of the Potomac. Peering through the thick foliage of magnolia branches, he caught sight of the mansion's grand, covered porch. It stretched the entire length of the two-story structure, its large white pillars supporting the overhanging roof blanketed with red wooden shingles. The porch offered a commanding view of the finely manicured lawn that gently sloped to the banks of the Potomac. Jack could picture a serene afternoon scene: General Washington and his family leisurely playing cards on that very veranda, enjoying the panoramic view and gentle, cool breeze as they gazed across the river to the Maryland shore. Jack hoped that peaceful times would return, yet he realized it would not be today.

He carefully surveyed the rear of the house, observing four redcoat guards—two flanking the rear door and two patrolling the length of the long, white-planked porch. Assessing the situation, Jack weighed his odds. Subduing two, perhaps even three of the guards seemed possible, but all four?

As he waited in anticipation for the signal, beads of sweat

rolled down his back. A welcome breeze blew across the river, providing a brief reprieve from the oppressive midday heat.

What was the reason for the delay? Had the chief been spotted?

Jack regretted not going himself.

Gentle ripples danced across the surface of Potomac. In the distance, upriver, a vessel with a solitary sail made its way gracefully toward General Washington's dock.

Jack was out of time.

As he readied himself to take action, dark gray smoke spiraling high into the sky suddenly seized his focus. The corn had been lit!

Jack breathed a deep sigh of relief, the sight signaling the long-awaited commencement of their plan.

The sharp crack of a gunshot shattered the relative calm. Jack's head snapped toward the sound. Shouts and commands were called out as men's voices filled the air. Instinctively, Jack's muscles tensed, his grip on the rifle tightened, and his eyes locked onto the soldiers anxiously pacing back and forth on the porch. A familiar feeling swept through his body, reminiscent of the inner force he felt during the Battle of Charlestown when British gunships commenced their bombardment. The fight had begun; the moment had finally arrived.

Seconds later, the air was filled with musket fire erupting from every direction.

The redcoat guards on the porch quickly shouldered their rifles, sweeping their aim across the estate's sloping rear lawn, but it wasn't long before they realized the action was unfolding at the front of the house. Drawn by the billowing smoke, they sprinted, their heavy, black, knee-high boots pounding against the wooden porch. Pausing, they stood watching the towering plumes of smoke rise into the air.

Suddenly, a thunderous barrage of rifle shots erupted from the direction of the distillery. The guards whirled around, raised their rifles, and pointed toward the river's edge. A sloop, with its sail loosely flapping in the brisk westerly wind, bobbed alongside the dock. A dozen soldiers stood along the deck with rifles in hand and bayonets fixed, poised and ready to disembark.

Jack smiled with satisfaction as he recognized the stunning blue and white uniforms of General Washington's Continental soldiers aboard the sloop. On the porch, the British guards quickly knelt, took aim, and unleashed a volley of musket fire. Plumes of white smoke burst from their muskets. The Continentals in the sloop instinctively ducked at the sound, but one soldier wasn't quick enough. He tumbled headfirst over the railing, creating a splash as he hit the river. Jack watched, tense with concern. Miraculously, the soldier resurfaced, his arms flailing in a desperate attempt to stay afloat. On the dock, a fellow Continental extended a hand, reaching down to rescue the struggling man.

Jack inspected his powder and readied a round for his shot. He raised his rifle, steadied his stance, and stared down the smooth iron barrel. Narrowing his focus, he closed his right eye, centering the front bead sight on the center of the tallest redcoat's chest. His hand moved swiftly to draw back the hammer and, with measured pressure, squeezed the trigger. A sharp crack rang out as the powder ignited, propelling the lethal lead ball toward his unsuspecting victim. The ball struck the soldier squarely in the upper body, the force hurling him backward onto the wooden planks.

Jack quickly pulled another musket ball from his side pouch and primed his weapon, readying it for the next shot.

Startled by the sudden noise, the remaining redcoats spun toward Jack's position, fumbling to reload their muskets. Meanwhile, the disembarked Continentals, seizing the moment, dashed down the dock to the center of the grassy lawn. With disciplined precision, they dropped to one knee and took aim at the British guards.

The air exploded as the Continentals fired. Bright orange flashes erupted from their muskets, and brilliant clouds of white smoke billowed into the blue Virginia sky. Sensing the exhilaration of battle, Jack drew his knife from its hip holster and readied himself for close-quarters combat.

Two redcoat guards crumpled to the ground, struck down by the Continentals' volley.

Seizing the moment, Jack, with his long rifle in one hand and his knife in the other, sprinted from the cover of magnolia trees. The last redcoat reacted to Jack's charge, fumbling and dropping his powder horn in a frantic attempt to reload. As Jack closed the distance, the redcoat dropped his musket and drew his long sword.

Jack leaped from the edge of the lawn, his boots landing hard on the porch. He steadied himself, preparing to engage, but his attention was drawn to a pair of redcoat regulars advancing toward Jack's position quickly from the far opposite end of the estate.

Jack leveled his rifle, took careful aim, and fired a shot at the lead soldier charging him from a distance. The ball found its mark, sending the redcoat tumbling to the ground.

Jack sprinted the length of the white clapboard porch, leaping over the body of a fallen British soldier. The redcoat reared back and swung his blade with force. Reacting with equal speed, Jack ducked under the blade as the lethal blow whistled past. He lunged forward with a powerful stride, tackling the redcoat to the ground. Jack quickly pinned his adversary and, with a decisive thrust, plunged his knife deep into the redcoat's chest. The blade pierced the thick, red wool jacket until the handguard was firmly against the soldier's torso. Jack watched the life fade from the soldier's eyes and felt a release of tension in his muscles.

Jack's attention quickly turned toward the sound of heavy boots crashing on the wooden porch. With bayonets at the ready, two redcoats charged toward him. He pulled the knife from the soldier's lifeless body and slowly rose to his feet. Clutching his knife tightly, Jack widened his stance, and his eyes locked onto the two men with a fierce, unwavering stare.

The sudden roar of a musket blast rang out, causing Jack to duck and turn. The blast had come from the direction of the Continentals' position on the lawn. One of the shots struck a charging redcoat, who collapsed and writhed in pain. Another shot missed its mark and flew high, splintering a section of the mansion's white clapboard siding.

The remaining redcoat, bayonet drawn, charged Jack. Out of nowhere, a half-naked man lunged through the air and broadsided the redcoat with full force. The two men tumbled to the floor and rolled, slamming into the mansion's sturdy exterior wall. The Shawnee warrior overpowered the redcoat and pinned him to the ground. His face was filled with intense rage and adorned with striking war paint.

He raised his long-handled tomahawk high above his head and, with a swift downstroke, struck the redcoat with the ferocity of a crazed man. Blood splattered across the white floorboards, splashing onto the warrior's face and bare chest. Then, raising his head to the sky, he unleashed a violent, primal scream.

The Shawnee warrior stripped the lifeless redcoat of his woolen battle coat and turned to face Jack. In response, Jack offered a slight nod of gratitude for the warrior's timely aid.

He took a moment to survey the aftermath of the skirmish, drawing in a deep, steadying breath to calm his pounding heart.

Near the river, the Continental soldiers advanced cautiously up the lawn toward the mansion. Distant sounds of muskets and cannon fire filled the air, a stark reminder alerting of the battle unfolding.

WASHINGTON'S SERVANT

AUGUST 15, 1781
MOUNT VERNON, VIRGINIA COLONY

With both hands, Jack pushed open the heavy oak doors and stepped into the grand central hall of Washington's mansion. Moving cautiously with his knife in hand, he made his way down the hallway. Through the open front door, he could see a small contingent of redcoats standing shoulder to shoulder, unleashing a barrage of musket fire toward the distant tree line.

Colonel Boone and his band of sharpshooters were effectively returning fire from the cover of the woods. Jack watched as they skillfully took down a pair of British regulars. The attack was progressing according to his plan: Boone and his men had successfully drawn the regulars away from the estate, luring them into the line of fire and leaving the mansion unguarded, allowing Jack time to search for the "Butcher," Tarleton.

Jack ducked as a volley of shots erupted from behind. On the rear lawn, the Continentals were in a fierce skirmish with mounted Green Dragoons who had ridden in from the east.

Searching for any sign of Tarleton, Jack moved forward. The knife held firm and ready. Lund Washington rounded the corner and stammered backward at the sight of Jack and his blade.

"Lund, where is Tarleton?" Jack demanded, his voice raised to be heard over the battle raging outside. He advanced two steps toward Lund, turning the point of his knife, bringing it level with the bridge of Lund's nose.

Lund's eyes darted rapidly, and his hands trembled with fear. "In the cellar," he stammered, pointing toward the open door leading to the stairs. "There's a passageway that runs the length of the house and exits near the old distillery."

"You are a miserable traitor," Jack said, barely resisting the urge to plunge the knife into the man's throat.

Lund shook his head frantically. "He would have killed me," he said, his voice strained with his plea.

"Liar! You conspired to ambush General Washington. Betraying your kin and country. How could you?"

Lund's eyes filled with cowardly tears. "Does it matter? My cousin never appreciated my sacrifice, my years of loyalty. To him, I've always been just a servant."

Jack swiveled at the sound of footsteps pounding on the floor. The Shawnee warrior wearing the stolen redcoat jacket burst through the rear entrance, his face blood-streaked, wild eyes fixed on Lund, hatchet raised, ready to strike.

"Stop!" Jack said with force.

The Shawnee, not comprehending Jack's words but understanding the language of the knife, hesitated and lowered his tomahawk.

At that moment, Lund seized his chance, bolting toward the front door.

Jack exchanged a glance with the Shawnee, who recognized Jack's firm nod as a silent approval. With a ferocious battle cry, the warrior sprinted forward with his tomahawk held high and, in a swift motion, tackled Lund at the edge of the mansion's lawn, bringing the traitor to the ground.

ECLIPSE

22 FEBRUARY, 1545 HRS — TEN MINUTES EARLIER
MIT DATA CENTER, BUILDING W91 — CAMBRIDGE, MASSACHUSETTS

A silhouette appeared in the murky green glow at the server room's entrance. Instantly, Hassan's survival instincts kicked in. He threw himself to the ground just before the room erupted in the roar of large-caliber gunfire. The bullets sliced through the air, hammering into the metal computer racks with overwhelming power.

Each impact sent shockwaves reverberating through Hassan's body. Pain exploded in his thigh, sharp and unbearable, as if someone had plunged a dull knife deep into his leg. Gritting his teeth, he pounded the floor with his fist. The gut-wrenching pain was a familiar sensation.

He'd been shot.

With survival fueling his resolve, he rolled behind a row of servers. With his back against the cold metal, he closed his eyes and channeled the pain deep into the recess of his consciousness. He slowed his breathing, focusing on oxygenating his body, and pulled himself to his feet. A warm, wet sensation ran down his leg—the unmistakable feel of blood. He carefully tested his weight on the wounded leg. Relief dawned, mixed with pain; the bullet had missed the bone.

He refused to let the pain win. He'd come too far and sacrificed too much.

He had to escape to find his men and rejoin the fight.

Through the shadows, he moved quickly, dragging his injured leg down the service ramp. Searching for an exit, his Glock banged against the glass window of the door. With a swift jolt, he slammed the emergency release bar, throwing the door wide open.

A gust of warm air washed over his face as he stepped through. His lungs were immediately filled with the sting of fuel-laced smoke. He coughed in a desperate attempt to expel the toxic fumes. Bright, flickering white lights danced against the ceiling and walls. Their dizzying motion threatened to overwhelm his sense of balance. Fighting the urge to pass out, clutching the USB drive tight in his fist, he covered his mouth and staggered toward the haze of sunlight seeping from underneath a distant door.

Reaching the end of the hallway, Hassan pushed open the building's exit door. The abrupt flood of daylight poured in, momentarily blinding him. Then, from behind, he heard the distinct sound of a door unlatching and swinging open. He spun, his heart pounding, only to see an ominous figure advancing toward him.

Gunshots rang out as Hassan hurled himself through the exit, his body crashing onto the rough gravel outside. Bullets hammered into the reinforced metal door as it slammed shut behind him. Each breath was a struggle against the searing pain radiating from his shoulder.

Hassan slowly rolled onto his back. The sun's rays gently warmed his face, a stark contrast to the chaos he had managed to escape.

As he opened his eyes, a spirit-like image of his brother Yousef appeared against the bright, cloud-speckled sky.

In disbelief, Hassan closed his eyes, trying to drive away the ghostly image.

He opened his eyes again, only to be met with a vision of Yousef smiling. Yet, his expression was devoid of joy and unsettling. Silently, Yousef's lips moved, repeating a single word in a slow rhythm, over and over.

Hassan watched, transfixed and troubled by his brother's silent question.

Why?

The last word his young brother had uttered.

"Forgive me." Hassan's weakened breath forced the words out as sorrow flooded in.

As he repeated the words, the image of Yousef faded away.

A towering figure eclipsed the sunlight. Hassan's eyes widened as he looked up at the man standing over him, pointing a long-barreled shotgun at him.

A commanding voice shattered the tense silence. "Forgive you? Hell no! Drop the gun. Now!" The words were sharp, cutting through Hassan's fog of pain.

Gritting his teeth, Hassan struggled to his feet. He assessed the dire situation. The man was alone.

Fighting through the pain, Hassan opened his hand to reveal a USB thumb drive. Once a symbol of his conquest, it now meant nothing to him. To Hassan, it represented the weakness and Khalid's betrayal. It represented the false hope of his mentor's teachings.

Could this man be bought, like Khalid and the greed of others?

"Take it. This is wealth to last for a million lifetimes. You must let me go," Hassan said, his proposal mixed with desperation and calculation.

The man's response was cold and unwavering. "Not a chance." He raised the shotgun, aiming its barrel at Hassan's head.

"You must. It's untraceable," Hassan said, undeterred, extending an open hand while his other hand tightened on his Glock, ready to exploit any sign of weakness.

"I'll say it one last time. Put the gun down. Now!" the man said, lowering his head toward the shotgun's rear sight.

In that instant, Hassan's world narrowed. He closed his eyes, inhaling deeply. The familiar scent of his childhood flooded in. His mother's cooking in the predawn hours, the warmth of the desert breeze, and the sun's penetrating early rays. He imagined his mother in the kitchen, preparing food, the laughter of his younger brothers echoing, a ball thudding against the stone wall.

With a profound sense of destiny, Hassan embraced his fate.

He raised his gun for the final time.

A blinding white light flashed.

CANDLELIGHT

AUGUST 15, 1781
MOUNT VERNON, VIRGINIA COLONY

As the booming echoes of the skirmish outside faded into the background, Jack's focus narrowed to the task at hand—the pursuit of Banastre Tarleton. Jack carefully lifted a lit candle from the table, its flame casting ghostly shadows onto the cellar's gritty sandstone walls. The air cooled with each step deeper into the cellar, and the musty smell of rotten vegetables grew stronger.

Reaching the cellar's stone floor, Jack noticed a dim light at the far end of the passageway. The thundering roar of cannon fire shook the floorboards above, raining dust and debris onto his hat.

Amidst the darkness, Jack's concern briefly turned to his friends, Ben and Julius. Would he ever see them again?

The urgency of his mission refocused his mind. The British had taken so much, including his father. He pressed on, determined to bring the one man who represented the worst of the tyrants to justice.

Jack walked cautiously down the uneven stone passageway. He listened closely for any sign of Tarleton amid the continuous musket and cannon fire rumble.

The air was thick with the pungent odor of the unmistakable scent of vermin droppings. Jack shined his candle into the storage rooms as he passed. The brick-lined rooms with arched, vaulted ceilings were sparsely filled with barrels of spirits and baskets of corn and potatoes.

A faint sound of footsteps and metal clinking caught Jack's attention. Holding the candle out in one hand and gripping his knife tightly in the other, he moved forward, his heart beating faster with each step.

Suddenly, a woman's voice cried out. Her cry of distress jolted Jack. Another round of cannon fire roared above, sending vibrations through the rafters.

"Who's there?" Jack called out.

About twenty paces ahead, a figure emerged from the darkness, a sword clenched in his left hand. His attire was disheveled—not wearing a jacket, shirt unbuttoned and untucked. The candlelight cast shadows on his face.

Out of an adjacent storage room, a female servant darted out, clutching the top of her dress with both hands. Sobbing, she rushed past Jack toward the safety of the cellar's exit.

"Tarleton, I presume?" Jack said, his voice steady, determined.

"You may address me as Lieutenant Colonel Tarleton," the man replied with a calm smile.

"A title such as 'the Butcher' would be more fitting," Jack said, subtly adjusting the grip on his knife.

Tarleton's smile broadened. "I accept the compliment." He advanced a few slow steps.

Jack held his ground. The polished blade in Tarleton's hand caught the candlelight and glistened.

"And how shall we proceed?" Tarleton asked with a sly confidence. "You can meet your end at my hand or scurry away like Lund Washington, that cowardly mouse. From the sounds above, my royal reinforcements have arrived to finish the day. Soon, I will have the pleasure of capturing your esteemed General Washington."

His words hung in the air as Jack's anger simmered. He shifted his stance and, with a firm hand, pointed the knife at Tarleton.

"This ends now. Surrender or die. You may choose," Jack said, prepared to follow through on his words.

"Very well," Tarleton smirked and sliced the air with two

CANDLELIGHT

expert swipes of his sword, whirling the dust cascading from the floorboards above.

Jack quickly assessed the situation, realizing his disadvantage—his knife was no match for Tarleton's long blade. Jack glanced left, then right. In the dim light, a large, dark shadow became visible on the cellar floor.

Tarleton, with eyes glared with animal-like rage, thrust his blade toward Jack's chest. "No one is coming to rescue you."

The candle wax softened as Jack's grip tightened. The flame flickered, casting eerie figures on the stone wall behind Tarleton.

In a swift motion, Jack hurled the candle at Tarleton's face and dove toward the circular shadow on the cellar floor—the opening of an old storage well. Darkness engulfed the cellar, followed by the wisping sound of Tarleton's sword cutting through the air.

"You cannot hide. My blade will find you," Tarleton said calmly.

Jack pressed himself against the cold sandstone wall and moved laterally with careful side steps. He held his breath to avoid discovery and evade Tarleton's blade. Reaching into his pocket, he retrieved Jefferson's coin. Its surface was smooth under his thumb as he recalled Jefferson's words—to present the coin when confronted by those challenging his loyalty. This was undoubtedly such a moment.

With a calculated flick, Jack sent the coin spiraling into the well. It clattered against the stone, echoing sharply as it struck the bottom.

Reacting to the sound, Tarleton lunged, his sword scraping the stone floor, sending sparks flying.

"Tell your king we will never surrender," Jack said boldly.

Tarleton let out a cry of surprise, followed by a resounding thud as his body slammed into the bottom of the dry well.

◆ ◆ ◆

Above, boots pounded the floorboards. Jack cautiously stepped out into the dark passageway, his knife drawn, prepared for the enemy to emerge.

Light cascaded down the cellar steps, followed closely by two men carrying lanterns hurrying toward him. As they drew closer, the lantern light revealed familiar faces.

Jack lowered his knife and breathed a sigh of relief.

"Jack, is that you?" Colonel Boone's voice broke the tense silence.

"Yes, sir, it's good to see you. You're a sight for sore eyes."

Ben stepped past the Colonel and wrapped his arms around Jack in a firm bear hug, lifting him off the ground.

"What's the situation upstairs? Outside, I mean?" Jack asked, realizing the cannon and musket fire had ceased.

"Julius managed to locate Generals Knox and Washington, who promptly sent reinforcements," Ben said with a wide grin.

"The remaining Dragoons and the British regulars retreated to the east. General Washington dispatched the cavalry to round them up," Boone said.

"But we haven't found that scoundrel, Tarleton," Ben said.

"May I?" Jack took Ben's lantern and directed its light into the dry well. The golden glow illuminated the mossy stone lining, and at the bottom, Tarleton lay on his back. His long, disheveled hair partially obscured his face as he stared, in a disoriented daze, at his captors.

Ben kicked loose dirt and stones into the well, his attention drawn away by the clap of hard-heeled boots descending the cellar stairs.

Straightening, Jack brought his feet together and saluted as the estate's proprietor approached with long, dignified strides. The lantern's light gleamed off his polished black boots and his uniform's golden buttons.

"Gentlemen, indeed, today stands as a most remarkable and gratifying day," General Washington said.

SUNLIGHT

22 FEBRUARY 1550 HRS
MIT DATA CENTER, BUILDING W91 — CAMBRIDGE, MASSACHUSETTS

Paul froze at the crack of a shotgun blast, his heart hammering in his chest. He stood motionless for a moment, waiting, listening, with his Colt trained on the exit door. Uncertain of what he'd find, he slowly opened the data center's exit door, shielding his eyes against the harsh sunlight. The air outside was heavy with the strong scent of diesel and spent gunpowder.

He stepped out, his grip on the gun firm, prepared for whatever might come next.

"You can lower your weapon, Mr. Knox," said a voice, steady and familiar. It was Agent Johnson, with the Remington lowered at his side. He stood over a bloodied, lifeless body sprawled on the ground.

Paul's tension gradually dissipated as he lowered his weapon and slid his finger off the trigger. As he stared down at the dead man, he braced himself for a flood of emotions—satisfaction, relief, or perhaps even a grim sense of delight. Yet, he felt nothing for the man lying dead at his feet.

"Who is he?" Paul asked.

Agent Johnson pointed the barrel of his Remington down toward the motionless body. "This terrorist mutt?" he said, his tone laced with disdain. "He commanded what we believe was ISIS's North American network. A Syrian national, Hassan Ali Hamadei, had a long history of extremist ties, reaching into the upper echelons of the Iranian government."

Agent Johnson's voice took on a serious tone. "He was the trigger man behind the O'Hare Thanksgiving Day bombing.

I've been tracking him ever since that terrible day. Our intel led us to Detroit, where he ran a sophisticated cyber-terrorist operation."

Paul processed the information, connecting the dots. "So, he was also behind the power and internet breaches?"

Agent Johnson nodded. "We think so. The evidence points to Hamadei as the one who executed the master plan. But the brains of the operation was Khalid Ahmed Ghlam, or as he was known, Allessio Urbani. An Iranian, a former member of the Army of the Guardians of the Islamic Revolution. He was the ringleader."

Paul's focus narrowed. "Do you have any leads on where this Khalid might be?"

"Dead. Taken out in an FBI raid yesterday morning."

"Well, whoever took down that bastard certainly deserves a medal," Paul said.

Agent Johnson, visibly in pain, reached out and leaned against the building, shifting his weight, trying to get some relief. "I'm sorry, just give me a sec. My back is killing me. It's been a long couple of days."

His voice took on a serious tone. "There's something else. The FBI suspects the late congressman from New York was deeply involved with other insiders in the government and possibly foreign agents who funneled top-secret information to Ghlam and Hamadei. In exchange, he was likely promised a cut of the ransom or maybe something else. We'll know more once we dig deeper."

Agent Johnson continued to speak, but his words faded. Paul's attention was drawn to a beautiful young woman running toward him. In that instant, the fatigue that had gripped him since Sara's cancer diagnosis seemed to vanish. He reached out, catching Emma as she jumped into his arms. Gently lowering her to the ground, he noticed blood smeared on her arm and shirt.

"Are you okay?" Paul asked, checking her for injuries.

"I'm fine, are you?" Her voice was filled with worry.

"Now I am." He smiled but noticed a troubled look on her face. "What's wrong?"

"It's your father. He didn't look good, and that woman, Lia...she drove away with him."

"Did she say where they were going?"

"She said she'd be in contact soon. Dad, who is she?"

"It's a long story. She's...a friend."

"What kind of friend?"

It was the kind of question a daughter asks her father when another woman is involved. Paul thought about it for a minute.

"Yes, Mr. Knox, what kind of friend is she?" Agent Johnson asked with a hint of sarcasm.

Paul thought it best to redirect the conversation. "What matters is that you're safe."

"Here." Agent Johnson tossed Paul a set of keys and motioned toward his unmarked sedan. "Go find your father. I've got things covered here. The Feds will want to debrief you, but that can wait."

Gratefully, Paul shook Agent Johnson's hand and looked down one last time at the dead body, wondering if it was—finally—over. With Emma beside him, Paul walked quickly to the car. As he started the engine, the radio played a familiar Steely Dan song. "Ah, grapefruit wine," Paul said.

"What?" she said, looking puzzled.

"This song is one of your mom's favorites."

"You mean 'was' one of mom's favorites."

"Sorry. I know she's listening. She's in a special place looking after us, and she would want us to move forward. Together." His smile returned as he turned to Emma. "Let's go find your grandfather. He has a lot of explaining to do."

"And Lia?" Emma said.

Paul smiled and through the car's windshield, the traffic light turned green.

The power was back on.

THE END

ABOUT THE AUTHOR

SCAN TO VISIT
GEORGEMEHOK.COM

GEORGE MEHOK is an author, technologist, and entrepreneur with a distinguished career in designing software and leading high-performing teams in the financial services, telecommunications, and aerospace industries. His insights have been featured in the *Wall Street Journal*, *CIOReview*, and *InformationWeek*, covering wireless communications, cybersecurity, and data analytics. George's expertise has earned him accolades, including Crain's *Business Magazine* CIO of the Year award, and his work has been recognized in *InformationWeek*'s Annual Elite 100 ranking of the most innovative technology users in the United States. George lives in Cleveland, Ohio. When not reading and writing, he enjoys fly fishing and competing in US Masters swimming. He can be reached at gmehok@gmail.com.

ABOUT ATMOSPHERE PRESS

Founded in 2015, Atmosphere Press was built on the principles of Honesty, Transparency, Professionalism, Kindness, and Making Your Book Awesome. As an ethical and author-friendly hybrid press, we stay true to that founding mission today.

If you're a reader, enter our giveaway for a free book here:

SCAN TO ENTER
BOOK GIVEAWAY

If you're a writer, submit your manuscript for consideration here:

SCAN TO SUBMIT
MANUSCRIPT

And always feel free to visit Atmosphere Press and our authors online at atmospherepress.com. See you there soon!

Milton Keynes UK
Ingram Content Group UK Ltd.
UKHW031400011224
451790UK00011B/143/J